River of Gold

By the same author

River of Gold

Empire: Volume Eleven

ANTHONY RICHES

**HODDER &
STOUGHTON**

First published in Great Britain in in 2020 by Hodder & Stoughton
An Hachette UK company

1

Copyright © Anthony Riches 2020

Maps © Rodney Paull

A CIP catalogue record for this title
is available from the British Library

Hardback ISBN 978 1 473 62884 7
eBook ISBN 978 1 473 62886 1

Typeset in Plantin Light by Palimpsest Book Production Limited,
Falkirk, Stirlingshire

Printed and bound in Great Britain by Clays Ltd, Elcograf S.p.A.

Hodder & Stoughton policy is to use papers that are natural, renewable
and recyclable products and made from wood grown in sustainable forests.
The logging and manufacturing processes are expected to conform to the
environmental regulations of the country of origin.

Hodder & Stoughton Ltd
Carmelite House
50 Victoria Embankment
London EC4Y 0DZ

www.hodder.co.uk

For Helen

ACKNOWLEDGEMENTS

My first thanks must go to the editorial staff at Hodder & Stoughton, led by my long-suffering editor Carolyn Caughey, who manages to stay eternally cheerful even when the author, not the most reliable of deliverers, is forced by external pressures to delay manuscript completion by months at a time. My agent Robin Wade remains a constant, reassuring presence even if, after fourteen books, I'm quite laid-back about the whole thing.

For inspiration of much of the storyline, this book's first prize has to go to Malcolm Quartey, whose amazing web page (detailed in the historical note – warning, contains spoilers) on the Wildfire Games website (and thanks to Wildfire too, for that matter) came at just the right time when I was scratching around for a new enemy to give Tribune Scaurus and his familia a suitably hard time in Aegyptus. The discovery of this new and (to me) unknown power in the ancient world was something of a revelation, and all the result of a chance mouse-click. I love those moments of sudden clarity and have the deepest of respect for the people whose assiduous hard work makes such apparently effortless serendipity possible.

Most of all I owe the usual debt of gratitude for patience, encouragement, and occasional therapeutic browbeating, that is my wholly undeserved reward for having lucked into the life-partnership that keeps me from the distractions which would otherwise only serve to delay delivery by an even worse fraction of the calendar. Thank you, Helen, for everything.

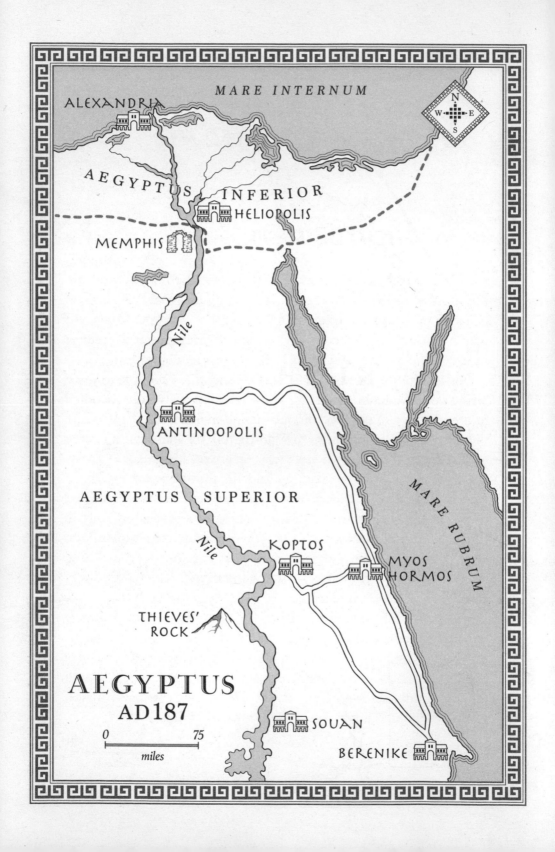

MARE INTERNUM

ALEXANDRIA

AEGYPTUS INFERIOR

HELIOPOLIS

MEMPHIS

Nile

ANTINOOPOLIS

AEGYPTUS SUPERIOR

Nile

KOPTOS

MYOS
HORMOS

MARE RUBRUM

THIEVES'
ROCK

AEGYPTUS
AD 187

0   75
miles

SOUAN

BERENIKE

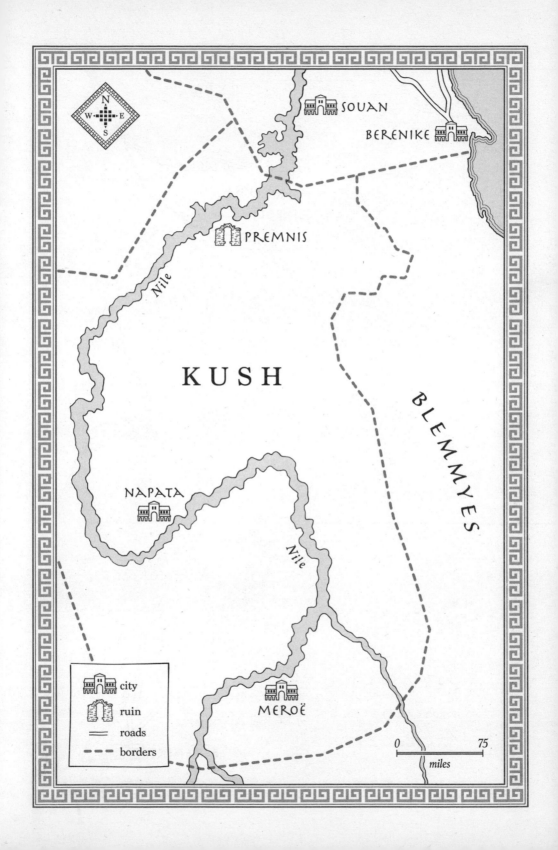

Prologue

Aegyptus, February AD 187

'Isn't that just typical of the blasted cavalry. Give them one simple job to do and you can be sure that they'll find a way to gallop off into the landscape and not be seen all day. Although what they could have found to chase around this barren landscape, I can only imagine. What do you think, First Spear? Is it the usual wild goose chase, or might they have found something to drink all the way out here?'

The senior centurion marching beside Prefect Servius's horse barked a terse laugh. Ten years older than his commander, and close to the end of an illustrious career, his curly black hair was greying above a nut-brown face, his skin lined and seamed by both age and the elements. He reflexively turned to look back down his cohort's line of march before answering, nodding to himself in satisfaction that his centuries were still in a tight formation, despite the arid, stony terrain across which they were advancing. The soldiers were silent, other than for the rattle and scrape of their equipment, and the occasional curse as a hobnailed boot slipped on a loose pebble, their eyes fixed alternately on the men in front of them and the stark, treeless line of the horizon. Their discipline on the march was something he had inculcated into them over several years of training across thousands of square miles of desert, land empty other than for the trading caravans working the road from their base at Koptos to Rome's southern-most trading port, Berenike, hardening them for the desert's harsh conditions. Toiling across a limestone plain, under a sun which, if not anywhere close to summer's full heat, was still warm enough to make them grateful that they had not yet been ordered to don their helmets, they looked every bit as capable as he expected, trained and drilled to the height of efficiency and obedience.

'Our mounted brethren, Prefect? I doubt that lot could find anything so useful if they were led to it by Mithras himself. But I don't think we'll miss their presence all that much. If their scouting report was accurate, then we should come within sight of the Blemmyes village when we cross that next rise. And we'll hardly need a few dozen horse thieves to help us triumph against such a ragged opposition. We are going to attack?'

Servius nodded decisively, replying in the spoken Greek that was the army of Aegyptus's main language, no longer requiring any conscious thought after two years of constant use.

'Of course, I have to make an example of them, something I can point out to their king wouldn't have been necessary if he'd kept a better grip on his subjects this side of the great river. So yes, once we're within four hundred paces we deploy into line and then go through them without any pause, other than for the customary challenge and response to get our men's blood up.'

His first spear nodded agreement.

'The sooner we get this done, show these thieving bastards what happens when Rome gets tired of their constant robbery, and then make our way back to civilisation, the happier I'll be.'

The prefect grinned at him.

'Thinking about your daughter, are you, Khaba?'

The older man grimaced.

'Thinking about her mother, more like, and the amount of money she seems determined to spend celebrating the girl's betrothal. It's not like I haven't already provided a decent dowry, but all I hear is silk dresses and spiced cakes whenever I see them.'

Servius laughed.

'At least there's no shortage of either, or of merchants willing to give a man of your standing a healthy discount. And if you couldn't take a joke, perhaps you shouldn't have had the child?'

His subordinate nodded, his face creasing in an apparently mournful look of ruefulness.

'Something I am reminded of by her mother every time I question each new expense. Never before have I agreed quite so strongly with the rules against marrying before retirement from the service.'

'Quite so, Centurion! The wisdom of our elders and betters, eh?' The two men shared a smile, the easy familiarity between them the result of the two years of hardships involved in drilling the cohort as close to perfection as could be achieved with native auxiliaries. The senior officer had initially faced a bigger challenge than his men, daunted by the loneliness of command in a distant outpost, and that he had adapted to become an efficient and respected commander was due in no small part to his subordinate's patient and tactful guidance. 'If there's one thing that my own domestic life has shown me, it's that being a married man and being a soldier are somewhat incompatible. All I hear whenever I reach for my helmet is "how long will you be away *this* time?"'

The centurion nodded knowingly, warming to a familiar theme.

'That, or "when will you be back *this* time?", as if I had the choice. She seems determined to assume that I prefer the company of five hundred unwashed men, and the joys of eating cold food and shitting behind rocks to the comforts of my home. And of course she's convinced that I have a woman out here somewhere, when the most attractive creatures I ever see on patrol are the donkeys carrying the water. With no disrespect to your horse, Prefect.'

They shared a moment of amusement before Servius spoke again.

'At least this ought to be simple enough. We flatten the Blemmyes village, kill anyone that stands against us, enslave the rest, burn whatever can't be carried and head for home. Leaving a clear and unmistakable message for every member of their tribe.'

'Steal from Rome, and Rome will make you pay the price of admission to the game?'

'Exactly, First Spear. Ah, there they are.'

Cresting the shallow ridge in the desert's seemingly unending, gently undulating terrain, they had come into sight of a small desert settlement. Not the sprawl of buildings that surrounded the wells further to the south and east where most of the Blemmyes people lived, but a mean cluster of huts and tents that would provide shelter for no more than a hundred people at the most.

'I'll deploy the cohort into line, if I may, Prefect?'

Leaving his subordinate to what he did best, the swift and efficient transmission and enforcement of orders, Servius dismounted and hammered a notched iron stake into a crack in the rock, tethering his horse to it before pulling on his crested helmet over a clean, and momentarily sweat free, linen arming cap. Taking a swift drink of tepid water from his bottle, he turned to find the cohort completing its deployment from column to line, and walked across to join his subordinate in front of the soldiers, calling out an order that was more for show than any need to tell such an experienced centurion what to do.

'Get that line dressed, First Spear! Let's not show these animals any sign that they might have the faintest chance of beating a cohort of Roman troops in a straight fight!'

The prefect watched with satisfaction as the older man saluted crisply and stalked away down the cohort's line, bellowing orders and striking out with his vine stick at those of his soldiers who were slow to respond. His auxiliaries were arrayed in an extended battle line, two men deep and two hundred long, waiting with the patience of men habituated to standing in formation, seemingly untroubled by the ragged band of desert warriors who had emerged from their dwellings to face them. His task completed, the first spear strode back down the line to rejoin his prefect, his dark, sun-blasted skin beaded with sweat from his exertions.

'The cohort is ready for battle, Prefect!'

Servius nodded gravely.

'Very well, First Spear. Since the enemy haven't just fled at the sight of so many soldiers, I suggest we get this unpleasantness over and done with. The sooner we have the cohort back in Koptos doing what they're paid for, rather than chasing around the desert after this bandit scum, the better!'

He walked forward to stand before his men, turning his back on the desert tribesmen waiting for them two hundred paces away, up a slight slope that led to the settlement his cavalry scouts had discovered the previous day.

'Men of the First Macedonica Equitata!'

The soldiers tensed, knowing that his address was the final preparation for battle, and Servius looked across their line, seeing fear, eagerness, bloodlust and even boredom on their faces, as his men readied themselves to fight.

'These desert dwellers before you have pushed their luck with Rome one time too many!'

Word had reached the fortress at Koptos two days before, borne by a merchant who had been by turns irate and disconsolate at the size of his loss. His caravan, over one hundred beasts laden with an entire ship's cargo of valuable trade goods, had been stripped clean at sword point only two days into its journey up the long road north from the port town of Berenike. Trade goods that had been shipped a thousand miles across the Erythraean Sea, carried by captains willing to brave the treacherous tides, turbulent waves and rock-studded waters that made any voyage to the kingdoms of the distant east an act of faith, had been stolen with what Servius considered breathtaking daring, given how far the Blemmyes had penetrated into imperial territory to carry out their raid. Not only that, but the threat of violence used to cow the caravan's guards had been shockingly credible, scores of armed bandits springing a well-planned ambush that had totally overwhelmed the twenty hired swordsmen who had been employed to fend off any attempt at robbery. Faced with such a change in the desert-dwellers' customary opportunistic banditry, the prefect had known that he had no option but to make an example of the band in question, and had marched at dawn the next day in cohort strength, using his cavalrymen to scout ahead and follow the robbers' tracks to their village.

'These criminals before us have stripped an entire shipment clean at the point of their spears, hoping to sell their gains to the highest bidder! They have stolen those goods, not just from their rightful owner, but from Rome too!'

He paused for a moment to allow time for his men to think on that. A crime against trade was a crime against the empire, denying the imperial treasury the taxes that would result both from their import and re-export across the sea to Rome itself. And there was one last reason for them to want these desert bandits dealt with just as much as he did, a sentiment he weighed carefully before putting it before them.

'And consider this, men of the First Macedonica! As *praefectus praesidiorum et montis berenicidis*, my responsibility is to safeguard both the port, and the quarries to our east, *and* the roads that lead north from them across this desert! I can assure you that if you and I fail to provide these vital imperial assets with the protection we are paid for, our place here will be re-garrisoned with legion troops, and we will be marched away to guard dusty road forts in the middle of Aegyptus. We will be stationed so far from civilisation that we will never again see those who have come to depend on us, not unless they choose to accompany us to whichever desolate outpost we are sent to!'

And that, he knew, would be the most convincing reason for them to show the bandits no mercy. The prospect of losing the familiarity and comfort of their fort, in a town filled with the entertainments and diversions traditionally enjoyed both by the men of the caravans on their way north and back again and, in their absence, his own men, would horrify them.

'But that will never happen, men of the First! We are going to rip through these poor, deluded fools, who believe that they can defy the might of Rome and make them rue the day they decided to try! Those that we kill will be left here as a feast for the vultures! Those we capture will be sold into slavery, to work as labour in the quarries! And the profits from their sale will be divided up between those of us that survive this battle!'

His men cheered their approval of that last roared promise, and his first spear bellowed the order for them to start making some noise, a rhythmic rapping of their spear shafts against the wooden boards of their shields. The sound would, so the military manuals said, calm the nervous, and give strength to men whose legs were trembling, but Servius had long since decided that the intention was mainly to give them something to do, to distract them from contemplating the horror that awaited the first battle any of them would ever have fought in. He drew breath, then shouted the challenge that was routinely practised on the parade ground prior to mock battles, so that every man present would know what was expected of him.

'Are you ready for war?'

The reply was almost instant, his soldiers keen to get the ordeal over and done with, and see who would live and who, against the odds that were stacked in their favour, would die.

'Ready!'

'Are you ready for war?'

The second time, less of a question and more of an imperative.

'Ready!'

'ARE YOU READY FOR WAR?'

And one last time, a full-throated challenge to his soldiers' manhood, their pride and their right to inhabit their privileged world – but as he shouted the words at them, he saw facial expressions in the cohort's front rank change in the time it took him to roar out the words. Eyes which had been fixed on him, in accordance with orders drilled into them on hundreds of occasions, were suddenly looking past him, up the slope to the place where their enemy waited. As Servius turned to follow their shocked stares, a horn sounded from behind him, a long mournful note whose

implications sent a shiver up his spine. On the ridge behind the
waiting Blemmyes men were moving into position, hundreds
strong, each of them holding a bow and a sheaf of arrows, while
at either end of their formation horsemen were walking their
mounts into position. Some among them were holding up objects
on the points of their spears, and after a moment staring up at
them in perplexity, Servius realised, with a sickening shock, that
they were severed heads, more than one still carrying the gilded
helmet of a Roman cavalryman. Shaking off the momentary
paralysis that had gripped him, shock at the speed with which
the situation had catastrophically changed for the worse, and
realising his own personal danger, he turned back to his men
and started walking briskly across the twenty-pace gap to the line,
fighting his instinct to run for the illusory safety of their ranks
and in doing so start a panic that would see them all dead. The
first spear pulled a soldier aside to make a gap for him to slip
through, then pushed the man back into place, stepping back
alongside his superior and shouting loudly enough to be heard
along the entire length of the cohort's formation.

'Get your bloody shields up! *Shields!*'

The first spear's bellowed order broke the spell that seemed to
have gripped the auxiliaries with the appearance of the new threat,
his men raising their shields as ordered.

'This is a death trap, Prefect! We need to back away, if they'll
let us, and then speed march for the nearest water fort as fast as
we can!'

'But this is *our* ground . . .'

Knowing even as he said it, and without needing the negation
in the other man's eyes, that he was, at least temporarily, utterly
wrong. The first spear pointed at the forces mustering on the
slope above them, the dull weight of certainty in his voice.

'No, Prefect, this is *their* ground now. That many archers, and
cavalry, the only way we get out of this trap is if they let us re—'

The horn's mournful note sounded again, and, with a hiss of
arrow fletching carving the air, the archers loosed their arrows.

The centurion dragged Servius into the cover of the rear rank's shields, shouting at his men to take cover as the deadly iron sleet plunged down onto the Roman line. Curses, imprecations, exhortations to stand fast and shouts of agony and terror erupted along the quailing cohort's length, arrows punching into shields and flitting through the gaps between them to deal indiscriminate death among the auxiliaries. A soldier reeled from his place in the rear rank with an arrow's shaft protruding from his neck, managing half a dozen disjointed steps before collapsing lifelessly at Servius's feet, while all along the line his men were falling, mostly writhing in pain at the shock of their wounds as another volley hissed down to repeat the carnage inflicted by the first. The first spear pushed the dead man's shield at his superior, flinching as a pair of arrows hammered into the board that he had raised over his own head, lethally pointed iron heads protruding a clear six inches through the layered wooden boards.

'You have to get away, Prefect!'

Servius shook his head in prompt negation of any such idea.

'I won't run!'

'They're five times our number and more! The only choice we have is being slaughtered by the archers if we stand or ridden down by the cavalry if we run! But one man can still escape!' He pointed to the prefect's horse, tethered fifty paces back from the embattled Romans, the beast shying at the battle's sudden cacophony but held in place by the iron stake Servius had hammered into the rock only moments before. 'Go! Take the only chance we've got and get word out as to what happened here! You of all people know what all this must mean!'

The prefect nodded reluctantly, knowing that once on the horse he would be uncatchable by the enemy cavalry, almost certainly already part-blown by their exertions in the desert's harsh environment.

'Surely the cohort will break, if they see me run for it?'

Khaba shook his head grimly.

'Not if I lead them forward at the same time.' He shook his

head tiredly. 'This is a knife in Rome's back. You have to get word of this treachery out to Alexandria.'

The prefect nodded, his mouth a tight slash in his pale face. 'Very well.'

'And if you make it, see that my woman and the child are looked after?'

'I will. And I'll dedicate an altar to you.'

The first spear smiled weakly, flinching as another volley hammered at the cohort's shields, and yet more of their soldiers fell under the deadly hail. The volume of shouts and screams was already reduced, most of the soldiers focused simply on staying in the cover of their shields, while those who had failed to do so, and paid the price, were for the most part dead, each successive volley reaping more of the men whose wounds had left them helpless on the bare ground. He pointed at the horse.

'I always wondered what a man had to do to get himself immortalised in stone! I'd have been happy never to have found out though. Now go!'

He turned to face the enemy, roaring a command over the confusion and terror.

'With me, First Cohort! Advance!'

Along the line the remaining centurions and watch officers began echoing his orders, pushing their men forward in what Servius guessed they would instinctively know was a doomed attempt to counter-attack. He watched for a moment as the men of his command followed their example, shaking his head as several wounded soldiers somehow managed to follow their comrades forward up the slope, limping, staggering and in one case literally crawling in their wake. Turning away with a prayer to Mercury for divine speed, he sprinted for the horse, straining every sinew against the weight of his armour and weapons, mentally rehearsing the three swift actions that would see him escape: unhook its reins from the iron tether, leap astride the beast, and put his boots into its flanks once he had it facing away from the battle. Halfway across the gap between his doomed cohort and the animal, running so fast that he felt as if he were floating over the limestone's hard surface, perpetually on the edge of falling, such was his breakneck pace, and at the very instant he began to believe that he would make it to the animal unnoticed in the battle's chaos, an arrow flicked past him a pace to his right. The second, loosed after him an instant later, did not miss. The shaft pierced his thigh with such force that the iron head protruded a hand span above the knee, sending him sprawling across the rock hard enough that he bit through his lip with the impact. Rolling onto his back, the instinct to survive still strong, despite the shocking pain making the wounded leg all but useless, he stared for a moment at what was happening on the slope beneath the village. From the ridge's vantage point, the enemy archers were pouring their arrows into the advancing auxiliaries with sufficient venom to put their shafts straight through the thin wooden layers of their shields at such close range, aiming high to put their spiked arrowheads into the faces of the men behind such flimsy protection.

Rolling onto his knees, gasping as the arrow's shaft scraped across the rock, Servius managed to get to his knees and drew his sword, putting one hand on his unwounded thigh and the weapon's point against the rock, pushing himself upright. Tottering on the spatha's wobbling support, he snarled at the pain before starting a slow, painful limp towards the waiting horse, dragging the useless limb behind him as he lurched, one slow pace at a time across the sandy ground. Without any apparent transition other than a brief sensation of being struck hard in the back, he found himself struggling to work out why the world was suddenly at right angles, sky to the left, ground to the right. An overwhelming sense that none of it really mattered had settled on him, the sensation's crushing weight like the reassurance he had enjoyed from being placed under heavy blankets as a small child, seeming to pin him where he had apparently fallen. There was bare rock under his helmet, grating on the finely engraved metal, and he wondered briefly how he was going to get the scratches polished out before abandoning the thought as irrelevant, as he realised what had bludgeoned his body into immobility. Something was inside him, its intrusion beyond simple pain, and he put a hand to his chest to feel the first inch of an arrow point protruding through the armour, the hole slick with his blood.

'I'm . . . *dying*.'

The realisation was comforting, in a way. The indignity and distress he was feeling, through the numbing, enervating shock of having an arrow pierce his body from back to front, would soon be over. The loss of his command, still visible on the village's slope but now reduced to little more than a hundred embattled men, their drive up the slope halted as they clustered together in a doomed attempt to survive the continual barrage of arrows that was pecking steadily away at their numbers, was no longer a personal disaster, but simply something that happened when men went to war. Servius would be with his ancestors soon enough and, he realised, the only thing he had left to worry about was that his death wound was in his back. He watched, detached from the events by more than distance, as the remnant of his cohort gathered themselves for one last, magnificent, shambling attempt to attack, their pitiful advance failing in the space of a dozen paces as the archers reaped them without pity and felled every last one.

The Blemmyes came down the slope to start picking over the dead and wounded for the contents of their purses and the bounty of their equipment, a wealth of iron armour to men used to fighting without any such protection, prizes to be displayed, he mused, for centuries to come. Or perhaps to be discovered and punished with death, when the legions came to take Rome's revenge for their theft. A pair of running men passed him, both seeking to take the magnificent prize waiting for them, the horse still tethered to the rock behind him. After what sounded like a brief scuffle, one of them came back to stand over him, muttering something vicious and pulling the dagger from his belt. He knelt on one knee, looking the dying Roman up and down for a moment and nodding, perhaps calculating that the wealth to be had from his gleaming bronze breastplate and heavily decorated equipment would, perhaps, compensate for the loss of the horse. He put the weapon's point to the dying man's throat, ready to deliver the mercy stroke that would finally end the prefect's pain, and Servius smiled faintly, readying himself to die.

A fresh voice barked, an unmistakable command, harsh and pre-emptory, and the cold sensation of the knife blade against his skin withdrew, the Arab standing and looking with venom at several heavily armed men escorting someone towards him. Realising who it was he was about to defy, presumably at risk to his life, he fell to one knee, then withdrew hurriedly at the bark of another terse command. The bodyguards halted, their ranks opening to allow their charge to approach. Dressed in magnificently ornamented battle armour, intricately chased with silver and decorated with gems, the enemy leader knelt to look into his eyes.

'You are dying, Roman.' The words were Greek, heavily accented but recognisable, the voice soft and yet shot through with iron. 'A wound such as that which my men have inflicted upon you is invariably fatal, although it might be hours before the shock and loss of blood take you to your ancestors. You will lose your ability to think soon enough, but you might hover here, caught between life and death, for as long as a day, as your life leaks away from the holes we have put in your body.' The eyes seemed to bore into him, above the veil of chain mail that covered the speaker's nose and mouth, covering skin so dark as to be almost black. 'I can hasten your journey across the river to meet those that went before you, if you assist me with the answer to a simple question. Will you do that, Roman?'

'*What . . . question?*'

The eyes narrowed in a smile that to Servius's fading consciousness looked almost affectionate.

'What more forces does Rome have in the field in the land of my allies, the Blemmyes? Just answer me that, and I will cut you free from this unhappy end myself. And I will put the blade in your throat, a death wound with honour. No man wishes to meet his grandfather bearing only the marks of having been shot in the back as he ran from battle, does he?'

The soft voice hardening, the eyes staring down at him without compassion, without any emotion other than the need to have the question answered.

'You . . . swear . . . it?'

A nod.

'I swear it on the life of my son. I swear it to Amun, the Lord of the Thrones, and to Nut, the sky goddess, mother of Osiris, Isis, Set, Nephthys and Horus, that I will give you the mercy stroke, here and now, if you answer this one simple question honestly. And this is not a vow any ruler would make without the most serious intent.'

'You . . . are . . . a . . . king?'

The brown eyes stared down at him dispassionately, unblinking.

'No questions. Only answers.'

Servius thought for a moment, weighing the twin evils of betraying his oath to serve the emperor, no matter how small the treachery, with the need for some vestige of honour in his death.

'No . . . other . . . forces.'

'Then the fortress at Koptos is empty, and the port of Berenike is undefended.' The eyes stared down at him for a moment, assessing the truth in his eyes. 'Your part in this is done. Go to your ancestors.'

The blade under his chin moved swiftly, tugging at his windpipe, and with a hot rush of blood onto the rock, Servius felt the last of his consciousness depart, his killer's eyes the last thing he would ever see as life left his failing body. The armoured figure stood.

'Prepare your men to march, General Tantamani. There is a rich prize to be taken, and I want our appearance at the gates of the port to be unheralded. Leave our enemies to pick these poor fools clean, they have served their purpose and can only delay us if we demand they join us in this conquest. Not to mention the evil that they would inflict on the innocent womanhood of the city, where I know I can trust our own soldiery to act with decency. Can I not?'

The man to whom the question was addressed nodded, meeting his leader's eyes in the manner expected when questions of life and death were put.

'Very well. As we planned it, take our cavalry to the east; there is water to be had on the main trade road. Allow your horses to drink, then turn them to the south and east, following the road until you have Berenike in sight, but remain out of view. Allow any passing caravan to go unmolested. The last thing we want is for an alarm to be raised before our arrival, and any ships in the harbour to escape. We will only declare our presence at the last possible moment, when it will be too late to retrieve their sailors and oarsmen from the taverns. I will follow with the infantry and archers at the best sustainable pace, and once we catch up with you, we will march into the port and explain the facts of conquest to our new subjects. Rome has held this ground since the days of my ancestor Amanirenas, two hundred years ago, and has on occasion even bound us to treaties signed at that time, that have required our horsemen and archers to fight alongside them. But now that is all just history.' A hand swept through the air to dismiss such irrelevance. 'The time has come for these invaders to discover that when the dwellers of the lands further down the great river named our kingdom *Ta-Sety*, "the Land of the Bow" in their ancient language, they did so not from a sense of respect, or kinship, but from fear!'

The same hand pointed to the northern horizon.

'Rome's rule here is ended, and I dream of a day when our dominion stretches from the pyramids of Meroë to those of distant Memphis. I will bequeath my son the great river's entire length, and make him the ruler of a dominion that stretches as far north as under the rule of my ancestor Taharqa, to the distant sea itself. I will drive the Romans back into that sea and declare myself ruler of the Black Lands that are watered by the great river. Their rich, dark soil will no longer be Rome's to pillage, to feed a city of idlers, but ours to cherish as our true homeland once again! Cavalry, ride!'

I

Mediterranean Sea, March AD 187

'The thing you must remember about my homeland, gentlemen – and this above all other facts – is this.' The speaker paused portentously, looking around himself to be sure that all the men around him were listening. 'Aegyptus is not like any other province in the empire.'

The imperial secretary had been marched aboard the praetorian flagship *Victoria* by a party of praetorians shortly before the tide had turned, with the sacrifices already made and declared favourable, and the crew in the final stages of casting off from her mooring. Olive-skinned and with the dark eyes common among his countrymen, finely boned and with a faintly avian cast of features, he nevertheless wore his status as an official in the imperial court with a somewhat bumptious confidence. Having swiftly introduced himself to the nonplussed members of the party which had preceded him aboard the warship some hours before, the secretary had set about their education with breezy gusto, evidently believing that he was both expected and entitled to do so whether his insights were desired or not. Now, with the praetorian fleet's flagship an hour out from Ostia, making good speed to the south-east under sail with its tiered banks of oars inboard, and with its rowers relaxing on their benches in the morning sunlight, he had embarked upon an explanation of what it was that made the emperor's own province, on the far side of the sea dominated by their navy, so unique. He looked around his small and somewhat bemused audience with the self-satisfied look of a learned man in the presence of the less educationally privileged.

'Not for no reason was it that the first emperor, whose name was Augustus, declared the province to be his own. He decreed that it was to be ruled by a man of the equestrian class, and not by a senator, for it was too precious a territory to risk losing to the control of a potential usurper. It is the empire's breadbasket, no less, and were it to be lost then—'

'Rome would starve. We *know*.'

The imperial functionary looked at the party's leader, a tall, thin man wearing a tunic edged with the thin purple stripe of the equestrian order. His grey eyes were locked on the secretary in a flat stare that might have been described as pitying, were his features not set rather more kindly.

'These were only my opening remarks, Tribune Scaurus.'

'You know my name, from which I am to presume that you have been briefed as to who we all are?'

The secretary nodded.

'You are Gaius Rutilius Scaurus, a tribune of the equestrian class. You have an infamous reputation for having played no small part in the fall of the last praetorian prefect, and for having helped the current chamberlain to be promoted into his position.'

The tribune nodded his head in agreement.

'That much is true, more or less. Not that your master recognises my part in his elevation to ultimate power with any fondness.'

'Indeed not. It is the talk of the palace secretariat that our master Cleander is somewhat ambivalent with regard to your eventual fate. He places you into situations where your death seems inevitable, with the added benefit that your unlikely survival can only be achieved by the defeat of Rome's adversaries. And yet, despite your having been commanded to challenge the odds on three occasions, here you are, sailing on another imperial mission from which there ought to be no return.'

Scaurus shrugged.

'And perhaps this time your master will achieve the result he so clearly—'

He frowned as the official raised a hand in correction.

'With all due respect, Tribune, I find it best to be clear about matters such as that you refer to. And so for clarity, I am forced to point out that Chamberlain Cleander is not my master. I have no master, as such. I am a man raised in the Greek tradition, in the great city of Alexandria which, as every man knows, is the world's centre of learning. I am a *philosoph*, literally, a—'

'Lover of wisdom. With Socrates, Aristotle and Plato as your guiding lights.'

The Aegyptian inclined his head in agreement, apparently failing to recognise Scaurus's gently sarcastic tone.

'Indeed. I am a man of the intellectual tradition, a citizen of the world of ideas and knowledge just as much as I am a man of Aegyptus. And I have no master.'

The tribune smiled tolerantly.

'Your point is taken, although, were I in a disputative frame of mind, I might point out that Chamberlain Cleander is every man's master with the exception of just one. Shall we compromise as to his part in your life, and refer to him as the man who orders your every waking moment with even his slightest whims?'

The secretary nodded slowly.

'In that much I am forced to agree, Tribune Scaurus. In truth, the chamberlain might as well be my master, even if he lacks the formal title.'

'And your name is?'

'Ptolemy. My mother named me for the great man who rescued my country from the disaster of the wars that followed the death of his friend Alexander.' He drew himself up to his full height, still half a head shorter than the shortest man in the party. 'She told me that I have it in me to be every bit as great as the king himself.'

'Every man does, if he knows how to access the best in himself.' Scaurus smiled, ignoring the sounds of stifled mirth from behind him and putting out a hand. 'Well met, Ptolemy of Alexandria. And now, if you have been briefed as to who we all are, perhaps you could share that briefing with us?'

Ptolemy nodded happily.

'It would be my pleasure to share that knowledge.' He studied the men standing behind the equestrian, pointing to a man in his mid-twenties wearing a tunic bearing the same thin purple stripe as Scaurus's. 'You, Centurion, are Marcus Valerius Aquila, adopted son of a murdered senator, and you go by the assumed name of Marcus Tribulus Corvus. I know this by the two swords you wear, one of them given to you after the death of your birth father, a legatus who died in Britannia. You are of *special* interest to the chamberlain.'

Marcus regarded him for a moment before replying. Lean and yet graced with a soldier's muscle, his body hard and wiry, his hawk-like face was marked by scars on the bridge of his nose, and under his gaze the secretary visibly shrank slightly into himself.

'Of *special* interest? Is that a way of saying that he has a *special* interest in my death?'

'No, Centurion Aquila.' The secretary stared back at him for a moment. 'Forgive me, sir. Opportunities to converse with a living legend are not granted to a man many times in this life, so I may seem a little awed.'

'A little awed?' A man in full centurion's equipment leaning on the ship's rail spat over the side, taking a lungful of the salt-edged air before speaking again, with a hard smile that was as much menace as it was amusement. 'What you seem, friend, is cock-struck.' He switched to speaking Greek with the ease of a man long accustomed to the language, although his idiom was the clipped, hard tones of a soldier. 'Since you say that you're as much a Greek as Aegyptian, are you perhaps one of those Greeks we've all met? A man with a taste for men? Or do your tastes incline instead to young boys? Or ducks, perhaps?'

Ptolemy shook his head, clearly intent on not taking offence.

'No, Centurion Cotta. And were it not for your friend, it would be you I would be regarding with a degree of reverence. Not many men, after all, have had both the nerve and the gods' given blessing to kill an emperor.'

Cotta shook his head in disbelief.

'That *again*? He wasn't a fucking emperor, he was an idiot general who made the mistake of allowing his men to put a purple cloak around his shoulders and prance up and down shouting "rich soldier" at him, until he genuinely believed that he was the right person to replace his master. Who was, unfortunately for him at least, not actually dead. I was ordered to take Cassius's head off his shoulders by my legatus, to spare him the indignity of the public punishment that would have preceded his death, had he caused the expense and loss of life of a civil war. All I did was what I was legally ordered to do, by a man invested with the authority to issue that order. You might as well blame the knife I used!'

Ptolemy smiled knowingly.

'I read the official report from the imperial agent who gave you the order to deal with Legatus Augusti Cassius. You killed half a dozen men—'

'Five men, and one would-be god.'

The secretary ignored Cotta's interruption with the grace of a man well used to being verbally harassed by men less fortunate than himself.

'After which you carried Legatus Augusti Cassius's head back to your own legion's lines in a bag, walking brazenly through his men's guard posts without anyone realising what it was you had done. You are a fascinating man, Centurion.'

Cotta snorted, tipping his head at Marcus.

'Go back to kissing that young idiot's arse, before I tire of your attentions and put you over the side.'

The secretary bowed.

'As you wish, Centurion. It is a long voyage, and given time, I have no doubt that you will soften sufficiently to tell me your story. And perhaps your friend's taciturn companions will be more forthcoming in the meantime. The officer next to you, for example.'

The man leaning on the rail next to Cotta shot a sideways glance at Ptolemy before going back to contemplating the passing sea.

'Avidus? I doubt it. He's a man of few words, unless there's a ditch to be dug or a siege engine needs building, and then you can't shut the bastard up.'

'Indeed, Centurion Avidus who, I believe, has what's left of his century with him. A century which Tribune Scaurus "borrowed" from the Third Augustan Legion a few years ago and has apparently conveniently forgotten to return. The Third's legatus has written in complaint to Rome more than once, but it seems that the chamberlain is reluctant to break up a winning team. It was also fortuitous that the centurion and his men were left behind in Rome when you marched to deal with the bandit Maternus, since it meant that they, unlike most of your command which is still on its way back from Gaul, were available to join you in your mission to Aegyptus.'

'For all the good they'll be. Unless we need a wall putting up, that is.'

Ptolemy turned to three other men in the group, singling out the man who had spoken, a tall, muscular figure clad in a white tunic with the silver studded leather belt of an officer, an intricately decorated dagger sitting on his right hip, and bowed unexpectedly.

'Dubnus, prince of the Brigantes. My felicitations to you, Your Highness.'

Cotta barked out a laugh, genuinely amused.

'If only Julius were here. He'd have stained his tunic with joy at that.'

Dubnus, a man in his mid-thirties with more of the warrior about him than any of the secretary's implied regality, shook his head in flat rejection of his new supplicant's sympathy.

'That's *Centurion* to you, Scribe. The days when I was usurped as successor to my former tribe's throne are so distant as to be nothing better than uncertain memory. And long since avenged.'

Ptolemy bowed again, an obliging expression on his face.

'Of course, Centurion. I completely understand your desire not to be reminded of the past.'

Cotta laughed cynically.

'Which makes a man wonder why you would raise it? In a hurry to find out the colour of your own guts, are you? Or just eager to swim with the sharks, perhaps?'

The big Briton ignored the interjection.

'I have no problem recalling it. No sense of pain or loss, not after this long. It's simply that when I walked up to the gates of the Roman fort and gave my life to Rome, I was reborn. The days when I was Dubnus, son of Cynbel, rightful ruler of my tribe, are nothing more to me than a dream. The last time I went back to my tribe's city it was as a Roman officer, to make my peace with the man who succeeded my father and have revenge on the men who killed him.'

Ptolemy leaned forward, his eyes narrowing with evident fascination.

'And will you tell me more of this? It would be a valuable addition to our understanding of your people.'

Dubnus eyed him with evident amusement, reaching out and tapping the official's tunicked chest with a thick forefinger.

'I *know* what you are, Scribe. I've met men like you before, book learned and as bright as gold buttons. You think you know all there is to know, and that everything that matters can be hidden in the scrolls you write, like a code for men like you who can decipher it. You observe, you note the details and you scribble them down for others to read. But most of all, you like to *watch*.'

The secretary nodded agreement, pursing his lips in apparent ambivalence.

'What you say is true, more or less. I . . . *we* . . . do believe in the importance of the written word, to pass the lessons of the past down through generations, information that might otherwise be lost to the grandsons of the men who discovered what makes the world the way it is.'

The Briton leaned back, looking down his nose at the smaller man in a way that his comrades immediately recognised.

'Oh, dear gods below, can you not resist the temptation to do your warrior king impersonation *just* this once?'

Dubnus waved Cotta's complaint away.

'I understand the power of words, freedman. They are part of the secret to Rome's empire, words, and roads, and legions, but I believe that in putting your nose to a scroll for all your waking hours you miss the essential truth of this life.' He patted the shaft of the axe whose heavy iron head rested on the ship's planking, and which he had politely but firmly declined to store in the vessel's hold. 'This is the instrument with which I write my destiny. And my stories are written in the blood of my enemies, and that of the men who stand alongside me. You should exchange the stylus for a sword and see whether you too might find a purer calling.'

He grinned down at the scribe, evidently seeking to intimidate the man, but Marcus was intrigued to see that Ptolemy's answer was a simple birdlike nod of his head.

'I will take you up on that kind offer, Centurion. It would be a matter of the greatest honour to learn the secrets of the sword from you.'

Dubnus shook his head, drawing breath for some retort, but the man behind him, fully a head taller even than the massively built centurion, was faster to react. His barked laugh made the secretary jump, loud enough to narrow the Briton's eyes in momentary discomfort.

'By the gods, Lugos, if you're going to bellow in my ear at least do me the favour—'

'He have you, Dubnus!' The long-haired tribesman simply ignored his complaint, his booming voice effortlessly overriding the Briton's. 'You make like big man, he find your heel of . . .' He turned to Scaurus in question. 'Who is man you tell me of, immortal except for his heel?'

The tribune smiled up at him with an affection born of years of shared hardship.

'Achilles, Lugos. Half-man, half-god.'

'Hah!' The giant clapped a hand on Dubnus's shoulder, the comradely gesture tipping the Briton's body to one side momentarily. 'He find your heel of Achilles. Your pride make you his prisoner. Now you must teach him sword!'

Dubnus turned his irritation on the scribe.

'Were you trying to catch me out, you devious little sh—'

'Not at all, Warrior Prince!' Ptolemy raised his hands in protest, eyes wide with conviction. 'But tell me this, I implore you! Who, if offered the opportunity to learn from a master of their art, would do anything other than accept the kind gesture with the utmost alacrity?'

'I think he means that given you were stupid enough to make the offer, you—'

'I know what he means, Cotta!' Caught between his own frustration and the danger of appearing churlish under the secretary's deluge of praise, Dubnus capitulated, albeit with an obvious reluctance. 'Very well, Scribe, tomorrow morning, and every morning, we will practise with the sword. Let's see what can be made of you.'

He turned away, then, caught by a sudden inspiration, returned his gaze to the freedman.

'One more thing.'

'Anything!'

'My comrades here.' Dubnus hooked a thumb over his shoulder at the massive bulk of Lugos looming behind him, and the watchful figure of the tribune's servant Arminius at his side. 'What did your briefing tell you about them?'

Ptolemy bowed to Lugos, who stiffly returned the gesture with an expression of genuine interest in whatever the imperial functionary was about to say.

'With regard to this man, my briefing was simply this: a barbarian giant, extremely dangerous. Not to be provoked or trifled with.'

Dubnus shook his head in disbelief.

'So *I* can be provoked, but not this monster?'

The subject of his ire shook his head briskly.

'Far from it, noble Centurion. I was instructed to treat you with the utmost of respect, but to engage you in discussion at any opportunity. You are one of us, and therefore open to rational discussion. The barbarian Lugos, however, I was told to avoid any discourse with at all costs. Apparently his sort are prone to fits of rage, presumably as the result of their realisation that they can never match the grandeur of Rome.'

Lugos looked down at him in silence for a moment, ignoring Cotta's attempts to muffle his laughter with the scarf that protected his neck from the edging of his armour. When he spoke, his voice was curiously muted, the point he wished to make evidently rooted in sadness rather than anger.

'You are right, little man.' He leaned forward to put his big face so close to Ptolemy's that the scribe could see the pale detail in the long scar that carved a furrow through the flesh of his right cheek. 'My people do not live in palace of stone. We do not eat from bowl of silver. We do not even wear coat of iron, like Roman warrior. We are poor people. But we have . . .'

He looked at Scaurus, seeking assistance with what he was trying to express.

'Dignity?'

The giant nodded, but before he could repeat the word Marcus spoke into the charged silence, his voice charged with emotion on his friend's behalf.

'And pride. Pride in who you are. And what you were before Rome turned your lives upside down.'

Ptolemy frowned and opened his mouth to argue, only to be interrupted by Arminius.

'A fate avoided by my own people, the Quadi, only at a high price in our blood. Like every people who have surrendered to Rome and found themselves assimilated. Conscripted. *Taxed.*' The German stepped forward, looking down at the secretary with an unreadable expression. 'You might find us untypical subjects of the empire, Scribe. We have seen Rome's rule in Britannia, Gallia, Germania, Dacia, Syria and half a dozen other provinces. And we have travelled in the east, as far as Ctesiphon, and looked back at Rome through the eyes of our enemies. We see what Rome is, and what she does to the peoples her armies conquer.'

'I know. I have read of your exploits, Arminius of Germania.' Ptolemy's voice was abruptly soft. 'And I have many questions for you on the subject of those travels.' He nodded slowly. 'And I understand your point. Rome is a hungry beast, with an appetite for conquest, regardless of the consequences for others.'

'No.' They turned back to Lugos, who had straightened to his full height and was staring out over the warship's side at the distant smudge that was all they could see of the receding coast behind them. 'Rome not hungry. Rome got all it ever need. Rome is like a jealous neighbour, want you land, you wife. Want to enslave you children and take you gold. And very few people got strength to tell Rome no.'

He turned away and walked to the ship's side, leaving them staring after him.

'I had no idea that a barbarian of such apparent brutality could be so thoughtful. I must speak more with that man. And perhaps with you as well, Centurion Qadir?'

The Syrian archer bowed slightly.

'I cannot imagine what it could be that I could say that would be of any interest to a man as full of knowledge as you.'

'And yet I do have questions for you. The secretariat has been interested in you ever since you came to our attention.'

'Me?' Qadir appeared genuinely puzzled. 'What is there to me that could attract the interest of your scholars?'

Ptolemy smiled back at him kindly.

'It is not the scholars among us who are interested in you, Centurion, but rather the record keepers. When your presence in this familia was first noted by the men set to watch the tribune and those who accompany him, the usual searches of the records

pertaining to your province were made. The secretariat is most
diligent in such things, as I'm sure you can imagine. And the
mills of imperial record-keeping do grind slowly, but they also
grind very finely. And yet with regard to yourself there was nothing
at all, not until the time you joined the army as an archer, under
what appears to have been a pseudonym. That is an invented
name, used for the purpose of disgui—'

'We know this, Scribe. And your point is? I'm sure my colleague
wouldn't be the first man to join up with a new name.'

Ptolemy nodded earnestly.

'The secretariat, Centurion Cotta, hates a mystery. Perhaps
Centurion Qadir can illuminate his origins and put their concerns
to rest. Nothing troubles an administrator more than a lack of
certainty as to particular facts, as I am sure you can imagine.'

His matter-of-fact statement, made, apparently, without any
intent to threaten, left the party momentarily nonplussed, a
silence which the single-minded Aegyptian completely failed to
recognise as a reason for concern.

'Doubtless we can talk more on this subject at some point.' He
turned to Scaurus with the determined expression of a frustrated
teacher. 'And now, sir, with your permission, I will resume the
briefing I have been ordered to deliver to you.'

'Oi, what about us?'

Both men turned to face a pair of soldiers standing at the rail,
their tunics rough compared to the finer cloth worn by the officers,
the fabric much repaired with off-coloured patches taken from
other garments, their belts and daggers utilitarian rather than
decorated.

Ptolemy looked at them both blankly.

'What about you, legionaries? You seem unremarkable, other
than your somewhat surprising status as barbarian legionaries
who have the ability to speak Greek.'

The shorter of the two, a man in his late thirties with a sly,
calculating look, shook his head in disgust at the response.

'Of course we speak Greek, we learned it in the east. How else was we supposed to get fed, or get a drink, or a woman? So what were you told about Sanga and Saratos, eh?' He opened his hands wide. 'Spies, brawlers and fighters, we are, with stories to tell!'

'Stories like "How I spent all the tribune's gold in a brothel and told him it was used bribing secrets out of other men when all I actually did was get them pissed and listen to their drunken babble"?' Cotta raised an amused eyebrow. 'I can see how the imperial secretariat would be keen to get that one onto paper for generations to come to marvel at.'

Ignoring the jibe, the soldier stared at Ptolemy, who shook his head slowly.

'No mention was made of either of you, legionary.'

'I ain't a legionary, I'm a watch officer!'

His companion tapped him on the shoulder and shook his head.

'Leave it. Is same as always.'

'Too bloody right it is.' Sanga turned away and leaned over the side, muttering to himself, and Cotta barked another laugh, if a little more sympathetically. 'Not every man can be a figure in this fool's history of the world. And trust me, Sanga, you're better off sticking to the simple life you enjoy so much, calculating time by how long it'll be before you have a drink in your hand and a woman pretending to laugh at your stories while she prays that the contents of your purse are larger than what's under your tunic. Because when the time comes that we all fall foul of some evil bastard, you'll be able to slide out from under.'

Ptolemy waited for a moment, listening politely to the soldier's aggrieved muttering before turning back to Scaurus.

'As to that briefing, Tribune, I—'

The tribune raised a hand.

'Before you continue, tell me, Scribe, just how far is it from Ostia to Alexandria?'

Ptolemy answered without hesitation.

'Fifteen hundred miles, more or less.'

'And how long will the *Victoria* take to cover that distance?'

'Given the prevailing winds, I believe that we can expect a crossing of approximately fourteen days.'

Scaurus nodded.

'As I thought. So, given that we have two weeks to fill, more or less, perhaps we might defer the pleasure of receiving your extensive knowledge of the emperor's province to some later date?'

Ptolemy inclined his head in solemn acceptance of the point.

'I will look forward to that opportunity to share my knowledge with you.'

'Thank you. Although there is one question that I would appreciate an answer to, in the meantime.'

'Name it, sir, and I will answer, if it is within my power to do so.'

'We have been hurried aboard this vessel and shot like an arrow from the imperial bow at Aegyptus, with orders to deal with "a minor problem in the province". A *minor problem* that remains utterly unspecified, with no further briefing having been provided by the praetorian detachment that escorted us to the docks. Can you illuminate us as to the nature of whatever it is that requires our very particular skills?'

The scribe's face fell.

'With the deepest apologies, sir, I must admit that I am unable to provide you with any further detail as to the nature of the task entrusted to you by the imperial chamberlain. Perhaps you will be more completely briefed by the prefect commanding the province?'

The *Victoria* made landfall on the day her tribune had predicted, much to the pleasure of his crew, who were keenly anticipating the opportunity to sample the city's delights, although the prospect of making harbour was apparently not one that gave their fleet commander any joy. A taciturn, heavily bearded man, known to Scaurus's familia from previous journeys at Cleander's command, he stared over the vessel's side as her navarchus alternated between barking out a succession of steering and rowing orders and directing a steady stream of invective at the smaller craft obstructing her path. The entrance to the city's eastern harbour was less than a quarter of a mile distant, the four-hundred-foot-high lighthouse of Pharos towering over its entrance in its scarcely credible three-tiered grandeur, the gap through which the flagship would have to pass crowded with traffic. Scaurus gestured to the vessel's captain, as he paced the deck with the look of a man ready to assault anyone that gave him the slightest excuse.

'Wishing that was you, Tribune?'

The naval officer shot Scaurus a disbelieving glance.

'Do I look like a fucking idiot?'

The soldier inclined his head gracefully, conceding the point.

'Not every man who manages, by good fortune and his own skills, to be promoted to the height of his competence, is necessarily happy to leave the performance of his skills to other, lesser men.'

They watched in silence for a moment as the navarchus ordered a swift change of course, guiding the flagship's stately progression into the city's Great Harbour around a group of small boats whose occupants seemed determined to seek their deaths under the beak of her copper-sheathed ram.

'You think I wish I was the one shouting the orders and cursing the bum boats?' The sailor shook his head. 'I spent ten years being the man responsible for sailing this unwieldy monstrosity around Our Sea, forever wondering when I was going to run it onto an uncharted rock and end my days begging for spare change outside the arena with the other failures. And now, thanks to you taking the fleet's last commander ashore with you and leaving him six feet under the dirt of wherever it was in Persia that you took him, I command the fleet. Me, the son of a butcher, who ran away to sea rather than put up with the stink of offal and the perpetual buzz of flies.'

'How was it that you kept your temporary command? I had expected that there would be a queue of suitably qualified gentlemen for such a prime position.'

The dark-faced seaman raised an eyebrow at Scaurus.

'How do you think? I was summoned to an interview with the chamberlain, in which I was informed that the position was mine for the rest of my time at sea, but only if I was willing to undertake certain *secret operations* without asking any awkward questions.'

'Smuggling?'

The sailor's expression remained impassive.

'I have no idea, Tribune. From time to time I receive orders to bring the fleet here, or a squadron, or sometimes just the *Victoria*. Showing the locals the strength of Rome, as my orders put it. After all, there's no point having a navy and allowing it to rot at anchor, or at least that's the chamberlain's stated position on the matter. How else could my navarchus be so familiar with this shoal- and rock-strewn channel as not to need a pilot?'

'And while you're docked, and your oarsmen and marines are ashore doing their best to plant a crop of little sailors and soldiers in the local women, the odd unofficial cargo comes aboard?'

'Sometimes the items in question are small enough to be tucked under a visiting dignitary's cloak. Sometimes five hundred men will labour for a full day to bring them aboard my ships. We once loaded twenty-one vessels to their full capacity with bags of what I can only presume was grain.'

'I see.'

Both men were silent for a moment, Scaurus staring up at the towering lighthouse on the ship's right-hand side.

'You've heard the name of Alexander the Great, I presume?'

The naval officer nodded scornfully.

'I may live for the sea, Tribune, but I'm not a total fool. And yes, I know that he commissioned this city from bare sand, marking out the street plan with flour. Which is funny, given the amount of grain that comes through here to keep Rome from starving.'

'And Ptolemy?'

The big man smiled ruefully.

'Some Aegyptian or other. There are limits to a sailor's interest in the doings of lesser mortals.'

Scaurus returned the smile.

'Ptolemy was a Macedonian, just like Alexander. And he was the great man's closest friend, allegedly the bastard son of Alexander's father Philip. They grew up under the teaching of a genius called Aristotle, and a good deal of that wisdom must have rubbed off on him, because when his friend died, Ptolemy was the first of his generals to realise there was no way to keep the empire he'd built in one piece. He staked out Aegyptus for its wealth and strategic position, and he took it for his own. He made himself a king, to start with, the most that could be tolerated from a Greek by the population, but he was astute enough to rule wisely, better than the Persians before him, and made this city into a centre of philosophy and the arts. And in time, through clever association with the local deities, he made himself and his successors into living gods.' He shot a grin at the sailor, who was listening with the expression of a man being lectured. 'Which is a good trick. Our emperors have to die before being admitted to the imperial cult. How much better to attain godhead while you're still alive, eh?'

'It's a good story. Are you sure you're not just passing the time with a history lecture for a dumb oarsman?'

'Stay with me, there's a point to my story. Ptolemy was a clever man, not just a warrior, and his time at the feet of one of the greatest philosophers that ever lived had gifted him with a lifelong love of the civilised way of life. He built this city to last, to be a place of splendour for all time, and one of the challenges he decided to tackle was this . . .' Scaurus waved a hand at the harbour before them. 'You know what a difficult bay this would have been to enter, what with the island of Pharos and the offshore reefs that stud the harbour mouth. And so he decided to put a light on Pharos, tall enough to be seen from thirty miles away at night, to guide sailors to safety and mark out the rock.'

He gestured to the lighthouse, now less than a quarter mile distant as the warship stood into the bay at a dignified walking pace under the steady propulsion of its banked oars.

'The man who designed that thing for Ptolemy was called

Sostratus, or so the historian Plinius would have us believe. It cost eight hundred talents of silver to construct, which, when you bear in mind that the Parthenon of Athens is said to have cost around half as much, tells you what a dent that must have made in the royal finances. And when it was complete, or so the story goes, Sostratus had his own name carved into the building, then covered it with plaster into which the king's name was inscribed.'

The sailor nodded approvingly.

'Clever bastard.'

'Quite so. He reasoned that by the time the render fell away, both architect and king would be long dead, meaning there would be neither an insult, a victim, nor indeed anyone left to be accused. Rather like the relationship between our emperor and his current chamberlain.'

'What are you trying to say?'

Scaurus shrugged, a faint smile touching his lips.

'I suppose my point is that Cleander is like the architect. While Commodus takes the plaudits, and lives the life of a magnificent ruler, the man who is managing the empire for him intends that his name too will echo down the centuries. At least if he has his way.'

The naval officer turned to look at him.

'You think these acts of smuggling are part of some plot to put Cleander on the throne?'

'Who knows?' Scaurus smiled again, raising his eyebrows in question. 'Perhaps he's just one of those men for whom no amount of wealth can ever be enough. But an abundance of riches, or of gifts bestowed by the gods, or just simple luck, is a strange thing. It tends to make a man view the world differently. He starts to consider men not blessed with the same good fortune as lesser beings, to be disposed of as he sees fit. Who knows what ambitions are harboured in the chamberlain's mind? After all, with each dawn he wakes to the task of bending his ferocious talents to the ceaseless and unforgiving management of one hundred million subjects, while the emperor busies himself only with his own pleasure.'

'If you put it like that, I see your point. But what else am I to do?'

Scaurus nodded.

'There is little alternative, that's clear. You must continue to perform the small favours that the chamberlain requests of you. But keep a record, my friend, and if at all possible, find out what it is that you are carrying for him. Who knows, one day that knowledge might be the difference between being able to defend your actions and a less happy outcome, if Cleander falls and the man that succeeds him comes looking for cronies to deal with.'

The warship was rounding the pier that struck out from the lighthouse's base, and Scaurus looked across the strip of water that separated ship from land at the crowd of citizens who had gathered to watch the powerful vessel's passing, wondering what they were thinking as such a powerful symbol of Rome's imperial might swept through the harbour's entrance.

'We still have a little time before you're called on to play the fleet commander for the local officials, so let me tell you another story. You'll see my point soon enough.'

The sailor gestured for him to continue.

'In his early days on the throne Ptolemy needed money. He was only a king at that time, rather than a god, and a kingdom like this one needs constant attention if it is to be efficiently milked of the sort of money that builds four-hundred-foot-high stone lighthouses. And so, to assist him with that milking, he enlisted, or rather he tolerated, the services of a man by the name of Cleomenes. Greedy, corrupt and completely untrustworthy, he was nevertheless an expert at the art of taxation, of plucking the goose without being pecked, and under his control the imperial authorities generated all the money Ptolemy needed. Albeit at a price, which was Cleomenes's own enrichment, and his not-so-gradual rise to grandeur. And for a time the king tolerated his venality, until the time was right for him to upgrade himself from ruling as a mere mortal and assume the role of god. At which point he turned on Cleomenes, sided with the men who accused him of extortion, and had him executed. At his trial, the king's former favourite was accused of having accumulated eight thousand talents, enough to build that lighthouse ten times over, making him quite possibly the richest man in the world. But all that wealth was no defence against the wrath of a living god.'

'You're telling me that Cleander might go the same way?'

Scaurus looked out over the Great Harbour's bustling waters.

'Who can tell? Commodus has ignored the machinery of state for so long that he might well have forgotten what it is to actually rule. And he might continue to ignore his duties to the degree that Cleander can simply slide the empire out from under him and into his own pocket. But a man in that position needs to tread softly, because an emperor wakened to the danger of harbouring a usurper tends to strike hard, and fast. All I'm suggesting is that you keep a record of the jobs Cleander asks you to perform, ready to detail for the men who might come to question you when he falls from grace, as I suspect he surely will. And now, Tribune, you must go and perform your duty as the fleet's commander. And we, as ever, must go and find out just how deep the bucket of dung we've been dropped into is this time around.'

2

Scaurus's party went ashore, once the docking formalities had been dealt with, having spent the previous hour preparing for their interview with the province's equestrian prefect. While the officers had taken turns to lace each other into their scaled armour, meticulously checking each other's shining finery for any smudge or finger mark that might reduce their collective magnificence, Lugos and Arminius had combed and plaited each other's hair and inspected each other's tunics for any mark that would embarrass their tribune, while Sanga and Saratos had invested equal care with their equipment in support of the former's determination to impress any ladies they might meet. Walking out from the docks into the city, they looked about them with various expressions of wonder and appreciation for the grandeur of the wide streets, the imposing buildings that rose on either side. Teeming with the city's population, the broad thoroughfares had a subtly different aroma to that they had most recently experienced in Rome, the faint trace of a sweet musk underlaying the usual smells of any city where hundreds of thousands of people lived cheek by jowl.

'You would do well to keep a hand on your purses at all times, gentlemen.'

Dubnus snorted at Ptolemy's warning, looking about him at the throng of people going about their business with the jaundiced expression of a man well accustomed to the thievery that he believed to be a way of life in every city.

'If any of these idlers so much as lays a finger on me, I'll have his hand off with this . . .' He patted his dagger's hilt meaningfully, having been persuaded to leave his axe on the warship for later delivery to wherever it was that they would end up spending the night. 'And then I'll put it where its owner won't easily retrieve it. And besides, having a beast like Lugos along with us does seem to have the effect of discouraging anyone from getting too close.'

The Aegyptian nodded his agreement with the big Briton's sentiments.

'Our barbarian colleague's presence does seem to have something of a deterrent effect on the usual plague of beggars and street urchins. And then there is the fact that we are all clearly both armed and capable of using our iron to good effect.'

Cotta smirked at him disbelievingly.

'I can see the entire street cowering away from you, master swordsman.'

The Aegyptian raised a haughty eyebrow at him in return, the man's innate belief in his own abilities self-evident in the set of his head. His daily tuition at the hands of Dubnus had, Cotta would have been the first to admit, resulted in a commitment to mastering the use of a short infantry sword that had surpassed any expectation. Exercising twice daily with the weapon provided to him by the *Victoria*'s marines from the warship's inventory, he had become a familiar figure on the deck in the light of dawn and late in the evening, practising the lunges, cuts, parries and stabbing blows that Dubnus had taught him.

'I may not have had the benefit of your life experience, Centurion, but I have worked hard to build the familiarity with my blade and, as is usually the way, my persistence has been rewarded.' He shooed away a supplicant with a hard look and a tap of his sword's hilt in self-conscious imitation of his tutor's brusque method of repelling unwanted attention, putting an even broader smile on Cotta's face. 'This weapon already feels like a natural extension of my arm when I wield it.'

'This is good progress.' Ptolemy beamed at Arminius's straight-faced praise. 'If you have come that far after only two weeks of

Dubnus's teaching, then it is my expectation that you will only need another nine years and fifty weeks of practice to become the expert you hope to be.'

The Aegyptian frowned, unwilling to accept his new comrade's opinion.

'But . . .'

'Consider it this way.' Marcus turned back to smile tolerantly at the scribe. 'You spent a good deal of time throughout the voyage lecturing us all on the history and geography of this province, did you not?'

'That, and shamelessly pumping anyone that would tolerate his constant whining for information.'

Marcus twitched his lips in a smile at Cotta's comment.

'And, when you were not enriching your own knowledge at the expense of your new comrades' undoubted patience, for which I am sure you will be keen to make some recognition in liquid form, you did manage to impart some learning to each of us, did you not?'

'I did.'

'And would you now consider any of us to be a master of your chosen discipline of philosophy?'

Ptolemy shook his head in bafflement.

'Why, no. You have barely scratched the surface of the myriad subjects that are avail . . .' He saw Cotta grinning at him and fell silent as the trap into which he had stepped became apparent. 'Ah.'

'Indeed. *Ah*. Your beginnings of skill with the sword are heartening, like the progress I'm sure you made when first you were set to learning your letters, but knowing your alphabet is a long way from being able to read, fully understand and then conduct a learned discourse on the subject of the thought and works of Aristotle.'

'I suppose that's a fair analogy, Centurion. But ten years? I learned my letters when I was a small child, and every philosopher knows that the body's energy is spent growing itself to adulthood, rather than on the development of the mind. Surely I can master the sword in less time than that?'

'Possibly.' Marcus gestured to the dagger at his waist. 'But the sword isn't all you have to consider, if you wish to become a warrior like your tutor Dubnus.'

'It isn't?'

The prospect of there being other disciplines to be mastered put a look of dawning realisation on Ptolemy's face.

'Fighting with a dagger at close quarters is a skill all in itself, as much about the eyes as the blade, learning to fight with your instinct as much as any learned skills. And then there's the spear. Putting a spearhead into a target the size of a man at twenty paces, that takes practice.'

'Months of it. Years.'

The Aegyptian looked from Marcus to Dubnus, who had stepped closer to add his flatly stated opinion.

'But how . . .'

Marcus raised a hand to silence him.

'I do not wish to be unkind. Or no more so than would be your reaction, were you faced with Dubnus here declaring an intention to master Euclidean geometry in a week. Be happy that you have made a solid start to your training, and that you have shown yourself to be a capable and diligent student. But do not fool yourself into believing that you could stand alone against anyone who has been handling blades for more than half their lives.'

Ptolemy made a small bow to both men.

'I consider this to be a part of my education. And, coming from two such learned exponents of the art, I can of course only accede to your counsel.'

'I think he means that he agrees.'

The Aegyptian turned to Cotta with a bright smile.

'I'm heartened, Centurion, to discover that just a little of our learned discourse over the last two weeks has worn off on you.'

The veteran centurion grinned back at him.

'Likewise, Scribe, that you've adopted a little of our sense of humour.' He paused significantly. 'While retaining enough of your caution to avoid someone taking offence and beating the very shit out of you.'

'Shall we, gentlemen?' Scaurus, if not impatient, was clearly keen to be moving on. 'While we stand here debating, I fear I am at risk of losing a certain German at the hands of an outraged lady's bodyguard.'

He turned to bark an exasperated order at Arminius who, having drifted away from them with a bored expression on his face, was ignoring a pair of bemused black-skinned men to engage a beautiful woman in his version of artful conversation. Clearly both intimidated, and to some degree intrigued, by the sight of the German and the pale-skinned giant standing behind him, the lady's guards were clearly steeling themselves to intervene, hands on the hilts of their daggers. The lady herself, having ascertained that there was no transaction to be entered into, was shaking her head with a friendly but insistent reluctance to waste any more valuable time. The tribune interposed himself, bowing to the lady who, impressed by his shining bronze armour and evident status, simpered in reply, managing to further excite the German's ardour before he and Lugos were ushered firmly away.

'I've told you enough times for it to have sunk in, Arminius, they expect to be *paid*! All your manly posturing will ever achieve is to have their bodyguards' knives out faster, especially with a seven-foot-tall beast of a man at your shoulder.'

With his servant complaining bitterly at having his enjoyment so rudely curtailed, loudly enough to be heard but carefully pitched to nevertheless be ignored, they walked further into the city, following Ptolemy's directions towards the praetorium.

'What are they queuing for?'

The Aegyptian answered in a bored tone, waving a dismissive hand at the line of men that stretched away down the street from an imposing building constructed with blocks of marble.

'It is the tomb of the great king, Alexander. They queue for a moment to stare at his embalmed body.'

The queue's order was being maintained by half a dozen imposing acolytes in priests' robes, each man carrying a brass-shod staff with the look of a useful enough weapon in the event of a brawl. Scaurus stared at the building with a look of longing, a wistful note in his voice.

'That is a thing I would dearly like to see.'

'I've seen it. It was rubbish. Just the dried-out husk of a man with a crooked nose.' They turned to look at Cotta, who was looking at the mausoleum with a bored expression. 'We all went for a look eventually, when we were posted here. After all, he was the master of the world until some crafty Greek bastard had him poisoned.'

'The rumours that Aristotle and the general Antipater murdered Alexander are forgivable.' Ptolemy nodded his respect for Cotta's apparent insight. 'Both men had good reason to wish the master of the world dead. Although a simpler explanation is surely more likely. And the tomb is indeed not the experience you might expect, Tribune. I have seen it more than once and must admit that the body is most sadly reduced. As for his nose, it is a regrettable and carefully denied fact that, in placing a diadem on the great man's head as a form of homage from one great conqueror to another, the divine Augustus managed to break it off completely.' He sighed. 'The damage was repaired hurriedly, and without artistry, to support the narrative that it never happened. You might be better off leaving the whole thing to imagination.'

Scaurus nodded.

'Another time, perhaps. For now I must follow my orders and report to the emperor's prefect.'

At the next intersection of roads they came upon the bustling vista of a market, but as Ptolemy went to lead them around the edge of the throng, Lugos, his stature allowing him to look over the heads of the crowd, tugged at Scaurus's sleeve with a look of dismay. He pointed at something in the market's heart which only he could see, shaking his head angrily.

'Is not right. Women, children, be torture.'

The tribune looked at their guide questioningly, but the Aegyptian seemed unperturbed.

'In this place, at this time of the day? It is likely to be a tax collector of the city at work.'

Scaurus led them through the watching crowd, any protests by the citizens he pushed aside quickly dispelled by both the magnificence of his armour and helmet and the threat carried by the men at his shoulder. On catching sight of the unmissable and angry-looking giant pressing close in behind the Roman, the look on his face promising violence to anyone that stood in his master's path, the crush of people melted in the face of the familia's advance. In a wide circle at the crowd's centre, what appeared to be a family were cowering under the cudgels of half a dozen hard-faced men dressed in drab tunics and heavy boots. Two adult women, one, Scaurus guessed, the wife of a man who was being held away to one side, the other old enough to be his mother, and five children of varying ages, were struggling to keep a large iron basket off the ground inside their circle, while another thug circled them with a short whip. Unlikely as the Romans would have thought it, the scene was playing out under the watching eyes of a tent party of legionaries with a disgusted-looking centurion standing out in front of them, his vine stick held in a white-knuckled hand in front of him.

As they watched, the smallest of the children allowed the basket's base to touch the cobbles at his feet, prompting an angry shout and a flick of the whip at his calves that made him stagger, weeping with the pain. The pinioned man struggled, earning a punch to his gut that would have doubled him over had he not been held upright. He gasped for air, croaking a protest at his family's treatment.

'The money is on its way! Keep me, but let them go, in the name of Jehovah!'

Another blow silenced him, expertly placed in his sternum, leaving him fighting to breathe at all. The gang's leader stepped forward and raised his hands to quieten the crowd's growing buzz of outrage.

'This man owes the state money! He and his filthy Jewish brood will stay in our custody until the full sum is paid! And anyone that doesn't like that can consider it an example . . .' He turned a slow circle with his truncheon held high for all to see the iron capping gleaming dully in the sunlight. 'That, or step forward to complain to me, if you're bored with life!'

The crowd simmered with resentment, but as the gang's leader had clearly calculated, nobody was brave enough to take him up on the challenge.

'What the fuck are they doing, torturing those people?'

Ptolemy looked at Dubnus expressionlessly, clearly familiar with the scene.

'They are collecting taxes. They call themselves "tax farmers", because they reap wealth from the people like a farmer scythes wheat. That man probably owes the tax farmer whatever has been assessed as his debt to the state, plus his profit. He will release the man's family when he has paid the required amount.' He looked dubiously at the victim's oldest daughter. 'Or at least he should . . .'

'And the amount is assessed by who, exactly?'

The Aegyptian looked at Scaurus with a puzzled expression for a moment, then nodded with realisation.

'I had quite forgotten that this is not the way it works elsewhere. The rest of the empire has its taxes administered by officials, whereas in Aegyptus, the emperor's own province, we have what you see here. It has been decided by the governor, with the approval of Chamberlain Cleander, that the old system of tax farming is more appropriate.' He shot Scaurus a knowing glance. 'The emperor guards the privacy of his officials' doings here like a jealous husband, and without senatorial oversight, Aegyptus is a very fat goose indeed, with a lot of feathers to be plucked. And so the governor awards the contract to levy taxes to the highest bidders, who must then submit enough income to cover their contracts, but are allowed to keep the remainder for themselves. And, to answer your question, the taxes are assessed by the farmers themselves. Theirs is a great skill, to extract enough money to pay off their contracts and make a profit to keep, while not inspiring the people to defy them in open rebellion.'

'And they practise this *great skill* by preying on women and children?'

Ptolemy shrugged at Marcus.

'The tax will be paid, the citizen's family will be freed from their temporary inconvenience. It is customary and, as the divine Julius noted, soldiers and taxes are indivisible. It is impossible to have the one without the other, and for the lack of either the other will fail. And it is the way of the world. Come, the praetorium is this w—'

'This *normal*?'

Something in Lugos's voice made the Aegyptian flush bright red, his hand trembling as he raised it to deny the question.

'No! They usually only do *this* to the Jews!'

The giant's eyes slitted, but, before he could act on his sudden fury, Scaurus nodded his understanding, and raised a hand to forestall the giant's impending expression of the rage that was clearly coursing through him.

'Not yet, Lugos, or any of you.' He turned back to Ptolemy. 'Our comrade is angry, because, like all of my familia, he does not react well to the sight of innocents being victimised' – he shook his head at the baffled Aegyptian – 'whether they be Jews or any other people. For now, however, we must go to the praetorium, after a further brief detour. I have some questions for the governor, once I have sought out the man my banker recommended to me.'

An hour later, with his personal business completed, and free to focus solely on the matter at hand, he allowed Ptolemy to guide them through the city's thronged streets to the seat of Roman power in the city. Once inside the gates of the governor's official residence, admitted by armed legionaries to the cool, shaded precincts of the sprawling marble edifice to imperial rule, Scaurus left the bulk of the party to relax in the shadow of a high wall, drinking from the courtyard fountains. Taking Marcus with him, he ascended the stairways that led to the governor's office, situated on the building's highest floor with a view over the city that, under happier circumstances, he would have been eager to enjoy for as long as possible. Strolling into the office's anteroom they were presented with the predictable sight of two long benches of men, supplicants awaiting their turn to petition the emperor's representative in the province.

'Greetings, gentlemen. You have an appointment with Prefect Faustinianus?'

The two men stared flatly at the diary scribe who was blocking their path, Marcus stepping forward with a look to Scaurus that made his superior smile inwardly, while he composed his face to present a stern expression.

'Tribune Scaurus and I have travelled across Our Sea for two weeks, to attend on the governor and receive his instructions.'

The secretary shook his head, the very picture of a regretful inability to allow them access to his master.

'Gentlemen, if you have no appointment then I am not at liberty to admit you. Indeed, if you persist with the request, I have standing instructions to summon the sentries and have you escorted—'

He fell silent as Marcus leaned in close, although the Roman was impressed with the degree to which the secretary's apparent lack of interest in their circumstances was otherwise unruffled. Doubtless they were not the first men to have attempted to jump the queue, doubtless they would not be the last. He had, Marcus mused, probably already been worn smooth by the constant friction implicit in his role, and he did, after all, have his orders.

Nevertheless, Marcus was unprepared to retreat in the face of the man's obduracy.

'This officer, Scribe, is Tribune Gaius Rutilius Scaurus. He is a hero of the empire more times over than I can recall, his most recent exploit having been the defeat and capture of the infamous bandit turned would-be usurper, Maturnus, in the act of attempting to assassinate the emperor himself. Tribune Scaurus has risked his life for the empire on a multitude of occasions, and now, at the express wish of Imperial Chamberlain Cleander, he has voyaged here aboard the flagship of the praetorian fleet, ordered to be of service to this province. He has sailed a thousand miles and more, commanded to deal with whatever matter it is that has spurred this province's prefect himself to ask for assistance, and now you seek to deny him a meeting with the very man who has called for his help?' He shook his head at the secretary, who was finally starting to wilt under the heat of his anger, although the man was still clearly clinging to his increasingly shredded authority. 'Next you'll be telling me that the earliest you can fit him in is three days from now, and suggesting that we await the pleasure of a few minutes in your master's presence by taking in the sights of the city. To which my answer is to invite you to consider a sight yourself!'

He turned and pointed through the open archway at the Great Harbour, where the *Victoria* was dominating the smaller craft around her with her imposing size and martial grandeur, the sun gleaming on her polished fixtures.

'If we're not the next men into that office behind us, then we're going to leave. Immediately. We will board the emperor's praetorian flagship, and immediately order the navarchus to muster his crew from the dockside taverns and prepare for our prompt return to Rome. It will then be up to your master to decide how best to inform the chamberlain that the help he requested was turned away at the door of his office. And then, presumably, to determine the best way to pay you out for bringing about his dismissal from this most exalted and *lucrative* of all the positions available to a man of the equestrian class. I'd imagine that his repayment for your bringing about the termination of his career in such an abrupt manner will be both inventive and long-lasting, wouldn't you? Although he might just command his ceremonial lictors to beat you to death with their rods, as his last command to them before relinquishing the role.'

He fell silent and fixed the hapless functionary with a level gaze, waiting for the other man to speak, while Scaurus stood to one side examining his fingernails.

'I . . . er . . . that is to say . . .' Realising that he was dithering in a manner hardly suited to either his role or self-image, the secretary made his mind up with commendable decisiveness. 'On this one occasion I will make an exception, for a hero of Rome.' He turned to the waiting citizens with a forced smile that invited any of them to provide him with an opportunity to revive his dignity by taking equally swift action in the event of any dissent. 'After all, I feel sure that not one of these gentlemen could offer a word of complaint at being requested to undergo a short delay in order to facilitate matters of such pressing importance to the emperor himself?'

Under Marcus's equally questioning stare the gentlemen in question shook their heads, the most senior among them standing to shake Scaurus by the hand and state in florid terms that it would be his absolute pleasure to forego his turn in the queue in favour of such a pressing appointment, being careful to drop his own name into the statement for future reference. With such an example, every other citizen present nodded even more vigorously, and the two men were grateful that it was at that moment that the inner office's doors opened as the prefect's previous appoint-ment left, revealing the man himself. Dressed in a formal toga and evidently expecting to greet his next supplicant in a suitably magisterial manner, he looked at the diary secretary with an expression that did not bode well, evidencing that Marcus's predic-tion of violent unhappiness, should they have chosen to decamp back to the flagship, had been better founded than he had guessed.

'Tribune Scaurus, Prefect, and his aide. They claim to be here at the command of Chamberlain Cleander, and your other appointments have spontaneously agreed to forego—'

The light of realisation dawned in the prefect's eyes.

'Gentlemen!' He gestured to the inner office with a smile so sudden and broad that Marcus wondered whether there might perhaps be some hint of mania behind it. 'Please, come and join me!' He made a fractional bow to the waiting men. 'My apologies, citizens, these officers are here to discuss matters of state which are of the highest possible importance. I'm sure you all under-stand?'

Closing the door behind him he ushered them to a pair of chairs beside his desk, clicking his fingers to order his assistant to provide them with glasses of chilled wine.

'Introductions, gentlemen. My name is Lucius Pomponius Faustinianus, and I have the singular honour to be the *praefectus augustalis* of this magnificent province. I know who you both are, since Cleander was kind enough to dispatch a letter for me on the same vessel that conveyed you across Our Sea.' He waved a hand at an opened message container lying on his desk with a pair of scrolls beside it. 'I must say that, for men who are supposed to be dedicated servants of the throne, his descriptions of you both make interesting reading.'

His servant served the wine in glasses, rather than the more usual cups, and Marcus took his with a flash of memory to happier, more innocent times. The exotic drinking vessel was every bit as fragile and beautiful as those he remembered drinking from in his youth, never having truly appreciated the wealth required for the provision of such luxuries before the doom that had enveloped his entire family. Dismissing the servant with a wave of his hand, Faustinianus took a seat on the other side of the desk and looked at them with an expression of calculation, his effusive bonhomie falling away to reveal the man's true nature as he took up the heavier of the two messages and read from it out loud.

'"I am sending you a party of men, among whom Rutilius Scaurus is the foremost, and the man I expect to deal with the problem on your southern border. He is an upstart equestrian who will insist on taking a hand in affairs of state . . ."' He fell silent, reading on without speaking until he came to another line that he evidently felt impelled to share. '"The other man you should consider as both hostile and dangerous is the centurion who goes by the name of Tribulus Corvus, but who is more accurately named Valerius Aquila, the son of a traitor who should have died alongside his father."' Both men stared back at him impassively, having heard much the same words from too many mouths for them to carry any sting and, with a shrug, he continued. 'Cleander's choice of instruments with which to resolve this problem are novel, but then the man has always been the arch-pragmatist. Although I'm forced to observe that you're not exactly what I asked him for.'

Scaurus leaned forward in his chair, fixing the other man with his grey-eyed stare.

'And what was it that you requested, Prefect? What is the problem to the south that can't be resolved by your local legion commander?'

'The problem, Tribune Scaurus, isn't exactly clear. The trade route through the port of Berenike seems to have been cut in both directions, apparently by hostile action. I have received a series of somewhat garbled messages from the fortress at Koptos, apparently written by a centurion, telling me that there's been some sort of invasion from the south, unlikely though that might seem. And what I asked for was a legion, Tribune. Enough strength to prosecute a swift war on the province's southern border and resolve a local difficulty that has stopped the flow of commerce from beyond the empire's edge. Tenth Fretensis and Third Cyrenaica are both within a month's march of here, and I had expected that Cleander would have them both provide a detachment to make up a full legion. Instead I have you, a practised exponent of the art of war, it seems, but lacking in any strength . . .' He raised the scroll. 'Other than what the chamberlain describes as "a ragtag handful of disaffected officers and barbarians". Quite how he expects you, with the strength I can spare you, to master whatever it is that has cut us off from the far south of the province, I have no idea. But no matter, I have instructions for you, direct from the chamberlain, and so I suggest you follow them to the letter.'

Scaurus took the second scroll as Faustinianus passed it across the desk, breaking the seal and reading the few short lines before looking up again.

'It's the usual order, more or less. Do what you need to do, using whatever forces you need to use, and let no man stand in the way of discharging your duty to the throne on pain of death. Which, as you say, I must follow to the letter. So, what strength can you *spare* us, do you think?'

The prefect shook his head, lips pursed, missing the barbed hook that Scaurus had dropped into the discussion.

'Not very much. I am granted a single legion to control this province, much reduced from the three that were once deemed necessary. There are garrisons of auxiliaries dotted around at strategic points, but the real strength is here, commanding and controlling this city.'

Scaurus raised an eyebrow.

'You need to keep an entire legion for the purposes of policing Alexandria? Surely the city watch will suffice for that task?'

Faustinianus shook his head with a knowing smile.

'If only. Alexandria, like all the biggest cities, is a barely tamed animal, crouching under the whip of its masters. And this city is especially ready to erupt in violence, due to the nature of its population. There are three parts to Alexandria, gentlemen, all constantly bickering with each other and occasionally taking up arms against each other, or even the state itself, depending on the circumstances. The Greeks have ruled Aegyptus since Alexander conquered the country, through the descendants of his lieutenant, Ptolemy. They are a class unto themselves, like

Greeks everywhere, and naturally consider themselves to be better than the rest of the populace. When we conquered Aegyptus, the divine Augustus pragmatically allowed them to continue in that role, albeit it under our rule. The Jews – of whom there are a multitude, which, of course, breeds incessantly – are their usual selves, money-grubbing and ever ready to take offence at the merest of slights. Jewish uprisings are hardly unusual in this part of the world, and when they happen they tend to be soaked in the blood of anyone who gets in their way. And then there are the locals. Good for nothing more than manual labour and street theft, and prone to a strong sense of being outsiders in their own country. A mob, when roused, happy to burn and loot without discrimination. And if all that wasn't enough, there are also the blasted Christians, who infest the population with their "one God" nonsense, which is the perfect spark for a disastrous uprising by any or all of them.'

'Which would, of course, risk delaying the grain supply to Rome, and see you replaced without delay. And which might be provoked at any moment by the taxation fraud that you and Cleander are using to make yourselves rich at the cost of brutalised citizens.' Faustinianus stared at Scaurus in angry surprise at the candour of his comment, but the object of his ire returned the gaze without any apparent concern. 'Prefect, let us be very frank, because I have no intention of letting good manners – which you have already abandoned in your comments as to our provenance – get in the way of reality.'

He leaned back in the chair.

'I have been sent here by your master – indeed, your co-conspirator in the systematic robbery of the imperial treasury . . .' He raised a hand to prevent the eruption he saw building in the man sitting opposite him. 'Please don't try to appear outraged, Pomponius Faustinianus. A truly angry man loses the blood in his face and goes white with rage, a reaction to his body preparing for the fight. Whereas you have gone red and look nothing more than guilty. You skim off a good portion of the trade that comes through this city, and send it to Rome aboard vessels of the praetorian fleet, unseen and untaxed, straight into the pocket of the chamberlain and from there, in some measure, to your own. And you sell the rights to farm taxes – an archaic practice that I had believed had long since been ended across the entire empire – to criminal scum who pose as tax collectors. You ignore the injustices they do in your name in return for your share of the gold they extort from the population, and you use the threat of your legion to legitimise and enforce their theft.'

Faustinianus stared back at him through anger-slitted eyes but said nothing.

'Your silence, Prefect, is eloquent.' Scaurus pointed at the scroll from the desk in front of the other man. 'And now, of course, you're wondering whether to bring forward the quiet execution that Cleander recommends for us both in that message, when the matter we've been sent to attend to is done with. But that would be unwise, *Praefectus Augustalis*. For one thing, your guards neglected to take our weapons from us when we entered this magnificent building. After all, what soldier is going to think to disarm a superior officer? And on top of that . . .'

He took a wooden whistle from the purse on his belt.

'Legion centurions use these to issue commands in battle. And battle, as I very much doubt you'd know, is a *very* confusing place. You'd be surprised how hard it can be to even think straight. All that shouting and screaming, the stink of blood and shit, your friends dying right in front of you . . . It's enough to unman the strongest minded among us. Which is why they make these things so loud. If I blow this now, it will be heard all over the building, and the "ragtag handful of disaffected officers and barbarians" I left waiting downstairs will run wild, and redecorate your magnificent murals with the blood of every man in the building. Not yours, of course, your fate would be a little more protracted. Centurion Corvus, or "Two Knives" as his soldiers named him the very first time they saw the quality of his swordplay, will easily hold off your guards while I use my blade to show you the colour of your own intestines. Being strangled with a rope of your own guts would be a novel way to leave this life, I'd imagine?'

Faustinianus raised his hands, palms forward.

'Your execution? The thought hadn't even entered my head!'

Scaurus shook his head disbelievingly.

'I find that somewhat hard to believe. It certainly entered mine, when I saw Cleander's message to you go ashore the moment the *Victoria*'s bow touched the quayside. So I went to see my banker's counterpart here in Alexandria, and deposited a letter of my own with him, with instructions for it to be sent to Rome immediately by various routes, land and sea. It will be received by several people who have the ability to place the facts of what you and Cleander are doing here in front of the emperor, with a request for them to do so in the event of my untimely death. And as we both know, Prefect, Commodus is well known for his lack of patience with anyone he perceives to have done him wrong. If we fail to return to Rome in a sufficiently timely manner then he will undoubtedly be informed of the theft that his chamberlain and you have been perpetrating ever since Cleander put you into this magnificent role, with your complicity the price for your undeserved advancement over the heads of other, better qualified men.'

He smiled without a trace of humour, the same dead-eyed twitch of his lips that Marcus had seen him employ before when his anger was close to the surface.

'But of course there's no need for any of that, if you behave in a rational manner. Cleander sent us here to do a job, doubtless with the expectation that the task in question stands a very good chance of killing us all. So why not roll the dice alongside him, send us south to deal with whatever it is that irks you both? After all, we might not survive the experience. Although you'd better hope we do, if you're to avoid being executed for defrauding the throne.'

The prefect nodded slowly.

'You're an impudent bastard, aren't you? I can see what it is that makes Cleander put you to use, with all that self-belief. And it's not hard to see why he wants you dead either, although the reason why he hasn't simply had you executed eludes me. Very well, I can spare you five hundred men.'

Scaurus smiled again, shaking his head in grim amusement before leaning forward and delivering his response in a deadpan tone that belied the evident anger in his eyes, a glare of disgust that set the prefect back in his seat.

'I'll be marching south with *six* cohorts. And all the cavalry you have. The other four cohorts will be more than enough to maintain order in the city, if you cancel all leave and pull back the hunting parties.'

Faustinianus stared at him in dismay, groping for a reply.

'I . . . you . . .'

'Will be taking whatever I want. Unless, perhaps, you'd care to roll those dice on a different outcome. One involving your painful demise.' Scaurus stood suddenly, leaned forward and plucked Cleander's message from the desk in front of the gaping prefect. 'And I'll have this. It'll make for interesting reading.' He raised the whistle to his lips. 'You can either call for your guards and start the excitement, or sit there, drink your wine and hope I manage to deal with whatever it is that's troubling your province *and* get myself killed in the process. Good day, *Praefectus Augustalis*!'

He turned away from the desk, then remembered something and readdressed the stunned prefect.

'One last thing, Pomponius Faustinianus. I saw one of your tax farmers being a little, shall we say, *overzealous*, in pursuit of the gold that you and Cleander are generous enough to share with the imperial treasury. I plan to chide him just a little, on my way to your legion's camp. I thought I ought to warn you, just in case the report of that chastisement makes you wonder if the revolt you've done so much to foment in the city's population has begun. So you might be wise to order the other "farmers" to reap their crops a little less enthusiastically, because when word of what I plan to do to him gets around, who knows what it might incite your subjects to do?'

3

'Good afternoon, Centurion . . .?'

The officer in question sprang to attention, unsure as to where the immaculately dressed and equipped officer in front of him had appeared from, and with no idea whatsoever who the man was, but with no intention of providing him with any cause for dissatisfaction. Senior officers, as he knew all too well, were completely capable of being unreasonable, incompetent and, in some cases, downright dangerous to themselves and those around them without ever knowing it, and he hadn't made it to command of a century without learning when it would be sensible to keep his mouth shut, and wait to see what sort of man he was dealing with. The late afternoon sun was mild enough that he had ordered his men to put their helmets back on a few moments before, and he snapped his right hand to the brow guard of his own crested headgear as he answered the newcomer's question.

'Petosorapis, sir!'

'At ease then, Centurion Petosorapis. I'm Tribune Scaurus, your new commanding officer. You've been detailed to keep an eye on these *bastards*, have you?'

The centurion started, surprised both by the vehemence in Scaurus's voice and his unexpected statement of authority, but was careful to keep his reply neutral despite the tribune's jocular tone.

'Standing orders, Tribune. Tax collectors are not to be hindered as they go about their duties.'

The man standing before him, resplendent in shining bronze

and crisp white linen, turned away to watch the scene before them for a moment before speaking again. Watched by a crowd that was, in anything, larger than before, the debtor's family were still struggling to keep their burden off the ground. Their efforts were being brutally encouraged by occasional, casual flicks of the overseer's whip, while the gang's leader was sitting outside a nearby taverna with a jug of wine and a bowl of food in front of him, the hapless debtor sitting unhappily beside him.

'There's no sign of anyone paying off the tax debt then?'

'No, sir.' Petosorapis lowered his voice. 'Sometimes the tax collectors name an amount that can't be paid off, because they fancy something the debtor owns. Or one of his family.'

He tipped his head to the group fighting to keep the iron basket off the ground, and Scaurus saw that the oldest child was in the first flush of her womanhood.

'You don't mean they plan to . . .'

'Wouldn't be the first time, sir. We see a lot of what they get up to, as we escort them round the city. Sometimes they make fun of us, if a soldier looks like he doesn't agree with what they're doing. If it weren't for our orders, there's more than one of my colleagues would have had his lads take their iron to the bastards.'

The tribune nodded slowly.

'In which case, you might find what I'm about to do refreshingly at odds with your orders. And all you have to do, Centurion, is stand here and do one thing.'

'What's that, sir?'

Scaurus smiled bleakly.

'Nothing, Centurion.'

He strolled away from the detachment of soldiers and stopped a few feet from the debtor's family, looking about him with an expression of dissatisfaction.

'Help you?'

One of the thugs was walking towards him with his cudgel held behind his back, the tax collector glancing at him over the edge of his wine cup before returning his attention to the bowl of stew.

Evidently the man addressing him was deemed to have authority in their group, and neither man expected any trouble from a military official who was expected to be aligned with the prefect's expectations of them. Stopping in front of Scaurus with a look of bored condescension on his face, he repeated the question with a slow, deliberate insolence.

'Can. I. *Help*. You?'

'Yes.' The Roman looked him up and down. 'You could bathe, for a start. You stink like a pig's arse. And a recently washed tunic wouldn't hurt, you've piss-spotted that one too many times for it to have been clean any time this week.'

He smiled beatifically, the expression so much at odds with what he had just said that the man in front of him was momentarily lost for words.

'You . . . *what*?'

Scaurus pounced, putting a hand on the hilt of his sword and stepping forward to put his face so close to the other man's that the thug recoiled at his shouted invective.

'I am a *fucking* tribune of Rome, you diseased piece of shit! Get out of my *fucking* face, and fetch the man who holds your rope before I air my *fucking* blade and use it to open you from your chin to your *fucking* balls!'

Caught between the urge to run, confronted by a ragingly furious man of infinitely superior standing, and the urge to follow his instincts and fight, the thug dithered, turning to look beseechingly at his master, who, shaking his head wearily, made a great show of taking another drink before getting up and strolling across to greet the Roman.

'I don't know what this is, but we have the protection of the provincial prefect himself, so I suggest that you find something better to—'

'Had.'

The tax collector frowned, uncomprehending, the final traces of his patience dissipating in the face of the officer's truculence, where only a subservient response was expected.

'What did you say?'

'You *had* the protection of the prefect himself. And of all the tribunes who suck from the same teat he does, and turn a blind eye in return. But, as of a short time ago, that misguided provision of imperial favour for your actions was revoked. By *me*.'

The tax collector looked past Scaurus at the legionaries behind him.

'Are you lot just going to stand there and watch this nonsense?'

'No.' Petosorapis shook his head, then barked a command at his men. 'Tent party . . . about-face!'

The thug's jaw dropped, as the soldiers smartly swivelled on the spot and turned to face the crowd behind them.

'It looks like the ultimate enforcers just turned their back on you. Which just leaves you and me.'

The tax collector scowled, unwilling to be cowed by the threat of a single man, no matter how exalted.

'You're forgetting that I'm not alone, friend. I don't need that bunch of barracks tossers to run my business.' He shrugged off the hand his deputy had put on his shoulder, clenching his fists in readiness to attack. 'I'm going to give you a practical demonstration of just what it means to upset the wrong person, you . . . *What?*'

The last word was almost shouted, as another tug at his tunic, too hard to be brushed off, made him turn to see what it was that his second-in-command wanted.

'What the fuck is it th . . .'

His bark of anger died half born at the sight of the men who had stepped from the crowd, standing close enough to his own men that a couple of paces would be enough to put them face to face. Five were uniformed, some with cross-crested helmets identifying them as centurions, and another two were heavily built barbarians, one so large that the men closest to him were already backing away and looking behind them for escape routes, both men finely dressed and with their hair oiled and plaited.

All were armed with drawn swords, and each of them was looking at his men with expressions somewhere between anger and eagerness. Their body language, to a man raised on street fighting, screamed their readiness, perhaps even a need, to do violence. The oiled hiss of polished iron against the throat of a scabbard raised the hairs on his neck and arms, and he turned slowly to find the tribune looking at him down the length of a shining blade.

'You can't do this. The imperial prefect—'

'Will learn to deal with the disappointment. After all, there are doubtless other tax farmers every bit as efficient as you. Whether they're scum like you is a different matter. And, as my father used to tell me, a man can only deal out his god's justice to whoever his god chooses to put in front of him. And my god, the Lightbringer, has chosen to give me you.' He raised his voice to shout a command. 'Put down your weapons or you will be forcibly disarmed!'

After a moment the thugs dropped or lowered their cudgels to the ground, looking at each other in bafflement.

'And the knives! Don't take us for fools.'

Their reluctance more pronounced, the gang divested themselves of an assortment of blades, some with metal knuckle guards.

'Search them!'

His men sheathed their weapons and moved in with the look of experts, cowing the thugs with minimal but expert brutality – a slap, a kick to spread a man's legs wide for searching – with nothing to give any indication that they were anything other than ready to use their dangerous expertise to its fullest extent. The tribune put the tip of his sword against the tax collector's breastbone and smiled, a look of great enjoyment replacing his previous anger.

'Are you mad? If you kill us, the prefect will—'

'Kill you?' The Roman shook his head with evident amusement. 'Why should I *kill* you? You're much more valuable as an example to others.'

He strolled forward into the centre of the circle, surrounded on all sides by confused citizenry. The tax collector's victim was gathering his family about him, and showering his thanks on a bemused Ptolemy while the other members of Scaurus's familia herded the thugs into a tight knot, roping them together with cord taken from a market vendor to prevent any of them making a run for it.

'People of Alexandria! The emperor's taxes are required to pay for the legions that protect you, and the administration of our empire! Obedience to tax collection is a duty we all share! But these men have gone beyond their authority and acted like nothing better than common criminals!'

'But we *have* the authority—'

The erstwhile tax collector's shouted protest ended violently, Lugos casually backhanding him into silence before pivoting at the waist to sink a massive fist into his gut, in just the way their victim had been treated earlier. His victim vomited his meal across the cobbles and sank to the ground, submitting to being tied to his associates without fully comprehending what was happening to him.

'So, like common criminals, they will be subjected to the imperial code of justice.' He turned to the sullen prisoners. 'You are hereby sentenced to service in the army. You will be taken far from here, hopefully to be replaced by others who will be more inclined to behave like imperial officials rather than robbers and rapists!' He turned to Ptolemy. 'Lead us to the city's garrison.'

'But you can't . . . we can pay you!'

The captive tax collector gestured beseechingly, hampered by the rope tied around one arm, and Scaurus shook his head at the desperate offer.

'Your gold has no allure for us. You stole it from the emperor's treasury, which makes it tainted.'

'But there'll be others to take our places!'

The Roman gestured to Ptolemy, who led them through the

crowd, which parted as Dubnus strode forward into their ranks behind him at the small column's head.

'Undoubtedly so. But as I told you, a man can only deal with the evil that's put in front of him. I'll have to trust that this will act as an example and moderate the behaviour of your fellow farmers. And let's face it, you're getting off lightly.' The tax collector stared at him in disbelief. 'I know, it doesn't feel that way, but trust me, this might all have been much worse. One of these days this city's population will decide that they've had enough. And on that day, as your colleagues will discover, a few sticks and daggers won't protect you against the wrath of an enraged mob.'

'From now on my name is Lucius. The name Cotta probably hasn't been forgotten by the officers of Trajan's Second Legion, given what I did to "their" emperor. So if they were to find out that they had the man they think denied them their imperial payday among them, then I wouldn't last much longer than a virgin boy in a Greek soldiers' mess. Have we all got that?'

The veteran centurion turned to Ptolemy with a forbidding look, and after a moment the scholar realised that he was expected to reply.

'Of course, Centurion!'

Cotta nodded grimly.

'Just don't forget. Because if I find myself in imminent danger of having my wind stopped because you managed to drop my name at the wrong moment, then you can be sure that you'll be crossing the river ahead of me.'

The party had left Alexandria through the eastern gates, walking the mile-long road from the city's walls to the legion fortress, the sullen file of prisoners looking around themselves in growing horror at the depth of their predicament. The crowd of eager citizens which had followed them through the city streets, presumably in the hope of further violence being done to the former tax collector and his men, had gradually thinned out as the lack of any such entertainment became apparent. By the time they passed through the gate only a single figure was walking behind them, albeit at a respectful distance. As the party approached the white painted walls of the legion's camp, Scaurus looked back and then hooked a thumb back over his shoulder.

'Now that we've established who you are, Centurion *Lucius*, perhaps you'd like to go and see what it is that our shadow back there wants?'

Cotta nodded and turned back, placing himself firmly in the path of their follower. Wearing a clean white linen coat, his beard grown long, he was in the middle years of his life with a calm, regarding expression. He stopped at Cotta's raised right hand, putting both hands behind his back and studying the veteran's clothing and equipment with apparent interest.

'That's far enough, friend.'

The other man bowed slightly at the command, smiling disarmingly.

'Greetings to you, Centurion. May the peace and blessings of Our Lord Almighty be upon you and give your soul rest from the trials and tribulations of this life.'

Cotta nodded, his expression knowing.

'Christian. I ought to have known it just from the look of you. Let me guess . . .' He paused theatrically, putting a finger to his chin in an exaggerated show of thought. 'You saw us deal with this scum and thought, these are the men for me. If I can just convert them to my superstitious little cult, then my fellow canni-bals and incest-mongers will be pleased with me. Is that it?'

The other man smiled slowly, his eyes alive with the pleasure of religious debate.

'I have long enjoyed the stories of how the Christos evicted the money changers from the temple. And after all, if the meek are to indeed inherit this world, it will be up to men like yourselves to not only provide a salutary example of how it is right and fitting for men with authority to behave, but on occasion to punish the unworthy.'

He gestured to the shuffling prisoners.

'And if there is a better example of the unworthy being punished, I have yet to see it. I was hoping to speak with your tribune, and to volunteer my services in whatever it is that has brought you here from Rome.'

Cotta frowned, then turned back to the men waiting behind him.

'He's a Christian! And he wants to know what brings us here from Rome!'

Scaurus walked back to join him, frowning at the apparent ease with which their mission seemed to have been uncovered.

'Your name?'

The bearded man bowed respectfully.

'I am called Demetrius.'

'And you are a Christian?'

'Yes, Tribune. I was called to follow the saviour's path ten years ago and have never wavered in my belief from that day to this.'

'And before that?'

The Christian paused momentarily, looking straight at Scaurus.

'I was a persecutor of my brothers and sisters in the Christos. I served in your army, recruited in Greece to serve in Judea, and before I came to see the unavoidable truth of their beliefs, I was responsible for the making of more than one martyr for God's truth.'

'More than one?' Cotta shook his head in dark amusement. 'How many more than one? And how is it that you come to be accepted by them, if you have done them such harm?'

Scaurus spoke first.

'One or one hundred, the number is immaterial. This man has pursued the members of a religious cult only to find himself unable to resist becoming a part of it. As to your other question, I have some familiarity with Demetrius's faith, born of my desire to understand what drives its members to make martyrs of themselves. I believe that forgiveness is at the heart of your beliefs?'

'It is.' The Christian beamed with pleasure. 'It is central to our

faith that no man can be refused forgiveness, if he truly repents
of his sins. Our Lord Jesus the Christos himself forgave the man
who betrayed him and condemned him to die on the cross at the
hands of—'

'We know.' Scaurus interrupted with the air of a man who knew
that a sermon was imminent, and who had neither the time nor
the patience to listen. 'And I know what it is that you hope to
gain from this conversation.'

Demetrius raised an eyebrow.

'You must be a very perceptive man, Tribune, to know what is
in my mind.'

'It doesn't take a genius, Christian. After all, even if we weren't
in the company of a pair of fearsome northern barbarians, my
officers obviously aren't from around here. On top of which, I've
already seen you once today, haven't I?'

Demetrius nodded.

'Yes. I saw you on the deck of the *Victoria* as the warship
entered the harbour, along with your companions.'

'You were standing on the island on which the lighthouse of
Pharos is built.'

'I was drawn there today, without knowing why. When your
ship approached the harbour I knew immediately that this was a
moment of importance to me. To my faith. God spoke to me at
the instant that I saw you.'

'What did he say? There's a man with plenty of gold, why not
go and see if you can charm some of it out of him with the usual
wild tales of a man being crucified and then rising from the
dead?'

The Christian ignored Cotta's jibe as if he hadn't heard it.

'He told me that you are his vessel – his unwitting but faithful
instrument in spreading our faith to the unbelieving peoples.'

He stared at Scaurus levelly, and the Roman shook his head
in polite but firm disbelief.

'I follow a different path. The Lightbringer is my god.'

'Our God is everybody's god, my friend. He smiles on you

no matter what path you follow. And he will judge you in the afterlife according to the good you do in this one. I see much good in you, Tribune. You would make a fine addition to our church.'

Scaurus laughed softly.

'Flattery is unlikely to get you very much from me.'

Demetrius spread his hands wide in a gesture of innocence.

'Not flattery. Sincere appreciation for the acts of a just man. You have been in this city for less than a day, and already you have freed a family from the threat posed to them by an emperor's wrongdoings.'

The Roman shook his head, no longer amused.

'I wouldn't go shouting that praise too loudly, friend, or you'll find yourself emulating your one-time leader and joining the list of martyrs to your cause.'

The Greek shrugged.

'I would not be the first, nor would I be the last. We have something in common, my brothers and sisters in the Christos, which is that we are all willing to give our lives for our beliefs.'

Cotta snorted another laugh, but Scaurus's expression remained stern.

'You're hardly the first religion to inspire the authorities of the day to execute men they see as zealots. The word martyr is itself Greek, not Latin.'

'Which makes the prospect an honourable one, does it not.'

Scaurus shook his head in exasperation.

'I do not have the time to debate with you. I suggest you return to the city and go about the task of being a good, loyal citizen.'

Demetrius bowed deeply.

'Please do go about your business, Tribune. I will be here when you emerge, ready to follow you wherever it is that your mission takes you. When the time comes for your part in Our Lord's plan to be made clear to us both, I must be ready to play my part. Whatever that may be.'

★

Scaurus and Marcus were ushered into the lamp-lit office of the legion's commanding officer, to be greeted by a tall, watery-eyed man dressed in a uniform tunic to which he seemed not entirely suited, lacking any of the physical self-confidence that was usual in men of his exalted position, whether justified or not. He stuck out a hand somewhat self-consciously, as if he were emulating the expected demeanour of a legion commander rather than actually performing the role.

'Greetings, gentlemen, I am Lucius Caesius, *praefectus legionis* of the Second Traiana. There's no legate rank to be had in Aegyptus, just as there's no governor, just prefects appointed by the emperor from the equestrian class. A glass of wine, Tribune?'

Gesturing to the chairs facing his desk, he nodded to his steward, a uniformed soldier who, apparently well accustomed to the senior officer's habits, stepped forward with two cups before retreating from the room. Scaurus took a sip, watching over the wooden cup's rim as the other man drank deeply, noting his expression of pleasure mixed with what looked somewhat like relief. Their arrival had been notified earlier in the day by an advance party consisting of Qadir and Avidus's engineers, and the party had been admitted with a minimum of fuss, swiftly allocated to a barrack block, and their prisoners taken away for processing into the legion's ranks without comment, once Scaurus had declared their fate to the duty centurion. The camp seemed, on the surface at least, to be efficiently run, its guard posts manned and its streets spotlessly clean, exactly as defined in the military manuals by which the army's centurionate discharged their responsibilities. Such neatness and order seemed at odds with the prefect's apparent lack of any spark of martial vigour, and the Roman found himself wondering just who was the source of the legion's discipline.

'So tell me, Tribune Scaurus, what is it that I can do for you?'

Scaurus set the wine down on the table before him.

'You have no word from the governor, Prefect?'

The other man shook his head.

'Other than a one-line message to grant you all realistic assistance with your mission, no. What is it that you've been ordered to do?'

'Go south and find out exactly what it is that has cut communications with the trading port of Berenike.'

The prefect leaned back in his chair, taking another deep drink from his cup.

'Ah, that. I was wondering when that was going to excite some interest from Rome.'

Scaurus shook his head in bafflement.

'Ah, that? You've been aware of this apparent invasion from the south for how long? A month?'

'At least.'

'And yet—'

'We've done nothing? You've met *Praefectus Augustalis* Faustinianus, have you not? You should already be very clear as to his priorities. They are made abundantly clear to me every time we meet.'

Scaurus nodded.

'I can imagine. And yet . . .'

'I should have found a way to investigate? Despite his repeated orders to maintain a grip of the city and ensure the flow of tax revenue to Rome? Perhaps I should.'

'But you haven't done so.'

'No.'

The legion commander drained his cup and called for another. His steward, clearly well drilled in this evidently frequent request, entered the room with a full cup and removed the empty. When he had gone the senior officer spoke again.

'Look at me, Rutilius Scaurus, and tell me what you see.'

Scaurus nodded his understanding.

'You invite me to excuse you from your duty on the grounds of what, an uncontrolled love for wine? A position that you neither expected nor desired? A role that you have unexpectedly been granted mainly to ensure your legion's loyalty to Cleander, and his various means of extorting money from this province?'

'And there you have it.' The prefect drank again. 'I am purely a figurehead here. A conduit for the orders that flow from above. As to what I'm doing here, I'm every bit as bemused as the look on your face tells me you are. My family is rather better known for producing scholars than for its military men. I was appointed without an expectation of being so honoured, after a career that was at best average, and with no more experience than a military tribunate in Dacia fifteen years ago. I am almost completely unqualified to command a legion, and yet here I am: unqualified, unwanted and, it has to be said, unneeded, for the most part. The Second is run for me by a most efficient body of officers, centurions for the most part, and the keenest of my tribunes, and this is, I am sure you will agree once you have seen them exercise, a fine body of men, well trained and with the purest of motivations. There is no fraud within these walls – indeed, my first spear would rather fall on his sword than participate in any of those schemes involving recruits who don't exist or mythical hunting parties to explain absent soldiers. But neither is there any opportunity for us to do what is usually expected of a legion. My men march around the city keeping the peace and ensuring that the tax collectors can go about their task unobstructed, and . . .'

Seeing Scaurus's expression change, he raised a questioning eyebrow.

'You'll have one less tax farmer to protect after this afternoon.'

Caesius listened with a growing look of amazement as Scaurus told him what he had done on his way from the praetorium. Emptying his cup, he called for another, shaking his head in amazement.

'You've got balls, Rutilius Scaurus, I'll give you that! You do realise that Faustinianus will appoint another tax collector as soon as he finds out about this?'

Scaurus shrugged.

'As I told the vicious bastard who was victimising the people of the city this afternoon, I can only deal with the injustices that are put before me, Prefect.' He sipped at his own wine. 'Which are your six best cohorts? If your first spear is a traditionalist, then perhaps he's adhered to the old rule that the Second, Fourth, Seventh and Ninth Cohorts are those which contain the youngest and rawest recruits?'

The other man shook his head languidly.

'I really have no idea. I'm sure he will have an excellent grasp of the legion's capabilities. Shall I have him report to us?'

'That would be helpful, Prefect. How much I will be able to achieve here depends on what sort of legion he and his officers have built for you, and whether I will be marching south in command of lambs or lions.'

The Second Legion's first spear's craggy features were carefully composed as he stood at the head of his senior centurions, his brown skin creased and wrinkled from exposure to the elements. Leaning against the praetorium's wall off to one side of the Second's assembled centurionate was a man of about twenty-five, dressed in the same thin-striped tunic that Scaurus and Marcus wore, his face carefully neutral as the legion's officers regarded the new arrivals with a mixture of curiosity and uncertainty.

'If I may, Prefect?'

Caesius smiled wanly at Scaurus, waving a hand.

'By all means, Tribune.'

The Roman turned to face the line of men.

'Gentlemen, I suggest you stand at ease. This might take a while.'

The first spear barked a terse order, and his men settled into a marginally less stiff posture while the military tribune smiled knowingly and met Marcus's glance with a nod of greeting.

'Thank you.' He turned to the assembled men, his next words stiffening the centurions' backs as his expectation of primacy in their small world became clear. 'Officers of Trajan's Second Legion, I bear orders from the emperor himself! They are orders that I, and you, are expected to follow without either question or hesitation.'

The officers kept their gazes level, clearly unwilling to deviate from their senior centurion's expectations of iron discipline, and after a moment their leader spoke, his voice the same iron-hard, grating rasp to which Scaurus and the men of his familia were accustomed in men who expected their commands to be both heard and instantly obeyed at a hundred paces. His Latin was almost unaccented, as if spoken from birth.

'There has been speculation, Tribune.'

'I can imagine, First Spear . . .?'

'Abasi, Tribune.'

'Let me put that speculation to rest then, Abasi. If the inveterate gamblers among your cohorts have been accepting odds on a march south with any sort of generosity then they are likely to regret that decision.'

The other man nodded curtly.

'That is as expected, sir. How many cohorts?'

Marcus raised an eyebrow at the lounging tribune, who smiled fractionally and nodded agreement with his unspoken sentiment.

'Straight to business, First Spear?'

'Why waste time in discussion, Tribune? Tell me how many men you want ready to march, and when, and I will make it happen.'

The watching tribune levered himself off the wall and stepped forward, raising a hand in salute.

'First Spear Abasi is, as you will already have noticed, almost laconic in his brevity.' He flashed a grin at the senior centurion. 'It might not entirely surprise you, *Sese*, if I don't share your enviable lack of concern with where we might be going, and what we might be expected to achieve. It isn't every day that men like these step off an imperial flagship and stroll into the fortress carrying marching orders straight from the Palatine Hill. So forgive me, gentlemen' – he half bowed to Scaurus and Marcus – 'if I'm just a little keener than old leather lungs here to know what's afoot? My name is Julius Fabius Turbo, senior tribune of the legion.'

He glanced down at the thin purple stripe that lined his tunic, obviously drawing attention to the social status that allowed him to feel comfortable in bestowing an evidently fond nickname on a man ten years older and with a good twenty years more military experience. Marcus shot a glance at Abasi, only to find his face set in the same expressionless mask.

'Well then, Tribune Turbo, since you ask . . .' Scaurus was choosing to play it straight, ignoring the jocularity that invited him to treat the younger man as an equal. 'I do indeed carry orders from the palace, orders given to me in person by the imperial chamberlain, along with the command to either resolve the matter causing him great distress on the emperor's behalf or, put simply, not to return.'

'*I tan, I epi tas?*'

The younger man had switched from Latin to Greek to reference the ancient Spartan command from a wife or mother to her husband or son on handing him his shield, something that all educated Romans learned as part of their grounding in the classics.

'With this, or upon this?' Scaurus nodded solemnly, choosing not to match the tribune's knowing smile. 'Yes, that's very apt, given your reference to Spartan brevity a moment ago. I am indeed invited to return with my shield, or else on it. Victory or death. And Chamberlain Cleander, being the pragmatist that I can assure you from previous experience he is, has left it up to me to determine how to discharge my orders, as is his habit. On the one hand, it can make for unexpected conflict, when it becomes clear that I can only discharge those orders at the expense of other men's dignity. On the other, the very lack of their specificity means that no man can point to them and try to tell me that their commands are out of bounds to me as they are not listed in the order. I am simply empowered, as always, to demand complete and unquestioning cooperation from all and any servants of the throne, whenever and wherever I should require it. Cooperation which, from the stream of irate complaints his office receives from wherever it is that his orders send me across the empire, the chamberlain knows I am somewhat adept in procuring. One way, or another. Easy or hard.'

'And your demands of us are . . .?'

'The Second Legion's six most competent cohorts, fully manned, two cohorts of auxiliary light infantry and a wing of cavalry, at least to start with. Oh, and all of your artillery with the exception of the catapults. We can gather up more strength as we march south.'

'I see. And Augustal Prefect Faustinianus was agreeable to this requirement?'

Scaurus smiled, showing his teeth.

'The augustal prefect, Tribune Turbo, had no more choice in the matter than I did, when I was ordered to board a warship and flung across Our Sea at breakneck speed, ordered to resolve a problem that the augustal prefect is apparently incapable of dealing with. That might be overly harsh, of course. Perhaps Pomponius Faustinianus is simply forbidden to abandon his first responsibility, which is evidently to wring as much tax as possible from the province. Either way it makes no difference, as it results in my having been ordered to take whatever steps are required to restore normality to this part of the empire. I trust you understand the position that puts us both in?'

The other man inclined his head.

'I think I have a grasp of it. I will be subordinate to you in all matters for the duration of your mission to investigate this matter.'

Scaurus nodded, twisting the blade of his advantage with his next statement.

'Correct. And to whoever I choose to appoint to command in my absence. Which will be my colleague Tribulus Corvus here, a man of our class who has previously filled the role of tribune to my legatus in the past. Rank can be somewhat fluid, when operating under the chamberlain's orders.'

Turbo shot a swift, startled glance at Marcus's centurion's uniform, but if Scaurus was looking to defuse a potential conflict by provoking confrontation, he was disappointed.

'As you say, your orders are all encompassing.'

'Indeed.' The Roman turned back to Abasi and his men. 'So, First Spear, how quickly can you have my six cohorts ready to march?'

The senior centurion's expression didn't change from its studied impassivity.

'Twelve hours, Tribune.'

'You're sure that's enough time, First Spear? You must have men on passes in the city who will have to be called back, and every legionary must be properly equipped, blades sharpened, boots shod, armour riveted, supplies packed . . .'

Abasi nodded at Scaurus with the certainty of a man in complete command of a legion he considered his own.

'Twelve hours will be enough.'

Scaurus nodded equably.

'Very well, First Spear, in that case we will march soon after dawn tomorrow. I trust that the legion's young gentlemen can be ready to the same schedule?'

Abasi's smile was barely detectable, more a reflection of his new tribune's attempt at humour than genuine amusement.

'As ready as they can be, Tribune.'

Scaurus nodded his agreement.

'Very well. Start making your preparations, gentlemen, and we'll discuss the ins and outs of how to go about dealing with whoever has deprived the empire of its southernmost port later this evening.'

As the meeting broke up, Dubnus tapped Ptolemy on the shoulder.

'Earn a little of that sword tuition you insist on receiving, little sparrow. What does the word "laconic" mean?'

Ignoring the nickname with the flicker of a frown, the Aegyptian dropped into his customary didactic style.

'It comes from the name given by the Greeks to the kingdom of men we call Spartans. Lacedaemon was the name of that land, and its people were famous for their use of half a dozen well-chosen words where anyone else would use a hundred to less effect. It has become known as "laconic", in their honour. An example that I am fond of is their response to the king of Macedon, Alexander the Great's father, who, having invaded southern Greece and received the submission of every other city-state, sent a message to the Spartans asking them whether he should come to them as a friend, or as a foe.'

Dubnus nodded.

'A good approach. It has a threat, and yet promises peace under the right terms. How did they reply?'

'With one word. *Neither.*'

'Neither? By the gods, that's good! But surely this king just invaded, having been put down hard?'

Ptolemy shook his head.

'Not at all. Even a hundred and fifty years after the heroic stand of the three hundred at Thermopylae, and bearing in mind that Sparta was no longer the pre-eminent state in Greece, their reputation in battle was still enough to deter Philip from attacking. And so he sent a further message, warning that if he brought his army to Lacedaemon he would destroy their farms, kill every Spartan and raze the city to the ground. And can you guess how many words the Spartan responded with?'

'Two?'

Ptolemy shook his head with a smile.

'One. *If.*'

The Briton smiled slowly.

'That's . . .'

'Laconic. One word with enough meaning in it that neither Philip nor Alexander ever invaded.'

'I like this. You can teach me all the "laconic" that's in your head, and in return I'll show you how to emasculate a man with a single thrust of your blade.'

The Aegyptian nodded slowly, his thoughts dragged abruptly from the pleasure of being a teacher to the tribulations of being taught by so exacting a master.

'Thank you. I think . . .'

4

'The port of Berenike is situated here . . .' Ptolemy pointed to a spot on the map laid out before the officers far to the south of Alexandria, on the shores of a narrow sea whose name was marked as *Mare Rubrum*.

With the fortress a hive of frantic activity, as Abasi's centurions strove to make good on his promise to ready the legion for the march by the next morning, Scaurus had called his key officers to the *principia* to discuss his proposed approach to the task at hand. The scribe had unexpectedly found himself the focus of the room's collective attention, having been ordered to make all present familiar with the geography of the problem that faced them.

'Why is it called the Red Sea?'

'Because, Centurion, in the right light it has a red tinge. The reason is unknown, although many philosophers have attempted to explain the phenomenon.'

He looked at Dubnus questioningly, but the big Briton simply nodded at his answer and remained silent.

'The port was founded four hundred years ago by Ptolemy the Second, the son of the Greek warrior king who took Aegyptus for his own after Alexander's death. He named it after his mother, with, we are told, the suffix *Troglodytai*, referencing the local inhabitants of caves in a range of hills. Although from my readings of the writers of his day I am convinced that the original name was *Trogodytai*, and that lazy copyists have identified these ancient tribes as cave dwellers rather than the term's original meaning, people of the desert.' He looked around the group of officers in evident hope of some reaction, waiting in vain for a moment, and then continued with a slight shake of his head at their lack of interest in his academic prowess. 'It was built at the head of a bay, which the geographer Strabo named *Sinus Immundus,* after the Greek *Akathartos Kolpos.*'

'The Unclean Bay.'

'Indeed, Tribune Scaurus. Something to do with the currents, doubtless. It is separated from the valley of the river Nilus by a range of mountains which contain emerald mines, the *Mons Smaragdi.*'

'Literally, the Emerald Mountains?'

'I believe that the gems are prolific in the area, and mined, of course, under the control of imperial officials. The port stands on the flat ground between the sea and the mountains.'

'It is used for the import of goods from the east, I assume?'

Ptolemy nodded at Marcus.

'Yes, Tribune. It is the most important port on the eastern coast.'

'But why there? Surely a port further up the Red Sea and closer to the capital would make more sense? Why spend money carting goods up the coast when a ship could take them north so much more quickly and cheaply?'

'It is a safe anchorage, and being further south than the other major port on the Red Sea, Myos Hormos, it can often be easier to reach from the south. The winds, you see . . .?'

'The winds?'

The scribe waved a hand over the map.

'There is a weather phenomenon in this part of the world that we call the *mawsim,* with a pattern that repeats every year and brings the rains that make the river Nilus flood, and washes rich black soil downriver from the highlands of the far south, giving the farmers of the river's delta the most fertile land in the world. In the winter the wind blows from the south-west, making it easy to sail up the Red Sea but hard to sail down it, whereas in the summer that position is reversed, and a laden merchant vessel heading north up the Red Sea, returning from a trade voyage begun in the spring, would be hard-pressed to make a more northerly port unless by good fortune or the painful labour of its oarsmen. Being further south is a definite advantage for a trader based in Berenike, as he will often be more easily able to make port when laden, and find the tricky winds and frequent storms easier to cope with for the same reason.'

'But all the same, this port is hardly critical to the empire's survival, is it? Or even for the continuation of the trade that puts silk on rich women's bodies and spices in their kitchens?'

Ptolemy smiled at Marcus's question.

'And expensive steel-edged weapons in your hands, Centurion. The finest iron in the world comes from the east.'

'The port's loss is a flea bite for the empire.' Scaurus looked down at the map for a moment before continuing. 'But no empire which suffers even the slightest reverse can afford to ignore the discomfort of that flea bite, for fear that other fleas will be encouraged to bite in their turn. And that's before we bear in mind that a good-sized portion of the money that the emperor depends on comes from this province. And that much of that will be taxation of the traders importing luxury goods from the east at the point they bring those goods into the empire, where they are more easily identified by means of their transportation and therefore easily taxed. This port has a prefect in command, I presume?'

'Indeed it does.' The Greek was eager to display his knowledge. 'The *praefectus praesidiorum et montis berenicidis.*'

'And nothing has been heard from this prefect for how long, Prefect?'

Caesius, who had made a point of waving away the wine that each of the officers was sipping from, much to his senior tribune's poorly hidden amusement, answered in a tone that was almost brisk.

'Word came from Koptos, an auxiliary fort five days march to the north-west of the port, that contact had been lost with the prefect and his command, a full part-mounted auxiliary cohort.

This came five days after the last message received from the prefect himself, that a trader's caravan had been stripped clean by desert raiders, and that he was taking his force to the south, with the intention of finding and destroying the bandits involved.'

'Which he seems to have failed to do, and probably at the cost of his command and his own life. A dismal failure, if the enemy involved were no more than a ragged band of opportunistic robbers.'

'That's an easy charge to lay at a man's door without actually placing yourself in his boots, Tribune Scaurus.'

All eyes turned to the young tribune, whose opinion had been voiced in a questioning tone. Scaurus nodded curtly, his expression unchanged.

'I understand your point, Turbo. But in the absence of knowing anything about him beyond his name and official title, it's hard to know how competent a job he would have done, is it not?'

The younger man stepped forward, his eyes bright with the certainty of his social rank's equality to that of his new commander.

'On the contrary, Tribune, his competency seemed evident enough, to me. Prefect Servius was the model of a Roman officer and gentleman.'

'You know the man?'

'I have met him.' The young tribune smiled. 'My father paid for me to undertake a journey up the Nilus prior to joining the legion, and when I reached Koptos I decided to spend some time getting to know the area.'

'Did you indeed? In which case you must have much to share with us. Tell me about this prefect, if you will.'

'He is a decent man, a member of our class, Tribune. And, I would add, a man to whom I warmed as being devoted to his duty, with a firm grasp of his role. We dined together on more than one occasion, and became friends. Indeed, he took me out on patrol into the desert, and across the river into the land of the desert dwellers who occupy the oases far to the west of the Nilus. He was more than kind, introducing me to their royalty on a routine show-of-force visit, and indulging me in all manner of discussions as to his role in the region.'

To Marcus's eye Scaurus's expression softened slightly, perhaps in recognition of a kindred spirit, of sorts.

'And your conclusion, from what he told you?'

'His command is positioned to protect the road from Berenike to the river crossing and port at Koptos from the depredations of the local desert bandits, in addition to keeping an eye on the dwellers of the western desert. These bandits are from the same tribe as inhabit the oases to which he took me and go by the name of Blemmyes. They live in the desert between the road and river, a barren waste without roads where we are unable to control them, and they take every opportunity to raid the caravans that carry trade goods, as the merchants transport their cargoes north from Berenike. They are a stubborn people, and difficult to control, well familiar with the desert, and of late it seems that they have become a good deal bolder in their forays. Servius knew he would have to deal with them, sooner rather than later.'

'I see.' The Roman stared up at the map thoughtfully. 'And I suppose that—'

'A further thought occurs to me, Tribune?' Scaurus turned back to the younger man, gesturing to him to speak. 'I had quite a good look at the forts situated along the road north from Berenike, and it seemed to me that they were there for two reasons.'

'One being to protect the trade passing up and down those roads, I assume?' Turbo nodded. 'And the other?'

'Each fort is built around a well.'

'Your colleague is right, Tribune Scaurus!' Ptolemy pointed at the map with fresh animation. 'These watering stations are called *hydreumata*, or *hydreuma* in the singular. The course of the road is determined by the presence of wells or springs to provide water to the men and beasts of each caravan making their way to and from the ports.'

Scaurus jumped to the point that he suspected Ptolemy was about to make.

'How much water can each fort provide?'

'More than enough to refresh a hundred camels and the men guiding them.'

'Camels? What's a *camel*?'

They turned to look at Dubnus, Scaurus smiling at his centurion.

'Our comrade here hails from the far north of the empire and is unfamiliar with the beast.'

'Ah, yes.' The diminutive scholar adopted the lecturing tone with which they had become familiar, clearly eager to demonstrate his expertise to his tutor. '*Kamelos* in Greek, from the ancient local term, *gamal*. A beast introduced to Aegyptus by Rome, a truly marvellous creature that can go for as long as ten days without drinking, due to its ability to store large quantities of water in a fleshy hump upon its back. It is further blessed with a third eyelid, which is transparent, with which to clear sand from its eyes when blown there by the wind, and—'

The burly Briton interrupted with a look of disbelief.

'You wouldn't be inventing any of these magical properties, would you, sparrow? Because if I discover you to be attempting to deceive me for the purpose of humour at my expense, I'll take that sword you're so fond of waving around and sheathe it where the sun never shines!'

'It's true!'

Dubnus looked from the scribe to Marcus, who nodded encouragingly, reluctantly ceding the point with a sour expression.

'You can show me one of these amazing creatures, one day soon.'

'And you will be amazed when you do set eyes on such a beast. An adult camel can drink a dozen amphorae of water in less time than it would take you to run a mile, and can—'

Scaurus coughed ostentatiously.

'Returning to the point of our discussion?' Ptolemy bowed apologetically, gesturing for him to continue. 'So, if these *hydreumata* can provide sufficient water to keep a trading convoy on the road, then presumably they might also serve to keep an army in the field. Is that your point, Tribune?'

Turbo nodded his agreement.

'My point exactly, Tribune Scaurus. An army that had taken Berenike would be able to push north and take the waterline points, and therefore be able to keep itself in the field as long as it was supplied with food.'

'But surely that prize will turn to dust in their hands?' Prefect Caesius pointed to the trading city of Myos Hormos, well to the north of the captured Berenike. 'After all, word will spread quickly enough, as ships meet each other at sea and in foreign ports. Their masters will soon know not to sail back to Berenike, but to take their cargoes to other ports, such as this one, if they want to be paid for their efforts?'

'I'm not so sure.' All eyes turned back to Scaurus. 'Think it through. Whoever it is that has Berenike in their grip will have taken the port for a reason, and with a plan of what to do when they have succeeded, do you not think? Nobody goes to war with Rome without having first worked out what to do under all of the eventualities that they can imagine. In the event of a such victory, were I the victor, my approach would be business as usual, just under a different rule and with a different customer. Merchants will be encouraged to keep trading, taxes on their profits reduced or dropped altogether to encourage them to support the new order of things. Under such circumstances they would be likely to send out smaller vessels to encourage their returning ship masters to make port in Berenike as usual, rather than running north to a different port, and to cooperate with their new rulers.'

He looked around at the officers before speaking again.

'Make no mistake, gentlemen, this is a serious state of affairs. That port receives a significant proportion of the total trade the empire conducts with the eastern lands, across the ocean we call the Erythraean Sea, does it not, Ptolemy?'

The scholar nodded knowingly.

'There is a *periplus* of the trade with the east, literally a "book of sailing around" that was written by one of my countrymen a century ago, a denizen of Berenike itself, as it happens. It provides us with a full description of the goods traded with other countries and cities. It is somewhat poorly written, it has to be said, with confusion between Greek and Latin words and some very poor grammar—' Scaurus raised an eyebrow, and the Aegyptian hurried on to answer the question. 'The port of Berenike receives trade goods such as spices and metals from the kingdoms of the Dakinabades on the far side of the ocean, gemstones and cloth from Ariaca, silk from Thinae and gold mined in Gedrosia. Indeed, it is in and itself akin to a metaphorical river of gold, a river which runs all the way from the kingdoms of the east to Rome!'

'Meta . . . what?'

The Aegyptian turned to Dubnus with a slight smile.

'Metaphorical. It means that the trade routes are *like* a never-ending flow of money, at least to the people who live along its banks, so to speak.'

Dubnus opened his mouth to deliver a rebuke to the scribe, presumably for his habitual wordiness, but Scaurus beat him to it.

'It is a good analogy, if a little convoluted. And this is a river of gold into which the imperial chamberlain has set up more than one watering point for the emperor's private finances. Which explains why he has sent us here, and what he expects of us: nothing less than to allow this river to continue delivering its bounty.'

He held up a scroll.

'These, gentlemen, are my orders. And at the risk of being tediously repetitive, this is the point at which we usually have to waste a good deal of time arguing as to who outranks whom socially, and, by association, who should command such a mission. It seems that no man of any rank can bear to have his position usurped, no matter how justifiably, without feeling the urge to fight the apparent loss of his prestige. You, Prefect Caesius can argue, and with some justification, that the Second Legion is yours to command. It is my decision, however, that you would be better placed to remain here in command of the remainder of the legion.'

Caesius inclined his head in acceptance, possibly grateful, of the order.

'And you, Tribune Turbo, might well be of the opinion that, in the absence of your legion's commander, your position as his second-in-command, coupled with your undoubted local knowledge of the area in question, makes you the more suitable man to lead. Which might also be true. But before you bring out those arguments, you should be aware of some irrefutable facts.'

The officers remained silent as he raised a finger.

'Firstly, I carry a written and personally signed instruction, addressed to whoever it may concern, from the imperial chamberlain, signed and sealed in the presence of this member of the Palatine secretariat . . .' He gestured to Ptolemy. 'Who is here for the sole purpose of pointing out to you all that my orders are both legal and binding on every imperial citizen in commanding you to afford me every cooperation. I hope that's clear enough for you but be in no doubt that I will order your centurions to detain any man that stands in my way. And I have no doubt that First Spear Abasi and his officers will be unhesitating in their eagerness to follow an order from Rome.'

He looked at Abasi, smiling tightly as the senior centurion nodded tersely.

'But there is another factor that I think you might want to consider before deciding whether you want to dispute the command of this mission with me.' He waved a hand at his familia. 'These men behind me, who have gathered around me over the last few years, all of them veterans of a dozen battles and skirmishes, share an unenviable social status with me. We are all, gentlemen, just one step from being exiled or executed.'

He raised a hand to forestall any questions.

'The reasons for that looming death sentence are not material to this discussion, and neither do I have much patience in explaining the injustices involved to men who might struggle to even believe them possible, so I'll ask you simply to consider the fact of our being subject to deep imperial opprobrium. The empire turns the sternest of gazes upon us, even as it somewhat hypocritically demands the fulfilment of yet another task which is likely to end in our deaths in its service.'

'That would seem . . . perverse . . . were it to be true.'

The Roman nodded at Turbo.

'It would, rather. And to be clear, I have no interest whatsoever in proving that injustice to you. Believe it, or refuse to do so, I've learned that it makes no difference. My point is that I am expected to succeed in liberating Berenike from whoever it is that has taken it from Rome, and that if I fail I am expected not to return to Rome. And so I ask any man who thinks that he would be better placed to command in my place whether he feels brave enough to risk the same fate? After all, it seems that Chamberlain Cleander has a very personal reason for wanting the normal trade conditions re-established as quickly as possible. Given that uncomfortable fact, are any of you really brave enough to try taking responsibility for this from me?'

The legion's officers looked at each other for a moment before Caesius replied.

'No, Tribune Scaurus, I don't think anyone here feels like challenging you to drink from such a poisoned cup.'

'As I expected. Command has a siren quality to it, until the ugly reality of the facts behind missions like those which have been entrusted to us of late is laid out. So, gentlemen, with that settled, perhaps we might turn to matters of practical interest?'

'Good evening, Tribune.'

The western gate's centurion saluted Marcus and nodded to Cotta as they walked along the wall overlooking the city, still clad in their armour. Night had fallen, and Alexandria's myriad lights pricked the gloom, illuminating the city's dark bulk to the degree that it was hard to pick out from the blaze of stars against which it was silhouetted.

'Good evening, Centurion, stand at ease.' Marcus stared more closely at the man in the wall's pale torchlight. 'I recognise you from earlier today. You were on duty in the agora when we dealt with the tax farmer and his men, were you not? Petosorapis?'

The other man nodded with a grim smile.

'Yes, Tribune, although my comrades call me Peto. And you should know that the whole fortress is buzzing about what you did. It's about time someone showed the scum who've been recruited to collect the empire's taxes the right way to behave! The Second Legion's newest recruits will be getting a hard time of it from now until the day they manage to run away or get themselves killed.'

Cotta nodded approvingly.

'That sad collection of goat fuckers will have realised they've just stepped into the deepest shit in their miserable lives . . .' He frowned at the centurion, whose face had creased with a look of puzzlement. 'What?'

Petosorapis shook his head.

'It's . . . nothing. Just something you said that sounded familiar.'

The older man shrugged, grinning at the other man's discomfiture.

'Happens to me all the time. You talk to enough men, then over the years you're going to hear something that takes you back to a different time.'

'Yes . . .' The Aegyptian nodded slowly. 'I suppose you're right. It just had the feeling of words I'd heard before though.'

A soldier strode up, saluting and addressing him in an urgent tone.

'Begging your pardon, Centurion, the chosen man sent me to find you. He's found two men—'

'*Thank you*, legionary.' Petosorapis overrode the man before whatever crime he had detected became public knowledge. 'I presume he has them both in the guardhouse?'

'Yes, sir!'

'Very good. On your way, and if you want to avoid an uncomfortable encounter with my vine stick you'll keep this to yourself, whatever it is. Understood?'

'Sir! Yes, sir!'

The soldier bolted away, and his centurion shook his head in disgust.

'My apologies, Tribune. No matter how well you watch them, the bastards always find a way to upset the apple cart.'

Marcus waved a dismissive hand.

'Of course, Centurion, no apology needed. I've stood in your boots in my time, and wondered just what it is that motivates some men to such acts of idiocy.'

Petosorapis strode away with the legionary trailing in his wake, and Marcus turned to his friend with a knowing expression.

'That looked like a close call to me, even if I didn't quite know what was happening?'

'I do.' Cotta shook his head in disgust. 'I realised what I'd done the moment the words were out of my mouth.'

'Which was what, exactly? Is this something to do with your killing Avidius Cassius?'

The veteran centurion sighed.

'I've always tried to keep the details to myself. Like I said on the ship, when that idiot scribe reminded me of the whole bloody affair, you kill one false emperor' – he shot his friend a rueful grin – 'and no matter how stupid the bastard was in allowing his centurions to drape him with purple, no matter how righteous your orders, then you're marked for life.'

He shook his head, sighing at the memory.

'I've never discussed it with you, as much to protect you as from a desire not even to think about it ever again. Thirteen years ago, this mob and my own legion were camped down in the delta, in the aftermath of the herdsmen revolting. They started cutting the guts out of Roman officers and cooking them up for their dinners, or at least that was the story we were told. Which is why the rules about no senators being allowed in the province went straight out of the window, and the empire's biggest-balled legion commander was given *imperium,* blessed with the title "Supreme Commander of the Orient", and sent in to teach them a lesson. The emperor clearly thought he could trust the man to renounce that absolute power once it was all done with.'

'This was the uprising of the *boukoloi*?'

'Yes. We put them down hard too, mainly due to Cassius being such a bright lad. He sowed a few lies and turned those country boys against each other, and the whole revolt just seemed to collapse in the space of a few weeks. Which was just as well, because there were a lot more of them than there were of us. But then, of course, his cleverness got the better of him, like it does with most of those fools that crave power. Marcus Aurelius was dead of some sickness or other, or so we heard, and when the inevitable pack of idiot centurions decided to put him on a throne he was stupid enough to actually let them do it. And I was the mug who got picked to take him off it, when word arrived that the emperor wasn't dead after all.'

'Who was doing the picking?'

'My legatus. Seems he'd been put in command of the Third mainly to keep a careful eye on Cassius.'

Marcus nodded.

'The last emperor was nobody's fool. And his man on the spot's choice of assassins was impeccable.'

Cotta spat over the wall.

'He fucked me every bit as efficiently as a bolt thrower at twenty paces. I went from the life of a centurion, with a decent chance of making it to first spear given time, to being an outcast. The legatus gave me a bag of gold and cordially advised to me to piss off double quick, get my head down and keep it down. Except that men who murder emperors, even idiot pretenders, don't tend to have that luxury. This lot, Trajan's Valiant Second Legion, tried to kill me twice in the first few years.'

He smiled wryly, his teeth agleam in the torchlight.

'No good deed goes unpunished, right? I took a handful of my closest mates back to Rome with me when I left, after putting Cassius's head on my legatus's desk, to avoid them paying the price for my crime. But word of where I was to be found got back to this lot soon enough, probably down to my friends' incessant bragging about what a big man I was to anyone that would listen when they'd had a few. Which meant I spent all my time looking over my shoulder, and being ready to deal with the men who were sent to take revenge on me for spoiling their dreams of being rich soldiers. I saw it coming, of course, and set up my own little army of ex-soldiers under the disguise of a bodyguarding business, and spread plenty of money around to make sure that anyone asking questions was given answers that made them take risks to get to me. And each time I stopped the wind of a fresh party of would-be killers, I sent their heads back here, along with the message that they were wasting their time, their gold and their blood. Eventually the bastards seemed to take the hint and stopped trying. But now that we're here . . .'

'All it takes is for one man to recognise you.'

'Exactly. And what I just did there was a big mistake.' The older man shook his head disgustedly. 'I remember Centurion Petosorapis well enough, and what I said to him thirteen years ago, when I was fronting up to a guard post that stood between me and my legion, and me with their emperor's head in a bag. He was just a watch officer then, which made it easy enough to stare him down and be on my way with nobody any the wiser, but you can be sure they made the connection as soon as my name got round the camp. And it'll probably only be a matter of time before he remembers what it is that's nagging at his memory.'

'I see.' Marcus thought for a moment. 'I think all we can do is bluff it out, in the event that he makes the connection. Just deny all knowledge of whatever it is he thinks he knows, and in the end it'll be forgotten. After all . . .'

A moment in the gloom below them caught his attention, and he leaned over the wall.

'Is that . . .'

Cotta followed his pointing hand.

'That Christian who was following us earlier? I think it is. And he's not alone either.'

A small group of robed figures were gathered at the side of the road that led from the fortress's western gate to the city, close enough to be dimly discernible in the light of the torches blazing along its rampart, and additionally illuminated by the flickering flame of a brand held by one of them.

'They're worshipping? In public?'

Cotta nodded.

'You get used to it. There isn't very much of it in Rome, not that you see in public, but here the bastards are shameless. It'll be one of their rites. Not only are they superstitious, talking about a dead man getting up and walking around, but they get up to all sorts of filth.'

Marcus stared down at the huddled knot of men.

'They look harmless enough.'

'They do now, but you only have to listen to them, the animals. They're cannibals, and worse, they practise incest as well.'

'Ah. You may find that you've been somewhat misled on those topics.' Cotta stared at Marcus with the look of a man unwilling to be parted from his beliefs. 'Come on, let's go and have a look, shall we?'

'*What?*'

The Roman laughed softly at his friend.

'They're not flesh-eaters, they just have a rather individual approach to religion. One they continue to practise despite all the warnings they've had on the matter. Come on!'

The chosen man commanding the gate sentries insisted on accompanying the two men out into the darkness, ignoring Cotta's protests that they were more than capable of looking after them-selves in the face of any threat a few underfed-looking religious perverts might have to offer.

'All I know is that if anything happens to either of you two gentlemen it'll be *me* bent over a post for a fucking good scourging. Sir.'

The two men strolled out into the night with a handful of men behind them, their spears held ready in unmistakable threat, closing to within a few paces of the huddled figures before stopping. Marcus raised his empty hands as he addressed the group.

'My apologies for disturbing your worship. Please ignore the armed men behind us, they simply seek to ensure our safety.'

Demetrius stepped out of their midst, clearly untroubled by the threat of the legionaries' weapons.

'To be a Christian, Tribune, is to make the decision never again to allow oneself to worry about the potential dangers of following the one true path. Were one of your soldiers to pierce me with his spear and take my life, he would simply be sending me to join the Christos in heaven, where my judgement awaits me.'

Marcus smiled at the man's transparent belief in what he was saying.

'That must be helpful, when pursuing a faith that puts you at odds with the empire's rules of what is seemly in a religion.'

Demetrius shrugged.

'Our faith does not seek to threaten Rome, Tribune, but rather to make her stronger in the worship of the one true God, and the inherent justice of that state of mind for all men. But I do not believe you came down here to be converted, did you? Your time is not yet here, I feel.'

'Nor will it ever be. There is too much of the fanatic to your beliefs for my taste, too much appealing to the common man in shameless proselytism. I fear for a world with only one god, whose demands are interpreted by men whose authority will be absolute. Your Christos might be the most beneficent of deities, but I have seen enough of human nature to be less than convinced that his priests will necessarily follow his teachings. The priests of Ahura Mazda in Parthia, men whose baleful influence I have seen at close quarters, perpetually struggle for power against the men who lead the king's army. They seek to control their king, and through him the kingdom.' Marcus smiled and shook his head. 'Imagine an empire as powerful as Rome, but led by a man susceptible to the urgings of the priests of a single god.'

Demetrius nodded, his face creasing into a similar smile.

'I can imagine such a thing, but I do not view it with fear. Quite the opposite.'

'And so there we find our fundamental difference. You wish to unite the world under the priesthood of one god, whereas I would fight against such a thing to my last breath.'

The Greek inclined his head respectfully.

'And yet you too will come to see the justice and glory of our faith, Tribune, given time. You will bow your head to the Christos, and his father, the one true God.'

'We shall see.' Marcus gestured to the darkness, and the stiff breeze that was dragging the flame of their torch away from its pitch-soaked head at a right angle. 'What is it that you are doing here, you and your brothers? You were advised to return to the city and go about your life, and yet here you are in this inhospitable place.'

The Christian gestured to the knot of his fellow believers clustered behind him.

'Not just my brothers, Tribune. My sisters in the Christos have also joined me, to say farewell before my journey, and to share with me the body and blood of Our Lord.'

Marcus frowned.

'Ignoring the foolishness of your apparently barefaced declarations of incest and cannibalism, which we both know are at the root of Rome's distrust of your faith, *what* journey? Where is it that you think you are going?'

Demetrius extended a hand into the darkness, pointing to the south.

'I will go wherever you go, Centurion, and I will follow you until such time as the purpose of my calling becomes clear to me.'

'No. You cannot accompany us. My commander will not allow

it, for one thing, and we will not feed you, nor allow you to share our camp.'

The Greek smiled broadly, his teeth a flash of white in the torchlight.

'My blessings on you for providing such a clear warning of the hardships to come. And yet were you to have counselled me that the road ahead was winding, hemmed in by thorns, parched and beset by hunger, I would still be required to take it.' He rubbed at the thick, greasy wool of an outer garment that had evidently been provided by his brethren. 'My cloak will suffice for shelter, and I carry enough coin to feed myself for months, if I eat frugally.'

'And what if you encounter robbers, on the road?'

'Well then, there is this.' Demetrius pulled his cloak aside and patted the hilt of the short sword concealed beneath it. 'I am no stranger to the use of a blade, indeed before my conversion I was the strongest adherent you can imagine of its primacy in the affairs of man. If the unworthy attempt to deflect me from my path, I will not hesitate to use it to defend myself, and in as forceful a manner as needed to preserve my service to my God.' He grinned at Marcus's surprised expression. 'Did you think that I was some sort of pacifist, Tribune? The Christos did indeed teach his followers to turn the other cheek in the face of aggression, when he spoke on the mount, but sometimes the older teachings of the Hebrews are right. I will absorb all and any insult, endure abuse and even casual blows, from those who do not know better, but when the time comes that my purpose in this life is threatened, then I will smite the unbeliever and leave them to the mercies of Our Lord when he comes to judgement!'

'There you go . . .' Cotta leaned close to Marcus and muttered in his ear. 'Just another religious maniac. What did I tell you?'

'And, ignoring the wilder accusations of those around you . . .' Demetrius flashed an undaunted smile at Cotta. 'In truth, you cannot stop me from following your path. A body of legionaries will hardly be difficult to follow. Unless you choose to nail me to a cross and leave me to God, of course. And I do not see that sort of cruelty present itself here, not in you, Centurion, and neither in your superior. And you may trust me when I tell you that I am very much an expert in the expression of physical cruelty. But now, if you will excuse me, I must complete the ceremony that I have begun, with my brothers and sisters. There is bread and wine to be blessed, and the guidance of Our Lord to be sought once the physical needs of this fragile shell have been satisfied.'

Marcus looked up at the sky.

'There is cloud drawing in, from the north. It may rain later.'

'In which case it seems likely that I will get wet. But the sun is never absent from our sky for long, Tribune, and when it re-emerges I will dry out again. Such is the way of things, as I learned a long time ago, and in much the same way that you did.'

'Very well. I see that you are set on this course, and that only physical restraint will prevent you from following us to wherever it is that we are going.'

The Christian shook his head.

'Not even that, Tribune. You could bind me, that is true, but another man would take my place. Perhaps less hardy, perhaps less resourceful, but one of us will follow you, no matter how many others you detained. And when, upon the road, that individual was set upon by the bandits you warned me about, and was less able to defend himself than I, his death would be on your conscience. And, I must add, noted for your judgement, when the time comes for you to stand before Our Lord and account for your sins.'

'You have it all worked out, I see.'

Demetrius smiled.

'I have the certainty of true faith, Centurion. It burns brightly in me and inspires all that I do. You should try opening yourself to the teachings of the Christos, and enjoy his radiance in your soul.'

Marcus turned to Cotta with a wry grin.

'It seems that you were right. Religious fanaticism conquers common sense every time. Come on, let's go and find something hot to eat.'

'You do not intend to hamper me in my holy task?'

The Roman turned back to regard Demetrius levelly.

'It will be for my tribune to decide, not me. But for my part, given what I believe we will be marching towards, if you lack the wit to comprehend the risk you're taking, then there's little that I can do other than to afford you a decent burial, when the time comes.'

5

'I'm obliged to admit, it's been a while since I've seen a legion as well drilled and turned out.'

Cotta raised a jaundiced eyebrow at Marcus's observation.

'Trajan's Valiant Second always was *shiny*. The problem with them was that they were also *shy*.'

'You are saying they were . . .'

Qadir paused, uncertain how to phrase the criticism, and his friend pounced with the speed of long practice.

'Scared of a fight? Liable to move backwards in the face of the enemy?' Cotta stared across the parade ground at the neatly turned out soldiers marching across the flat surface under the watchful eye of First Spear Abasi. 'Yes, I am. Their spearheads might have been polished to a mirror finish, but they shook so badly when they took to the field that it looked like an imperial message relay tower with the crew working double time.'

'You might not want to allow those views to be overheard, Centurion.' Scaurus had approached from behind them, unannounced, a smile wreathing his lips at his officer's bitter condemnation of the men parading before them. 'I doubt that our colleagues would be all that delighted to be described as lacking backbone, and they were, let us remember, awarded the title *Fortis* for their defence of Alexandria during the revolt of the *boukoloi*, were they not?'

Cotta shook his head, raising his eyebrows to indicate that he had expected better from his superior.

'There was face to be saved, Tribune. When the peasants ran amok across the delta, slaughtering every soldier and official they could get their hands on, this lot just locked themselves up in the city and left them to it.'

'And withstood a siege that lasted several months.'

The veteran centurion shrugged, unimpressed.

'Standing steadfastly behind the city's walls against a mob armed with pitchforks and scythes. With enough grain in the city's warehouses to feed them for years. It's not my definition of the word *fortis*, with all due respect, sir.'

Scaurus smiled and kept his own counsel, recognising from long experience the tone and inflection of a centurion, a class of men he knew only too well to never knowingly be in the wrong, who was obdurate in his opinion. Marcus exchanged an amused glance with his superior before breaking the slightly awkward silence that had resulted.

'What do you think of their first spear? I suspect that Julius would be doing that thing he does when faced with another warrior king at this very moment, were he here.'

Cotta guffawed, forgetting his enmity for the Second Legion.

'That thing where he leans back, puffs out his chest, puts his hands on his hips and stares down his nose at the other man?'

'Exactly. They seem as alike as two peas in the pod to me.'

The veteran officer nodded, pursing his lips judiciously.

'Yes, I see the resemblance, for all that Abasi is somewhat darker of skin and more economical with his language. He has that same swagger about him, and the look of a man whose subordinates really don't want to disappoint.'

With the last of his cohorts in place, the ritual shouting of orders and close, intimidatory supervision of their ranks by glowering centurions completed, and the whole formation standing in perfect silence under the morning's sunshine, Abasi marched briskly across to where Scaurus was standing and snapped to attention, saluting punctiliously.

'The Second Legion is ready for war, Tribune.'

Scaurus took his measure for a moment, nodding his satisfaction at the man's pugnacious declaration of his cohorts' readiness, then strolled forward to survey the ranks of men awaiting his command.

'You are to be complimented for putting the legion on the road in so short a time, First Spear. And your cohorts appear to be at their establishment strength. All legionaries are fully equipped as per regulations, all carrying two days' rations? Their boots are freshly nailed? Every tent party has checked their gear, repairs have been made and new equipment issued where necessary?'

He gestured to the lines of carts neatly lined up to one side of the parade ground, their teams of donkeys prevented from making any of the usual braying protests by the judicious application of their morning feed.

'The legion artillery, rations, tents and animal fodder are all correct, all pack animals are present and ready for the road?'

Abasi nodded confidently.

'They are, Tribune, and so' – he added, anticipating the inevitable follow-up question – 'are the cohorts we're leaving to control the city.' He leaned closer to the Roman and lowered his voice to make what he was about to say private. 'There are no non-existent soldiers on *my* legion's payroll.'

Scaurus nodded, meeting the other man's direct stare.

'As it should be, First Spear. And as it will need to be, over the next few months. I hope your men are as well drilled with their weapons as they are smartly turned out?'

Abasi turned to look back at his cohorts.

'The legion practises with weapons every morning for four hours. And marches the daily distance three times a week.' His face creased into a faint smile. 'Sometimes twice that.'

Scaurus nodded, raising an eyebrow at Cotta before speaking again.

'Your men must regard you as a hard taskmaster, First Spear. I'd imagine that some of those training marches must see you back on this parade ground well after darkness has fallen?'

Abasi shrugged.

'They are ready for war. I have sworn never to permit anything else as long as I carry this.'

He raised a vine stick unlike no other that Marcus had ever seen, its ends capped with riveted gold ferrules that gleamed softly in the morning sun.

'Your badge of office is a piece of craftsmanship, First Spear.'

Abasi turned to face him with a hard smile, offering the stick for inspection.

'The legion's centurions compete for this trophy once a year, Centurion Corvus. I have held it for the past nine years.'

'I see.'

Turbo was the first to speak in the resulting awkward silence.

'And now you're wondering how it can be possible for any such competition to be fair, aren't you, Tribulus Corvus? Even if it's too early in your relationship to say so to his face.'

Marcus inclined his head in acceptance of the point.

'You raise a fair point, Tribune.'

'I had the same doubt as to such a competition's honesty, obviously, when I first arrived. But my cynical expectations of some bias in the award of this prize were soon disproved. The Second's centurions hold a boxing tournament for the honour of carrying that bauble, and I can assure you that there isn't one of them who would give that contest anything less than their best. Abasi oversees the fights himself, with the exception of his own bouts, and in deciding who will fight whom in each successive round, he always contrives to meet the most effective competitors on his way to the final. He has, I can assure you, battered the biggest and nastiest of his officers for the right to carry that stick, and taken his share of their return blows. That's why they call him "Sese".'

'Sese?'

'It means "vanquisher" in the Aegyptian language, does not, First Spear Abasi?'

The big centurion nodded, his expression unchanged, neither embarrassed nor displaying any hint of pride.

'It does, Tribune.'

Turbo grinned.

'His men love him, Tribune Corvus. They worship the ground he walks on. He submits them to more hardship than any other legion in the empire, I'm guessing, and yet they regard him as some sort of warrior king. I've heard men say they'd die for him in a heartbeat, and sound deadly serious in the promise.'

'You are a throwback to harder days, it seems, First Spear.'

Abasi shrugged expressionlessly at Scaurus's comment.

'This legion disgraced itself during the uprising. We were rescued from a mob of peasants by legions from other provinces. And our general was murdered in our own camp.'

'Avidius Cassius? The man was an imperial pretender, was he not? Surely his life was forfeit, and his fate earned?'

Abasi shook his head.

'The legatus was misadvised.' He shook his head. 'But, regardless of his murder's imperial sanction, I have sworn an oath to Mars never to see such ignominy fall upon the legion again. Not while I have breath in my body.'

'And so you have made the Second over in your own likeness.'

'Not in my image. That of Hercules, the demi-god who will be the legion's inspiration long after I have gone to the dust. I simply provide my legionaries with an understanding of their part in achieving that glory. And now that the time has come for battle, I do not intend to miss the chance to fight. Who knows when it might come again?'

'Who indeed?' Scaurus gestured to the paraded soldiers. 'In which case, First Spear, I suggest we get on the move. How far can your men march?'

'Thirty miles a day, Tribune. And every day, as long we don't dig out a marching camp at night?'

Scaurus considered the point.

'Is there a need, while we're still in the Nilus's delta? I presume that the peasants are unlikely to revolt again?'

The centurion shook his head.

'The plague that came back from Parthia with the army reduced the population so much that most villages are hard pressed simply to feed themselves.'

'Aegyptus was as hard hit by the plague as the rest of the empire?'

'Worse. One in three people who were taken sick died, and most men were infected. No repeat of the uprising is likely.'

Scaurus nodded.

'Very well, we will proceed south without the use of marching camps, at least until we reach Koptos. Although we will assume a military posture on the march from the start.' He turned to Turbo, who had been appointed to lead the legion cavalry as a means of softening the blow of his apparent demotion. 'Your horsemen are to lead the march, Tribune, and ensure that the road is clear of civilian traffic as we pass. I don't want to find myself held up behind ox carts, given the prodigious pace I believe First Spear Abasi's men will prove capable of achieving.'

'That's it. I'm spent.'

Dubnus looked up at Marcus from his place by their fire, bone-dry cordage burning brightly in the near total darkness of the Second Legion's camp. The night was illuminated by the dozens of fires that dotted the ground on which the cohorts had set up camp for the night, the ridges of their tents forming black triangles against the blaze of stars above the resting soldiers. The countryside around them was silent apart from the occasional distant bray of a donkey, and the fitful barking of farm dogs.

'I'm serious. I think that march might have broken me.' The Briton winced, stretching out his legs gingerly and rubbing his calves. 'Quite how these bastards manage to look so cheerful after reeling off a thirty miler in that heat is beyond me. It's been as hot as the best summer day I can recall in Britannia . . .' He paused and stretched his arms out, grimacing at the tension in the muscles. 'Although at least the nights are cool enough.'

'That heat was actually quite mild, for Aegyptus.' Cotta smirked at him from the other side of the fire, leaning back against his pack. 'After all, it's only spring. Wait until we get further south, and into the desert. It can be so hot in the summer that you can literally cook an egg in your helmet, if you leave it in the sun for a few minutes first, and even at night it never gets cold enough for a man to need to sleep under his cloak.'

'Bullshit!'

The veteran smiled knowingly at Dubnus's disbelief.

'I know, it seems impossible. Just you wait and see. No cloud, you see? There's nothing to stop the sunlight in the day, so it just beats down without any respite, until a man would give a month's pay for a cloudy day. And there's no water for hundreds of miles, other than what we can take from springs and cisterns. Give it a month and you'll see that the most important thing in your life will stop being that axe you cuddle up to every night, and start being your water bottle.'

'He's right.' Turbo appeared out of the darkness with Centurion Petosorapis at his back. 'Forgive my butting in, I'm just doing my rounds of the camp before I turn in and leave Peto here to keep the guards on their toes, not that they need much encouragement given the punishment Abasi has said he'll inflict on any man caught sleeping. Mind if we join you for a moment?'

The Tungrians made space for him, and he grunted with pleasure at the fire's warmth.

'In two weeks' time – because that's all it will take at the pace we kept up all day today – we'll have left the delta behind us and be will into the interior. And the desert is unlike anything you'll ever have seen.'

'We've seen wastelands, Tribune.'

'Not like this.' Turbo shook his head emphatically. 'Bare rock and windblown sand, without any water other than what comes out of a spring or a well that reaches a hundred feet or more into the ground. Which means no vegetation. At all. Military action will be a fascinating thing, I suspect, more like a game of robbers than anything you might be used to.'

'We've already played that game, on the grasslands of Parthia.'
Marcus stood, turning to look out into the darkness. 'Without
trees there can be no hiding place, if an enemy scouts with sufficient thoroughness. Which, as you suspect, will turn war into a
long, devious series of manoeuvres to gain the advantage. So what
do we know of the enemy we will face across this empty land?'

'Assuming that Blemmyes are responsible for the capture of
Berenike?'

'It seems from everything that I have read, and from the opinions of our man of letters, that they are the most likely adversary?
Are not the people of the far south only a shadow of their former
martial abilities?'

'Such is the received wisdom. I have never laid eyes on a man
of the city of Meroë, which makes it hard for me to have an
opinion. But I can tell you what I was told by Prefect Servius.'
Marcus nodded. 'Meroë is the latest ruling city of an ancient
kingdom called Kush, which at one time grew so powerful that
it came to dominate Aegyptus as well as the territory to its south.
And this at much the same time that Rome was little more than
a village on the Palatine Hill. The rulers of Aegyptus were black-
skinned men from the south, it seems. They were eventually driven
out by the Assyrians, and settled back into their homelands,
which are rich in both high-quality stone for building and gold,
and have the water and wood needed for the smelting of iron
traded with the kingdoms across the Erythraean Sea to the east.
Indeed the name the Aegyptians have given the land to their
south, Nubia, is derived from their word for gold, *nu*. By quar-
rying and trading these resources they have retained their position
in the world, and resisted even the advance of the empire. So
now we trade with them, a relationship so obviously beneficial to
both parties that Servius thought any war with them most unlikely.'

'They are a peaceful people?'

Turbo shrugged.

'I do not know, but the kingdom is, he told me, not only ruled
over by kings, but, on occasion, by women. If the prince in

question is not yet old enough to rule, then his mother will take the throne, using the title "Kandake" to indicate her position. And any kingdom ruled by a woman is hardly likely to seek war with an empire like Rome.'

Dubnus grunted his disagreement.

'You have clearly never travelled to Britannia, Tribune. My tribe, the Brigantes, were ruled by a woman a hundred years ago, at much the same time as another queen led her tribe in revolt against Rome and burned out more than one city. Never under-estimate the fury of a woman, if you give her both power and the reason to use it.'

Turbo smiled at the Briton's gloomy tone.

'I see your point, Centurion, although I was attempting to point out that most women have more sense than to start wars they must know are unwinnable. Unlike the multitude of kings that Rome has been obliged to put in their place, over the centuries.'

'And the Blemmyes? What sort of people are they?'

Turbo shrugged.

'They are a tribe of desert dwellers, used to hardships, a widely distributed people whose dispersion makes them hard to rule. I found their king to be a welcoming and civilised man, even if the more easterly of his people do sometimes prey on our trade routes.'

'Although any scholar will tell you that they are also a race of monsters.'

'Really?' Dubnus perked up noticeably with Ptolemy's prim statement. 'Monsters? What sort of monsters? I hope your descrip-tion will be of something whose head would look good nailed to a roof timber?'

The Aegyptian shook his head.

'If heads are what you seek, then the Blemmyes will leave you severely disappointed. Their heads, you see, are non-existent.'

'What? How can a man not have a head?'

'By having his mouth, nose and eyes in his chest, Centurion.'

Marcus exchanged glances with Turbo, who shook his head in baffled amusement but said nothing.

'Bullshit! Just when I thought you might be starting to be some use there, you go to spoil my improving opinion of you. And besides, what would you know of such things, Scribe?'

Ptolemy bristled at Dubnus's disparaging tone.

'This, of course, is where the man of letters has an advantage over the man who relies solely upon the evidence of his eyes for his understanding of the world. The Blemmyes, as we may well discover, are *akephaloi*. By which I mean, of course, men without faces. The existence of such a people was first described by the Greek philosopher, Herodotus, five hundred years ago and more.'

'And this Greek saw such people with his own eyes?'

'No, as a scholar unable to travel the entire length and breadth of the world he was forced to depend upon the accounts of those who had seen those benighted people. His assertion of their exist-ence was supported, however, by the learned geographer Mela, who called them Blemyae, and by Pliny, whose *Natural History* describes them in just the same way. And these are learned men, Centurion, not to be questioned by the likes of you . . .' He flinched at the sudden intensity of the Briton's glare. 'Or I, for that matter.'

'And did any of these other learned men, whose feet I am clearly not fit to wash, actually see these creatures with their own eyes? Or were they too, I wonder, merely *informed* of them, perhaps by men they paid well to provide the description?'

'Your tone, Centurion, implies disbelief?'

'Too fucking right it does!' The Briton shook his head in total refusal to accept his swordsmanship pupil's story. 'One philosopher accepts a story about something he's never seen, and then another pair of equally "too educated to travel" scribblers copy that story, simply because they're too lazy to get off their arses and go and see for themselves! All it takes then is for men like you to bow down at the mention of their names, and accept it all as the truth. And where's the real truth in all this?' He pointed a hand out into the darkness to the south. 'Out there! Along with men, before you mention it, with the heads of dogs and every other piece of nonsense ever written that says a man has anything other than two legs, two arms and one *normal* fucking head!'

He turned to Turbo.

'Tell me, Tribune, did you ever see any of these monsters on your travels?'

The Roman shook his head with a look of regret.

'Sadly, Centurion, I did not.'

'But that does not disprove the writings of the ancient philosophers! Surely the tribe would be likely to keep such a creature out of sight from the casual visitor? Herodotus was clearly informed by men with a better familiarity with the tribe, who were able to see behind that veil of secrecy.'

Dubnus shook his head in disgust and got to his feet.

'I give up. There seems to be no mind as closed as that which has too much education. But there is one benefit to all this rubbish, however, which is that it's given me the need to empty my bowels.'

Staring out into the night after him, Ptolemy shook his head in apparent sadness.

'A shame.'

'What is?'

The Aegyptian smiled ruefully at Marcus's question.

'Such an independent thinker, and yet so opposed to the works of great men, whose skill with words may never again be matched.'

The Roman shrugged, resisting the temptation to grin at his slightly pompous tone.

'Make the most of the opportunity to learn from him, Ptolemy. Perhaps something more than simple swordplay will rub off on you?'

He stood looking out into the darkness at a lonely fire burning fifty paces away.

'I see our Christian managed to keep up throughout the day's exertions. Which means, I presume, that he wasn't exaggerating when he described himself as having some form of military training.'

'What difference would that make, Centurion? Either a man can walk this distance or he cannot, I would have th—'

'The difference, Ptolemy, lies not here . . .' Marcus pointed at his feet. 'But rather *here.*'

He tapped his head, and Ptolemy raised his hands in bafflement.

'The secret of marching lies in the head? But surely it is the feet and legs which become conditioned?'

'You might think that, if you'd spent the day lolling listlessly on the back of a donkey and wondering what all the fuss is. As was your good fortune, given that we knew all too well that neither your legs nor your head would have been fit for the purpose of a thirty-mile march.' The scribe accepted Marcus's acerbic comment with a show of good grace, inclining his head in a solemn signal for the centurion to continue. 'That man out there will be in pain, most likely soaking his feet in a ditch to wash away the blood. His feet will have blistered, and the blisters then burst and bled, because years of relatively easy treatment will have allowed the callouses of dead skin that protect men accustomed to marching to have worn away. But, and this is my point, he is a man unlike anyone who has never marched such a distance before, sometimes without any fire or food at the end of the day. Because at dawn tomorrow he will get up, put his boots back on and march on behind us, ignoring the pain in his feet and the aching of his legs. Because he knows, deep inside him, that these discomforts are both irrelevant to what he has determined he must do. And that, given a few days of marching, they will pass. That Christian, Scribe, is a soldier of his god. And he is prepared to suffer for his beliefs.'

'I'm not sure I'm ever going to adapt to the Second Legion's ferocious appetite for covering ground.' Scaurus grimaced at the stiffness in his legs. 'I'd hoped that by three days into the march south I'd be starting to come to terms with it, but it seems as if my legs are going to be protesting all the way to Koptos.'

From his place on a donkey behind the marching Tungrians, Ptolemy, unusually quiet in the wake of his disagreement with Dubnus even two days after the event, ventured an opinion that made the Romans turn and look back at him in bafflement.

'From my elevated position, Tribune, I am happy to inform you that you will very shortly see something that will banish all thoughts of physical discomfort. Instead, your mind will find itself reeling in amazement at the sights, the glorious edifices that are about to reveal themselves to you.'

He fell silent again, refusing to comment further but simply commending the party to be attentive to the southern horizon. After a further mile of marching, Lugos, by far the tallest of the party, called attention to something only he could see.

'Is something on horizon. It is triangle, like top of monument in Rome, but . . .' He fell silent momentarily before continuing, his tone thoughtful. 'It not on horizon, but far away. Which mean . . .'

'That it is very tall indeed?'

The Briton turned to look at Ptolemy, whose gaze towards the object was close to reverential.

'Yes. What is?'

The scribe smiled.

'It is a pyramid, a man-made structure that took thousands of craftsmen twenty years to build. There are many of them in my country, and that one is the pyramid of the Great King, his final resting place. I will tell you all that I know of it, although that might not be enough to satisfy your curiosity. But first let us simply enjoy the pleasure of discovery as the object in question – and those around it – come into clearer view?'

The legion's unrelenting progress brought the pyramid closer through the late afternoon, and with every mile covered, the true size of the colossal monument became clearer to the Tungrians, as the sun began to dip lower in the sky to silhouette its other-worldly shape.

'I hadn't realised that we would reach it so soon.'

Ptolemy shot Scaurus a disbelieving glance.

'You are aware of the pyramids?'

'Of course.' The Roman smiled back at him tightly. 'My tutor was a Greek, and he insisted on attempting to make a philosopher of me, despite both my own and my birth family's lack of interest in my becoming an academic. My mother was already dead, having expired giving birth to me, and my father's sister was too consumed with grief at his loss in Germania to care very much about me. And so I was allowed to run wild, more or less, without any education other than that delivered by the fists of the local street children.'

'How did he die?'

Scaurus raised an eyebrow.

'There's that ever-demanding need to know the facts of any matter, eh, Scribe? If you must know, he killed himself by falling on his sword. He had taken upon himself, in the absence of any other officer feeling any culpability, responsibility for the loss of a fortress he had been ordered to relieve without also being afforded the necessary resources with which to do so. And so it was, that after several years in the miserable existence that followed, being in a household but not part of one, I was taken under the wing of a senator of note and afforded an education somewhat better than I deserved. Part of which was a thorough grounding in the world's seven wonders, none of which I ever expected to see in this life. And yet there it is, refuting that expectation. The Great Pyramid of *Suphis*, in all its glory.'

'Suphis?' Ptolemy looked startled. 'You surprise me, Tribune. Until this moment I had yet to meet a Roman who did not use the Greek name for the pyramid's builder.'

'I was taught not to refer to the Pharaoh as Kheops, but by his actual name, Suphis. My tutor was a genuine philosopher, proud of the depth of his learning, and for all that he was a Greek, he would never use the Hellenised term for a man whose true name was known. He had me read your countryman Manetho's "Dynasties of the Gods", in which the author insisted on using the king's real name, and not that distorted by thousands of years of historical interpretation.'

They stared at the magnificent structure, now less than a mile distant, the cladding of white marble facing stones that made its sides almost impossibly smooth coloured a rosy pink by the descending sun, and Ptolemy leaned forward across his mount's neck, lowering his voice reverentially.

'Truly awesome, is it not, Centurion Dubnus? It is almost five hundred feet high, built from millions of blocks of limestone each as large as an ox cart, each one quarried far from here and delivered by boat, then manhandled into place over the decades. It is the tallest structure built by man in the world, and surely by far the most magnificent.'

'For once, Scribe . . .' The Briton stared up at the looming edifice. 'I am forced to agree with you.'

'And consider this . . .' The Aegyptian continued his lecture, more than a hint of pride creeping into his voice. 'This mighty construction was built over two thousand years ago, at a time when your people of the north were still living in huts built from reeds and mud.'

His moment of quiet admiration shattered by the scribe's triumphalism, Dubnus barked a terse laugh.

'For one thing, scribbler, the halls *my* tribe lived in were built with the trunks of trees, every bit as hard to move and lift as blocks of stone. And for another, you can be grateful that there are oceans between my people and yours, because while your ancestors were preoccupied building a house of stone, mine would have been into them with sword, spear and axe to make them *all* slaves, not just the army of workers that must have been required to build such a thing!'

Silence fell over the party, Ptolemy sitting erect on his donkey with the look of an affronted man, while Dubnus grinned broadly at the offence the Aegyptian had taken to what had been, he considered, a reasonably run-of-the-mill put-down. The legion stopped to camp for the night in the shadow of the largest of the three pyramids, and, as Scaurus had expected, his familia were quick to abandon the fire once lit, leaving a protesting pair of soldiers to keep it fed and stir the pot in which their evening meal was stewing, Dubnus firing a piece of advice over his shoulder at them as he walked away.

'And if that pot smells of piss when we get back, I'll use the badge on it to emboss your face!'

Making their way over to the largest of the massive structures, they stood and stared up at its impossible height and size, Scaurus stepping over the humped remnant of a wall that had once surrounded the massive pyramid to keep out casual trespassers.

'How long did it take to build it, do you think?'

Still sulking, Ptolemy kept his own counsel and refused to even acknowledge Dubnus's question. Scaurus shook his head.

'Nobody really knows. And in the absence of facts, opinions on the question are varied, as is usually the case when learned men see the chance to argue over something that is not fully understood.'

The tribune placed a hand on one of the facing stones, shaking his head in admiration as his fingers traced the almost imperceptible hair lines where it joined with those around it.

'The joints between these stones are so fine as to be almost undetectable, either by eye or by touch. Can you imagine the feats of engineering and transport, and sheer muscle power that must have been required to erect such a towering monument to the king? The massed craftsmanship needed to polish so much stone to a perfect finish on all six sides of every block? And yet the pyramid was, it seems, born of great evil. Will you tell the story, Ptolemy, or must it fall victim to my admittedly imperfect recall?'

The scribe inclined his head respectfully.

'The tribune's memory of his lessons is correct. Suphis, we are told by Herodotus, broke with a noble tradition of fine governance of his people upon ascending to the throne. He closed the temples and compelled the people to undertake slave labour for him. The great pyramid was built at such great cost that, it is written, the king commanded his own daughter to lie with whoever could pay the sum demanded as a contribution to the building works. And yet she was a wily one, and demanded that each of her suitors gave her in addition a stone, like those that were used to construct this pyramid, and these she had placed in a monument of her own in the same form.'

Dubnus shook his head in disbelief.

'She'd have had to have been on her back from dawn to dusk every day for ten years to even pay for a tiny fraction of this! Were there even that many men who could have afforded to pay her father and still be able to fund an additional month's work by a skilled mason?'

Ptolemy flicked his fingers, dismissing the Briton's question.

'You might not have it in you to respect one of the greatest historians of all time, but you cannot deny the truths of the men whose spoken history he was the first to commit to paper.' He continued, ignoring Dubnus's evident amusement. 'And of course this is simply one small part of the magnificence that is the mightiest city that has ever existed on this earth.'

'Which city is that?'

The scribe shot his sparring partner a pitying glance.

'Memphis, of course. It was founded three thousand years ago, by the first of all the Pharaohs, Menes. It was he who diverted the river with earthworks, to build the city on the land that he reclaimed. And who unified the two lands that became Aegyptus, the river delta and the uplands. This is a fact on which both Herodotus and Manetho have agreed in their own times, which means that it is indisputable, and—'

'So they both heard the same story and decided to copy it as their own? We're back to that way of getting to "the truth", are we?'

Ptolemy turned and walked back towards the legion's campfires in evident disgust, and Marcus watched him go for a moment before turning back to his friend.

'You could just indulge him? He's obviously proud of what his countrymen have built here, and you have to acknowledge that this monument is the most fantastic thing you've ever laid your eyes on, don't you?'

Dubnus shrugged.

'Yes, but funded by a king's daughter turning whore? Do you believe that nonsense? There's no king would have ordered such a thing, for fear that his throne might be taken by the bastard child of one of her clients! And as for a three-thousand-year-old city founded by a king who built dikes to divert a river that powerful? I no more believe that than all that bullshit about Rome being founded by a man suckled by a wolf!'

Scaurus gestured to the camp.

'Hopefully by now those two miscreants will have managed to make something at least partially edible from the evening ration, so I suggest we go and sample their cooking before they take the opportunity of our absence to consume the lot. And you, Dubnus, might be advised to needle our colleague just a little less, or he might decide to keep the remainder of his knowledge to himself.'

The Briton shrugged.

'I could probably live without the pearls of wisdom he lets fall, unless he can point us at a tavern that sells a decent beer. All this date wine is loosening my guts in a manner every bit as spectacular as that pile of stone.'

They turned to walk back to the camp to find the Christian Demetrius standing a dozen paces behind them, staring up at the pyramid with a curious expression.

'Well now, it's our shadow. How are your feet, Demetrius?'

The Greek smiled at Cotta knowingly.

'My feet, Centurion Lucius, have, as we both knew would be the case, hardened up nicely, thank you for asking.'

'So has your footwear, I see.'

'These?' Demetrius looked down at the military boots on his feet, smiling at the Roman. 'I have become accepted by the men of the legion, it seems. They consider me to be an eccentric, and

my tales of my service to Rome have amused them well enough
that they have taken pity on my disintegrating footwear and found
me a spare pair of *caligae*. They even provided some hobnails
with which to make them fit for the march.' He opened his hands
in a gesture that was part gratitude, part blessing. 'It is as I have
told you, the Lord will provide for the needy traveller, if he has
sufficient faith to cast himself on the mercy of his fellows.'

'And what do you make of this?'

The Christian looked up at the pyramid's looming bulk before
speaking again.

'I find it chastening, Centurion.'

'Chastening?'

'Indeed. I am chastened by the very presence of such an idolatrous edifice and when I consider the thousands of men who
must have died in its construction. The man who commanded it
to be raised from the desert floor was considered a god, and yet
for his sins I expect that he will not have found any place in Our
Lord's paradise. Any man who considers himself a god will face
a powerful reckoning, when the time comes for him to be judged.'

'Our own emperor will one day be among that number,
Demetrius. You might do well to remember that.'

The Greek smiled at Scaurus.

'As have been many others before him, I believe. Both those
who ruled and those whose rule was terminated by untimely
assassination. But all will be judged by God, when they stand
before him after their deaths. As will their killers.'

He bowed, turned and walked away, his gait showing no sign
of the discomfort that most of the party were still prone to even
after two weeks on the road.

'What did he mean by that?'

Marcus looked at Cotta, who was staring after the Greek with
a thoughtful expression.

'What?'

'He said that his god will judge everyone, emperors and their
killers alike.'

'It's just his rhetoric. You ought to know that by now.'

'Perhaps.' The grim-faced centurion watched the Christian's receding figure with a hard stare. 'Or perhaps he was trying to be clever. Too clever.'

6

'Second Legion . . . HALT!'

The Tungrians, marching behind First Spear Abasi's vanguard century, stopped at the shouted command and stretched, mopping the sweat from their foreheads with rags already soaked from the day's march. Staring at the city on the river's distant eastern bank, Sanga spat on the ground at his feet.

'Another day's march, another shithole town pretending to be a city. So what makes this one so special? Which emperor put the crown on his own head here, eh?'

Ptolemy leaned out of his donkey's saddle with a conspiratorial expression.

'The city of Koptos has one feature that I think you're going to find very—'

Saratos interrupted, rolling his eyes.

'Oh really? Is another three-thousand-year-old man bury here?'

Sanga turned to his comrade gleefully, ignoring the disgusted looks that Ptolemy was giving them both from atop his mount at being so rudely interrupted.

'Now you're getting the hang of it, you dozy Dacian ape! If it didn't happen more than five hundred years ago, then it just don't count round here! We can be burning hot, sweating until our balls rub raw, feet pounded to ribbons from walking on rock all day and every day, sand up our arses and flies up our fucking noses, and still, all *some* donkey riders give a shit about is who did what, where, and how long ago!'

Dubnus, having taken a long draught from his water bottle, stoppered the container and looked up at the scribe, seeing that his usual irritation was somehow more righteous than was usually the case.

'Well, gentlemen, I see you two have decided to give us yet another illustration of why it is that neither of you will ever make it beyond the dizzying rank of watch officer.'

'Eh?'

Sanga found himself cross-eyed, as the end of the centurion's vine stick came to rest under his nose with a speed and precision that belied the big man's outwardly relaxed demeanour.

'What was that, Watch Officer Sanga? Quickly now, before I accidentally demote you and you lose all that lovely extra pay that's mounting up in your records.'

'I meant, "I'm sorry, Centurion, I seem to have missed your point." Sir.'

'Better, Sanga. Just about good enough, this time. And the point that I was trying to make, albeit far too subtly for you to grasp, is that I suspect our comrade Ptolemy was just about to tell you something you'd be as keen to hear as any man here. Is that right, Scribe?'

The imperial secretary smiled slyly down from his mount's back.

'Perceptive of you, Centurion. I doubt I'll bother now though.'

'As you wish. Understandable too, given the cruel way this pair of donkeys have just treated you.'

Smiling smugly at them, the big Centurion turned away to stare across the Nilus at the walled city on its far side.

'Look at that, eh? A great big place it is too, compared to some of the genuine shitholes we've passed through on our way up the river in the last three weeks.'

'Oh now, that's hardly fair to a city like Antinoopolis.' Marcus strolled forward to join his brother officer in his contemplation of the bridge. 'The architecture. The statues. The sheer audacity of a city built from nothing in the middle of nowhere. You could hardly call that a shithole, could you?'

Dubnus inclined his head.

'I grant you that. Although it should be all that and more, shouldn't it, given it was built to celebrate the life of Hadrian's dead boyfriend? After all, if your favourite catamite is stupid enough to drown himself in the Nilus, what else are you going to do but build an entire city as his monument? Gods, but that man was an emperor to make builders everywhere rich! A ninety-mile-long wall in Britannia, a city in the desert in Aegyptus . . .' He smiled ruefully at the thought. 'But, brother, it has to be said, nowhere we've been in all of these two weeks of incessant marching has been quite as alluring' – he extended a hand theatrically – 'as this!'

Sanga frowned at him, tipping his head on one side in puzzlement.

'What's so great about it then . . . Centurion? It looks tatty enough to me. Just another desert town.'

The Briton grinned at him wolfishly.

'And that, Watch Officer Sanga, is because you have eyes that work well enough when you're looking for the obvious, but not when a thing is even a little bit less than clear.'

Sanga turned and shot his fellow soldier a despairing glance as Scaurus joined the discussion, equally as amused as his officers.

'Look at the scene before you, Watch Officer, and tell me what you can see. In your own time; I'd imagine Abasi will be a good few moments waiting for the duty centurion from the fort across the river to cross' – he paused portentously – '*by the ferry.*'

Sanga followed his pointing hand, shaking his head in bafflement.

'Errr . . . a ferry, Tribune? Across the river . . . and a walled town . . .'

'And there, if only you knew it, is the answer to the question, Sanga.' Marcus looked at the baffled Briton for a moment, and then continued. 'What are ferries for?'

The soldier's frown of incomprehension deepened.

'Crossing rivers, Centurion?'

'Indeed. And what is it that might require there to be a ferry of that size, do you think?'

Sanga shook his head in mystification, but behind him Saratos nodded slowly.

'Pack animals.'

The Roman pointed at him with the air of a man who has discovered something he thought lost.

'Yes, there's the intelligence I was hoping for! Pack animals! A lot of them! And what are walls usually built around towns for, Sanga? After all, it's not like any of the other cities we've passed have been walled, is it?'

'To keep out . . . enemies?'

The Dacian, now apparently having realised what it was that Sanga was missing, interjected with an air of impatience.

'To keep out thieves and robbers.'

Dubnus nodded vigorously.

'Exactly, Saratos! To keep out the Blemmyes, who, I recall from Ptolemy's lectures, are the pre-eminent thieves and robbers in this part of the province even if' – he raised a hand to silence Ptolemy before the Aegyptian had the chance to protest – *'even if* they do not have faces in their chests, as some people might have you believe! So, what does that tell you about the town?'

'That many trade caravans cross river here.' Saratos, confident he knew the answer. 'Which mean they come here from ports on distant sea. A long journey.'

'Indeed, which means that they will have to stop here for a day or two to allow their animals to rest, and while the payment of customs duties is sorted out, I'd imagine? And that means—'

Sanga's face lit up.

'Taverns! Taverns and—'

Dubnus rolled his eyes theatrically as Marcus interrupted the suddenly gleeful soldier.

'Yes, taverns *and* the women who frequent them. Well done, Sanga, you got there in the end! But there is one more piece to this puzzle.' Sanga shook his head, his deductive powers exhausted. 'The port through which all that wealth flows has been captured, by the Blemmyes, we're presuming. Which means that there aren't any caravans coming north up the road from the coast. And while there may be caravans waiting to head down the road to Berenike, waiting for the army to make it safe again, their men are likely to have spent whatever money they had to spare for such entertainments.'

Sanga grinned hugely, prompting a world-weary interjection from Dubnus.

'There's a large part of me wishes we'd never told him.'

The Briton nodded gleefully, turning to his Dacian comrade.

'Empty taverns! Empty taverns offering cheap drink to pull in customers, and full of lovely women all desperate for a little coin. Get that purse open, Saratos, it looks like it's time for you and me to go to the rescue of the local economy!'

'You have no idea how relieved I was to see you march up the road, Tribune. It's been a lonely couple of months since the First Macedonica marched out and never came back.'

Scaurus returned the centurion's salute, looking around the headquarters' office keenly for signs of neglect or disarray in the commanding officer's absence. The man standing before him looked steady enough, with none of the signs of being under more stress than he could manage that might have been expected from his small command's precarious position. The shadows under his eyes, however, and the haunted look of a man who had spent months waiting for an attack, told their own story. The Roman clapped him on the shoulder reassuringly, then pointed to the painted wall map of the area around the city.

'You are to be congratulated on the state of your command, Centurion. Some men would have been tempted to absent themselves, or to allow this outpost to become slack and demoralised, but you and your men are a credit to your cohort. Perhaps you can explain what you know of the current situation to us?'

The officer pointed at a point on the map, well to the south and west of the town.

'Prefect Servius was heading in this direction when he marched. A caravan had been robbed by Blemmyes, stripped of everything by over a hundred of them. The prefect was determined to find and kill or enslave every last one of them by locating their lair and wiping them out to the last man, to teach their tribe a lesson for getting above themselves . . .' He caught Scaurus's look of bafflement. 'It wasn't like what they usually do, Tribune, it was different. Dangerous.'

'What do they usually do, Centurion?'

The other man responded to Marcus's question by pointing at the map again, putting a finger on the long road that led from the port of Berenike to Koptos.

'Each of these settlements on the track is a watering point, with about twenty miles between each one. The way the Blemmyes usually operate is to track the progress of a caravan by watching the watering points, working out how many guards each one has, and then stopping them on the road with just enough strength to make it easier for the man in charge to pay a small fee to be allowed to pass, rather than fight and risk losing the entire consignment. Some of those merchants are moving the entire contents of a sea-going ship at a time, fifty or more donkeys all carrying a hundred pounds of goods, a load which could earn millions of sesterces when it gets to Alexandria. They call it "the Blemmyes tax", just enough to make it worth the bandits' effort, not so much that fighting them off is the better option. After all, the businessmen running the trade pay tax at the port, and again to cross the bridge across the Nilus here, and again in Alexandria to sell their goods there to the merchants who will ship them onto Rome, so what's one more levy to pass onto the end customer? But this caravan came in bare, everything taken from them, including the guards' weapons. The caravan master was still raging four days after it had happened and demanded that the prefect do something about it immediately.'

'And Prefect Servius agreed.'

'Yes, sir. I don't think he had much choice in any case. If we'd failed to react, then it looked likely that the cheeky bastards would repeat the trick. There's a ready market for stolen goods to the south, and the Blemmyes roam pretty much wherever they want on both sides of the river, so it wouldn't be all that hard for them to turn their haul into gold.'

'So your prefect marched with a full cohort, other than your century?'

The centurion nodded.

'Yes, Tribune. He left all the men approaching retirement and anyone carrying an injury here and stripped out most of my century's combat effectives. Four hundred men and a double-strength squadron of cavalry looked like more than enough to deal with a hundred or so of those ragged-arsed desert savages.' He shook his head in disbelief. 'But they marched away and just never came back. Four days later, without any word from them, when I would have expected them to have sent word that they'd dealt with the problem and were marching for home, riders came up the main road. For a moment I thought it was a message party from the prefect, but I soon enough realised that they weren't like any cavalrymen I'd ever seen before.'

'What did they look like?'

All eyes turned to Ptolemy, who had stepped forward with a look of excited curiosity.

'They were darker skinned than we are, for a start, some of them quite black, some dark brown. I could see that they weren't our men while they were still a mile away. And they were wearing felt armour, dyed red, except for—'

'Felt? What bloody use is felt?'

Ptolemy ignored Dubnus's question, his eyes strong with the certainty of what he had deduced from the description.

'They were Kushite cavalry, men of the kingdom of Meroë, that much is indisputable. The black men among them come from the far south of Aethyopia, while the brown-skinned are from the northern part of the kingdom, not so very far from here.'

'Meroë?' Scaurus shook his head in dismay. 'I'd hoped that these were only Blemmyes raiders.'

'It is certain, Tribune. If the skin colour of these riders were not enough, then their felt armour makes if doubly so. The Blemmyes do not use the material, but rather choose ox hides that have been cured to make them as hard as wood.'

'I still want to know what sort of idiot wears felt in this sort of heat, for all the good it would be in stopping an arrow or a blade.'

'All in good time, Dubnus. You might find the practice more effective than you expect.' Scaurus turned back to the centurion. 'So what did these riders have to say for themselves?'

'They rode up to the gate a hundred strong, as bold as you like, despite the fact that we had half a dozen bolt throwers manned and aimed down at them. Their leader demanded to speak with the commanding officer, so I ignored the fact I was close to shitting myself and went out to speak to him. And he was a big bastard, bigger than him . . .' He gestured to Dubnus. 'And evil-looking with it, like he hadn't got much patience for anything that wasn't just right for him. He was wearing scale armour, unlike the rest of them, and it looked like the scales were gold to me, and his sword was the strangest thing I've ever seen in a soldier's hand. I got a good look at it because he drew it while he was telling me what had happened to the cohort, waving it around and going on about the crushing might of the god Amun or some other crap. I was half relieved but half disappointed that the boys on the wall behind me didn't put a bolt through the mouthy bastard. I suppose they wanted to live just as much as I did.'

'This sword. Was it shaped like a sickle moon on a short, straight blade?'

'Yes. But how did you—'

Ptolemy turned to Scaurus.

'That man was a temple guard, Tribune.' The scribe shook his head solemnly. 'And the temple guards are the elite of the army of Meroë. Whatever it is they want, they must really want it, if they have their best warriors in the field.'

Scaurus nodded grimly.

'So what was the message this man had for you?'

'More or less what I expected, to be honest with you, sir. The cohort was ambushed, slaughtered and their bodies left for the vultures. He showed me Prefect Servius's helmet as the proof. And he told me to pass a message to my emperor . . .' The centurion smiled wanly. 'Perhaps his relationship with his king is closer than mine.'

'And the message?'

'I wrote it down. He said this: "Berenike is ours now. The emerald mines of the desert are ours now. All the land south of this city is ours now. The kingdom of Meroë will destroy any and all forces sent to attempt to reverse this change of rule." There was more, a lot of prick-waving about how many horsemen and war elephants they have, and some lordly stuff about how trading between the Rome and Meroë was going to work, but to be honest I just kept looking at the prefect's helmet and imagining all my comrades scattered across the desert. The gist of it was that if we want the goods that ship into Berenike, or the emeralds from the mines, they'll come at a price.'

'It's a sound strategy, and cleverly executed. Lure most of our strength out into the desert in pursuit of bandits, and then confront them with an army instead.' Marcus looking questioningly at Ptolemy. 'In your lectures on the province's history you have mentioned a war against Meroë, back in Augustus's day. How many men did they manage to field against Rome, back then?'

'Several tens of thousands of men, if Strabo had it right, Centurion. It seems that the ruler of Meroë reacted badly to Rome's conquest of the land south of here, and the loss of tax revenue that resulted. So when some of our forces were withdrawn to fight the Arabians, they saw their opportunity and invaded. They took every city on the river as far north as Souan and enslaved the inhabitants, carrying away the statues of Augustus. A greater insult would have been hard to imagine.'

'Which meant, of course, that the emperor couldn't ignore their challenge.' Scaurus smiled lopsidedly at the thought. 'I have read of this war. Augustus sent Gaius Publius Petronius south in just the sort of counter-attack that a great general would undertake, pitching his ten thousand men against thirty thousand in the Merotic army. Of course these were battle-hardened legions, fresh from the last of the civil wars only five years before, and it seems that they went through their enemy easily enough. After which Petronius led them south to sack the city of Napata, the former capital and northernmost of their cities. With that punishment inflicted, he withdrew to the north, rather than risk getting bogged down among hostile tribes, and fortified a hilltop stronghold on the river Nilus, at a place called Premnis.'

Ptolemy inclined his head in recognition of the tribune's historical knowledge.

'Indeed so. Although this seems to have inflamed the situation somewhat. The ruler of Meroë, a queen called Amanirenas, raised a fresh army from her peoples of the south, and came north three years later intending revenge by destroying the fortress. It is suspected that her husband Teriteqas had been killed in the first battle, and that she was ruling as Kandake in his place. Petronius seems to have beaten her to it, however, and reinforced his position with every bolt thrower he could lay hands on. Enough to cut any serious attempt to attack the fortress to bloody ribbons. And so, it seems, a stalemate resulted.'

Scaurus turned back to the map, pointing at the land to the far south.

'And eventually, as is the way of things where neither party can gain the upper hand, Meroë and Rome decided to be allies, rather than enemies. Rome paid a handsome tribute to the queen and her successors, and Meroë sent troops to fight for Rome when requested. Premnis remained as a Roman fortress inside territory that was nominally Kushite, and the guarantor of security for the cities along the Nilus south from here. It was garrisoned until about a century ago, and even when the army in Aegyptus was reduced to a single legion, and Premnis was abandoned for them to reoccupy, it seemed as if the rulers of Meroë were content with their northern frontier. Until now.'

He stared at the map for a moment with a thoughtful expression.

'I wonder what it was that convinced the current king to change his policy towards Rome?' He shrugged, turning back to the centurion. 'No matter, the question that matters isn't what caused this war, but how we go about ending it. First Spear Abasi.'

The grizzled centurion stepped forward.

'Tribune.'

'I want this city sealed tight. Double the guards on every gate and close the ferry to all traffic. With no exceptions.'

Abasi nodded, saluted and left the room to carry out his orders, leaving Turbo to voice the question that was on every man's lips.

'Why seal the city, Tribune? Surely the real threat lies far from here?'

Scaurus stared at the map with a faint smile.

'Because, Tribune, when the plan that's forming in my head becomes apparent, there's going to be a stampede of men wanting to get their property away from here before it's too late.'

'So what do we do now? It seems as if we've marched all this way to be presented with a choice that's no choice at all, given there's an army in the field that would probably wipe its arse with us in less than an hour. Although I'd dearly love to see an elephant again, a proper war beast and not like those poor tired things they have in Rome. Just not from close enough for it to get the chance to stamp me flat.'

Marcus, Dubnus and Qadir were standing on the fortress wall, looking out over the river at the watch fires burning in the legion's camp on the Nilus's western bank. The cloudless night sky blazed in the glory of countless stars above them, and all three men had donned their cloaks to keep out the desert night's chill.

'What do we do now?'

Marcus stared across the river's black water for a moment before replying to Dubnus's question, watching as the reflections of a million stars shimmered in the dark rippling water. 'We do what Rome expects of us. We're not the first men to be faced with such an unenviable choice, and we won't be the last. Republic or empire, it's always been the same. A man faces whatever it is that Rome needs from him, knowing that his decision isn't whether he lives or dies, but how he goes about satisfying the city's expectations of its sons. Even today, when most citizens of Rome have never seen the sun rise over the city.'

Dubnus shrugged.

'I understand. Uncle Sextus spent the first five years of my time with the cohort beating exactly that lesson into me, may the gods rest his departed soul. That and threatening me with death for trying to get out of the camp to kill the men who conspired to murder my father. And I have no problem with dying, not when we've refused to accept it so many times in the past. When the time for me to die comes, I'll face it with a snarl, not a whimper. But surely one legion can't take on an entire kingdom? I'm all for not allowing the bastards to just annex parts of the empire whenever they feel like it, but it seems to me like we've stumbled into something that's bigger than five thousand soldiers can hope to deal with.'

Marcus grinned at him.

'Go on then, *Legatus*, what are the options?'

The Briton shrugged.

'I can only see two, and neither of them are any good. We can advance down the road to this port they've taken from us, face an army several times our own strength with the equivalent of a single legion of unblooded men, and see how that plays out. The likely result being that we all die and have our bones picked clean by the vultures, like those poor bastards that marched out of here a few weeks ago. Or we can sit here and defend what's effectively Rome's new southern frontier, leaving these southerners in possession of the port we were sent to retake. The likely result of that being that we find ourselves recalled to Rome for execution, or just killed here, once that bastard Cleander hears that we've failed to retake the source of his precious tax revenue. And neither option feels all that good to me, since they both mean I'll never see home again. It just doesn't seem like much of an end to our stories, does it?'

'No, brother, it does not.' Qadir's soft voice was underlaid with an amused tone. 'But in all the years that we have marched with him, can you honestly tell me that you've ever known Tribune Scaurus to lack for an idea in situations like this? I'll be surprised if he doesn't have an answer to this that involves neither suiciding on the spears of our enemy nor accepting this new status quo.'

'What other options are there? We either go out to fight, and die, or we stay here and live, for a little while longer.'

Marcus shook his head in amusement at Dubnus's blunt assessment.

'Were you so outraged at the idea of felt for armour that you actually stopped listening to anything else that was said?'

'I heard the scribbler and Scaurus exchanging notes as to some battle from history or other, but I will admit that I wasn't listening as closely as I might have done, had I realised there was a third option involved. So what was it?'

The Roman looked out across the starlit darkness for a moment.

'The tale they told was of the war fought between Meroë and Rome two hundred years ago. When Rome took control of the province, and reclaimed territory that the southerners had taken as the Ptolemies' rule weakened.'

'These Ptolemies being the Greeks who replaced the previous rulers hundreds of years before that?'

'Exactly. If you read enough history books, it becomes clear that power ebbs and flows like that. At one time the rulers of Aegyptus regarded the land far to the south of here as their own,

but as their dynasty declined, the rulers of Meroë came in turn
to view it, and the money that flowed from it, as having passed to
them, as if by right. Saying that the arrival of Rome, and the loss
of that land, came as something of a disappointment to their king,
would be putting it mildly. To use Ptolemy's metaphor, it must
have been as if a river of gold had been diverted from their
treasury, to flow instead to Rome's coffers.'

'And he didn't take that disappointment well?'

'No. He invaded, with three times the strength that Rome could
muster, given all the other wars that were being fought at the
same time.'

'But we won, right?'

Marcus grinned.

'*We?* You really have become a Roman, haven't you?'

'What do you expect? I've been risking my life for Rome for
more than half my life. Rome feeds me, Rome pays me, and one
of these days Rome is going to bury me. So, this war . . . ?'

'Was fought, and won, in a manner of speaking. Even if the
emperor then chose to bribe the Kushites into making peace to
avoid having to risk fighting again with such a numerical disadvantage on the ground. He knew that his general Petronius won
because of a very particular set of circumstances and I suspect
that our Tribune, ever attentive to the history books, is going to
take that lesson and play it out to see if he can remind the current
king of the mistakes made by his predecessors.'

'You can't do this! These beasts are our property!'

'And our livelihoods too!'

'You're taking the bread out of our children's mouths, you
thieving bastards!'

A group of a dozen irate men were railing at Scaurus and his
officers in the fortress's praetorium, the barrier of a pair of crossed
spears all that was preventing their protests from being even more
personal. To one side of their seething group a similar number
of men were standing apart, watching their employers' fury with

the knowing looks of men who had either done business with or served in the army, and understood the only likely outcome of the traders' rage. The leaders of the various teams of bodyguards who would, in happier times, have been dispersed across the province, escorting the traders' caravans to and from Berenike. They had respectfully requested admittance to the meeting, a request which had puzzled Scaurus until the Romans realised that, far from having vanished on their arrival in the city, as had seemed to be the case, Demetrius was among them. Ignoring the merchants' fury, Marcus watched him, leaning on the office's wall with a look that combined amusement and disgust at their anger, as they railed at the indignities that were being heaped upon them.

Scaurus raised an eyebrow at Abasi.

'Perhaps, First Spear, you might like to restore a little decorum to this meeting before we continue?'

'Tribune.'

The veteran officer stepped forward, raising his vine stick in one hand while the other rested casually on the hilt of his sword. He swept the gaggle of outraged merchants with a cold-eyed stare for a moment and then, when his attempt at silent intimidation failed to produce the instant result he had clearly been hoping for, he stepped forward again, closing the gap between the pack of furious traders and himself to less than two paces.

'*Silence!*'

The parade ground roar stunned the complainants into moment-ary quietude, before one man, braver or more foolhardy than his fellows, opened his mouth to renew the verbal onslaught that had been prompted by Scaurus's pronouncement. Lunging forward, Abasi beat him to it, putting the vine stick's gold-capped tip up under his chin and tensing his arm, ready to thrust it upwards.

'You are one word from dying! One word! Don't even breathe!' The merchant goggled at him, raising both hands in silent suppli-cation, his face slowly reddening while the senior centurion stared intently at him until, with the other man starting to visibly shake, he lowered the stick fractionally. 'You may breathe. Do *not* speak.'

A long, shaky breath hissed from the frozen man's mouth, his eyes bulging as Scaurus stepped forward to stand alongside his first spear.

'We'll try that again, shall we? Without the chorus of disapproval this time, so that we can all discuss the matter in a rather more civilised manner. As I was saying . . .' He paused for a moment as if savouring the silence, then nodded to Abasi. 'I think you can allow the gentleman on the end of your vine stick to stand unaided, thank you, First Spear.'

The hard-faced senior centurion stepped back with a warning stare at the terrified merchant.

'So, gentlemen, for those of you who might not have heard what it was that I said a moment ago, before that unseemly excitement, I shall repeat myself. All of your beasts of burden are being requisitioned until further notice, in pursuance of an urgent military priority. If you wish to comment, I suggest you select a representative to make your views heard in a civilised manner.'

The traders went into a huddle, selecting one of their number to be their spokesman and telling him what it was they expected him to say on their behalf.

'Well then? I have a war to be fighting, so if you want your point to be heard you'll have to make it quickly.'

The spokesman stepped forward.

'Honoured Tribune . . .'

'That's a good start. Keep it up and my first spear might be able to contain his temper.'

The trader flicked a nervous glance at Abasi before continuing.

'My fellow merchants have asked me to make it clear to you that they view this confiscation of their property with the utmost dismay.'

'Because . . .?'

'Tribune?'

The spokesman looked puzzled, and Abasi's voice took on an impatient tone.

'*Why?*'

'Ah. Because, Tribune, our mules are the means by which we transport the commercial goods on which our livelihoods depend.'

'I see.' Scaurus nodded his understanding. 'No mules, no transport. No transport, no gold.'

'Exactly, Tribune. So you can see—'

'Except there is nothing to transport. Is there? You came this far south and didn't dare push onto Berenike, once the soldiers here told you that the port has been occupied by Rome's neighbour to the south. You fear that the kingdom of Meroë will confiscate your beasts, and use them to trade with their own cities instead. Which means that you are in fact stuck here, until the port is retaken, or at least abandoned by its occupiers. Correct?'

The trader nodded reluctantly, unable to argue.

'Yes, Tribune.'

'Which means, I presume, that what you would very much like to see happen is for me to take my legionaries away to the south, and either defeat the enemy or at least make them leave the port. After all, you're telling each other, that's what you pay all that tax for, isn't it? It's hardly your fault that the army was stupid enough to lose the port, and cut you off from your main source of revenue . . .'

The spokesman remained silent, afraid to agree with such an opinion even if it was true enough.

'Yes, I thought so.' Scaurus smiled at the group, the hard smile of a man with the whip hand. 'Except the reality, gentlemen, is this: your taxes, heavy though you may believe them to be, do not in fact fund anywhere near enough force in this province to protect it, should its neighbour to the south decide to unexpectedly declare war. One legion is all we have, and a part of that legion is needed to keep a grip on the port city of Alexandria. The port though which Rome is fed. Which means, gentlemen, that if I am to reopen the trade route across the Erythraean Sea, I must find a way to put an army of, at a guess, thirty thousand infantry, archers, horsemen and, for all I know, war elephants, off balance. I need to make them react to me, rather than submitting to the role their king has planned for me.'

Silence fell over the room as Scaurus contemplated the office's wall map for a moment.

'See that?' He pointed at a point on the river, far to the south of the border town of Souan where Rome and Meroë's lands officially met, the unmistakable symbol used to denote a legion fortress. 'That's the impregnable stronghold of Premnis. For a long time it was held by the empire as an outpost in Meroë's territory, a clear statement of Roman superiority, but since the time of Trajan it's been held by the army of Meroë, because when Rome decided to pull one of the two legions that held the province out and send it to Syria, there wasn't the manpower, or the perceived need, to hold it any longer. And here's the thing, gentlemen.'

He turned back to look at the now silent traders, his relaxed manner of a moment before replaced by an intense, predatory stare.

'It might be the best part of a month's march to the south, and deep in territory they consider their own, but I'm going to take it off them despite that. Or perhaps even just *because* of it. I'm going to march south with every man at my disposal, and every mule too, yours included, loaded with enough grain to feed my legion for months. So that even if I find the fortress empty, and devoid of supplies, I will be able to fortify it and hold it for long enough that the enemy have no choice but to come to remove me from their supply route.'

'Tribune, if I might speak on behalf of the other party to this discussion?' Demetrius pushed himself away from the wall, raising his open hands to show Abasi that he meant no disrespect as the first spear pivoted to face him. 'There's no need for excitement, Sese.' He gestured at the fuming merchants. 'These men, who will clearly never enter the kingdom of Our Father in heaven as long as they remain as selfish and greedy as they so evidently are, do not reflect the views of my brothers here.'

'Your *brothers*, Demetrius?'

The Christian nodded beatifically at Scaurus, pulling a necklace from beneath his tunic, a rope of silver with a dull iron ornament hanging from its links. Appearing to be a wheel with six spokes, it was evidently immediately familiar to Scaurus, and several of the traders, who shot knowing looks at each other and shook their heads in disgust.

'I have seen this before, in Rome. The Greek letters Iota and Chi combined to form the first letters of your martyr's name in that language. Am I right?'

The Greek bowed respectfully, opening his arms as if to preach.

'Indeed you are, Tribune, Iota and Chi, Jesus Christos. The symbol of my faith. We are followers of the Christos, Tribune – some old, some new, but we all wear some form of the badge of our faith. And we choose to do so in the simplest of forms: wood, or non-precious metal. One of my brothers here wears a symbol woven from reeds.' He smiled at the Romans' nonplussed faces. 'That is the beauty of our religion, gentlemen. I had only to find the church of my beliefs in the city to make a connection with these men, my brothers in faith and devotion.'

'I see.' Scaurus shrugged. 'You know that I am unbiased in this matter, neither for nor against your sect. So tell me, what is it that you and your new brothers wish to input to this discussion?'

Demetrius inclined his head in thanks before continuing.

'You see, the thing is, Tribune, these herders of donkeys . . .' He waited for the traders' protests to die away under Abasi's uncompromising stare before continuing. 'I mean you no particular offence, gentlemen, but that is what you are when your earthly wealth is removed from the equation. Your utterly meaningless wealth, which will forever blind you to the necessities of this life, if a man is to find meaning and, in your cases, redemption. You are, of course, unused to having this undeniable fact pointed out to you. We all know that in normal times, the men with swords who protect your gold, your silk and your spices, are nothing to you but tools, men you employ to keep other men's hands off your goods, to be discarded after use. And these men, for their part, know well enough not to point it out to you, because they know that in your vain glory you will punish them for such temerity.'

His smile broadened.

'But now, when the times are hard, and every man with a sword is of value, and those among us who have served with the army doubly valuable, the need for any such restraint is dispelled like mist in the wind.' He put a finger to his lips. 'Which might make it better for you to reflect on your new stations in life, and consider a little more humility on your own parts?'

'An eloquent rejoinder, if a little judgemental.' Scaurus pointed to the Christian's comrades. 'You speak for them?'

'Yes, Tribune. I speak for those previously downtrodden men. Each of them is the leader of a band of swords for hire, some smaller, some larger, numbering perhaps two hundred men in total.'

The Roman smiled, shaking his head in amusement.

'You defy all expectations, Demetrius. But, since these . . . your brothers in the Christos, it seems . . . have accepted you as their leader, perhaps you could outline to me what it is that this newly empowered group of men would like to bring to this meeting?'

'My brothers and I understand the situation you have been charged with rectifying better than these others, because most of us have served the empire in one way or another, and *all* of us have the intelligence to know what comes next, once you have separated these herders from their mules.'

'What does he mean?' The traders' spokesman stepped forward, ignoring Abasi in his irritation. 'What is it that comes next, and what makes you think that we can be—' He recoiled, as the first spear slapped his arm expertly with the vine stick's gold cap. 'Ah! Fuck! You can't—' The stick landed again, smacking the flesh of his thigh, and Demetrius smiled at Abasi with genuine admiration. 'You remind me of a senior centurion I served with in Judea, First Spear Abasi. He too was an artist with the vine stick, if not as pugilistically inclined as your good self. And as for what I mean . . .' He looked at Scaurus. 'Shall I tell them, Tribune?'

The Roman waved a hand, shaking his head in amusement.

'Be my guest.'

The Greek turned to face the freshly cowed merchants with a knowing expression.

'Well now, gentlemen, let me educate you as to the new reality that you face, and help lift the curtain of your incomprehension. Until a few moments ago, you considered yourselves to be the masters of all you surveyed, did you not? Doubtless some of you still do. You could buy and sell men like these behind me for the promise of a gold coin or two, and with a snap of your fingers make them yours to command, if they wished to collect on the promise of that sliver of yellow metal. But now, my friends, the big wheel has finally turned, as it always does. And now, it seems, you are the masters of hundreds of beasts for which there is no cargo. Which means that all you are is actual mule herders. And the worst of it is, not one of you has realised what that means for you all.' He gestured to Scaurus. 'You are part of this man's army now, whether you like it or not.'

The traders bridled, but, undaunted, Demetrius simply shook his head at their outrage.

'Please, gentlemen, tell me, what exactly were you expecting? That the tribune here would pay you out for the loss of the animals and leave you here, now that you know exactly where it is he's taking his legion? The moment he told us what his objective is, it was clear to me, if not to you, that all of us will be going along for the ride. Not one man who knows the plan can be left behind, unless he is in uniform and bound to the empire's service.'

The traders stared at Scaurus in horror, and the Roman nodded his agreement with the former soldier.

'He's right, I'm afraid. Secrecy really is of the utmost importance in this instance, since I have no desire to find myself confronted by a vastly superior enemy a hundred miles short of the objective and without any means of placing any defence between my legion and such overwhelming strength.'

'But surely . . .'

Demetrius laughed softly at the traders' spokesman, but Marcus could sense an anger arising within him, a fury of righteousness.

'What's that you're muttering? Surely a tribune of Rome can't imagine that you fine gentlemen would ever sell us out to the barbarians that took Berenike? Except he doesn't have to imagine, does he? Look at you all! You are empty vessels! Buying and selling is what you do! It is *all* you do! All you are capable of! If the tribune here were unwise enough to leave any of you behind when he marches south, you would be falling over each other in your eagerness to get some recompense for your lost animals before our dust had even settled on the horizon. You would be away down the road, vying to sell us out to the unbelievers without a second thought, because you lack any fidelity other than to gold.'

He fell silent for a moment, and Marcus suspected that he was suppressing the anger that had boiled up in him. Then, shaking his head, he laughed out loud at their affronted expressions.

'And don't dare to look unhappy, because you know my words are true! So, given your inevitable betrayal, if you have the chance to do so, Tribune Scaurus has only two ways to prevent that unhappy outcome. Either he kills you all, here and now.' He waited while the blunt statement sank in, as the traders cast nervous glances at the soldiers around them. 'It would best be done quickly and quietly, of course, before you try to make a bolt for it and have to be chased all over the fortress before you can be put down.' A profound silence gripped the room, and Demetrius allowed the tension to build for a moment before continuing. 'It's either that, or you are conscripted to march south alongside us, enabling your lives to be spared. I would recommend the second option, if I were you.'

'Nobody actually mentioned conscription, Demetrius.'

The former soldier turned back to look at Scaurus with a look of disparagement which Abasi contrived to ignore.

'Tribune. Please. Don't insult my intelligence, or that of the men behind me, or the men who work for them, for that matter. We are ex-soldiers, for the most part, and we can read the writing on the wall easily enough. We represent the best part of two centuries of trained men, and that's not something a man in your position can afford to ignore.'

'True.' The first spear spoke for Scaurus, putting the tip of his vine stick on the Christian's chest. 'I would conscript you all. But the tribune has other ideas.'

'Really?' Demetrius looked at Scaurus with a fresh curiosity. 'What ideas, Tribune? What is it that you'd value more than easily available trained men?'

The Roman smiled knowingly.

'You understand what I plan to do about this invasion from the south, don't you?'

The Christian nodded.

'Yes, I think I do. You're not the only man here to have read the histories, Tribune. You're going to take a lesson from what Augustus ordered two hundred years ago, and counter-punch where the enemy isn't strong, then tempt them into your trap. This place Premnis *was* a fortress, right?'

'It was. And, if we can take it, we can keep them occupied for months, possibly even make them think twice about the idea of trying to wrest Berenike from Rome. But I think we can be assured that the man commanding the army of Meroë isn't stupid enough to let the same thing happen to his army that happened two hundred years ago. He'll have scouts out, cavalry set to watch and report on any move south. The geography of this theatre of operations is strongly in favour of our enemy.' He pointed at the map again. 'Do you see? Even when we have marched two thirds of the distance between here and Premnis, following the river's course, we will only be eighty miles from Berenike as the crow flies. So if we are detected by the enemy's scouts before we cross the border with Meroë at Souan, we are likely to find the fortress manned and ready for us when we reach it.'

'You must avoid alerting the watchers.'

Scaurus shook his head.

'A more vigorous approach will be required. I must take the watchers unawares and kill or capture them. Either will do.'

'And you want us to make that happen?'

'Exactly. I'd imagine that your brothers in belief know the desert better than any of us. They're already equipped for the job, for the most part, and those that were stripped of their weapons by the Blemmyes can be re-equipped from this fort's armoury.'

Demetrius grinned.

'And you think you can trust them, do you, Tribune? Can Christians be relied upon to do the empire's bidding?'

Scaurus shrugged.

'I care little for the uncertain relationship between your sect and the empire. You consider yourselves men of your word, do you not? Indeed, I seem to recall reading that trustworthiness is a central tenet of your man the Christos's teachings. And besides, I'm a firm believer in both the carrot and the stick.'

'Let me guess.' Demetrius gave his fellows a knowing look. 'The carrot is a generous sum in cash – shall we say five in gold each, payable when this is all done with, legally signed and binding on both parties. That way, if none of these men come back, the money still gets distributed to their families. And the stick is the *sacramentum*. Am I right?'

'Not a bad guess.' The Roman nodded sagely. 'Five aureii might be pushing your luck a little, but we can come to a mutually agreeable number, I have little doubt of that. And yes, you'll be swearing the oath of allegiance.'

The Christian nodded, looking across at the bodyguards for confirmation, then straightened his back and saluted.

'We will join with you, Tribune. For my part I would have gone south with you in any case, and these men will readily serve, as long as you do not seek to subvert their beliefs.'

'Good. First Spear Abasi will muster you and your comrades, sign you up and have you take the oath. Come up with a name for yourselves; we'll need to call you something on the pay records.'

The merchants' representative raised a hesitant hand.

'What about us?'

'A good question.' Scaurus turned a less than beneficent eye on the traders. 'What about you? What is it that you have to offer, beyond the ownership of a few hundred mules, which, as I've already told you, are going to be requisitioned in any case?'

'But . . . why wouldn't we get paid as well?'

The Roman raised an eyebrow.

'You want to swear the *sacramentum* as well, do you?'

'*Sacramentum?*'

'The oath of loyalty to the emperor.'

'Will it get us paid?'

Scaurus smiled slowly.

'Oh yes, it'll get you paid *something*. Although the terms it imposes for breaking the oath are, to say the least of it, harsh.'

'How much?'

'How does a denarius a day sound?'

The traders' spokesman laughed at him.

'What do you take us for? That's barely enough to feed us!'

The Roman shook his head at Abasi's incensed glare, and the merchant's grin widened as he sensed an advantage, but his smile slowly faded, as the object of his derision walked slowly across the room and stood toe to toe with him.

'What do I take you for? I take you for *whores*, since you ask.'

'How dare—'

The spokesman abruptly fell silent, as Scaurus drew his dagger and raised the blade so that he could see his own reflection in it.

'Forgive me, I've always been unimpressed by false outrage. You might be good at calculating your profits and your losses, or posturing to get the advantage in a negotiation, but you're not all that clever when it comes to reading people. *Are you?*' The vehemence of the last two words made the other man flinch. 'I take you for whores, because that's what you are. You have offered to take the oath of allegiance to the emperor without any thought of actually obeying it, in the hope of getting the same deal as men who're going to risk their lives for that gold. Why do we call the oath of allegiance the *sacramentum*, Sese?'

Abasi stepped forward, barking out his answer loudly enough to make the traders flinch as one man.

'Because it is a promise before the gods, Tribune!' The centurion's eyes blazed with a passion that made the man before him take a step backwards, but Abasi reached out a hand and took a grip of his richly decorated tunic, lifting him onto the tips of his toes with an effortless strength. 'The most holy of all the oaths any man can swear! A promise to all the imperial gods who have gone before the current emperor! A promise to be held unto death! To serve the throne and its officers without hesitation! Never to desert the service of Rome! To accept death in the service of Rome, rather than dishonour the empire by accepting defeat!'

He looked the trader up and down with a look of disdain, lowering him back onto the floor and pushing him away with just enough power to put the hapless merchant on his backside. Scaurus smiled at the horrified men before him, sheathing the blade before he spoke again.

'My word, First Spear, that was quite a speech. And every word true enough to carve in stone for a soldier's memorial altar.' He turned back to the merchants. 'It all sounds a bit tritc to you people, doesn't it? You've spent your whole life laughing at men like us who keep you safe from men like the ones who've taken Berenike.' Scaurus smiled knowingly at the newly chastened traders. 'But trust me, the *sacramentum*, once taken, rolls over you with the power of a boulder that's rolled from the top of a mountain. So, *whores* – because we've established that's what you are – how much gold would make you happy to swear that sort of allegiance? How much does it take to buy your loyalty unto death? And before you answer, consider one question very seriously.'

He gestured to Demetrius.

'What my newest officer there said a few minutes ago, about the security risk you present us? It was true. My choice is either to take you with me as little more than ration thieves, or else to have you put to death to prevent the very significant risk that you'll betray us.'

The man who Abasi had sent sprawling had got to his feet, his reply a mix of offended dignity and desperate bluster.

'You would not dare to carry out such a brutal attack on free men! We are citizens of Rome, all of us, and we have the right to demand our day before a judge, in Rome! The empire would have you executed, were you to—'

'I doubt it.' The cold certainty in Marcus's voice stopped the merchant's protests as he strolled forward with both hands on the hilts of his swords. 'You might have been right a hundred years ago, under Vespasian, or even ten, under Marcus Aurelius. The empire had more time for the formalities in those days, and perhaps more of a regard for the ways of the Republic too, but the current emperor and his chamberlain are nothing more than bloody-handed pragmatists. If the tribune here tells Cleander that he had to have you all put to death, as the price of success against Meroë, then the only response he'll get is a shrug and an open hand, ready to receive the renewed flow of gold from the port. So I suggest you work out what amount of coin will be sufficient, combined with your being allowed to live, to reward you for the difficult task of leading mules down a road for a month or two. I thought a denarius a day was a more than generous offer, but if you insist on negotiating harder we can see where the discussion ends up. Possibly with a higher rate of pay. Or possibly lower. I'm sure that you can work out your best negotiating strategy, given the facts before you.'

'You're clear as to your orders, Fabius Turbo?'

The tribune stared down from the fort's walls at the legion's hundred-strong cavalry wing that was mustering in the street below along with an equal strength in men of Demetrius's newly formed *numerus speculatorum*, his mouth twisted into an expression of severe dissatisfaction. Shipped across the Nilus that morning, each horse had a rope net filled with brushwood tied to its saddle along with another of feed, and each rider a coil of rope twenty feet in length over his shoulder. Turbo returned his attention to Scaurus, but if his direct stare was intended to make his superior officer feel uncomfortable there was no outward sign that it was proving successful.

'Yes, sir. I'm not happy with what you've directed me to do, but I know what it is that you expect of me. I am to ride east with my horses, dragging those bundles of brushwood until I reach the Mare Rubrum. If I see any – and you have stressed the importance of that word more times than I can recall – *any* sign of pursuit by the forces of Meroë, no matter how insignificant, I am to evade to the north as the terrain allows, but not to abandon the ruse you wish me to perform, unless and until the enemy are close enough to realise that the dust they think is the sign of an army on the move is in fact a few dozen horsemen dragging bushes behind them.'

Scaurus nodded, looking out over the fort's walls to the south, smiling tightly at the note of disdain in his subordinate's voice.

'I understand your frustration, Tribune. Just consider the fact that in performing this distraction, you might be the one to make the difference between our reaching Premnis unhindered and being intercepted on our road south. It is imperative that you manage to lure them as far to the east as possible, in the belief that you are in fact the better part of a legion, and looking to outflank them by marching east and then coming at Berenike down the Via Hadriana, along the coast.'

Turbo nodded his understanding.

'And if they realise that it is a ruse, it might encourage them to consider the reasons for such a distraction, and perhaps look south rather than north.'

'Yes. So when you reach the coast road, turn north and head for Myos Hormos. With a decent-sized portion of luck, the king of Meroë will decide that we've decided to safeguard the more northerly port, and be lulled into thinking we've accepted the new status quo.'

'And you think they'll be fooled?'

'If you can stay far enough ahead of their scouts to be no more than dust on the horizon, then yes, I believe there's a fair chance of our achieving that.'

'And when we reach Myos Hormos? What are my orders *then*?'

The older man turned to look at him with a faint smile.

'Trust me, Tribune, I understand the severe disappointment I'm inflicting on you.'

'Do you, colleague? *Really?*'

Scaurus leaned back against the wall's parapet.

'It's not all that long ago, Turbo, that I was just like you. Fizzing with the violent urge to prove myself a man, to serve the empire and to die gloriously if that was what was required of me. Indeed I had it worse than you, because my father died in Germania in what I now realise to have been the most desperate and unfair of circumstances. He died at his own hand, because others failed to do their duty by him and his men. So you can only imagine the desperate anger that was bubbling in my veins at your age.'

Turbo shrugged.

'Which means that you understand my position, and yet you're still sending me away to drag bushes through the desert?'

'Yes. Because it's *important*. Because I want it done right, and not entrusted to a junior officer who might take fright at the first wisp of dust on the horizon and make a run for it. If such a man were to cut the ropes and dump the nets, then the ruse, most likely, would probably fail. Or if the decoys were to retreat from any contact too fast it might also give the game away, because a legion does not march at the speed of a trotting horse. What I need from you above all else, Tribune, is both a cool head *and* the bloody-minded determination to perform this vital task to the very best of your abilities. Fail me in this and you have probably condemned the entire legion to the sort of glorious but futile death that you're apparently determined to seek, except you won't be there to enjoy it. And, before you ask, yes, if you can perform this task in the way I've outlined it, if you can put a ring through the king of Meroë's nose, and use it to drag his army fifty miles further away from our actual objective, then you might just be the one man who makes it possible to steal the initiative back from him. Are you ready for war, Tribune?'

The younger man snapped to attention at the challenge, saluting formally.

'Very well, colleague, I accept your orders and will do my utmost to deliver the result needed!'

'Good man. But that's not all.' The older man grinned at his subordinate's questioning look. 'Don't look so surprised. It was you who asked the question as to what you should do once the ruse I've requested of you is completed. And as it happens, I do have a further request of you. Something that ought to appeal to that Roman sense of duty and adventure. A mission that could have been performed by an eager young man like you at any point in the last five hundred years and earned him a place in Roman history to rank with the most celebrated of the city's sons. Why else would I send half of Demetrius's men with you? It's certainly not for the purpose of dragging bushes around the desert. You're going to need some locals, men who know the ground and who have some other special knowledge that will make perfect sense to you once I've explained the idea I have. It's a roll of the dice, Turbo, and not without risk, but if you can make the gamble I have in mind pay off, you might just be the man who wins this war.'

7

Marcus, Cotta and Qadir stood and watched as the legion marched the next day, unheralded and without fanfare, heading south at the usual brisk pace. Dubnus was the head of the column, continuing his long disputation with Ptolemy on the subject of the scribe's refusal to accept any criticism of the received wisdom of the great scholars, toleration of which had become the price of the Aegyptian's tuition with the blade. With a screen of mounted scouts thrown forward to guard against an unlikely ambush, in accordance with standing instructions, the first four cohorts – Scaurus and the rest of his party at their head – were followed by the artillery train, the legion's compliment of bolt throwers augmented by the Koptos garrison's eight engines. Each of the deadly machines had been dismantled, carried piece by piece down from the battlements and loaded onto carts, leaving the fortress looking strangely denuded in the absence of their threat. The tribune had patted the disconsolate centurion's shoulder as they had watched the last of his artillery being carried down to the waiting ferries.

'I know, this makes you feel even more defenceless than before, but trust me, if the enemy king wanted to take this pimple of a city he would already have you all in chains. A wise general knows when not to overextend his advance, and in taking Berenike and the emerald mines, I'd say he's given himself enough to digest for the time being. And once it becomes clear what I'm planning to do, I think you will see their dust on the horizon as they come hurrying after me.'

Behind the artillery came the supply train, the legion's cartloads of supplies supplemented by hundreds of mules and donkeys, each one loaded with clay jars of grain taken from the Koptos stores which, the centurion had been forced to agree, were not needed by the First Macedonica's tiny remnant. Behind them marched the three auxiliary cohorts that had been gathered up from their forts along the Nilus, one unit of archers and a matched pair of five-hundred-man-strong infantry cohorts. The auxiliary officers had quickly become used to Abasi's direct methods of man management, as each of them had been collected from their forts along the route, their initial sense of dismay more than justi-fied given his constant close attention to their drill, equipment, discipline and battle-readiness. Finally, in the rearguard position of march, were the Second Legion's remaining two cohorts, their senior centurions all too well aware that the man who ruled their world was more than likely to stride back down the road towards them from his current place in the column's centre where he was unmercifully harassing the auxiliaries. Every officer present knew that, as was his wont, he would then order a no-notice deploy-ment into line of battle facing back the way they had come, simply for the pleasure of watching them sweat through the complex manoeuvre.

'The man is a force of nature. I only wish Julius could have met him, just for one day, if only to see both their faces as they took the measure of the other.'

Marcus grinned at his friend, watching as the last men of the second-to-rearmost cohort ground past the spot from which they were watching the long column's progress. The road ran along the great river's western bank, its ochre line vanishing into the haze of heat and the dust raised by the vanguard cohorts already miles further down the road to the south.

'And who do you think the smart money would have been on?'

'As to which of them was the more martial?' The Hamian shook his head in amusement. 'Neither of them. In my imagination I see them bonding over their mutual disdain for the rest of us "poor bastards" and combining forces to make this army's life a thing of constant military joy and wonder.'

They were silent for a moment as the last cohort passed, Peto marching at their head. The three friends stepped out onto the cobbles as the Tenth Cohort's leading ranks swept past, and Marcus raised his vine stick in salute at Peto, waving away the other man's attempt at saluting even as he raised his hand to the brow guard of his brightly polished helmet.

'There'll be none of that, Centurion. We're all equal here.'

'But you've been a legion tribune. Sese has made it very clear that we're to show the appropriate respect.'

'First Spear Abasi, much as I respect *him*, is not the master here. Even a thousand miles by sea and two weeks of march from Rome, Cleander is the man who determines our respective ranks.' He grinned at the other man's discomfiture. 'On the day that I am appointed to a rank which is your superior, Centurion Petosorapis, you may salute me until your arm hurts, but until then we are equals, and will treat each other as such. Agreed, *Centurion*?'

'Agreed . . . Centurion.' The Aegyptian looked at the river to his left before speaking again, the far bank over a hundred paces distant. 'So tell me, colleague, if you know the answer to two questions that I am asking myself. Firstly, I wonder why it is that our commander has chosen to take the road on the western side of the river, when the maps tell us that the fortress sits on a high rock on the eastern bank? Surely that will make capturing the fortress at Premnis so much harder than were we to approach it on the same side?'

Marcus nodded.

'Without a doubt, but it also means that we'll be able to make our approach with a much smaller risk of attracting the attention of the enemy. And, given that we're repeating a trick from history, were the king of Kush to predict the move and march to give battle, we will have a wide river between us and their much larger force.'

Peto frowned.

'But surely they won't just ignore this side of the river? I know I wouldn't.'

'Indeed, and neither would I. There will be scouts on this side, but probably in small numbers. It would be both impractical and pointless to place a force strong enough to fight even a single cohort, when it is clear that the river's protection works both ways. All the enemy really needs is enough notice to be able to move a large enough force and prevent us from crossing such a difficult obstacle. So there will be scouts on this side of the river, ready to alert their comrades on the eastern bank, with horn or flag signals I'd imagine. If we can find and deal with them we will be able to march south and cross the river at Premnis unopposed.'

The Aegyptian cocked a sardonic eyebrow at him.

'So it's that easy, is it? All that we have to do is detect these watchers before they see us, overcome them without giving them time to sound any alarm, and then find some way to persuade their comrades across the river that all is well? After which we have the simple task of moving a legion past the spot without some braying donkey or idiot trumpeter giving our game away?'

Cotta grinned at his fellow centurion.

'You could have been born a Tungrian, my friend. I knew from the first moment I met Tribune Scaurus and his men that they had just the right combination of disbelief in the pronouncements of our superiors and bloody-minded determination to make whatever they're ordered to do work. No matter how far from home this little jaunt takes us.'

Peto shot him an amused glance.

'You seem happy enough here, Centurion Lucius. It seemed to take you no time to adapt to the heat, unlike some of your colleagues.'

Cotta's reply was edged, to Marcus's ear, with unease at the prospect of his true identity being unearthed, but the words were jocular enough.

'Hah! A pig can be happy in whatever shit it's dropped in. I suppose what I was trying to say was that every step of this march takes us further away from everything we understand and further into the unknown.'

'Not all of us. There are men among the legion for whom this march represents a home coming. You will already have noticed the black faces in our ranks – not many of them, I'll grant you, but they're there nonetheless. Some of them are the children of parents who came north from Nubia decades ago, but some have made their way north up the river specifically to join Rome's army.'

'Can you blame them?' Qadir interjected, shooting Cotta a glance to indicate his chance to fade into the conversation's background. 'Regular food, dependable coin . . . the chance to feel like you belong somewhere . . . It can be a powerful incentive to service, even if is in the army of the overlord. And some of them will, I imagine, be running away from their previous circumstances. Doubtless there are men just like them in the armies of Meroë.'

Peto nodded his agreement.

'True enough. Debts to be avoided, woman trouble, the desire to be something more than one seems fated to be . . . the usual reasons for a man to abandon everything he knows and seek a fresh start in another country.'

Marcus looked down the length of the cohort's column, smiling at the sight of a familiar figure walking in the wake of the last century at the head of the newly formed *numerus speculatorum*. The Christian had attempted to argue with Abasi that a name freighted with less military meaning would be more acceptable to the band of former soldiers the Christian had brought to the legion's service, only to run into the brick wall of the big man's flat refusal to accept anything that referred to their beliefs. Looking down his nose at the older man, his opinion had been swift and final.

'You volunteered to serve as *speculatores*. Scouts, spies and executioners is what you are, so that's the title you get. Deal with it.'

Demetrius's purposeful gait at the head of his new command was instantly recognisable, having clearly lost none of his pugnacious self-confidence over the legion's two-week march to the south, and neither did the privations of the journey seem to have reduced him physically. Peto followed his amused gaze and nodded agreement.

'He's a tough old bastard, isn't he? I could almost respect him, if it wasn't for the nonsense he spouts at anyone who'll listen, given half a chance.'

Qadir smiled at the note of disgust in his voice.

'A religious oddity he may be, but someone must have been listening to him, judging from how well fed he looks, and the quality of his footwear. I'd say you have more than a few of his fellow believers in the one god in your ranks, Centurion? And since we saw little sign of him while we were in Koptos I can only assume he found someone to give him shelter. Perhaps these Christians are more widely spread than we've been led to believe?'

'More fool them.' The centurion shook his head in disbelief. 'One god? What sort of crap is that for a grown man to believe, eh?'

'Indeed.' Marcus and Qadir exchanged glances before the Hamian spoke again. 'You had another question?'

'Yes.' Peto's brow furrowed. 'I am confused by the fact that our cavalry has not joined us on the march, and half of Demetrius's men. They may not be strong numerically, but surely they will be important in the days to come?'

'Ah. That.'

The centurion looked at Marcus quizzically.

'Am I to gather that I have asked a question that comes under the banner of "you don't need to know"?'

Marcus nodded.

'That's perceptive of you, Centurion. As you have quite correctly guessed, they have been detached to carry out another task. It is one that I do not envy, but which has been allocated to them in the absence of any other unit having the same capabilities.'

'I see. I'm going to take a wild guess that they've been ord—'

Whatever observation it was that Peto had been about to make was lost in the sudden confusion resulting from the auxiliary cohorts marching ahead of them suddenly, and without warning, deploying to either side of the road in a shambolic manner that was more melee than manoeuvre. Barking for his men to halt, Peto stood with the Tungrians and watched grim-faced as Abasi strode out of the chaos screaming imprecations at the auxiliary centurions, who were in turn belabouring their men with their vine sticks and fists, pushing and shoving them into formation while the veteran centurion barked terse orders at them without seeming to pause for breath.

'He's never quite as happy as when he has the opportunity to "encourage improvement", as he puts it. It seems that this is going to be a long day, for some of us.'

Peto turned and looked down the line of his cohort again, raising his vine stick over his head in what was presumably a private and pre-agreed signal to his centurions that excitement and unhappiness in equal quantities were likely to be delivered to them all shortly. 'And all of a sudden I couldn't give a shit where some pricks on horses have been sent, or what they're supposed to be doing. As long as I don't end up with Sese in my face that'll be enough to qualify as a good day.'

'Here, put these on, Centurion. They might not be quite as fine as the equipment you are used to, but they have other qualities you will come to value just as highly.'

Marcus put the equipment Demetrius had offered him on the side of the waggon on which his centurion's equipment would be carried, unbuckling his sword belt and metal harness before turning to Dubnus for help in removing his heavy scale armour and placing it into his travel chest. Pulling off his woollen tunic, he stood naked in the dusk's relative cool for a moment before donning the coarsely woven replacement, then refastened his sword belt and put the battered bronze helmet Demetrius had passed him on his head, over a felt arming cap.

'It fits well enough.'

Demetrius examined the helmet's set on the Roman's head with a look of satisfaction.

'I guessed your head size and bought it in the market. And now you look like the rest of us, more like an Aegyptian hired sword than a Roman, which will be a good thing if we come under scrutiny. Although perhaps you should add this to your equipment, if you wish to look a little less like a disguised officer and more like the low-born man of violence you wish to impersonate.'

He handed Marcus a foot-long length of spear shaft with a heavy leather strap riveted to one end, the Roman hefting it with a look of surprise at its unexpected weight.

'It has been drilled out and filled with molten lead.' Demetrius grinned at the Roman's surprised expression. 'You still think a man of my God cannot arm himself against the unworthy?' He tapped the cosh hanging from his belt, a heavily stitched sausage of leather. 'Mine is filled with lead slingshot balls. It is usual for caravan guards to carry such weapons, for the settlement of disputes where the use of a knife might tempt fate a little too eagerly. Hit a man with that hard enough and he won't get up quickly.'

'Or possibly at all.'

'That too. At least with one of these a man can choose how vigorously to smite the unbeliever, whereas a knife often leaves little choice between life and death. Suspend it from your belt and let us be away. I think it would be wise for us to be forty miles down the road before the army has managed to drag itself onto the cobbles tomorrow morning.'

He led the Roman through the legion's camp to where the rest of his men were waiting, equipped and ready to ride. Dubnus, Cotta and Qadir were standing to one side, the latter already dressed and equipped much the same as Marcus.

'We should all be coming with you, not just this bow-waving easterner.'

Qadir raised an eyebrow at Dubnus with a faint smile.

'That's mild for you, brother. Should you not be challenging my manhood as well as my chosen weapon?'

'He has a point though, Marcus.' Cotta gestured to the gathered *speculatores*. 'They're not exactly likely to be the most dependable of allies.'

Marcus spoke before Demetrius had chance to object.

'They swore the *sacramentum*. Which means they're soldiers, and not for the first time in most of their cases. I think they'll be every bit as effective in their roles as our own men, were they here to do the job, and probably a good deal more efficient in their understanding of the way this place works. And in any case, we have to divide our efforts if we're to be sure that the tribune is to be kept safe. Make sure there's one of you beside him at all times.'

'Is that settled?' Demetrius looked at Dubnus and Cotta, who, glancing at each other, nodded their agreement, embraced their comrades and walked away through the camp towards Scaurus's command tent. 'They have no cause for worry, we will take as good care of you as would your own men.' The Greek paused, eyeing Marcus critically. 'Indeed it's not you I'm worried about, but rather my brothers in the Christos.'

'Why so?'

The Christian put both hands on his hips, his gaze hard and uncompromising.

'We should be straight with each other, Centurion. After your tribune told me what it was that he wanted my brothers to achieve for him, and that you would be leading us on this delicate task, I made a point of finding the two most outspoken men among your party and offering them drink in return for information.'

Marcus smiled knowingly.

'A wise choice. I very much doubt you had to make the offer twice.'

'They were indeed endearingly easy to persuade. I suspect that they would have been forthcoming even without the bribe, if not quite as volubly, such is their affection for you. All I had to do was mention your name, at which point they proceeded to entertain me with story after story from the campaigns you have fought across the empire. Heroic victories, dead friends mourned, imperial glory and all the women and wine a man could want. Or at least that was their version of events, once they'd managed to live through whatever battle had just made you and your tribune even more famous than you were before.'

The Christian raised a questioning eyebrow at Marcus.

'You don't seek to deny it, so at least you don't harbour any pride in the fact that your reputations are built on other men's lives. And your reputation goes before you, Centurion, you and Tribune Scaurus both. You are an officer of some repute, a war hero, a deadly swordsman . . . a man made into a myth by the things that your men whisper behind your back. Which might well make you as dangerous to my brothers here as to the enemy.' He paused for a moment. 'So, with no disrespect intended, I have a duty to the men I have brought to Rome's service. They are not afraid to risk death, and I know that *my* time to die is not at hand, but neither are they looking to throw their lives away following a hero either. Can you understand my concern on their behalf?'

Marcus raised a hand to quell Dubnus's angry retort.

'I respect you for making all of that clear. And to be fair, more than one of the men who insisted on following me has paid for it with his life, over the years.' He turned back to the hard-faced Christian. 'But let us make sure we understand each other, Demetrius, because while I do understand your concerns, there are some unavoidable facts for us to agree on. Firstly, I command here, and no other man.'

The other man nodded gravely.

'Granted, Centurion. There can only be one leader.'

'Secondly, I expect you all to provide me with your expertise. I've fought and won with men like these in half a dozen provinces, but your men's experience of Aegyptus might just save me from making a mistake we'll all regret.'

'No man could say fairer. We won't hold back from telling you if we think you're leading us into trouble.'

'Good. Last, I expect you all to fight like men who've taken the oath, when it comes down to swords and shields. And when the time comes for me to air these blades I expect to find you at my back with your own iron ready.' He turned slowly to play a piercing stare across the men gathered around them. 'We are soldiers of Rome, gentlemen, every last one of us, and we all swore the *sacramentum*. It binds us all to the empire's service, no matter which gods we worship. Caution, stealth, deception . . . all of these things can play a part in the way we go about fulfilling this task we've been given, but when the blood's flying I expect red-handed savagery from you all. Any man that doesn't have that in him should reconsider his part in this before it's too late.'

Silence descended on them, and Marcus waited patiently until Demetrius nodded.

'No man here can deny that duty to the emperor, given we took his coin and said the words. If you lead us into a fight, especially one we've had a part in choosing, you will indeed find me at your side. After all, where better to see all that fancy sword-play I've heard so much about?'

Marcus nodded, holding out a hand to the other man who, after a moment's faintly startled contemplation, shook it firmly.

'So, given it's fairly certain that there'll be watchers posted along the road south, what would you and your brothers recommend as our best approach to finding them?'

Demetrius shrugged.

'We've been discussing just that all day, Centurion. And it is fair to say that there is more than one point of view. On the one hand, there are a good number of us that favour advancing down the road at night, as one group. That way, when they challenge us, we'll be strong enough to get the better of them, no matter how many of them there are.'

'And the alternate point of view?'

'Is that if there are too many of us on the road, the men who will be watching for any sign of an advance down this side of the river will keep their heads down and let us pass, then signal a warning to their comrades on the other side, once we're out of sight. And that opinion comes with a suggested tactic to counter it.'

'Let me guess.' Marcus shot the men gathered around him a hard smile, judging from their expressions who favoured this second, infinitely more risky option. 'A small group of us to lead the way – enough to put up a fight, too few to scare anyone watching for an advance into hiding from us.'

'Exactly.' Demetrius grimaced at the prospect. 'Half a dozen men at the most, men who are not afraid to take a proper risk, rather than just ride around in a herd and frighten off the scouts we're looking for.'

The Roman nodded slowly, considering the idea.

'How many men would you have sent across to this bank, if you wanted to keep an eye on the road south at all times of the day?'

The Aegyptian thought for a moment.

'Two or three men to watch at any time, the same number or more to search for firewood and keep an eye on the desert to their rear, just in case, and then—'

'Just in case of what?'

'This is southern Aegyptus, Centurion. Just in case some desert tribe or other decides that taking a few Kushite prisoners would be good for business. Just in case some bright young Roman has the idea that sneaking around away from the road to take them unawares might be a good idea. A man who makes sure that his back is covered lasts a lot longer in this part of the world. So, two or three watching, a few sleeping, a few cooking and tending the fire and generally keeping an eye open. Ten men. Perhaps fifteen. And they'll have chosen a nice vantage point from where they can see the road for miles, with somewhere to camp out of sight and a tidy little ambush point close by. Which means that when they jump us there'll be no warning, just men in front of us and men behind us. And if they pick their spot carefully enough, we won't even have time to dismount before they're on us.'

'And we can't have reinforcements close enough behind us to even up the numbers, because the watchers will see them coming.'

Marcus nodded, deep in thought. 'I can see the point of those among your men who believe that it would be suicide to advance in anything less than enough strength to resist such an ambush. Although that clearly isn't an option if it means that the men we're looking for will simply give the alarm to their brothers on the other side of the river. But, on the other hand, scouting without enough strength to prevail in a fight against these hidden watchers would also risk failure. Neither of these options seems to be the right choice, to me.'

Demetrius inclined his head in agreement.

'And so you see the argument that has been troubling us since we accepted Rome's gold to serve once again. But we must choose, and now, for to sit here discussing the subject for much longer will render the entire discussion meaningless, will it not?'

'Yes. But I have the feeling that we're missing something here. Were none of you born on this side of the river?'

'These two.' The Christian pointed to a pair of men within the group. 'But they were born less than thirty miles from here. And it is two hundred miles to Premnis. The fortress at Premnis was allowed to fall under the control of Kush long ago, and any knowledge of the road that runs so far into their territory has long since been lost to us.'

'What of the trade caravans that deal with the kingdom?'

'They are frequent, or were, until this war began, but they all cross the desert from Berenike to the border city of Souan at the river's first cataract, where their goods are traded with Kushite merchants and then shipped up the river to the kingdom. This part of the river is an unknown to us, I am afraid.'

Marcus stood in silent thought for a moment, then smiled to himself.

'I have it!' He turned to walk back up the column, calling back over his shoulder. 'Wait here while I go to speak to First Spear Abasi! I suspect he's in possession of exactly what we need to solve this problem!'

*

'You're sure this is the man you want to speak with, Centurion?'

Marcus smiled encouragingly at the soldier in question, who had clearly already decided that keeping his mouth shut and staring fixedly to his front was probably his best hope of surviving an unexpected summons by Abasi without earning a flogging.

'We'll soon see, First Spear. Does he speak Greek?'

'He'd better, or I'll be sorely disappointed in both the man himself and his centurion, won't I, Petosorapis?'

Peto, knowing better than to attempt a witticism in front of an enlisted man, simply nodded curtly and acknowledged the point.

'Yes, First Spear.'

'Does this man speak the Greek language?'

'Passably, First Spear.'

Abasi turned back to Marcus.

'It seems that disappointment has been averted. What would you like to know from him, Centurion Corvus?'

'Soldier . . .?'

The hapless man took a minute to realise that a Roman officer was actually speaking to him, recognition dawning too slowly for him to avoid being prodded with the gold-capped end of Abasi's vine stick.

'Answer the question.'

'My name is Moise, Centurion, sir!'

'A simple "centurion" will be enough, Soldier Moise. Centurion Petosorapis tells me that you were born well to the south of here?'

The soldier replied quickly, eager to avoid a further application of Abasi's badge of office.

Yes, Centurion. I am the son of a boatman, and grew up in service to his owner, who was the captain of a ship trading between the first cataract and Koptos. The river is divided into sections by cataracts, which hinder vessels from passing from one section to another.'

'I see. And you ran away from this captain?'

'No, Centurion. He freed me when I turned fifteen years of

age, at my father's request. He said my father had given him thirty years of faithful service as his slave, and that he had earned my freedom.'

'He must have been a man of rare honour. And you came north to join the army.'

Moise nodded.

'There is little choice for a man on the Nilus in these days. If I had stayed I would have had to choose between working on the river or the land it waters when it floods.'

Marcus looked at Abasi, who nodded his agreement.

'The great plague. With so many dead, just growing enough food to survive on became paramount. What is it that you want from this man?'

Marcus explained the dilemma that his *speculatores* had outlined to him.

'How well do you remember the western bank of the river, Soldier Moise?'

The soldier smiled ruefully.

'As well as I know the lines and scars on my hands, Centurion. I spent the first fifteen years of my life travelling up and down the river from Koptos to Souan, and back. I must have made that journey five hundred times.'

'And you know the land on either side?'

'Of course, Centurion. We would moor up every night, when it became too dark to sail in safety. A young boy will always explore, when his duties are complete.'

Marcus nodded.

'Our enemy will be alert to exactly the strategy that Tribune Scaurus is attempting to carry out, and will have sent scouts to watch out for the legion marching south down the river. Can you think of any place where such a scouting mission would be best accomplished from?'

The dark-skinned soldier nodded without hesitation.

'A rocky peak known to those who live around it as Thieves' Rock, Centurion. It is a week's march from here, more or less.

From its top a keen-eyed man can see for thirty miles on a clear day. And most days are clear, on the river.'

'And a legion on the move will glitter like stars fallen to earth, with all that polished iron. Not to mention the dust we kick up on the march.' Abasi nodded grimly. 'Yes, if a man can see thirty miles, he will be in no doubt as to what he is seeing when a legion comes into view.'

'Indeed. I will need to borrow this soldier, with your permission, First Spear.'

Abasi nodded without hesitation, turning his forbidding stare on the Roman.

'Permission granted, Centurion. Just make sure you bring him back undamaged. We will need every man we have, when we get to Premnis.'

8

'So what was it that converted you from your life as a soldier
to . . .'

Marcus paused fractionally, searching for the right word. The
two men had taken the first watch after a long day in the saddle
during which the *speculatores* had outpaced the legion marching
behind them by a good thirty miles. The scouting detachment's
men were rolled up in their blankets and, for the most part, already
asleep, leaving the two officers to talk quietly in the silence of the
night.

'A man of God? A zealot?' Demetrius shot a hard smile at him
over the fire's flames. 'You're not quite sure what to call me, are
you, Centurion?'

The Roman nodded, amused by the sardonic tone in his
companion's voice.

'I'm not even sure that you know the answer to that question
yourself. You seem an uncertain mixture to me, a man seeking
his identity. You tell yourself you're changed from the days when
you were hunting the men with whom you now identify, but look
at yourself now and tell me that's the truth.'

The Christian laughed softly, looking down at his mail shirt
and military belt.

'These? This *mockery* of military equipment?' He leaned
forward, his smile hardening to a wolf-like grin in the dim firelight.
'I was a ten-badge centurion, before I saw the light and came to
Our Lord. I had the silver gilt helmet and scale armour, leather
polished to a shine you could see your face in – by my slave, of
course – and the gold I paid for my sword would have fed a

family of ten for as many years. Believe me, I wasn't just any centurion, brother Marcus, I was *the* centurion, the swaggering, vain, boastful veteran of a dozen battles. I had a sense of self-worth that would have put Abasi to shame, and a tendency to lay about me with my vine stick if even the smallest thing wasn't exactly as I expected it.'

'One of those.'

'Yes, one of *those*, spit polished to a gleaming shine and so full of my own importance it's a wonder I didn't burst.' The Christian leaned forward, eager to emphasise his point. 'I was a brutalist, pure and simple. A bully and a sadist, conditioned by the army, and by war, by life itself. No prisoners taken, no mercy offered. When my legatus told me to go and hunt down the Christians who were causing such an upset among the local population, I didn't stop to ask him what he wanted doing to them. It was simply obvious to me that they all had to die. Religious perverts was all they were, and the means of their punishment were as clear as day to me, given the manner of their leader's death. My legatus chose wisely in picking me, although I sometimes wonder if his selection was driven by my first spear's desire for a little peace and quiet . . .' He grinned at Marcus. 'I was an unpleasant mixture of piss and vinegar, in those days, and I doubt many of my comrades were all that happy when I walked into the mess. Or sad to see the back of me, for that matter.'

He leaned back, stretching luxuriously in the fire's heat.

'Had any other of them been chosen for the task, they would have seen it as their opportunity for an easy life. Ride around a bit, issue a few dire threats, scourge any follower of the one true faith foolish or slow enough to allow himself to be captured, but generally have a soft time of it. Not me though. I took the nastiest half-dozen men I knew with me, and told them that what they got up to with anyone we took prisoner would stay between us, if they helped me to sniff out the bastards. And believe me, brother Marcus, when I tell you that we became expert at sniffing them out. Dozens of them, some bleating for mercy, as I saw it then, some sticking their chins out and telling me to get on with it, all of them crucified and left to die as an example to others, their women and children used hard and then sold into slavery for the most part.'

'Left to die?'

Demetrius nodded.

'We stayed and watched the first few, to make sure they paid the full price for membership of what we called their dirty little cult, but have you any idea how boring a crucifixion is to watch? Trust me, I became an expert. Once you've nailed a man up there you have to settle down for a day or two of watching the poor bastard choking to death, standing up on the nails through his ankles to let himself breathe, screaming with the resulting pain, then slumping back onto the nails through his wrists, all the time babbling away to his god to take him. It's accepted practice to break their legs, of course, and stop them from pushing up on the ankle nails and let them suffocate, and they were forever calling to us to pierce them with our spears, like the soldiers that nailed up the Christos did to show him a little mercy, but that just seemed to miss the point of crucifying them in the first place. So we just nailed them up and marched off, warning the locals what would happen if we caught them helping the bastards.'

'Surely once you were gone their fellow Christians would have taken them down?'

Demetrius nodded, with a grimace of self-disgust.

'Of course, that became part of the game, as we saw it, once we were hardened to their suffering. We'd march out, wait a while and then march right back in again to catch the locals in the act of taking them down, so that we could punish them just as hard, rob them, rape them, then nail the Christians up again. Or sometimes we'd march out and keep going, just leave them to it, so that nobody could ever be sure whether we'd be back or not. I once hid in the hills and watched the occupants of a village argue with each other for the best part of a day as to whether to get one poor man down from his cross, while he begged them to either free him or kill him. And more than once we found men that had been released from their torture, their wounds healed, who'd taken up with life where we'd found them.'

'And?'

'What do you think? We nailed them up again, of course. There was no hiding place from imperial justice, not the way that me and my gang of conscienceless bastards exercised it. And the best thing of all was that it was all legal, approved by the local legatus. We would have been stopped eventually, of course, when word of what we were doing got to the governor. He was one of those soft, letter-writing gentlemen, forever asking the emperor for guidance, and of course Marcus Aurelius wasn't one for religious persecution. But life intervened first. Or rather God did.'

He stared at the fire bleakly for a moment.

'It was in a village, miles from anywhere. My band of thugs had persuaded me to take them back there after six months, and I knew why, of course. They wanted to revisit the family of the blacksmith we'd caught sheltering Christians the previous time we'd been there. His wife and daughters had all paid the price for his humanity, as you can imagine, and my men had returned to the subject of how much they'd enjoyed that day time after time, so I'd known the request was coming at some point. And frankly, brother Marcus, it hadn't bothered me one little bit. A repeat visit would help to cement our reputation as men who weren't prepared to let that sort of disloyalty to Rome slide. So we went back. They saw us coming, of course, and I can only imagine the fear they felt as we marched into that sad little collection of rude dwellings. Two men held the blacksmith at spear point while the rest of them took their time with his women, and I left them to it, kicked open the door of the tavern and demanded to be fed. And then it happened.'

He fell silent again, for so long that Marcus had begun to think he was unable to continue with the story when he spoke again.

'I was lounging on a wooden bench with a cup of wine and a half-eaten loaf of bread when the smith's wife walked in with her oldest daughter. Both of them were hollow-eyed and hobbling from the brutality the thugs who had raped them – with my full permission, remember – had visited on them. The woman was carrying a small bundle, wrapped in rags, and as she crossed the room towards me something in her eyes froze the blood in my veins. She was lost, beyond fear. Devastated. And whatever it was that had broken her had also made her invulnerable.' He shook his head at the memory. 'The man I was, right up to that instant, would have stood up and slapped her into the corner of the room, but I just sat and watched her walk towards me with a feeling of dread. I was rooted to the bench, my feet as heavy as lead and my heart pounding so hard I could feel it in my chest.'

He looked up at Marcus, and the entreaty in his eyes was palpable even in the fire's dim light.

'She put the bundle on the table in front of me and opened it with a contemptuous flick of her hand, her eyes boring into mine. It was a baby. A tiny, barely formed thing, dead and still on the table, covered with the blood of its birthing. The youngest daughter had been six months pregnant, carrying the child of one of my men, obviously, and they'd treated her so roughly that she had miscarried. I looked down at the poor little thing, begotten in violence and murdered in the name of Rome by a repeat of the disgusting act that had given it life, and something in me just . . .' he swallowed, '*broke*. And it let the light in, Marcus, it allowed me to see, and to feel, for the first time in my life, or so it seemed. I sat there motionless, while the women turned away and left me with their dead child. And I cried. Me, a man who hadn't shed a tear in thirty years. I sat there, and I wept helplessly.' His face hardened, his ire subconsciously surfacing with the memory. 'But then I stopped crying, and my despair was replaced with anger. With *fury*. Anger at myself, as I realised what an animal I had become, and fury at the depravity I had allowed the men who followed me to inflict on the innocent. The bestial cruelty they had visited on people whose only crime had been to care for their fellow men. And I decided to walk away from it all, then and there. But first I killed my men, to atone for their sins.'

'All six of them?'

The Christian nodded.

'All of them. Of course it was an act of practicality too. If I'd left them alive, they would have only pursued me, and tried to arrest me for desertion, and for the chance to strip me of my money, of course. But most of all I killed them because they were animals, not fit to be allowed to live and continue to practise their bestiality. I got up and walked across to the smith's forge, swaggering like the man I had been, to deceive the men restraining him that I was still the same bastard. I took up a hammer as if to inspect it, and then, without any warning, used it to stove in their heads, the first before he even knew what was happening, the other while he was goggling at the other's smashed face. The smith jumped up and reached for a weapon, of course, but I put up a hand to restrain him, and it was as if Our Lord's power flowed from me to quiet him. I took their spears and went to find the other four, still laughing and joking around the village well about what they'd just done, and I put the first two down before they even realised what was happening – one with a spear through the back, the other as he turned to see what was happening and took the second throw through his chest. And then I drew my sword and went at the last two.'

He smiled at Marcus, baring his teeth in a hard, wolfish grin that revealed the soldier underneath his drab clothing and other-worldliness.

'If they'd stood together they might have beaten me, even though I'd made sure to spear the most competent fighters first, but one of them saw the look on my face and took to his heels. I killed the other while he was still caught between fight and flight, gutted him with a single stroke, and then chased the last man down on the road and left him to die in a puddle of his own blood, with my sword sheathed in his back. And then I just walked away. Dumped my armour and equipment at the roadside and left my men to the tender mercies of the villagers. I heard a few months later that they were left to die where they'd fallen, unloved and unmourned, and I rejoiced in those cold, lonely deaths. I still do.'

Marcus stared at him levelly for a moment before speaking.

'And do you feel that you have achieved some measure of . . .'

He groped for the right word, but Demetrius spoke it for him.

'Absolution? The forgiveness of my wrongdoings?' He shook his head. 'I do not know. But I do know that I will fight for my God with all my strength from that day until the day of my death, and that I will be judged for my acts as is only right and fitting. As, Centurion, will we *all*. Can you say for certain that you have earned a place in heaven?'

The Roman shook his head.

'I do not seek a place with your god. I have other desires for the afterlife.'

'I know. Your men told me of your loss, and clearly you wish to be with your wife again when this life comes to an end. But consider this: if she was as good a person as has been intimated to me, and if you wish to see her again, then you must seek to join her in heaven, where she will surely be waiting for you. Our God will have seen the light that shone within her, and will have gathered her to his side, as he does with all his children whose actions in this life deserve such a reward. You can be reunited, but only by dedicating your life to his son the Christos.'

'You're sure you want to go through with this, Tribune?'

Turbo glanced at the man lying on the rock alongside him, the leader of that part of the *numerus speculatorum* that had accompanied his legion cavalry in their decoy ride to the east and then north. Judged to be a success by the two-hundred-strong unit of regular cavalrymen and their irregular comrades, mainly because they had managed to perform the ruse without being caught by the enemy horsemen they had seen following them in the distance, they had returned to Koptos to rest their horses before setting out again. This time, however, they had headed to the west, as instructed by Scaurus in his last discussion with the younger man. Now the two men were watching their objective from the vantage point of a rocky ridge, and even Turbo was forced to admit to himself that the supplementary task he had been charged with was every bit as daunting as anything he might have wished for in a quieter moment. But any qualms he might be feeling were, of course, not to be shared with his subordinate.

'Do I want to go through with this? Of course, Decurion! It would seem somewhat pointless to have come all this way across the desert only to turn around and head back to the Nilus without carrying out the task requested of us, would it not?'

The cavalry officer nodded dourly.

'We will do what is ordered, and at every command we will be ready. Sir. Not that I ever thought I'd be saying that lying down on a rocky hill looking at a load of tents.'

'That's the spirit.' Turbo stared out at the Blemmyes encampment for a moment longer before worming his way backwards until he was out of sight from the camp. 'And there's no time like the present. Remember, I want the *speculatores* to lead us in, as they're probably known to these desert raiders and therefore less likely to have arrows shot at them than our legion cavalry.'

'You make it sound so enticing, Tribune.'

The younger man grinned at his deputy.

'Come along, man! It isn't every day that you're handed the chance to be a history maker!'

The cavalryman looked at him with an expression verging on disbelief.

'If I might speak freely, Tribune?' Turbo gestured for him to continue. 'The problem with being part of history, I've noticed from all the stories I've heard on the subject, is that history tends to be full of men who died before their time was up. Glorious victory? Plenty of dead, more on their side than ours. Horrific defeat? The same, just this time most of them on our side. Taking part in the making of history, it seems to me, is no more than a succession of opportunities to get yourself killed. Or worse.'

'True enough. And quite fairly expressed as well. But the thing is, Decurion . . .' Turbo lowered his voice conspiratorially, 'we don't actually get much choice in the matter. We swear the *sacramentum*, and from that point the jolly old empire just assumes that we're all perfectly happy with the idea of dying – gloriously, horrifically or just plain tediously. So it seems we're rather stuck with the fact that death is a part of the job we're paid to do.'

The decurion raised an eyebrow.

'And, if you'll pardon me for saying it, sir, I think that's just the way you like it.'

The tribune smiled brightly back at him.

'No guts, no glory, eh, Decurion? It's as true now as it was all those years ago when the great men of the republic built what was to become the empire. Rome stands or falls entirely on the willingness of its young men – and indeed those not quite so young any more – to risk their lives in her name. Which, I'm neither happy nor sad to say, is where you and I find ourselves.'

The older man looked at him in silence for a moment, then lifted his right hand in salute.

'As I said, Tribune, we will do what is ordered, and at every command we will be ready.'

Turbo grinned at him, shaking his head in amusement.

'And as I said, Decurion, that's the spirit! So, shall we go and see if these Blemmyes remember me from the last time I was here? And, for that matter, if they do remember me, whether their memories are fond or not? And remember, you're not going to war, you're simply escorting a painfully young and irrepressibly cheerful Roman officer. Even persuading these fellows to listen to what I have to propose is going to be an exercise in subtlety, and having you scowling over my shoulder isn't going to help matters!'

'There it is. And your Nubian was right; it is indeed the perfect lookout post.'

Marcus nodded agreement with his companion's opinion,

staring hard at the peak rising two hundred feet above the Nilus's softly lapping water, silhouetted against the dusk's dark blue sky. In the last light of the setting sun, the red orb having already sunk beneath the western horizon, the river was a ribbon of pale pink tinged grey to their left, running away from them to the south. On the far bank, just visible in the failing light, a cluster of rough huts confirmed the presence of the farming community that Moise had warned them to expect, the likely base of operations for whatever force had been sent to watch over the roads down both sides of the river. It was two days since the Christian's tale of his conversion, and at noon of the second day the bulk of the *speculatores* had been left to make camp while Marcus, Demetrius, Qadir and Moise had made their way cautiously southwards, at a pace that the native soldier had believed, correctly, would bring them to a spot with a view of their objective towards the end of the day.

'If they're here, then whoever it was that made the choice was nobody's fool.'

Demetrius stared across the five miles of riverbank that separated them from the lookout post that the Nubian legionary had called 'Thieves' Rock', and Marcus realised that they were both crouching to stay out of view from its top, despite the twin protections of both distance and the deep shadow of the comparatively minor peak at whose foot they had their first clear sight of their objective. The Christian sighed, shaking his head in evident disquiet.

'It is as Moise told us it would be. A marching legion will stick out like lice on a blanket as far as the eye can see from that thing.'

'They might not be there.'

Even as he spoke, the Roman realised the likelihood of his statement being incorrect, and his companion shook his head with a small smile.

'You don't believe that, Centurion, and neither do I. If that's the lookout post of choice for this part of the river, then I would wager everything I have that they will be up there. The question now is how we are to get to them without their realising that they are being hunted, *and* without giving the game away to the men on the other side.'

They waited in silence while the last hint of light left the sky above them, and the landscape's shades of grey deepened and merged into deep black, the hills silhouetted against the cloudless night sky's blazing arch of stars. In the absence of any moonlight, the river's course past the outcrop on which he and Demetrius were crouching was no more than a gentle, glittering ripple of starlight on moving water, and the desert's rocky surface was all but invisible in the gloom. The four men had ridden south for four days, each man alternating between two horses to enable the beasts to be walked at twice the pace of a marching man, while the spare mounts carried the lesser weight of their supplies. Stopping frequently to water their animals in the day's heat, they had nevertheless managed forty miles a day, passing farming settlements scattered down the river's western bank whose occupants lived on the margin between river and desert. The fecund soil, the result of yearly flooding, Moise had explained, nevertheless required constant irrigation to produce a crop. Every mile had taken them deeper into territory that was effectively the frontier between Rome and Kush, land of little real value to either compared to the riches and prestige to be gained from possession of Berenike, a reality which explained the comparative lack of interest in it by the army of Meroë.

'Do you see that?'

Marcus followed the other man's pointing hand, just making out the faint flicker of light he was indicating by the side of the column of rock, at the spot where the soldier had told them to expect any watchers to set up their camp.

'Yes. I see the faintest glow. It is barely visible, but there nonetheless. Firelight reflected from a rock surface, perhaps. If we hadn't known where to look, I doubt we would have noticed it, but it can only be a watch fire, positioned so as not to be seen from the north.'

The two men turned away from their vantage point and walked

back down to the advance party's camp, where Qadir and Moise were tending a cook-fire carefully hidden from view in a hollow screened by bushes, in the shadow of the rock between them and the natural lookout tower, Marcus patting the latter on the back in congratulation.

'It seems that you have found the enemy lookout position for us, Moise.'

The soldier had drawn a rough map of the place where he suspected the Kushite watchers would lie in wait for them the previous evening, scratching lines into a flat rock with the point of an old knife. His illustration, showing both a high vantage point close to the river and a tumble of fallen boulders scattered about the road to provide plentiful concealment, had set heads nodding, as had his description.

'There are stories told about this place. Thieves' Rock was infamous for being a haunt for desert Blemmyes, who would mount a watch from it and spring ambushes on unwary travellers. And so it was that an alternate route began to be used around the peak by those with no choice but to pass it, a harder road than the one that runs beside the river but without any conceal-ment for robbers to wait in ambush.'

'And you know this alternate road?'

The soldier had sounded less sure, when faced with such a challenge.

'I have seen it in the daylight, and it is clear enough. In the darkness, without a moon, it would be harder to follow. I cannot guarantee not to go astray.'

Marcus turned to Demetrius.

'So, now that we know where the enemy is waiting for us, do you think we can do this in one night?'

The older man thought for a moment, his expression invisible in the night's gloom.

'I see little alternative. But if we fail to reach their hiding place before the sun rises we will be without any hope of avoiding detection, if the men waiting for us are alert.'

'And this mountain is what, five miles distant?'

'At least. And we have no more than eight hours to cross that distance, take the watchers unawares, and then discover whether they have a method of signalling to their comrades on the other side that all is well each morning.'

Marcus mused for a moment.

'We could simply conceal ourselves here and watch them for the day . . .'

The veteran soldier sounded amused.

'Indeed we could. But your voice tells me that you do not favour such a tactic. A day lost now might just be the day needed to win the campaign. And yet it seems the prudent thing to do.' He turned to Marcus, his concern evident more in the tone of his voice than his almost invisible features. 'We can easily become separated and spread out if we attempt to cross a desert at night, unable to coordinate our attack. And once we are committed to attack we have no choice but to go through with it. I can imagine a dozen ways that such a gamble might go wrong, and it will only take the watchers a moment to raise the alarm that will destroy your tribune's strategy. But I do not suggest inaction.'

'So what is it that you *do* suggest?'

'Consider, Centurion. Those men will have been watching the road for weeks now, if the Kushites have planned this theft of Roman territory in the methodical manner we suspect. They will have a camp routine, their boredom disturbed only by the occasional local traveller, with food being brought to them across the river at intervals. Which, by the way, could still undo any plan. Even if we manage to take the men on this side by surprise, some fool rowing across the river first thing tomorrow with fresh supplies would spoil everything.'

Marcus nodded his understanding.

'And so it seems that we must risk everything on a roll of the dice.'

Demetrius laughed softly.

'I have enjoyed, shall we say, something of a charmed life, Centurion. In my early days serving under the eagle, before I was set to persecute the Christians, I fought in the German wars, and was fortunate enough not merely to survive but to be singled out for praise and promotion. I rose from the ranks to hold a vine stick like yours. Later, with the war settled and the likelihood of further promotion dispelled by the peace, I was selected to join the ranks of the *frumentarii,* acting as my legatus's eyes and ears wherever there might be trouble fomenting in his legion's operational area. And finally, after more than a year of, shall we say, vigorous persecution of my brothers and sisters in the Christos, when I saw the light and decided to leave the empire's service, I did so, as I have told you, in a manner that would have been viewed as cause for the most brutal of executions, had I ever been captured. And in all that time, Centurion, through pitched battles whose stink of blood and shit pervaded the air for weeks after, and spying operations that often sent me hundreds of miles from my legion, and in all the years of being a hunted man that followed, I never once suffered even a scratch. And now . . .'

'Now you find that the good fortune you have enjoyed your entire adult life demands that you take this risk, with the potential to end in your death?'

The Christian shook his head with a sad smile.

'Not quite. The charmed life that I lived before I became a servant of the one true God has been replaced by the favour of Our Lord. He will protect his devoted servant, and give strength to my arm to smite the unbeliever, if it is necessary to save the souls of men who are yet to come to him. But we may not all live to see the sun rise over the horizon in the morning.'

'You believe this will work? Truly?'

Demetrius nodded at Marcus's whispered question, replying equally softly. The two men could see each other's faces in the grey light of dawn, and the looming shapes of the rocks and boulders strewn across the rocky ground to either side of the road had changed from the night's barely visible shadows to discernible shapes.

'Trust me, Centurion. We only have to be patient and wait.'

The four men of the scouting party had made their way from the outcrop to the base of Thieves' Rock over the course of the night, each of them holding a piece of rope tied to Demetrius's wrist to avoid any of them becoming lost in the gloom of the moonless night, their hobnails muffled by empty feed bags. Navigating solely by moving cautiously towards the peak's silhouette, a black tooth against the stars which had gradually loomed in their view as they had drawn closer to it, they had covered the distance from their hiding place to its foot without giving the unseen watchers at its top any signal as to their presence. By the time that the impending dawn had started to lighten the eastern horizon with its first, almost imperceptible, light, they had found hiding places at the mountain's foot among the debris of thousands of years of rockfalls, and camouflaged themselves against any scrutiny from above.

'Now you know why these men wear the scarves that your men found so funny back in Koptos.'

Marcus nodded, remembering the amusement his men had displayed on seeing the apparently dirty-clothed bodyguards for the first time. The party was crouched beside one of the larger boulders, the mottled headscarves draped across their upper bodies rendering them all but invisible. They sat in silence, Demetrius closing his eyes in a studied show of patience, his breathing slowing as he relaxed into an almost trance-like state. Moments passed, the rocks around them gradually lightening from dark grey to a paler shade, and when Marcus risked a quick glance from beneath his camouflage at the sky above them he saw that the vivid blaze of stars had dimmed to the point that only the brightest were visible. The older man opened an eye in response to the soft sounds of the movement, speaking so softly that his words were barely audible to the men around him.

'The far side of the river will be visible by now, or very soon.

And when it is, I expect that the men above us will communicate with their comrades.'

After a few more moments' wait, a horn sounded distantly from the other bank, and Demetrius peeped out from beneath his veil, pointing upwards at the peak's summit.

'Do you see?'

Just visible over the crag's edge, a flag was being displayed, the rippling white fabric crackling in the still air as it was waved back and forth. After a moment the trumpet blared again from the river's far bank, and the bodyguard put out a hand to order his men to remain in their places before glancing swiftly over the rock behind which they were concealed. He ducked back into cover and replaced the scarf.

'Their comrades on the far side are waving a single flag in reply . . .' The activity above their heads intensified as the watchers raised another banner and waved both to and fro, their passage through the air making the material flutter and billow. 'And the men above are waving two. So there, Centurion, is their code. Whatever number of flags their brothers on the far side display, they add one, for today at least.'

Marcus tipped his head in acknowledgment of the point.

'That is indeed a good start. And now . . .?'

Demetrius grinned.

'Follow me, while I follow my nose.'

He led them silently through the boulder field, sniffing the air with each careful footstep, until he detected the aroma he had been waiting for, and his nose wrinkled in disgust.

'Here. This is where they come to defecate. Take cover in the rocks behind me, and be very still.'

Taking the heavy cosh from his belt, he gestured for his men to ready their own weapons as he looped the thick, braided leather cord attached to the weapon's base over his wrist. Then, sliding into the cover of a large rock, he became immobile, as still as the stone itself, while Marcus and the other men hid themselves as ordered. After a few moments, the sound of hobnails on stone became audible, their sound strengthening as the boots' owner made his way down the crag's shallow lower slope, falling silent as whoever it was entered the sandier ground around the scattered boulders. Demetrius nodded to Marcus, tapping the bludgeon meaningfully before putting a finger to his lips to command absolute silence. The soft crunch of sand underfoot died away, and after a moment a soft groan of relief reached the scouts' ears. Nodding to Marcus, Demetrius risked a swift peep around the rock behind which he was hiding, then stepped swiftly out, raising the cosh and then swinging it in a vicious arc that ended with a dull thump as the heavy bludgeon connected with its target. Emerging from cover at the bodyguard's beckoning, Marcus saw a man's body sprawled face down across the rocky ground, and watched as Demetrius swung the weapon again to break his victim's neck at the base of his skull.

'Help me get his clothes off.' Turning the body over, he grimaced in disgust at the discovery that the lookout had fallen onto the excrement that he had been expelling, his tunic smeared with the foul substance. 'Nothing to be done about it. And in fact I can use it as a distraction.'

He pulled on the noisome garment, then removed the sound-muffling fabric from his boots and looked up the rocky slope.

'Do you smell that? They're cooking the morning meal up there, which means that there will be at least one other man to deal with, apart from those still asleep. Follow me, but stay hidden until you hear me attack, then come in behind me quickly, but quietly! Let us pray that the watchers aren't so keen to get their breakfast that they decide to start heckling the men below them while we're at it.'

He set off up the steps that had been crudely cut into the rocky slope, heading for a flattish section of rock a third of the way up the crag whose surface was invisible to them due to its elevation. Reaching the shelf's edge he set the scarf over his head to provide as much disguise as possible and then stepped out onto the rock platform.

'Gah!'

The convincing note of disgust in his voice as he wordlessly indicated the state of his tunic made Marcus smile despite the tension, and his grin widened as the scout hawked and spat in disgust, Demetrius using the classic tactic of distraction as he closed the gap between himself and whoever was tending the cook-fire. The cook's response was unintelligible to Marcus, but its softly spoken urgency spoke volumes as to the other man's desire to avoid waking the camp's remaining occupants. Marcus stormed over the shelf's edge as the sound of Demetrius's cosh striking home again reached them, just in time to see his first victim fall backwards, stunned or dead, while another turned, uncomprehendingly, to receive the heavy bludgeon's full force across his nose. He staggered backwards, clutching at his broken face and momentarily too shocked to protest, giving Demetrius a moment to point urgently at a pair of blanket-wrapped bodies even as he swung the weapon again, expertly crushing the reeling man's windpipe. Hefting the lead-filled spear shaft's unaccustomed weight, Marcus strode across the rocky platform and stood over the sleeping men for an instant before striking down with the heavy wooden club at the back of the closest man's neck. His victim's sleeping body, tensed in a subconscious reaction to the sounds of the fight, slumped back onto the rock like an emptied water skin, as he died without ever knowing what had killed him. His companion sat up, muttering a thick-mouthed imprecation in his own language with his eyes barely open, only realising what he was looking at in the last instant before the Roman felled him with a vicious blow to his temple. Hurriedly arranging the two bodies in sleep positions, Marcus moved back to the fire where Demetrius and his companions were waiting, the bodyguard speaking quietly as he peeled off the excrement-smeared garment and pointed up at the peak above them.

'They can't see us down here, the rock's overhang shields us from view. But we have no way to know what their morning routine is. If they usually come down for their food then we only have to wait, but if they expect it to be brought to them they will eventually get suspicious.'

Marcus looked around, his eyes alighting on a cloth bag with a long strap, made to hang from a man's shoulder.

'I would be prepared to gamble that the men up there are expecting to have their breakfast delivered to them.'

Demetrius nodded, but before he could reply, a call from above them broke the dawn's quiet, and both men looked up at the tower of rock looming over them.

'That sounded like a hungry man demanding to be fed, now that the sun's up. Give me that bag and I'll—'

'No, you won't.' Marcus unbuckled his sword belt and placed the weapons beside the fire. 'Look after these for me.' He scooped up the bag and put the strap over one shoulder. 'And be ready to follow me up when I call.'

Taking a headscarf from one of the corpses, he wrapped it around his head, then ripped another into two pieces and wrapped his hands in the thick material.

'Let's hope they see a man protecting his hands from the rope, rather than to hide the colour of his skin from their eyes.'

The rope ladder had been crudely fashioned from thin, rough cord, and creaked ominously as it took his weight, rough wooden rungs knotted into the ropes to make a serviceable means of climbing the rock. Forcing himself to ignore the sounds of its protests, Marcus climbed with deliberate care, slowing as he reached the point where the ladder reached the overhang, held clear of the stone surface by crudely fashioned wooden blocks that gave just enough separation from the rock for him to grasp the cord. His fingers were already aching with the effort of pulling his weight up the near vertical ascent, and he began to wonder whether he would be able to use them to grip a weapon when the time came. Approaching the top of the climb, keeping his gaze fixed on the ladder both to avoid losing his grip and to prevent the white skin of his face from being visible to the men above him, he heard a voice call out from close by. Looking up, he saw a dark-skinned hand reaching down to help him over the edge of the roughly flat surface that had been painstakingly chiselled into the peak's summit by the successive generations of its users. The man standing over him spoke again, amused, and despite his complete lack of comprehension the Roman realised that he was being gently chided, the tone of his would-be helper's voice edged with acerbic humour even as he reached out and took one of what he assumed to be a comrade's hands, hauling the Roman off the ladder and onto the relative safety of the lookouts' perch. Pausing for a moment to get his bearings, Marcus kept his gaze down, touching the bag and feeling the club's reassuring weight.

The lookout spoke again, his voice more impatient, demanding an answer to whatever the question was that he was asking, and Marcus knew that he had to act before suspicion set in. He stepped forward a pace and held out the bag, looking up to see the other man automatically reach for it. The lookout's face was devoid of any suspicion, brown eyes in a bearded, black-skinned face topped by slightly greying hair, cropped tightly in what looked like a military style. Taking another step Marcus lunged forward, putting both hands on the other man's chest and grasping his tunic, their faces abruptly close enough that he felt the startled man's breath on his face, and saw his eyes widen as he realised that he was looking at a stranger. Pulling the other man towards him, he used the soldier's immediate reflexive reaction of pulling away to assist his next move, summoning all of his strength to throw the Kushite bodily over the peak's side. Ignoring the falling man's shriek of terror, he pulled the cut-down spear shaft from the bag as the other watcher turned to face him with a look of amazement. When the Kushite spoke, after a moment's incredulity, his voice was thick with sudden rage at his comrade's brutal murder.

'I will kill you for that.'

A big man, he moved with deliberate care as he drew a long knife from the scabbard at his waist, ignoring the first, distant horn signal from the far side of the river, as the watchers' companions reacted to the fallen man's last, despairing scream in the dawn's silence. Marcus held the cosh out before him two-handed, knowing instinctively that his adversary was a seasoned knife fighter from the way he was slowly advancing across the rough surface. Feeling his way with his leading foot before bringing the other forward in its wake, the knife's point was weaving sinuous patterns to protect his advance, the blade held ready for a swift, deadly attack.

'I won't use this to kill you, just to cut you down.' The black-faced soldier's Greek was heavily accented but understandable, classroom learned, the Roman surmised absent-mindedly, as he focused on the weaving knife's blade, and his eyes were hard with the certainty of his intended revenge. 'I will throw you to your death, and you may accompany my brother in his journey across the river.'

Marcus risked a swift glance down and realised that he was barely a foot from the edge of the lookout point, and the Kushite laughed grimly as he crabbed forward another pace, eager to pen his opponent against the vertical drop.

'Yes, you see your doom behind you. I will—'

The Roman struck, feinting for the blade with his club and then, as the big man drew it away from the heavy weapon's arc, squatted low and released the cosh's handle, whipping it back at the fullest extension of its braided leather cord to impact hard against his enemy's kneecap. Grunting with the agony the Kushite staggered backwards, cursing in his own language before spitting a torrent of unintelligible abuse at Marcus and hobbling forward with the clear intention of overwhelming his opponent with his sheer size, to prevent any repeat of the blow. Swaying inside the path of the lunging blade, Marcus grasped the other man's extended arm and turned swiftly to put his back against his attacker's chest, reaching back over his shoulder to grasp a handful of tunic before pivoting at the waist to throw the big man over his shoulder. Helpless to resist the unexpected move, the soldier landed hard, barely a pace from the peak's edge, scrabbling for grip as he flipped onto his front and started to rise with a murderous roar that faltered as he realised that Marcus had swung the lead-filled spear shaft at him, then screaming in agony as the sweeping blow broke bones in the hand he had unconsciously raised to protect his face. Struggling to his feet one-handed, he tottered on the rough surface for a moment and then fell backwards, spitting out a curse as he disappeared over the edge and disappeared from view. Marcus sank to his knees and dropped the club, shaking with the exertions of the climb and subsequent fight, only to hear a voice shouting close by.

'Help me here! Move!' Turning back he saw that Demetrius had scaled the peak and was struggling onto the stone surface. 'Quickly! We must return their signal! See?'

On the far side of the river a single flag was waving to and fro in urgent sweeps, and Demetrius handed him a furled flag, unrolling the white linen of another banner.

'They show one flag, we must show two!'

Both men swept their banners from side to side, making the signal as vigorous as possible, and after a moment the signal on the other side of the river was lowered. After a moment's uneasy silence Demetrius shrugged, holding something out to Marcus.

'We'll know soon enough whether they're deceived into thinking all is well or not. While we wait, I suggest you eat this.'

Marcus took the warm bread and meat from him, chewing vigorously as they looked across the river's broad ribbon, grey in the early light.

'What would you do, if you were the commander of such a detachment and the sound of a man's scream had been heard from across the river, no matter how faint?'

The Christian nodded knowingly.

'I wouldn't be satisfied with a signal, that's a certainty. At the very least I would be across the river to berate my men for their actions.'

'Exactly.' Marcus swallowed the last mouthful of food and nodded decisively. 'A diligent man, with some regard for his career and his duty, would be across the river to find out what had happened. Help me onto the ladder, then keep watch and warn us if they show signs of investigating.'

Gratefully stepping off the ladder's last rung at the peak's foot, he found Moise and Qadir wrapping the corpses in their own blankets, ready for burial.

'These men deserve some dignity in the afterlife. We must bury them too deeply for the scavengers to reach them.'

'And the man I stunned?'

'Is awake, but unable to see. A result of the blow to the head that you dealt him. His Greek is limited.'

Marcus crossed to the stricken man, squatting by him and speaking in a conversational tone.

'Your friends are dead. All of them. And you, it seems, are blind.'

The soldier nodded disconsolately, utterly motionless when Marcus jabbed two fingers within inches of his eyes.

'I see nothing. Only black.'

'You will recover, in time, I expect. We can leave you food and water to consume while you recuperate, but first I need some information.' He raised a hand to forestall a refusal to cooperate, then realised that the soldier could not see the gesture. 'You will, of course, tell me to keep my questions to myself, and that you will not answer them. As any good soldier should. Which, of course, I must respect. And so it will be a matter of genuine sorrow to me, when I am forced to kill you, or as good as. Unless, of course, you can tell me a few simple facts about your comrades on the other side of the river? The choice is yours.'

'I cannot. My oath to my—'

'Your oath to your king will not save you from being torn to pieces by the vultures, when I take you down into the desert and leave you there, alone and in your darkness. It is your choice.'

He sat in silence while the terrified man spoke, then climbed to his feet and patted him on the shoulder before walking over to Moise.

'There are another eight men over there. They cross every two days to bring fresh supplies, and rotate the duty of watching, allowing the men who are relieved of duty to return to the village and enjoy its entertainment.'

The two men looked at each other, neither in any doubt as to the fate of the villagers.

'Which means that we will not be able to bring the legion through before they discover that we have murdered their comrades.'

Demetrius called down from above them, lying on his belly with his head over the peak's edge.

'A boat!'

'How many men?'

'Wait!'

His head disappeared from view for a moment before reappearing.

'Hard to say! Five! Six, perhaps!'

'Stay visible! Wave, and reassure them!'

Demetrius waved, and Marcus turned back to his comrades.

'We will have to allow them to get out of the boat before we take them. Qadir, if they leave a man with the boat he must die before he has the chance to get back into it. Soldier Moise . . .'

The Nubian snapped to attention. 'Centurion.'

'You must not die. You are the only man who can sit in the prow of that boat when we take it back over the river, and by the colour of your face persuade their comrades that all is well. Understood?'

'Yes, Centurion.'

'We will conceal ourselves, let them get out of the boat and into the rocks, where they will be hidden from view from the other side of the river, and then we take them. No hesitation, and no prisoners. Understood?'

The sound of a shouted question from the river reached them as they hurried down the roughly cut stone steps, followed a moment later by a deliberately incomprehensible response from Demetrius. Looking up, Marcus saw the veteran leaning forward as if straining to hear, a hand cupped at his ear, shaking his head as the question was barked at him again.

'This isn't going to fool them, not for one moment. Be ready to fight!'

Leading his men into the slabs of fallen rock that littered the ground between river and peak, Marcus cursed inwardly, knowing that such a hurried disposition of his forces was likely to remove any advantage they might have enjoyed had they had time to choose their positions more carefully, nodding at Moise as the Nubian slipped into the cover of a large boulder and hefted his sword, ready to fight. The man who had been shouting questions at Demetrius was talking to his men, clearly audible at a distance of no more than twenty paces or so as the boat ran into the riverbank's mud with a squelch, his words both commanding and urgent.

'They should have turned around and rowed back across the river to alert their general by now, surely?'

The Roman nodded at Qadir's whispered question.

'Yes. But these are no ordinary soldiers. They are good, but that makes them over-confident. Be ready.'

With a clatter of hobnails on stone the enemy soldiers were upon them, moving in short, disciplined rushes from one rock to another, and Marcus readied himself as the sounds of their advance drew closer.

'Go!'

The Syrian advanced around the left of the boulder with an arrow nocked and ready to loose, Marcus stepping out from its cover on the other side with his swords raised. In front of him, no more than five paces distant, a group of four Kushite soldiers were advancing in a compact group with their swords drawn, the man who was evidently their leader at their head, gazing furiously up at the peak's summit. His gaze snapped down from the waving Demetrius to the threat before him as the Roman stepped into view, and, barking a terse command, he rushed forward to attack. Parrying his hurried strike, Marcus went for the kill with his spatha only to have it parried by the man to his right, another stepping up on the other side to confront the Roman with three blades, the fourth man waiting behind them. Giving ground to tempt them forward, Marcus nodded in satisfaction as Moise stepped out of his hiding place and stabbed the closest man to him with his sword's point, then cursed inwardly as the blade stuck between the stricken Kushite's ribs for long enough that the man behind him had time to dance forward and lunge, putting the point of his own sword through the Nubian's thigh as he twisted away in attempted evasion, putting the soldier out of the fight. Faced with three blades again, and knowing that he would be unable to fight all of them at the same time, Marcus weighed the alternatives for an instant before – seeing the enemy commander looking behind him, ready to chase him down were he to run – he took the only other option available. Springing forward into the heart of the enemy, he lowered his head to butt the Kushite leader hard on the bridge of his nose with his helmet's iron surface, feeling bone snap as the officer staggered backwards momentarily. Raising the long spatha's blade, he reversed his grip on its hilt to leave the point downwards with the unconscious skill of the thousands of times Cotta had made him practise the simple movement in his youth, then attacked again even as the remaining two men lunged forward at him.

Sidestepping a sword thrust, he barged the man to his left against the rock hard enough to bounce his bronze helmet off the stone surface. While the momentarily stunned Kushite's fellow drew back his sword in readiness to strike, the Roman stabbed down with the spatha, feeling the resistance as his heavy iron blade's point cut down into his opponent's booted foot, then took a handful of tunic and manhandled him off the boulder's face and into the other's path. As the crippled soldier shouted in agony his comrade stabbed in with his own blade, intent on dealing out retribution, but only managed to put the point into his comrade's side. Stepping to the right the Roman sank his gladius's blade into the horrified Kushite's throat, opening the artery and leaving him staggering, dropping the sword as he tried to stem the flow of blood with his hands.

Something hit Marcus hard, sending him flying backwards to land hard with the weight of a man's body on top of him, losing his grip of both swords with the impact. Reaching for his dagger, he was almost too late in realising that the Kushite officer had already drawn his own close-quarters weapon and had it raised for the kill. He whipped up his hands just in time to intercept the blow, straining to hold the other's man's wrist with the weapon's point barely an inch from his throat. Growling angrily, his broken nose dripping blood onto Marcus, the Kushite put both hands onto the dagger's hilt and flexed his muscles, forcing the dagger's point down into the soft flesh of the Roman's neck, dimpling the skin as his weight and strength slowly but certainly overcame Marcus's ability to prevent the blade's remorseless descent.

With a sudden thud that Marcus felt through the other man's body, something shook the Kushite, and at the moment when it seemed inevitable that the blade would push down through the Roman's last vestige of resistance, the strength suddenly went out of his assailant, and he slumped lifelessly down onto his would-be victim. Rolling out from beneath the enemy officer, the Kushite abruptly having been transformed from hard-eyed avenger to lolling corpse, the Roman retrieved his swords before turning back to examine the dead man, raising an eyebrow at Qadir as he made his way back through the rocks.

'This was your doing?'

The Hamian shook his head in bafflement.

'The man guarding the boat had a shield. I was so long dealing with him that I feared you would be dead by now.'

'Then how—'

'It was me!'

Both men looked up at Demetrius, who was leaning over the peak's edge, so far above them that he was barely visible.

'But . . .' Marcus shook his head, looking around until he found a heavy stone close to the dead man's body, picking it up and raising it for Demetrius to see. 'You threw this?'

'Yes! Well, I dropped it more than threw it! It hit him on the back of his head!'

The two men bent closer, finding the Kushite's helmet flattened at its rear. Marcus straightened up, shaking his head in wonder. 'You *threw* this? Knowing that it would kill me, if it hit me?'

'There was never any danger, Centurion! Our Lord guided my hand, as I knew he would!' In the moment's pause that followed, Marcus could have sworn that he heard the sound of a poorly muffled laugh. 'And besides, he was on top of you. Had I not thrown the rock, he would have killed you before your brother officer could come to your rescue! Am I right?'

The Roman nodded tiredly.

'Come down! We have one more task to perform.'

The two men stripped the officer and two of his men of their equipment while they waited for Demetrius to make his way down from the vantage point, Marcus donning the officer's ornate armour and looking at Moise with dismay. The soldier had staunched the flow of blood from his thigh with his scarf, but was clearly quite incapable of standing without support, much less participating in a raid across the river.

'Without him I have no idea how we will get close enough to whoever remains on the other side of the river by surprise. Three men crossing the river without a black face among them will surely alarm them enough for them to run, and our chance of surprise to be lost.'

'Perhaps.' They turned to find the Christian standing behind them. 'And perhaps not. There is a trick that I pulled on a party of my fellow believers, in the days before I saw the light. It is a way to deceive them for long enough that your fellow officer will be close enough to let his arrows fly. But it can only work if you are able to control a man's natural instincts against doing such a thing.'

'What do you mean?'

Demetrius sucked in a deep breath.

'You must understand, Centurion, that I was a different man in those far-off days. Without scruple. Totally lacking in any regard for my fellow man.' He sighed. 'There is an act that I carried out, when I was hunting rebels at my legatus's command. There was a group of them hiding in a very secure place, high on a mountainside with a path barely wide enough for one man, rocky and uncertain, reducing that man's progress to little better than a walking pace. To attack it, in the face of determined resistance, would have condemned a dozen or more of my men to certain death, for there were archers among their number – and a shield, as you will know, is no sure means of defence against an iron-pointed arrow at less than a dozen paces. Other members of this troublesome Hebrew sect, as I saw them at that time, had taken their own lives rather than surrender, which only deepened my reluctance to throw lives away only to capture a cave full of corpses. And then, just as I was considering marching my detachment away, a latecomer fell into my hands. And, with a clarity that still shocks me today, I saw what it was I had to do.'

'Which was what?'

What Demetrius told the two centurions, factually and without attempting to justify his actions, made them stare at him in fresh amazement. The Christian shrugged apologetically.

'I told you, Centurion, that I was a different man before the one true God brought me into his light. And he has changed me, in so many ways, since that day. But at heart I remain the same person, with the same abilities, even if I am now the vessel of his plans rather than those of the empire which, by fortunate coincidence, now happen to be one and the same. Only say the word, and I will repeat the trick I have explained to you. After all, I already have to atone for the deaths of yet more men by my own hand; this will give me little enough extra penance.'

'They're coming back!'

The under-officer grunted, chewing on a piece of spiced lamb that he had cut from the half-eaten leg in the middle of what was serving as a mess table, and speaking through the mouthful of food as a question occurred to him.

'Ask him how many there are in the boat.'

The soldier sitting by the farmhouse's window shouted the question down at the riverbank twenty feet below, waiting a moment for the man at the water's edge, the sharpest eyed of them, to reply.

'He says five, Lord!'

'Which is the right answer. Ask him if there's anything out of the ordinary to be seen.'

After another moment's pause the answer was negative. The officer grunted, putting another piece of meat into his mouth and chewing vigorously as he spoke.

'I told him there was nothing to worry about. They gave the right counter-signal, and he's only been over there long enough to have a good shout and kick some arses, so that's that, from the look of it. You, woman!'

He held out his cup to be refilled with water, shaking his head at the state of the dead farmer's wife. Bruised about her face, her expression combined dejection and fear as she shuffled forward with a leather jug, her movements slow and pained.

'You lot have been going at this one too hard. You're going to kill her if you don't take it a bit easier. Which will mean that I'll have to wash my own clothes, and you'll have to make do with the donkey that works the irrigation wheel. What's wrong with her daughter?'

'She died two days ago, Lord.'

The under-officer shook his head again.

'You idiots! We're going to be here another month, at least, making sure the Romans don't come up the river to have a go at capturing the capital, and I don't plan to be that long without someone to cook and wash. Take a party upstream later on, and see what you can find, right?'

The soldier nodded equably, happy enough at the prospect, and after a moment the officer belched and stood up, brushing crumbs from his tunic.

'Right, let's have a look.' He strode to the window, looking out at the river to find the boat more than two thirds of the way back across, a pair of soldiers rowing hard, two more in the boat's stern, while his superior, as expected, sat in the small vessel's prow with his cloak wrapped around his shoulders. 'He must be getting old, if he thinks this is cold. Gods, but he's an ugly bastard.'

Both men watched as the boat came towards them, the under-officer smiling at the oarsmen's strenuous efforts.

'Look at them, rowing like athletes. He must be hungry, to have them laying into it like that. I did suggest he wait until after breaking his fast to go over and get those idiots by the balls, but no, you know him, always . . .'

He looked harder at the oncoming vessel, his brow furrowing as he tried to work out what he was looking at, the boat advancing to within a dozen paces of the riverbank with no sign of slowing down.

'His face . . . he looks . . . *wrong* . . .'

As he watched, caught in a moment of indecision as to what it was that was troubling him, one of the rowers let go of his oar and turned in the boat, raising a bow and loosing the arrow nocked to its string in one swift, fluid movement. The soldier standing watch on the riverbank had leapt to his feet an instant before, he too realising that all was not as it seemed, but as he turned to run his body jerked, then fell full length with the arrow's fletching protruding from his back. The man sitting in the prow no longer had a black face, but rather a mask of blood over pale skin that to the under-officer's eye gave him the look of a vengeful demon as he leapt onto the bank, a pair of swords gleaming dully in the dawn light. The men in the boat behind him were close behind him, all but for the one left slumped over the side, a corpse no longer held up by the man next to him.

'Shit! Quickly, we have to—'

He started as an arrow hissed through the window and dropped the soldier standing next to him to the floor, kicking and grunting in agony with the shaft buried deep in his chest. Starting away from the stricken man, he turned to run and found himself face to face with the farmer's widow, staring into her hard, embittered eyes for an instant before the pain hit him. Looking down, he saw the hilt of his own dagger, taken from the belt draped over the back of his chair, the entirety of its six-inch blade buried in his stomach.

'*You . . . bitch . . .*' Reaching down, he pulled the weapon free, roaring with the pain as blood spattered across his attacker's shift, then raised the weapon over his head, grabbing at a handful of her meagre clothing and cursing as she flinched away from him. Breathing hard with the effort and the pain, he backed her into the room's corner, showing her the knife's blade and spitting his fury in her terrified face.

'*I'll have your guts . . .*'

And abruptly found himself on the floor in a fast-spreading puddle of his own blood, staring up at the bloody-faced murderer who had worn another man's face until it was too late for the subterfuge's discovery to matter. Fighting to raise a hand that seemed heavier than he could ever have imagined, he forced the trembling fingers into the warding gesture.

'*Sorcerer!*'

The swordsman sheathed the shorter of his two blades, shaking the blood from the other.

'Hardly. All it really took was remaining steady enough to let a man I thought was harmless until a day ago skin a corpse, and then mask me with that skin.'

The Kushite opened his mouth to utter a curse, but the breath needed never came, and Marcus turned away from his blankly staring eyes to find the woman bowing to him. Putting a finger under her chin, he gently lifted her face in order to look into her eyes.

'This is over. You are free.'

'She does not understand you, Centurion. Allow me.'

Demetrius held his hands up, palms first to show that they were empty, stopping a respectful pace from the woman and holding up a thin blanket.

'I will care for her. Perhaps you should join your friend in looking for signs of any more of them, although I believe we have killed them all.'

Marcus nodded, turning for the door, then stopped as a thought struck him.

'The Jews that you sought to deceive, by taking a man's face from his body and wearing it over your own. Did it work?'

Demetrius nodded sadly.

'Yes, Centurion, it did. I was steeped in evil in those days, before I was washed clean of a lifetime's guilt by a man who could see past my earthly imperfections to the soul waiting to be delivered from that evil.' He met Marcus's eyes. 'You want to know how many of those poor benighted men, women and children I killed, hiding behind the face of a dead man to fool them that I was their friend until it was too late, and I was upon them? I cannot tell you. I was swollen by the glee of my deception to a thing of incarnate evil rather than a man, and the soldiers following up behind me flinched away when I emerged from the cave, painted crimson with the blood of a dozen victims. To this day I lie awake some nights, and relive the shameful memories of slaughtering innocents, lost in my lust for blood.'

He fell silent, still staring at Marcus.

'And yet you were willing to repeat the trick today?'

The Christian nodded.

'I knew that the day would come when I would be forced to compromise the teachings of my faith, in order to do what is necessary to bring new believers to Our Lord. That day was today.'

'And if you have to do so again?'

'Then I will pray to my God for guidance, as I did this morning in the dawn, when you thought I was napping, or pretending to. And if my God tells me that I must kill, then in his name I will do so.'

Later, with the bodies of the men they had killed buried in the farm's black mud, the Romans walked back towards the boat, leaving the sole survivor of the dead soldiers' depredations weeping over her dead husband's resting place. Demetrius bent, retrieving the mask he had cut from the dead Kushite officer's face less than an hour before, brushing away the flies before folding it into a triangle of bloodied flesh.

Qadir grimaced at the grisly trophy.

'Surely you can't want that?'

Shaking his head, the Christian gestured to the far side of the river.

'I must bury him intact. To send him onward to face judgement without a face would be the cruellest of insults.'

The Hamian raised a questioning eyebrow.

'His men murdered and raped the occupants of this farm, and who knows how many others? Surely that's cruel enough?'

'Possibly so, but it is not my place to judge. God himself will decide what punishment is to be meted out to the soul of such a man. My role was simply to send him to judgement.'

They climbed into the boat and pushed away from the river-bank, Demetrius rowing steadily for the distant western shore.

'One of the simplest but strongest teachings of the Christos was that it is those men who have lived blameless lives who will be the first to be admitted to paradise in the afterlife.'

The Hamian laughed sardonically.

'What does that mean for the rest of us? Our lives could hardly be described as having been blameless, no matter whether we believed that right was on our side or not.'

Demetrius kept rowing, and for a long moment it appeared that he would not answer the question, but at length he spoke again.

'God – the one true God, who sits apart from the plethora of idols and fakes that most men in the empire worship – does not simply judge a man on what he has done in his life, but rather on what was in his soul at the time he committed the acts. A soldier can fight, and kill, and God will not punish him for it if his desire was to protect his homeland from invaders, or to spread his word to the unenlightened. And surely, I would argue, this task that we are performing for your master in Rome meets both of those requirements. You are seeking to free your fellow citizens, are you not?'

'And you are here to convert the barbarians who have subjugated them?'

The Christian smiled enigmatically.

'I will provide them with the opportunity to see the light that shines from heaven.'

'And if they refuse to see that light? And consider your attempt at conversion to be grounds for your death?'

The answer was instant, having clearly been considered at length.

'As I told you, Centurion, I have lived, and continue to live, a charmed life. If God is watching over me so carefully, then it can only be with the intention of using me as an earthly vessel for his message, even unto my own death. And who am I, a reformed and forgiven sinner with the blackest of deeds in my past, miraculously forgiven and given another chance to make something from this life, to refuse?'

9

'It looks unoccupied to me.'

Demetrius nodded in agreement, the gesture just visible in the dusk's gloom. The scouts had ridden along the river to the south without any further sign of enemy scouts, replenishing their supplies at the border town of Souan by posing as well-escorted merchants looking to purchase emeralds. Bribing the gate guards to ignore their unconventional exit, they had slipped quietly away in the dead of night to resume their progress into Kushite territory without being spotted by curious eyes, friendly or not.

'It does seem to be empty, doesn't it? But that would surely be too good to be true, would it not?'

'Perhaps. And although I would happily accept that oversight on our enemy's side, the most important thing is that the fortress appears still to be intact. It was entirely possible that the king of Kush might have chosen to tear it down and remove a potential thorn in his side.'

The three men stared in silence across the river for a moment, taking in the fortress's looming silhouette brooding over the Nilus's course. Perched high over the river, crowning a rock outcrop that reared up from the river's edge to a height of two hundred feet above the water, it looked every bit as formidable a fortress as Scaurus's descriptions had led them to expect.

'Wait until our colleague Avidus lays eyes on that. He might just expire with the joy of such a natural strongpoint.'

Marcus nodded at Qadir's amused observation. Flanked on both sides of its four-hundred-pace frontage by steep-sided ravines, its western face an almost sheer drop to the riverbank, it was evident that the fortress could only be approached from the side that faced the desert to the east.

'Now I see how Augustus's general Petronius was able to hold it against the full strength of Kush for so long. They could only approach it from one side, and that so lacking in cover that a legion's bolt throwers would tear the heart out of an attack without even having to be aimed. But we don't have it yet.'

'And your orders, Centurion?'

He turned to find Demetrius grinning at him.

'Are you making fun of me, Christian?'

The older man shook his head, still smiling.

'Far from it. It is simply that we find ourselves with something of a choice to make, do we not? On the one hand, the fortress does indeed appear to be unoccupied. And it might be that a single small boat crossing the river in the darkness would go completely unnoticed, even were there men set to caretake it. On the other, the lack of visible illumination might be meaningless. A structure that large could harbour an infantry cohort without there being any sign of their occupation from this distance, if they were cautious enough not to display any sign of their presence on the walls.'

'Indeed.' Marcus stared at the fortress's looming bulk. 'We either cross now, a small party more likely to go unnoticed, or we wait for the legion's full strength to arrive.'

Qadir stared up at the fortress's brooding bulk for a moment.

'Waiting for the legion's arrival would at least put spears at our backs. They can only be a few days behind us, given they will cover the distance from Souan by river. Perhaps an approach in force is the most prudent answer to this question?'

The Roman shook his head.

'No. We have our orders, and they are well founded. The tribune was right – once he passes the first cataract, and the city of Souan on the far bank, the clandestine part of this advance is over.'

Scaurus had pointed at the frontier city on the map they had used to plan their strategy, the night before their departure from Koptos.

'We start at a disadvantage, gentlemen, which is why I intend to use subterfuge to tempt our enemy as far to the north as I can. It will take us ten days to reach the city of Souan, traditionally the border between Rome and Kush, because we are forced to follow the river's winding course to water our men and beasts. And when we reach Souan, we will still be several days march from Premnis, although we may be able to requisition enough shipping to reduce that travel time to a day or two. If all goes well, we will arrive at the fortress within a week of the advance party. *But . . .*'

He reached out and pointed a finger at the frontier city.

'Souan is riddled with the Kush. It is the point where Rome and its neighbour to the south have faced each other for the last two hundred years, ever since Augustus decided to make peace with Queen Amanirenas rather than risk another war when he had no legions available to fight it. Diplomats, priests at the temple, traders, informers . . . there will be hundreds of the enemy's civilians in Souan, and it will only take one of them to ride east with the news that a Roman legion has passed on the western bank to alert the king to our presence. How far is it from Berenike to Souan, gentlemen?'

The *speculatores* had conferred for a moment before delivering their opinion through Demetrius.

'The average of my brothers' estimations is two hundred miles. It looks a good deal less on the map, of course, but the road, such as it is, weaves its way through the mountains that run between them, and for every mile that you see there on the wall, there is more than another to be covered on the ground.'

Scaurus's response had been to emphatically tap the spot that he had determined was to be their objective with his index finger.

'So, perhaps three days' ride for a man willing to drive his horse into the ground. Allow an additional day for them to break camp and move west. After that they will have to cross the desert

to Souan and march south along the river, because I don't
intend to leave any ships for them to use. Which means that from
the moment word of our advance into their territory reaches their
king, we have perhaps ten days before his arrival in front of the
fortress gates. Or less, if word has reached him by some other
means. Which means that the advance party must take Premnis,
by whatever means, because we have no time for a lengthy siege.
If we fail to take the fortress, then our only option will be to
retreat back to Koptos and accept the loss of Berenike. So take
Premnis for me, gentlemen, at *any* cost.'

Marcus looked up and down the river's black ribbon.

'We must cross the Nilus tonight, while our presence here is
still undetected. And in doing so we might just succeed where
ten times our strength would fail in the daylight.'

'I must warn you that the crocodiles will be active, Centurion.'

The three men turned to Moise, whose voice bore the unmistakable signs of fear. He had expounded at some length on the
subject of the river's predators during their ride south, returning
to the subject any time that there was any hint of an amphibian
presence beneath the Nilus's water, and when Marcus had decided
to purchase a boat large enough to hold half a dozen men from
an amenable farmer, his warnings had become even more dire
than before.

'Surely if we stay in the boat we will be safe?'

'Not necessarily, Centurion. It is quite usual to hear stories of
the largest of them overturning small boats and taking the people
that were tipped out into the river. They carry their prey down
under the water and drown it.'

'It will be a swift death then?'

'Yes, but at night, in the darkness . . .'

The Roman put a reassuring hand on his shoulder.

'I understand. You can stay here, if you wish.'

Marcus gestured to the darkened undergrowth, but the soldier's
response was swift and emphatic.

'To do so alone would be even worse! Those monsters hunt

on the land as well! I will come with you, but by all the gods I ask you not to risk overturning the boat or we will never be seen again!'

They boarded the boat and set out across the now dark river, pointing the prow upstream to compensate for the Nilus's powerful current; Demetrius instructed his men to row steadily rather than risk attracting the attention of any lookouts by working their oars too vigorously. The fortress towered higher above them as they progressed, its unnaturally straight-lined bulk standing out against the starlit sky behind it.

'I see no watchers. No patrolling sentries. Surely a guard force would be more obvious?'

Marcus nodded at Qadir's whispered question.

'One might think so. But they may believe themselves immune from enemy action, this far south.'

Nosing into the river's eastern bank, the boat had no sooner touched its mud than the Christian, who had made the crossing perched in its bows, was ashore and holding onto the small vessel while his companions climbed over the side, carrying it into the cover of the rocks beneath the fortress's almost sheer northern face. Crouching in the darkness and looking up, Marcus held his breath for a moment and listened carefully, but the only sound was the lapping of the river's water against its banks and the occasional animal sound from the far side, as nature's constant war between predator and prey played out in the darkness.

'Nothing. Not a single sound out of place.'

Marcus listened for another moment before nodding his agreement with Qadir's opinion.

'Moise, you will struggle with such a climb as you are still healing. Stay to guard the boat at a safe distance from the river. The rest of you, with me.'

Leading the party up the steep ravine on the fortress's northern side, stepping carefully to avoid the larger rocks that had been strewn down its length during its construction, he stopped, breathing hard, at the point where a further slope branched upwards towards the walls above them. Pausing for a moment to get his breath back he continued the climb, cursing silently as rock scree slid away from beneath their boots to skitter down the steep slope. Gaining the level ground at the massive structure's north-eastern corner, the Roman peeped around the wall's corner at its northern frontage as the remainder of the party struggled up the treacherous slope, waiting until Qadir and Demetrius were at his shoulder before speaking, pointing at the curving run of the fortress's eastern wall.

'There's what looks like a gateway halfway down the wall. And if there's anyone here they'd have to be the soundest of sleepers not to have heard that racket. Either they're waiting in ambush or this place really is deserted. And there's only one way to find out.'

Moving quietly down the rampart's face, listening intently for any indication of a presence within the brooding fortification, they found that the black space in the wall's pale, starlit run of stone was in fact a gaping hole torn in the wall's frontage. Demetrius studied the opening, several paces wide and ragged-edged where individual stones had been torn out.

'The gate was probably no wider than enough space for a pair of armoured men to pass. And they have tried to make it impossible to defend by removing the doors. But are they still here? Why defend something you believe you have made useless for its purpose?'

Marcus drew his swords with a hiss of polished steel.

'Shall we go and reveal the truth of that question?'

Stepping through the opening he stood still for a moment, allowing his eyes to adjust to the gloom within the walls before moving deeper into the fortress's streets. Pacing slowly forward into the darkness he cocked his head to listen intently for any sound of occupation. A tall building rose on the right of the street down which they were advancing, and he led them through its open door into a high, vaulted space. Demetrius walked to the middle of the flat stone floor, turning a slow circle and inhaling deeply, pointing to a bronze statue gleaming dully in the shadows at its far end, fecund female curves and a proud featured face.

'It is a temple to their goddess. Do you smell the faint traces of incense? What a church to Our Lord this would make!'

A sound at the door caught their attention, the scraping scuff of metal on stone, and all three men turned to point their weapons at a man standing stock-still in the temple's doorway, frozen by the threat of Qadir's nocked arrow as the Hamian paced towards him with his bow raised.

'Move and I will shoot you. Do you speak Greek?'

'Yes, Lord.'

The newcomer blew out a shaky breath, his eyes wide with fear as Marcus stepped forward and used the flat of his spatha to push him into the tall, vaulted room.

'Who are you?'

'No one, Lord, a simple farmer.'

Demetrius shook his head in disbelief.

'A simple farmer who speaks the language of civilisation? How likely is that?'

'My mother taught me! A trader's daughter, she met a man of Kush and settled, although I believe she came to regret the choice when she realised what being the wife of a farmer meant. She hoped I would use the language to escape this life.'

'But you did not.'

'No. And when my father died, the neighbouring farmers drove me off my land. They said that I did not belong, and divided my farm between them. I worked as a labourer, scraping enough money to stay alive, and ended up in the work party that made this fortress unusable to the Romans.'

'And you stayed here when the army moved on?'

'It was not hard. Nobody would have expected any of us to want to stay here, and I had no friends to miss my presence. I had already found a hiding place, and concealed some of the grain which we were detailed to sweep out of the granaries, so it was easy enough to slip away and hide. Not that anyone came to look for me.'

Marcus stared at him in silence for a moment, then nodded as he made his decision.

'Show us where you have been living. And if you run, you die. What is your name?'

The Kushite relaxed slightly.

'Piye, Lord.'

'You may call me Centurion. Indeed you may call us all by that title. And don't imagine that knowing your name will prevent my colleague here from putting an arrow in your back if you try to run from us.'

Piye led them deeper into the silent fortress, apparently unable to stop talking now that the threat of death had been lifted, pointing at a tiny building sandwiched between a pair of what were evidently granaries, their walls buttressed against the weight of the grain that would have pressed against them when they were full.

'This was my hiding place when the army left, and I have lived in it since then.'

Qadir put his head into the small space, barely large enough for a man to lie in.

'His possessions are in there, such as they are. It seems that he is telling the truth.' He turned to the Kushite. 'What did the army have you do to render this fortress unusable?'

'You have seen the gates? We were ordered to tear away both doors and hinges, and then to pull out the stones in which the hinges were set. Then they had us break the cisterns that held enough water to provide for a garrison, and collapse the walls of the granaries into themselves. I recall the officer in charge of our work discussing it with his fellows. He was a proud man, dressed like a god in shining armour made of metal scales, like yours but larger, a man as black as the night from the far south. The officers spoke in Greek, which they believed none of us peasants could understand.'

'And what did they say?'

'They spoke of the coming war which their ruler had ordered them to prepare for. And they laughed at the thought of an invader seeking to use this place for protection, without gates, without water and without food.'

Marcus nodded.

'And they were right, all things considered. But their king has failed to consider the first rule of warfare.'

Piye looked him expectantly, but the Roman had already turned away and was examining the damage that had been wrought on the nearest of the granaries. Qadir spoke softly, his voice at once gentle but with an unmistakable undertone of threat.

'You find yourself part of another army now, Piye of Kush. You will show us where the damage has been wrought upon this fortress and help us to repair it, and make this place fit to defend once more.' He laughed at the disbelieving look on the labourer's face. 'You'll see. The army of Meroë may be a thing of terror in the field, when it outnumbers its enemy many times over, but it will be a different matter when its men are forced to attack in the face of a blizzard of iron.'

'Lor— Centurion?'

'You will understand, in good time. For now I am content to complete my fellow officer's statement. The first rule of warfare is that you must always endeavour to predict the unexpected, and to prepare for it.'

'But if it is unexpected . . .?'

The Hamian smiled.

'That will be the result of a failure to open one's eyes to the possibilities afforded by an enemy's strengths, and necessitated by his weaknesses. As the king of Kush may well be about to discover.'

'So Centurion, you've had a good look around the fortress, what do you think?'

Avidus pursed his lips in the manner to which his comrades had grown accustomed, looking up at the cloudless sky as he considered Scaurus's question. The tribune was standing on the broad, stony plain outside the fortress with his officers, considering the prize which his advance up the river had secured. Marcus smiled knowingly at Cotta as Abasi's hands reflexively tightened on his vine stick, the senior centurion clearly eager to be among his men as the shouts of the legion's officers reached them from the chain of soldiers laboriously passing the legion's disassembled bolt throwers up the ravine from the boats unloading at the river's eastern bank. The vessels had been commandeered in the river port of Souan by the simple expedient of a tent party being billeted on each one before their masters had the chance to sail, and several of them had been manned and sent to lurk on either bank in order to ensure that captains bringing their vessels down-river couldn't turn about and make a run back to the south, to avoid their being put into imperial service as well. Leaving the bulk of his legion in the riverside town, with orders to requisition every scrap of spare food, Scaurus had ordered his makeshift fleet to sail upriver with the disassembled artillery as their first cargo, accompanied by the legion's craftsmen and enough men to unload the powerful weapons and begin their assembly.

'Could you look any more like a Roman builder being asked to put right another man's failed work?'

The African smiled at Cotta's jaundiced observation, lifting a hand to point at the fortress.

'There is much to do here, Centurion. Where a city builder would be asking what the householder's budget was, I have a different question for my customer.'

'Which is?'

The engineer turned to address his tribune.

'I have walked the length and breadth of this fortress, Tribune. While she has been sadly abused by the barbarians, I am sure, given enough time, that my men and I can restore her to her former majesty . . .' he paused and tipped his head respectfully at Abasi, 'with the assistance of the legion's skilled tradesmen, of course.'

'Did you just call that pile of stones *her*?'

Avidus's lips twisted in disdain.

'You have no finer feelings for the beauty of a well-constructed building, do you, Cotta? The fortress has a spirit, a . . . presence, and like the sailor who terms his ship as "she", my men and I have a similar view. Scoff all you like.' He turned back to Scaurus, ignoring the veteran's mockingly blown kiss. 'How long do we have to restore her to her former glory?'

Scaurus shrugged.

'By rights we should have ten days, but our enemy has wrong-footed a perfectly competent commander once in this war already, so I see no reason to underestimate him. You have seven days at best, I think. What can you do with *her* in that time?'

'Seven days? It is not long enough, really.' Avidus beckoned his second-in-command over, a squat and fearsomely muscled chosen man whose prodigious strength had led to his being known by the not-entirely-humorous nickname 'Hercules', his hands scarred from a lifetime of manual work with the upper two joints of the index finger on his right hand missing from some accident in his past. The two men conferred for a moment, then the African nodded decisively. 'First Spear Abasi, I am presuming that your men will not require our assistance to assemble their bolt throwers?'

'They will not. I drill them in the assembly and use of their weapons on a regular basis, and there are strict rules which ensure that all components are always present. The tent parties that work them carry all the ironwork that holds their machines together, and spares besides, and they know that if I inspect them and discover as much as a single bolt missing, I will have them all bent over a post for a public beating, and their century on half-rations for a week. It seems to be an effective motivation, after a vigorous example having been made in the early days of my tenure.'

The engineer nodded.

'Then I will spare no thought for that side of the fortress's defence. Which leaves the obvious requirements for any such stronghold: a supply of water to ensure day-to-day survival, enough food to outlast the enemy, and walls that are strong enough to keep them from overrunning the occupants.' He looked around the gathered officers, inviting comment, before continuing. 'So, we are agreed. Let us consider them one at a time.'

He pointed at the nearest of the gaping wounds in the wall's run, where the gate that had filled the hole, and the stone which had formed the frame around it, had both been ripped away.

'The walls of the fortress are five paces deep, with well-cut and fitted block facings and rubble infill. They will resist anything that this enemy can throw at them, and I doubt that there is much chance of them having the time or patience to tunnel through ground this solid, and from outside of bolt-thrower range, to undermine them. Which means that the gates will undoubtedly be the focus of any besieger's attentions. There are . . . were . . . three gates, which have all been torn out. Without them we are defenceless against an army large enough to accept the casualties they will take from attacking into the teeth of our artillery. And the stones that were cut to fit around them have been carried away from here, which means that we will need to quarry and cut more, easily a longer task than we have time for. The best I can do is fill the gaps in the walls with rubble.'

Scaurus gestured to Marcus, who ushered Piye forward, the peasant labourer visibly wilting at being the focus of a dozen officers' attention, tapping him encouragingly on the shoulder.

'Speak.'

The Aegyptian quavered.

'I know—'

Marcus tapped him again, a little harder.

'No. *Louder.* Your mother gifted you with the Greek language, now speak out with the courage your father must have had to win such an exotic woman to be his wife.'

'I know where the stones are, Lords! All the Kushites did was throw them into the northern ravine so, if you know where to look for them, they are easily retrievable.'

Avidius smiled wryly.

'The word "easy" might be a little generous, but I understand. Did they throw the gates themselves down there as well?'

Piye shook his head.

'They were made of wood, so the officer in charge had them burned.'

The African grimaced, gesturing to the empty, barren landscape.

'Which will make them almost impossible to replace, given the lack of seasoned timber around here.'

'With respect . . . ?' The Romans turned back to Piye. 'The ships that pass this point are loaded with all sorts of trade goods that merchants in Souan know will bring healthy profits when shipped down the river to the north, such as gold, the tusks of the elephant, and exotic dark woods. And among these is a hardwood, *ebeninos*, grown in the lands far to the south, prized for its durability, that I believe would be especially suitable for the construction of replacement gates for the fortress.'

Scaurus smiled slowly.

'It seems that you have already proved yourself valuable.' He turned to Abasi. 'First Spear, would you be so good as to order an immediate blockade of the river? Use the larger of the boats we came upriver in to block the Nilus to all traffic, and only let them through once they've been searched and had anything of value requisitioned and unloaded. Give the masters promissory notes for anything of any value. Here . . .' He gestured to Piye. 'Take this man with you, he will translate your requirements to the locals and, I suspect, see through any attempt to deceive us as to their cargoes.' He returned his attention to Avidus. 'Which leaves the twin remaining issues of food and water.'

'Grain storage is easy enough, Tribune. The legion's craftsmen are numerous enough to have the granaries rebuilt within two or three days.' Scaurus nodded. Legion construction teams had been among the first men up the ravine's slope, and had been ordered to set to work repairing the storerooms in readiness for the grain that had been painstakingly carried south in the legion's baggage train. 'But water, I am afraid, is another matter. The fortress's cisterns have been broken and made entirely useless. The bastards set fires beneath them, then broke them with hammers when they became brittle, and where we will be able to find the right stone, quarry it and then cut it to shape in that amount of time is beyond me.'

Scaurus shook his head in frustration.

'And the matter of water is the most urgent of our needs. Every man's water bottle will have to be refilled once a day at least, more often for those taking part in the reconstruction. Which is an inconvenience now, but once the enemy are camped outside these walls we will be unable to set foot outside them, and will be completely cut off from the river. Do you have any thoughts, or is this final hurdle perhaps too high for us to jump?'

Avidus smiled tightly.

'Perhaps not, Tribune. I cannot repair the cisterns, not in the time available, but I reasoned that the lack of rain in this place means that its builders might perhaps have intended there to be another way to bring enough water from the river while under siege. And so I looked at the fortress's western side most carefully as we approached across the river, and saw that there is a gulley carved into the rock face, still lined with wooden planks. When I viewed this feature from above, in a chamber constructed at the highest point of the fortress, it was clear to me that it was designed to allow a bucket to be lowered to the water and raised again. The chamber is connected to the cisterns by channels which double as roof gutters, to collect rain when it falls in the seasonal storms. Such an elegant design.' He fell silent in contemplation of the system, only speaking again when Cotta coughed ostenta-tiously. 'The chamber has the marks in its floor of having housed a man-powered winch, but this has been torn out and presumably burned along with the gates, leaving nothing for us to work with.'

'And what would you need to reconstruct it, presuming you had the skills to do so?'

The engineer raised an eyebrow.

'I have the tools I need, thanks to our colleague's foresight in sending word back to Souan that we would require every kind of implement.'

Marcus had dispatched a message down the river with the news of the Premnis's abandonment, warning Scaurus that Avidus's men would need a wide range of tools, were they to bring the fortress back to a usable condition. The resulting mass door-to-door requisition had yielded up a cornucopia of construction equipment, from spades and picks for simple labouring to the finer tools required for carpentry and masonry. There had even been a blacksmith's forge, the latter perhaps a step too far in Cotta's amused opinion at the time, as his colleague had gloated over the equipment. The resulting widespread and genuine sense of outrage throughout the riverside town had been assuaged to some degree by Scaurus's gold, although the tribune had confided to his men that he feared the day would be remembered as a disaster by the local tradesmen for years to come, hardly helped by the way Avidus's men had been unable to restrain their glee at having tools in their hands again.

'And in the absence of the cisterns the system was designed to use, we can probably use the clay grain jars, once they are emptied into the granaries. What I do not have, however . . .' the African continued, 'is either the wood or the rope required to construct such a winch. Or, for that matter, a suitable bucket to lift the water up from the river. Although I may have found something that can be used to construct one, if we can get hold of enough charcoal to fire up that furnace we brought from Souan. Although the locals might be a little unhappy with what I'm going to propose.'

'All things considered, I'd say we've done about as well as I could have hoped for when we set out from Koptos. We have the ability to punish any force sent to break down our gates grievously, and in a day or two we'll be protected against their archers as well.'

Marcus and Scaurus were walking around the fortress's walls in the cool of the evening, as had become their routine after several long days supervising the myriad of tasks that needed to be completed before the enemy army's arrival curtailed their efforts to make Premnis defendable. Marcus stepped over the blanket-wrapped body of a legionary, raising his vine stick to recognise the salute of the sentry left awake to watch for any sign of an enemy presence on the plain to their east while his fellows slept alongside their ballista. The bolt-thrower crews were exhausted from a long day hauling wooden planks confiscated from the passing shipping up the ravine and onto the walls, and were sleeping like dead men, for the most part. Their loads were stacked neatly against the wall's parapet, ready to be used by the legion's craftsmen to raise a protective shield against the enemy archery that would almost certainly be directed at the artillery that had been installed on the rampart, engines having been installed in numbers so great that there was no more than a few paces between each one and its neighbours. Marcus nodded at his superior's statement, gesturing to the squat tower that inter-rupted the rampart's run behind them.

'And we have gates to keep them out, if they manage to reach the walls.'

The river blockade that Abasi had instituted at Scaurus's orders had proven remarkably effective at providing the materials needed for Avidus's reconstruction of the vital gates, more than one disgusted master unwillingly accepting a promissory note in return for their cargoes of timber, thick planks of a hardwood so dark it was almost black, and hard enough to stop an arrow dead at twenty paces. So dense had the timber proven that the carpenters had been forced to painstakingly drill guide holes before hundreds of heavily studded nails could be driven into the wood, as a further defence against any attempt to hack them down. Construction of the triple-layered gates had been overseen by the hard-eyed centurion, all trace of his usually relaxed character vanishing as he had inspected the work with the unforgiving air of a man who had no intention of being disappointed. Both his own men and the legionaries assisting them had breathed easier when he had disappeared back to the wall to check on the progress the building crew were making in reinstating the stones that would provide mounting points for the heavy slabs of wood. Their dead weight had been laboriously dragged up the ravines on either side of the fortress, Avidus noting with glee the iron hinge posts that had been left in place when the masonry in which they were fixed had been thrown down the steep slopes.

'The fools have made my job here so much easier, and all for the sake of a few hours with a hammer and chisel. Amateurs. An engineer would have left this fortress as a field of stones.'

Once the stonework had been rescued from where it was languishing in the ravine – gangs of legionaries toiling to drag each piece back onto level ground with ropes confiscated from the passing ships, their task made easier by the improvisation of wooden skids from the offcuts of hardwood – Avidus had ordered the forge to be lit. Watching with approval as the legion's smith had coaxed the fire from a small tongue of flame in a handful of kindling to a roaring blaze that made any man within a dozen paces sweat profusely, he had stripped to nothing more than a leather apron to protect his body from flying sparks, ignoring Cotta's jibes at the sight of his bare backside. Standing alongside the craftsman, he had assisted the burly soldier in the heating and hammering of iron scavenged from a broken sword, the two men working until it was formed into a massive pin which, bolted to a door, would allow it to hang from the barrel already embedded in the stone. Examining the resulting piece of ironwork, fresh from the quench and still warm to the touch, he had clapped the smith on the shoulder and told him to make another eleven exactly the same before moving onto his next task. Labouring in the sweltering heat of the water system's winch chamber with half a dozen of his men, he had not been seen for the best part of two days, and had answered all attempts at communication with instructions to be left alone other than to accept meals and pots of water.

The two men halted their progress around the walls to stare out over the plain that stretched out before the fortress in the only practical direction for an enemy to approach.

'It's strange to imagine that there could be thirty thousand men staring back at us when we look over this wall in just a few days.'

Scaurus nodded.

'Not for the first time, I find myself wondering if I haven't bitten off just a little too much to swallow. On all our behalves.'

'It's not as if you had very much choice. Staying in Koptos would only have got us all killed, and the town destroyed. To have pulled back down the river would have been to cede Berenike to Kush, and to advance out to meet them would have resulted in the destruction of the last body of men capable of resistance in the whole of the province. Which means that this is the only place you could have chosen to make a stand for five hundred miles or more, so it was either stop here or go on upriver and sack their cities one at a time until they caught and overran us. Augustus's general Petronius knew it, and it's as true now as it was then.'

The tribune grimaced out into the darkness.

'It being the only realistic option doesn't make it any more palatable, when you consider that it will undoubtedly attract our enemy onto us like flies onto fresh dung. Their king will be convinced that he has us in a trap of our own making, given his orders to make this place unusable. And Petronius wouldn't have been able to make peace without the fact that his master knew he couldn't spare the forces to fight and was willing to pay hand-somely to make friends with Kush instead. We quite obviously don't have that option, and the man commanding the enemy army will know that all too well. Once they're camped out there on that plain then that, I'm very much afraid, is likely to be that. Not that we'll even be able to offer them very much resistance, if Avidus can't get his water winch built and working.'

'The last I heard he'd sent his carpenters away to sleep and told them to leave him to it. Something about a ratchet mechanism.'

The two men walked around the wall, making their way carefully past the sleeping bodies, and tapped on the door of the
winch chamber, stepping back as a wild-eyed Avidus swung it
open with a bellow of something close to rage.

'Could you all just *fuck* off! I—' Falling silent in the face of his
astonished officers, he came wearily to attention and saluted,
his eyes red with fatigue. 'Tribune.'

'You look exhausted, Centurion. Is there anything we can do
to assist?'

The engineer shook his head wearily.

'No, thank you. I'm finished, more or less. I'm just making the
last adjustments to the . . .' He turned away, gesturing them to
follow. 'Quicker to show you.'

The two men followed him into the chamber, where the object
of his efforts over the previous two days sat in the centre of a
circle of oil lamps carefully positioned on small plinths in bowls
of water to remove any risk of fire from the sawdust strewn liber-
ally across the room's wooden floor. Evidently designed to be
powered by men, the winch had eight thick wooden bars protruding
from a central drum, a thick beam rising six feet above it.

'The winch will be turned by sixteen men at a time, one team
working and another resting. Working together they will have the
ability to lift a bucket of water as tall as a man from the riverbank
all the way up here a dozen times an hour. Once it's up here, we
simply pour its contents into the tank there' – he pointed at a
clay tank, still dark from its recent casting, a drainage channel
opening from one side and running away through the chamber's
wall – 'and it will flow out into the gutter network, which my men
have fixed so that the water can be diverted to the water storage
points as we wish. It would have been finished this morning if
only I could have made the ratchet work the first time.'

Scaurus calculated swiftly.

'We'll be able to fill every grain jar we have within a couple of
days. And keep filling them even once we're under siege, as long
as the artillery can keep the Kushites from interfering. So all you

need now, I presume, is rope and a bucket. And the rope's easy enough, but the bucket . . . ? They can't have been stupid enough to leave it, surely?'

'No.' The African pointed to the opening in the chamber facing the river, large enough to allow the bucket to be tipped into the channel. 'They threw it into the river, from what your tame Kushite told me. And even if I knew where it sank, there's no way I'd be going looking for it, not with the number of crocodiles I've seen break the surface from up here. Big bastards too, big enough to take a man under and never be seen again. No, there's no bucket, but I might have the answer to that, just as long as you managed to get me the beeswax I asked you for?'

'You're going to make a bucket. With beeswax.' Cotta stared at Avidus with an expression caught somewhere between disbelief and hilarity. 'When you're done with that, perhaps you could make a sword out of shit? I could drop you out a nice—'

'And you would care to place a wager on that? I mean as to whether I can make a bucket using wax, rather than your renowned ability to generate shit of all varieties?'

The veteran centurion recoiled slightly, his eyes narrowing at the African's response. The sound of men working on the rampart in the morning's relative cool was a dull buzz in the background as the legion's carpenters busied themselves building the protective wooden screens that Scaurus had ordered to be erected along the wall's length, although the activity on the ground below them was clearly attracting a good deal of interest. Avidus had led his work party out into the morning sunshine, and ordered the forge to be prepared for use again, directing his men to erect it only paces from the trestle table on which a piece of wax the size of a big man's ribcage had been placed to warm. The scene was completed by a freshly dug firepit, its steep-sided three-foot-wide bowl filled with kindling and fire logs, while a circle of short wooden posts had been embedded into the ground around it, protruding by no more than a foot.

'Would I care to place a wager on it? Of course I don't want to . . .' Cotta pondered the idea's impossibility for a moment. 'How much?'

'One of these.' The African opened his hand and tossed the aureus that had been hidden in his fingers up into the air, a glinting flicker of gold. 'Nothing, to a man as rich as you. Of course the main purpose of the wager wouldn't be the coin, it would be the look on your face when you are forced to cough it up. Unless, of course, you lack the stomach to back up your customary disbelieving humour?'

'Can you make a bucket with wax?' Cotta turned to Marcus and Scaurus, but found their expressions as uncertain as his own. 'If you can, then I'm buggered if I can work out how. So yes, I'll cough up a gold if you can make a bucket with wax *and* it holds water when it's being dragged up and down that cliff. If you think you can do that, then have at it.'

Avidus turned away, bellowing orders at his waiting men.

'Light the forge, and the fire! Legionary Zeno, to me! It's time to show us the result of all that fooling about with clay when you should have been doing something sensible like drinking and chasing women! And you, Hercules, go and do that thing you and I discussed yesterday!'

While his chosen man waddled off into the fortress with a purposeful gait, accompanied by several men carrying hammers and crowbars, a slightly-built member of Avidus's century walked over with a small canvas tool roll in one hand, saluting Scaurus and then turning to smile beatifically at Cotta, who shook his head at the soldier's smug expression.

'He's the one who gets the coin if this madness actually works, right? I always wondered what use a scrawny streak of piss like him was to a bunch of hairy-palmed latrine-diggers like you lot.'

Avidus smiled knowingly at his friend, extending an open palm to gesture at his soldier as the legionary unrolled his tool bag and laid out his equipment, an assortment of paddles and scraping tools with which to manipulate and shape the wax.

'It's true, he's not the biggest of us, the fastest with a pickaxe or the cleverest when it comes to numbers and designs, but I keep him around because he has a skill that no other man in my century can match.'

'Which is an ability to make useless fucking buckets out of wax, right?'

'Which is his artistry, you barbarian. He has a better eye than any of us, and an ability with his hands to express that vision in clay that would make a thirty-year-experienced potter weep tears of pure joy.'

Cotta shrugged.

'Doesn't matter how pretty he makes this wax bucket of yours, it'll still be as much use as a silk shield.'

Ignoring him, a look of concentration stealing over his face, the artist walked across to the massive lump of wax that had been placed on a trestle table in the sun to warm, walking around it and prodding with a finger to gauge its readiness for use.

'Don't tell me, like all great sculptors he can see the bucket inside the wax and simply has to free it from its prison.'

Scaurus shook his head.

'Do be quiet now, Centurion. If you put this man off his work it might well cost you more than an aureus.'

The veteran shrugged and fell silent, watching with the same fascination as the dozen men gathered around Avidus's artist, as the slightly-built soldier nodded decisively and set to work.

'You remember the specification?'

The soldier shot Avidus a meaningful look and turned back to his work, humming a marching song to himself as he used his tools to start working the soft wax, piece by piece, first creating a flat disc three feet across and then setting to work to build a rim around its edge. Under the coaxing of his skilled hands the shape of a bucket began to grow, but unlike anything anyone present had ever seen, larger and wider than any of them could have imagined. Avidus nodded his approval as the massive cylinder grew higher by fractions. After an hour or so, with a pair of steps built into opposite sides of the bucket's inner wall, to allow a man to climb into and out of it if need be, he stepped back and took a drink of water, nodding to Avidus who barked an order at the waiting engineers.

'Lower the table to the ground. Don't touch the fucking wax!'

Resuming work, the artist began to work faster, the object of his skills seeming to sprout from his fingertips as he worked with an intensity that reduced the watchers, who had previously conducted conversations under their breath to avoid disturbing him, to absolute silence. When the sculpture was four feet high he called for a stepladder and kept working, not stopping the process of building the bucket until it was as high as a big man's shoulders. Working with swift, confident skill he crowned it with a continuous circle of eyelets that rose from the rim, their holes large enough to take a stout rope, and sturdy enough to lift it from the ground even filled to the brim with water, had they been fashioned with metal. Cotta shook his head in bafflement.

'The design looks sound enough. But how will those eyelets ever hold?'

He pointed to the base of the bucket where a single wax loop protruded to the side, apparently to allow a cord pull to tilt the bucket's rim beneath the river's surface.

'I mean, it must be obvious to anyone that such a flimsy—'

Zeno stepped away from the sculpture and nodded to Avidus.

'It is complete.'

The African barked an order over his shoulder, the men working on the wall momentarily falling silent, such was its vehemence.

'Bring out the clay!'

Abasi shared a moment of amusement with his tribune, raising an eyebrow at his colleague's unexpectedly vigorous exercise of command.

'That's a powerful pair of lungs you have, colleague. Perhaps you have missed your way in life, Centurion?'

Ignoring the levity, Avidus shouted an order at the men

emerging from the fortress gates with heavy pots, each one held between two soldiers.

'Get it covered in mud before it softens too much and starts to sag.'

Obeying his order, a pair of men started scooping cool, barely viscous clay out of the pots, slathering it onto the wax with the speed and dexterity of long practice, careful not to damage the bucket's eyelets as they worked to cover it in an inch-thick layer of mud. Relaxing somewhat as the wax disappeared beneath its cool, wet covering, Avidus strolled across to Cotta with a grin.

'The secret ingredient, of course, is the volcanic ash I took from that builder's yard in Souan. The tenth part that I ordered to be stirred into the mud will prevent that mould from cracking when we heat it.'

'Mould?'

'What, you thought I was going to try to use a wax bucket to pull half a ton of water out of the river? I said I would make a bucket *using* wax, not with wax!'

Chuckling to himself, he walked away to supervise the lighting of the fire, watching critically as his men applied bellows to encourage the charcoal into incandescent life. Satisfied with their progress, he turned away and barked out a fresh command at the fortress.

'Barrels! And get some clay on the bottom of that thing, now the sun's dried out the first layer. And don't forget the drain holes!'

His chosen man emerged from the fortress through the newly repaired eastern gate at the head of two teams of men bearing a pair of wooden barrels, one heavier than the other to judge from the way the soldiers carrying it were straining under their load. Waiting until the two barrels had been placed beside the mud-covered sculpture, Avidus gave the empty container a close inspection, taking care to ensure that the fine wire mesh nailed to one end was suitably secured by the iron strips nailed across its diameter, and that the wooden beams by which they had carried it out of the fortress were firmly fixed to its body. Nodding his satisfaction to the men who had built it, he turned his attention back to the fire.

'Perfect. Start counting and give it a good puff with the bellows every time you get to fifty, just to keep it warming up. Right, let's get another layer of clay on that bucket.'

The wax sculpture's previously well-defined shape had vanished under the successive applications of clay, but the African ordered his men to continue until it was uniformly covered by two inches of the thick Nile mud, except for a pair of holes in eyelets on opposite sides of its circumference. Waiting until the clay had lost the dark colouring imparted by its water content, baked dry by the rapidly increasing heat of the sun, which was now almost directly overhead, he tapped at the mould experimentally and then nodded his satisfaction.

'Put it in the barrel. *Carefully!* The man who breaks it can go and refill the jars with mud, and if the crocodiles don't get him, the heat will!'

Working with delicate care, two of his men lifted the clay mould, now heavy enough to make them strain with the effort as they climbed onto steps placed either side of the barrel, carefully lowering it down onto the wire mesh at its bottom.

'Get the pebbles in! Quickly now, the fire's ready!'

A team of engineers worked swiftly to fill the barrel with handfuls of small, rounded stones from the other barrel, being careful to pack them around the clay mould, and once their level reached the top of the barrel, they fixed a disc of mesh the match of the one already installed at the other end with dozens of U-shaped nails, securing it with more iron strips. Avidus contemplated the finished result for a moment before shaking his head.

'Done, for better or worse. Pray to your gods that this works, gentlemen!' He waved his engineers forward. 'Get it on the fire!'

Eight men stepped up and positioned themselves, two for each end of the bars fixed to the barrel's side, then smartly lifted its heavy weight and positioned it over the glowing coals, resting its weight on the circle of embedded posts to suspend it over the coals.

'Turn the sand glass!' Avidus turned to his forgemaster with a look of enquiry, and the heavily muscled blacksmith nodded to confirm his readiness. 'Bring out the bronze!'

'Bronze?'

The African nodded at Cotta, examining the forge's incandescent fire carefully.

'It melts at a lower temperature than iron, which means that we can heat it until it becomes liquid and still keep it enclosed in an iron-pouring bucket, unless we're stupid enough to let it get hot enough to melt that as well.'

'But where did you get that much bronze from?'

A procession of soldiers was carrying heavy pieces of metal out of the fortress, stacking them neatly beside the iron bucket that would be used to heat them until they turned from solid to liquid.

'I had Hercules, a man famously lacking any regard for the gods which, of course, makes his nickname all the more amusing, take a hammer to the statue of whatever goddess that was in the temple.' Avidus stared levelly at the bemused veteran. 'What's the matter, Cotta? You suddenly look a bit pale.'

'You . . .' The older man shook his head in disbelief. 'You're going to use the statue of a goddess to make a bucket, for fuck's sake? Nothing good can come of such a thing!'

Avidus shrugged.

'It's a risk we'll have to take, if we're going to avoid being up to our balls in angry warriors once the Kushites turn up looking for our blood.'

'And you don't think melting down whoever that goddess was is going to piss them off just a tiny bit?'

'It's a risk I decided to accept, Centurion.' Scaurus stepped forward and looked at the pieces of shattered bronze with interest. 'Whoever she was, she's no deity of mine. The Lightbringer will protect us from her wrath, so I have sacrificed to him and sought his intercession.'

'And I have prayed to the Lord my God to protect us from the anger of this false idol's worshippers. No harm can come of this.'

Scaurus graciously accepted the Christian's statement of belief with a small bow.

'And as Centurion Avidus says, it's either this or we start running from the king of Kush – although quite where we'd run to is a difficult question to answer.' He turned to look at the fire. 'How long must that mould cook for?'

They watched in fascination as the goddess's fragments were placed into a large iron pot over the forge fire, the smith using a three-foot-long iron rod with a scoop at its end to prod the bronze as it softened and started to melt. Sporadic cracking noises issued from the fire barrel, as the stones that were holding the mould upright shattered into pieces, the intense heat finding their flaws and cracking them open with its brutal strength.

'That's the fifth sand glass empty, Centurion!'

Avidus examined the barrel containing the mould critically.

'It should be ready. Very well, let's get it turned. And in the name of all the gods, don't drop it!'

All eyes were on his men as they struggled with the barrel's weight, gingerly turning it over in a shower of dust and stone fragments. A stream of hot wax poured from the lower of the two drain holes, splattering across the sand in gobbets and strands as it flowed out of the clay mould, the initial rush quickly subsiding to a gentle trickle.

'Put it back on the fire that way up and give it another two glasses, then let's have it off the heat and see what we've got. How's that bronze doing?'

Waiting until their centurion's ordained timing had been fulfilled, the sweat-soaked engineers turned the barrel over again to present the mould's top edge, crowbarred the mesh off the wooden rim and then tipped it gingerly onto its side, using heavy, padded gloves to pull the remaining pebbles from inside the bucket. Avidus stared at the clay mould with undisguised nervousness, speaking slowly and clearly as he walked around the scorched barrel.

'All we have to do now is get it out without breaking it. So we're going to take our time. We're going to take it slowly. And we're going to treat that clay like it's the most important thing there's ever been in our lives, because it is. There's no more wax, so if we break this one we're done here, understood?' He knelt, taking a grip of the clay barrel's rim, tugging it towards him experimentally. 'One of you on either side, two of you ready to get hold of the other end when it comes out.'

Working with slow, careful movements, Avidus talking continually as they extracted the mould, they placed it in the pre-dug hole with the top third protruding above the ground, its base resting in a nest of blankets to protect it from the stony ground. Placing an iron funnel carefully into one of the drain holes, having painstakingly judged by eye which one was fractionally higher than the other, Avidus stalked across to the forge and eyed the bubbling pot of bronze critically.

'Let's get pouring.'

The four largest men in his century stepped forward with a pair of long iron bars, fitting them through loops set in the forge bucket's sides, while another four picked up smaller iron pots with heavily padded handles, their hands wrapped in glove-like coverings of similar materials, and came forward with wary but determined expressions. Avidus looked around at them, raising a finger in warning.

'Remember, once the bronze is in the pouring buckets it needs to go into that mould before you can count to fifty, so don't hang around admiring the stuff, get over to the mould and get it poured, then get out of the way to let the next man at it. And take it steady, right? Molten metal will have the skin off you to the bone, if you spill it.'

Each man placed his pot on the ground in turn and waited at

a respectful distance as they were filled by the straining engineers, tipping the forge bucket just enough to deposit a thin stream of the liquid metal into the pouring vessels, ignoring the splashes of bronze spitting on the hard ground and raising thin trails of smoke from their protective leggings. Picking up the filled pots, each man in turn carried his load across to the mould and poured its contents into the funnel with deliberate care. Once all four pots had been emptied twice, Avidus stepped forward and positioned himself by the funnel, beckoning the next man forward.

'Slowly . . . slowly . . .' The funnel, heated to a bright pink by the molten bronze, started to fill with metal. 'Stop, it's full. Get the funnel out and watch out for the overflow.'

Scaurus walked forward, putting an experimental hand close to the mould's clay.

'By the gods, that's hot. How long should we wait, Centurion?' Avidus shrugged.

'We usually leave it until the mould is cool to the touch, Tribune.' The Roman nodded.

'In that case I suggest we go about the business of getting the fortress ready to resist an attack until you call us to see the results of this magic? I'm sure Centurion Cotta will have a gold aureus ready by then.'

'We are as ready as we can be to receive our enemy, gentlemen. We have enough grain and dried meat to feed our garrison for months, a supply of water that ought to prove inexhaustible . . . and which only cost us a gold aureus . . .'

Scaurus paused for the inevitable laughs, and Cotta shook his head in disgust at a subject which had, to his mind, been raised a good deal more than necessary over the intervening days since the winch bucket's forging. As the first of the baked clay had been chipped away from the bronze beneath, revealing a smooth and unblemished surface of metal, he had tossed a gold coin at the waiting sculptor and conceded the victory to Avidus with a dismissive wave of his hand. And that, he had reasoned to Marcus earlier that morning, should surely have been enough recognition of his having lost the wager. Instead of which, he had that morning found a well-executed, if a little crude, miniature replica of an infantry pattern sword by his bed on waking, evidently fashioned from a flattened and dried human stool cut to the approximate shape of a gladius. He was willing to enjoy a little humour at his own expense, he had reasoned to his smiling friend, and it was true that a man shouldn't have joined if he couldn't take a joke, but this was a step too far for the disgruntled centurion.

'Some funny bastard . . .' he had cast a dark stare at Sanga and Saratos, lurking nearby with blameless expressions, and raised his voice to be sure they could hear him, 'or *bastards*, have got too much time on his . . . or *their* . . . hands, and when I catch him . . . or *them* . . . I'll put each one of his . . . or *their* . . . little presents back where they came from!'

'We've rebuilt the gates, better than before, and armoured our walls against enemy archery, which is just as well if the stories of their prowess with the bow are to be believed. And we have both sides of the fortress that aren't bounded by ravines too steep to be a route of attack covered by a legion's artillery strength. Unless our enemy has learned the secrets of siege craft over the last two hundred years, then I'd say we have a good chance of holding out for long enough that they'll think better of the whole thing and retreat back to their own lands.'

'And if they choose not to do so, Tribune?'

Scaurus turned to address Demetrius.

'If they choose to sit under the heat of the day, and, from what I gather, the rains that come in the mawsim, determined to wait us out? I will let the twin scourges of incessant boredom and disease play upon them until the very last day possible, then sally forth and give them a battle they won't forget in one lifetime. Petronius faced similar odds when he faced them in open battle two hundred years ago and killed their king, and it was old-fashioned Roman discipline that won the day then, just as it will now.'

The men around the repurposed temple nodded grimly at their leader's bellicose sentiment.

'Trust me, gentlemen, in making our unexpected strategic advance down the Nilus and taking this place in the name of Rome, we have achieved something that the king of Meroë will not have thought possible. We have given him pause for thought, and reasons to be concerned. The last time Romans advanced into Kushite territory they got as far as the city of Napata, and defeated the enemy in a battle that put the most important temple of their religion at our mercy. I'm sure even Demetrius here can make common cause with all us unbelievers in celebrating that achievement!'

He paused while the gathered officers chuckled, the Christian acknowledging his point with a raised hand and a wry smile.

'But, as he pointed out a moment ago, the king of Meroë is likely not to allow such a strategic reverse to stand without response. Even now I expect that he is marching his army, or a good portion of it at least, in this direction, with every intention of unseating us from our perch here above the river. He will bring tens of thousands of spearmen, archers, cavalry, possibly even elephants, and he will throw them at these walls with every intention of forcing an entry and putting us to the sword. He will know, as we do, that Augustus's general Petronius held off an army of thirty thousand the last time Rome and Kush fought for control of these walls, but he will be eager to test our defences, and to discover what strength we have in the artillery that bested his forebear back then. So make no mistake, gentlemen, we are going to have to kill a great many of his soldiers before he recognises that he faces an enemy every bit as implacable as that which defeated his predecessor. Which means that you will have to harden your hearts to the slaughter of a lot of hapless men, and ensure that your legionaries have it in them to keep murdering Kushite infantrymen even when they are packed against these walls like lambs in a pen. I know that we can do this, because I've watched in horror and pride on half a dozen battlefields as my men have visited death and destruction on proud armies, and sent them away bloodied and reeling from the shock of Rome's iron fist, but I need to know that you can do the same. Because any failure of our resolve will surely result in our deaths, alone and unlamented. Harden your hearts, gentlemen, and prepare to slaughter our enemies, because at this stage there can only be one winner. And woe to the defeated!'

'Their footwork is pretty enough. I wonder how well they'd stand up to a few cohorts of real men though?'

The assembled centurions nodded at Dubnus's musing, looking out over the plain that stretched away to the fortress's east for more than a mile until it ran up against a ridge that rose a hundred feet and more. The enemy army had spent two days setting up an armed camp designed to prevent a sally by the fortress's defenders from catching them unawares, but with that task complete, were now evidently under orders to prepare for an attack. Marching out over the wooden bridges that had been laid over a defensive ditch that ran the full length of their camp's frontage, they were marshalling into formation under the gaze of a magnificently armoured horseman standing out in front of them, apparently untroubled by any potential threat from the Roman artillery as he stared fixedly at the fortress walls.

'There must be twenty thousand of them. It seems that the enemy are considering a test of our strength.'

Marcus nodded at Qadir's flatly stated opinion, the two men watching as the army of Meroë paraded on the open space between their encampment and the point where, from trial and error and the loss of a dozen or so men, they had learned was the limit of the defenders' ability to strike at them. Along the fortress wall's length, ballista crews were waiting behind the wooden shields that had been erected in front of each engine with only a small slot through which to shoot, the legionaries peeping through the gaps between their protection and talking quietly among themselves about the engagement that now seemed imminent.

'They parade tidily enough, I'll give them that. I had expected them to be little more than a mob, but credit where it's due, that's not a bad effort. They might be due a surprise though . . .'

Cotta nodded in grudging respect for the enemy army's crisply formed line, turning to the one-eyed captain of the nearest bolt-thrower's crew.

'Think you can hit them from here, Cyclops?'

The veteran grinned back at him and stroked the words "Lady Chaos" carved into the wooden body of his ballista fondly, revealing a spectacularly uneven and gapped set of teeth that was testament to his long years of service.

'With this nasty old bitch wound right to the stops, Centurion? I reckon we could drop a bolt about twenty paces behind their front rank. Was you looking for another wager?'

Cotta shook his head with a laugh, raising both hands defensively at the soldier's good-natured reference to his recent losses. 'Gods no, I've lost enough gold to the unscrupulous for one lifetime, thank you! I tell you what, though, you knock that glittering ponce off his horse and I'll give you a gold all right, just for the pleasure of imagining the look on his face.'

'There will be no targeting of the enemy commander, Centurion Lucius.'

The four men turned to look at Scaurus as he walked down the wall towards them with Abasi close behind him, the tribune's grim smile betraying the same guilt he always felt when the moment came to spring a surprise on an enemy.

'For one thing it's hardly sporting, and for another, if I allow one crew to try then all thirty of them will put their shots into him and the enemy numbers will be more or less unchanged. I want forty bolts dropping into their ranks, and then another forty, and all before they've even moved from the spot they're standing on.' He turned and looked out over the enemy army with a contemplative expression. 'It seems that the time has come to educate our esteemed foes in the art of not allowing an enemy to know one's true capability until the time has come to throw off caution!'

He raised his voice to be heard along the wall's length.

'First Spear Abasi, if you'll give the order, perhaps we might begin shooting before they start coming at us?'

Abasi saluted and turned away, raising his voice in a bellow that could be heard along the length of the fortress's eastern wall.

'Bolt throwers! Wind to full tension and prepare to shoot!'

Lady Chaos's crew exploded into action with the eager vigour of men looking forward to seeing just what their machines could achieve with their iron bow arms cranked back to their maximum tension. With the bolt thrower wound to the very limit of its ability to store their energy, they stopped their frantic efforts, their captain turning his one eye towards his senior centurion and shouting the expected signal with an arm in the air.

'Ready!'

All along the wall, crew captains were raising their right arms, indicating their readiness to shoot, staring intently at their leader as he waited until the last of them put his hand in the air.

'*Shoot!*'

Every engine along the wall's length loosed their missiles with a collective hiss and thump that made the hairs on the back of Marcus's neck stand on end, the sound all too familiar from a succession of battlefields over the previous few years. The effect on the Kushite host was immediate, akin to poking an ants' nest with a stick, the ordered formation shivering as the speeding bolts arrowed down onto the waiting soldiers without warning. The screams and unintelligible imprecations of the men on the receiving end of such an unexpected assault were faintly but clearly audible even at such a distance, each bolt's arched, whist- ling trajectory carrying enough power to kill or maim more than one of the virtually unarmoured men in the enemy ranks.

'*Again! Keep shooting!*'

The legionaries threw themselves into the task of recranking their machines, arms bulging with the effort as their engine captains waited behind them with replacement bolts. As each machine reached its maximum tension, its commander moved forward at the same moment his panting men stepped aside, smooth choreography born of years of practice. Placing the missiles onto their machines' grooved sliders, each captain looked around swiftly to ensure that his crew had ducked below the level of the bow arms, a precaution against the risk of being caught by flying debris in the event of a failure of iron or bow cord, then pulled his machine's release lever again. The thumping salvo of bolts was a little ragged, as the faster crews started to outpace their comrades, but the impact on the Kushite army was every bit as powerful as before.

'Looks like you owe someone a gold, Centurion.'

Cotta raised an eyebrow at the engine captain waiting beside him, bolt in hand, while a fresh pair of men strained to recrank his machine. The Kushite general had been unhorsed, the beast bucking and kicking in uncontrollable circles at the pain of a missile embedded in its thigh, its rider stretched full length and unmoving on the plain's rocky surface.

'Possibly so, but not you. I saw you ignore the tribune's order and still miss that poor dead bastard by a foot and more.'

Ptolemy had pushed his way to the wall and was staring out from between two engine shields with the sickened amazement of a man watching his first battle.

'Surely they must withdraw? This is pure slaughter, is it not?'

Marcus shook his head at the horrified scribe's statement.

'This is nothing more than foreplay. Each bolt might kill or incapacitate one or two men, and we are shooting forty of them at the enemy every thirty heartbeats. Were they to stand and meekly submit to our barrage they would suffer perhaps five thousand casualties in an hour, if we could maintain our rate of shooting, but they will not stand there and let us keep this up for very much longer. At any moment their commander, whoever replaces that dead man, will order them to advance.'

'To advance? Into this storm?'

'Of course. It's either that or they will be forced to pull back, and no general is going to tolerate that sort of ignominy at the start of an assault.'

Another salvo of bolts thumped out into the clear morning air, drawing a fresh chorus of agony from the enemy ranks, and an armoured figure stepped out in front of them, raising a sword to point at the fortress before them and shouting a command whose intent was unmistakable. The Kushite front line lurched into motion, spear-wielding infantrymen obeying the command to advance with commendable speed despite the withering volleys of bolts tearing into their ranks.

'How is it that these men are moving forward?'

The Aegyptian shook his head in amazement, turning to Marcus with a questioning look.

'Their lives to this day have been as different from yours as yours is from mine.' The Roman looked out over the parapet as another salvo of bolts arrowed down into the Kushite host. 'They have been drilled from their first day to obey orders, just like our legionaries. Any man who disobeys is beaten, and any man who continues to disobey is executed, in front of his comrades, to make sure the lesson of his painful demise acts as a suitable motivation to them.'

'But to march forward into this?'

The Roman shrugged.

'Doing something, doing anything, is better than standing and taking this sort of punishment. Those men will be focused on staying in line, on stepping over the bodies of their dead, on whatever chant their under-officers have started to keep their minds off what we're doing to them. And they will believe that once they are within a hundred paces of our walls they will be safe from these bolt throwers, because they will have been told that we cannot point them that low. An illusion that will be shattered soon enough. But before that . . .'

He looked around at the archers waiting behind the ballista crews, sharing a moment's glance with Qadir and nodding to the Hamian, who turned to look at Scaurus as the enemy army advanced past the markers that had been placed two hundred and fifty paces from the fortress walls. The tribune nodded his approval, and the centurion raised his voice to be heard over the constant rattle of bolt throwers being cranked.

'*Archers . . . ready!*'

The bowmen nocked arrows and drew them back, pulling every last inch of tension into their bows, waiting for the command to loose.

'*Archers! At two hundred paces! Shoot!*'

Loosing their arrows blindly over the heavy ox-hide shields, the Aegyptians drew fresh arrows from their quivers and loosed again, and again, their movements both measured and swift with the assuredness of long practice.

'They do not look for targets?'

Marcus shook his head at the scribe's question.

'No, there is no need. The enemy ranks are packed so tightly that an arrow lofted over the shields will find a target as it falls to earth nine times out of ten. And once the infantry have passed through that rain of iron, the archers following up behind them will be forced to endure the same punishment. Our bowmen can empty their quivers without ever having seen the men they are shooting at and still know that they will have hit a man with most of their shafts.'

The Kushite line came on, seeming to accelerate as it passed the one-hundred-pace marker with an understandable eagerness to get inside the effective range of the ballistas that were pecking gaps in their ranks with every twanging thump of a bolt being spat across the plain. Arrows were beginning to slap against the ox-hide curtains that protected the ballista crews, as the enemy archers advanced into range behind their infantry comrades. An arrow flicked through the gap between the two sheets of leather protecting Lady Chaos's crew and took one of the winders in the throat, his look of puzzlement turning to first horror and then panic as blood welled from the wound and poured down his windpipe. The one-eyed crew captain turned away from the

machine, barking an order at one of the reserve winders to replace
him, pulling out his dagger as he gripped his soldier by the arm
and thrust the blade unerringly up under the legionary's jaw,
felling him instantly before lowering his body to the ground with
an almost reverential gentleness. Looking up to find the eyes of
the officers on him, he shrugged.

'I wouldn't let a dog die that way, much less a tent mate. Known
him ten years . . .'

Turning back to the bolt thrower, he re-galvanised his men
with sharp, barked orders, and Dubnus tapped the goggle-eyed
Ptolemy on the arm.

'It's rude to stare, and perhaps not wise when men have just
lost a comrade?'

'But he . . .'

'You heard what he said. That was a mercy killing. That's what
men who have come to be close do for their brothers when there
is the need. You might have to grant me that release, one of
these days.'

'And would you—'

'Oh yes.' Dubnus grinned at the horrified secretary. 'Without
a moment's hesitation.'

'Gentlemen?' They turned back to find Scaurus pointing down
the wall's length. 'The enemy have reached the gates.'

Hurrying down the rampart, they found Abasi leading a group
of men forward from fires at the fighting platform's rear, each pair
holding a heavy iron cook pot between them. Their hands were
covered in heavy padding to prevent them from being burned by
the pots, whose contents were roiling with slow, fat bubbles forcing
their way up through the thick, noisome contents. From the ground
below them the roar of the Kushites railing at the gate was shockingly loud, and Marcus stepped forward to crouch behind the
parapet, steeling himself momentarily before pushing his body up
to peer over the edge. The scene below was one of chaotic purpose,
the mass of enemy infantry pressed forward against the walls on
both sides of the gate while a space remained clear in front of the

massive black wooden doors. In that clear area, the massed infantry was held back by a semi-circle of ornately equipped temple guards whose terrible authority had the soldiers shrinking away from them. A dozen heavily built men were swinging axes at the wooden doors in turn, the bright silver blades of their weapons chopping fragments away from the heavy ebony planks.

With a flicker of motion, so fast that the Roman wondered if he had imagined it, an arrow bounced off his helmet in a moment that would remain with him for the rest of his life; he ducked back behind the parapet as another flicked over his head.

'The doors are holding, but given long enough they'll cut a way through.'

Abasi looked at Scaurus questioningly.

'Shall we end their efforts, Tribune?'

The Roman nodded dourly, and his first spear turned to the two-man teams squatting beside their iron pots.

'Run to the edge, hurl the contents of your pot over the men attempting to hack away the gates and then get down before the enemy archers use you for target practice! You and you' – he pointed to the first pair – 'go!'

The two men stood without hesitation, hauling their pot forward at the run and stopping a foot from the wall, heaving its semi-liquid contents out in a viscous arc that spattered the ground below with a sticky, boiling mixture of sand and animal fat. The axemen screamed in agony, their first bellows simple astonished outrage at the sudden incandescent pain, as the boiling fluid scalded their half-naked bodies, the screams that followed increasingly desperate as they fruitlessly scrabbled to remove the boiling sand that was continuing to flay their skin.

'Torch.'

Abasi held out a hand to take a burning brand, stepping up behind an ox-hide curtain and peeping around it momentarily to toss it into the middle of the thrashing axemen. The oil, puddled in the rocky ground's slight dips and already heated close to the point of its volatility, ignited with a crackle, and three of the writhing bodies were instantly wreathed with flames as the oil covering their bodies caught light. The tightly packed body of infantrymen pressed up against the wall shivered, as those that could see the agonies being experienced by the burning men before them began to cast anxious glances up at the wall, and Abasi looked back at Scaurus questioningly.

'Use it all, First Spear. Now is not the time for restraint.'

At the Aegyptian's command, the men waiting with the remaining pots came forward, pushing aside the curtains to empty their contents down onto the men hemmed in against the stonework below. One of them jerked with an arrow's impact and fell headlong from the wall, taking the pot he was carrying with him and nearly dragging his comrade over in his wake, but his falling scream was lost in the howling din of the infantrymen caught under the scalding rain. More torches were tossed over the wall, and within seconds, dark, oily smoke was billowing up as the Kushites' layered linen armour caught fire and turned the deadly mixture's victims into human torches. Marcus peered over the wall again, his stomach roiling at the smell of burned hair and flesh, shaking his head in horror as a dozen or more men, unable to scream as they lived out their last, agonised moments, staggered aimlessly among their comrades, who pushed them away in terror of suffering the same fate, then fell to the ground as the fire overcame them. No horn sounded, but no signal was needed to tell the Kushites to retreat; a sudden headlong dash away from the walls by those men closest to the defences swept the remainder of the army back towards their starting point. Abasi turned to the ballista crews, who had for the most part stepped forward to peer past their ox-hides at the horrific spectacle below, barking an order that was heard along the length of the wall.

'Who told you animals to stop? Keep shooting! Shoot down anyone trying to stop them from running!'

The archers, resupplied with refilled quivers by soldiers running to and from supply points in the streets beneath the wall, bent their bows and lofted arrows high into the air above the retreating army, their missiles falling indiscriminately among the fleeing infantry, while the ballista crews obeyed their leader's barked order and shot their foot-long bolts at any man attempting to stem the frantic tide of the enemy retreat. Scaurus looked around the shield behind which he and Marcus had taken shelter from the Kushite archers' sporadic harassment, then stepped out from behind its cover as it became evident that the enemy bowmen were no longer in any position to shoot up at the walls.

'They won't stop running until they're all back in their own camp. How many do you think we killed?'

'More than a thousand. Perhaps twice as many as that.' Cotta had joined them at the parapet, looking down at the scattered bodies of the dead and wounded. 'It's not the numbers that matter though, is it? We're never going to be able to kill them all, and even if we could, they probably have more men available. The point is that they won't come at us again in a hurry, not knowing that we can slaughter them like that.'

Avidus climbed the last steps up onto the fighting surface, coming from the direction of the gate.

'How did your new doors stand up to the attack, Centurion?'

The engineer nodded contentedly.

'Better than I expected, even after all the problems we had cutting the planks to size. The damage they managed to inflict before you set fire to them is minimal, pretty much. They won't be battering their way in here any time soon.'

Scaurus nodded, looking out over the strewn corpses of the enemy dead, grimacing as a blood-covered infantryman close to the walls, more corpse than man, falteringly raised a shaking hand in a familiar gesture, extending a thumb at his own throat in a silent plea for a merciful death.

'Indeed. We can only hope that they have sufficient fellow-feeling for their brothers-in-arms to come and retrieve them for a decent form of farewell to this life. And wonder what their next means of attack will be.'

★

'Here they come!'

The ballista crews leapt to their feet from the places where they had been sitting, playing dice and knucklebones, or curled up against the parapet to catch some sleep after the exertions of the day. Fed and watered at their weapons, they had waited for a second attempt on the fortress walls that had not materialised, and, with the sun sinking slowly into the west behind them, the advancing Kushites were perfectly illuminated. Two thousand strong, they were marching slowly, apparently weaponless, out onto the plain before the fortress, stopping when the man at their head barked a terse order without breaking his own stride.

Abasi walked to the wall's edge and stared hard at the advancing Kushite for a moment before shouting an order to his men.

'Track him, but do *not* shoot! I'll wield the scourge on any crew that looses a bolt at him myself!' He turned to Scaurus and Marcus. 'I suggest we see what he has to say for himself, before we decide whether to turn him inside out.'

The single figure walked steadily across the field of dead and dying men, one or two of them raising a hand to beckon him, diverting from his path towards the fortress gate only when forced to do so by a knot of bodies that seemed to have been cut down at the same moment by the remorseless flail of the defenders' artillery. He came to a halt twenty paces from the gate and looked up at the officers gathered on the wall, his bearing confident and erect. Dressed in shining armour, his helmet and the individual scales were inlaid with gold, and the hilt of his sword appeared to have been made from a solid billet of the precious yellow metal. His shining armour and black skin were clean, with no trace of the bloody rout that had been inflicted on his army hours before.

'It's not exactly the demeanour one might expect from a defeated enemy, is it?'

Scaurus stepped forward, Qadir motioning a pair of his men to flank him with their arrows nocked and ready to draw.

'Have you come to discuss terms on behalf of your king, officer of Meroë?'

The Kushite barked a laugh, his reply as dismissive in tone as if he were addressing a servant. His Greek was fluent, if heavily accented, the speech of a man taught the language by his own people, and from an early age, Marcus mused.

'I am Tantamani, Roman, priest of Amun, altar-master of Meroë and the leader of my ruler's army! In beneficent concern for all our people, I have been bidden to retrieve the bodies of our dead, so that we may mourn their loss and give them a fitting funeral! I assume that you will allow this!'

He stared up at Scaurus and waited for a reply to his assertion, and after a moment the tribune replied in an amused tone.

'I will, on this occasion! You were not to know that we would kill so many of your men! The next time, however . . .'

The Kushite waved a hand dismissively.

'And why would you imagine that we would be stupid enough to come at you in the same way a second time? Already my officers are discussing other ways to evict you from our property, and you will discover in due course that the army of Meroë is every bit as inventive as you seem to be!' He walked slowly over to the blackened remains of the men who had burned to death in front of the fortress gates, turning one of the carbonised corpses over with the toe of his boot. 'You have done a good job of preparing to repel our attacks, I will admit this freely! A man who cannot learn from the successes of others is doomed to repeat his own mistakes for the rest of his life! And we recognise the skill that you have exercised in outflanking us down the river, and making this place fit to defend! But we are not famed for our patience!'

He turned back to the men standing above the gate, putting his hands on his hips in a gesture of supreme confidence.

'There is an offer of peace on the table before you. You have only to swallow a little pride to be allowed free passage back down the river to your new border city of Koptos, carrying your arms honourably. You only have to agree to pass under a yoke and promise never to return to the lands ruled by Meroë, and you will all live to fight for your empire on another battlefield. Refuse, and we will simply hold you here until you are forced to surrender from simple hunger! Or possibly thirst! Accept this generous offer before it is replaced by another, whose terms will ensure that you never see your homes again.'

Scaurus stared down at the general for a moment before replying, shaking his head slowly.

'Put yourself in my position, Tantamani of Meroë. Can you honestly say that you would be willing to walk out of here and retreat back to the north, if you were me?'

The magnificently armoured general shrugged.

'We both know our duty. And we both serve rulers who would never consider retreating from such a contest. I simply came to offer you a means of escape one last time, before we retrieve our dead and grant mercy to the dying. What you do with that offer is for you to consider, not me.'

Scaurus nodded.

'And I thank you for your consideration of our likely fates, if we remain within this fortress. Not that my men's well-being is either any responsibility or concern of yours.'

'As I expected. And hoped. You will all die here, Roman, every one of you. Some quickly, some not.'

The Kushite general shrugged and turned away, raising his voice to roar a command in his own language at his waiting soldiers, who began to fan out across the corpse-strewn plain in pairs to collect the dead bodies and carry them back to their own lines. The Romans watched him walk back across the bloodied ground, still looking to neither left nor right and evidently uninterested in his men's bloody task.

'I can only imagine the resolve necessary to rise to the top of such an army. That man must be as hard as the ebony that made our gates impenetrable.'

Abasi stared after the receding figure with a hard expression.

'He spoke the truth, I believe. They may find other ways to come at us, but ultimately their strongest weapon is time. All they have to do is wait.'

'I can't believe they're actually going to try it. Surely any attempt to attack us from the river can only be suicide?'

Scaurus nodded at his first spear's incredulous statement, staring down from the north-west corner of the ramparts at the Nilus's gentle curve, the river's course stretching away into the lands downriver until it was lost from view in the heat haze. In the middle distance a flotilla of ships was forming up against the eastern bank, lines of oarsmen marching aboard to take their places on the rowers' benches. As each ship was crewed, it pushed away from the bank and turned north, just as had been the case for every one of the five days which had passed since the fleet's arrival from the south, the ships passing unseen but not unheard in the night. Behind the watching officers the winch was hoisting another bucket full of water up into the fortress, the encouraging shouts of the centurion commanding the men whose strength was turning the capstan underlaid by the rhythmic thudding of the capstan's ratchet mechanism, a sound the Romans had learned to ignore, so familiar had it become over the past month.

'I would imagine that those sailors are skilled enough – after all, they are, to judge from the various commentators, a riverine people. But will they retain those abilities when their ships are on fire, their captains dead and wounded, and half of them are lolling over their oars with arrows in them? I've seen the best the Roman navy has to offer over the last few years, and I can just imagine what the tribune commanding the Praetorian fleet would say if he were ordered to attack this fortress.'

Abasi snorted.

'You know as well as I do, Tribune, that if he were ordered to sail his fleet off the edge of the world, he would have no choice but to do as he was told. And neither do these poor fools. Whatever it is that their commanders plan will reveal itself soon enough, though. Although I'm sure you've noticed that there's been no sign of any infantry boarding being practised.'

Marcus looked down at the river, two hundred feet below them, allowing his practised eye to pick out the potential landing points, and the approaches to the fortress walls that would have to be braved.

'I would assess the odds of their being able to attack us success-fully from the river as being less than one in fifty. If they were to reach the only point of any value in an assault, at the bottom of that ravine, and attempt to unload soldiers to attack up that climb, then that attack would be into the teeth of our bolt throwers and archers. It would surely be suicide. As must be evident to their general, I would have expected.'

'Indeed.' Scaurus stared out at the line of vessels parading away down the Nilus. 'And yet some plan or other has made them spend the last month gathering what looks like most of their naval strength on the river. And they're rowing away downstream to conduct some sort of exercise where we can't see them, which I take as an indication that whatever it is they're planning will come without warning and be some sort of coordinated manoeuvre that needs to be perfected before they can unleash it on us.'

He looked up and down the lengths of the western and northern ramparts, both studded with a bolt thrower every twenty paces.

'Sixteen engines. Will that be enough, I wonder?' The walls facing the river had been reinforced by the doubling of their artillery quota on the day that the Kushite vessels had first been seen on the river to the north, and Scaurus had ordered the iron pots used to heat up the rendered animal fat to be moved across the fortress with the reinforcements. After a moment's thought he nodded decisively. 'Have another four machines moved to this wall, First Spear. Do it now, and do it quickly. There is a fresh purpose to the way those ships are manoeuvring that makes it seem as if they might mean to do some business today.'

The senior centurion saluted and turned away, bellowing orders for four crews to start disassembling their machines' iron frames for their movement around the fortress's broad ramparts. Scaurus turned to Marcus and pointed down at the river to the north, as worried as the younger man had ever seen him.

'Stay here and watch out for whatever it is that they seem to be planning, Centurion. The first spear and I will go about our morning rounds as usual, to let the men of the legion see that we consider ourselves to be the masters of this situation. Whatever it may be.'

Marcus saluted and watched as his superior walked away, the imperious senior centurion at his side.

'I'll miss Abasi, when the time comes to get out of this flea-infested shithole of a province.'

'Really, Cotta?'

The veteran scowled at Dubnus's amusement.

'What, will I really miss him, or is this really the most disgusting of all the places I've ever been sent to fight in the empire? Both.'

'It's not all that bad.'

'It really is. It was the last time I was here and it still is today. Too hot, too dry, too Greek . . . and now we can add "too African" to the list. I mean, how are we supposed to hold that lot out there off ad infinitum? I know we can hold them at arm's length for as long as we want to, but there's only so much grain in the stores and they don't show any sign of getting bored with waiting us out, do they?'

The Briton shrugged.

'There's a lot that can happen in the time we have left. But I was really asking how it is you're going to miss Abasi, if we do get out of here? For one thing, he's just the sort of spit and shine officer that you usually despise, and for another, you know as well as I do that he'd have you by the balls if he even suspected that you were *that* centurion. The one who killed—'

'Thank you, you oversized Brit. There's no need to be repeating that, not here, not now and not ever again. And as to why I'm going to miss him? Just look at the man.'

All three of them looked down the rampart's length to where

Scaurus had stopped to talk with the crew of a bolt thrower, Abasi looming behind him with his gaze fixed on the engine's captain in what they knew from experience would be a uniquely forbidding manner.

'It isn't often you meet a man who can intimidate just by breathing, but there he is. I always thought Julius was a warrior king among his men, but that man is the king of kings. The men of his legion fear him, and they hate him, but most of all they worship him. There'll be more tears shed for his passing among the old sweats of this collection of donkey-botherers than when the emperor dies at the hands of some catamite or other, because he and he alone gave them their pride back. No, I have to say that I—'

'Centurions?'

They turned at the nearest ballista captain's tentative enquiry.

'Soldier?'

He pointed over the wall to the north wordlessly, and Marcus strode to the parapet and stared hard upriver.

'The Kushites seem to have got themselves into some sort of formation. And they're rowing upriver. *Tribune!*'

Scaurus hurried back up the wall's length and looked out over the river with a frown of concern.

'It looks as if our esteemed enemy has worked out what it is they sailed all these ships down here for. But I'm damned if I can see what it is that they're planning. Hurry up those additional machines, if you can, please, First Spear?'

Abasi saluted and turned away, roaring encouragement across the fortress at the men working to disassemble their bolt throwers so loudly that several of the closest engine crew started visibly. Marcus and Cotta exchanged knowing looks, but Scaurus's concern with the developments playing out before them on the river was too great to allow for the humour of the moment. He stared at the enemy naval force as it rowed upriver towards them, still well out of bolt range but closing the distance with every well-drilled stroke of their oars.

'They've packed those ships in twenty abreast and five deep, like a riverine infantry line.' His brow furrowed in thought. 'It's almost as if . . .'

'As if they know that we'll start dropping fire bolts onto them the moment they're in range, and they want to give us too many targets to shoot at?'

Scaurus nodded at Marcus's opinion.

'Those are the tactics of a commander willing to lose some ships to get the others close enough to the fortress to do . . . what?'

They watched in silence as the enemy fleet worked its way upriver, Cotta grinning at Marcus despite the tension as Abasi strode back down the northern rampart behind the sweating crews of the relocating ballistas, his non-stop tirade of encouraging invective scourging any man that he deemed not to be giving his all to the task. Rushing to the indicated positions, the legionaries placed the bases of their machines down on the rampart's stone flags and set to bolting the shooting mechanisms to them.

'The first crew to be ready to shoot gets a silver apiece from my own purse!' The labouring men cheered distractedly at Abasi's unexpected largesse, while the waiting crews around them rolled their eyes in disgust at the newcomers' apparent good fortune. 'But if their first bolt doesn't fly long, straight and true then they'll be paying me back! With interest!'

'They'll be in range shortly, First Spear.'

The big man nodded at Scaurus's warning, stepping back to address the western wall's defenders.

'Bolt throwers! Load fire bolts!'

The crews leapt into action, heavily muscled winders labouring to force their strength into the machines' iron bow arms while other men took the first bolts from the racks in front of them, their slotted heads already loaded with folded strips of linen. Dipping the cloth into pots of warmed animal fat, they waited for a moment to allow the excess oil to run back before fitting them to the waiting engines' iron frames, stepping back and raising their arms to signal readiness to shoot, the men entrusted with the lighted tapers with which to set fire to the oil-soaked bolt heads moving forward into the spaces they had vacated. Abasi waited as the Kushite ships crawled inexorably up the river below them, calculating by eye the likely best range of his artillery.

'Bolt throwers! At maximum range! Target – enemy ships! On the command to shoot, aim for the middle of a target, light your bolts, let fly and then keep shooting!'

He waited a moment more, then nodded to himself and shouted the command for which every man on the wall was waiting.

'*Shoot!*'

The first volley sailed out over the river leaving greasy trails of smoke from their burning loads, arching down into the enemy fleet's leading ships at the furthest extent of their range. At least half fell into the water, vanishing with barely a trace, the better aimed or luckier shots striking home with immediate and dramatic effect as their oil-soaked cloths spattered burning fluid across whatever they hit. In every ship that was struck, men scrambled with buckets of river water to douse the fires that had been started, flames eagerly spreading across timbers made bone dry by long exposure to harsh temperatures and direct sunlight. Marcus watched in fascinated horror as one vessel's rowing benches disintegrated into chaos, as rowers sprayed with burning oil scrambled for the ship's sides in their desperate haste to dive into the Nilus's cool waters, heedless of the threat lurking beneath the water. Robbed of its motive power on one side, while the opposite benches continued rowing with all their strength, the ship veered to the left and collided with its neighbour, a chorus of distant screams reaching the watching Romans as the other vessel's oars were smashed abruptly forward, their butt ends smearing the hapless men working them across their benches.

'Keep shooting!'

The first of the relocated ballistas loosed its first shot, and a moment later the rest of the machines that could bear on the oncoming fleet loosed a second ragged volley. Their aim adjusted, with the benefit of the initial shots to guide them, the bolt-thrower captains struck harder than before, almost every shot striking home into timber or human flesh, and the Kushite sailors worked feverishly to extinguish the fires that threatened to engulf their vessels if not dealt with immediately. Despite their efforts, a handful of the enemy fleet were already ablaze, their crews steering for the banks on either side or simply abandoning ship and swimming for their lives to the closest vessels.

'Those poor bastards! They're being sacrificed to no purpose!'

Cotta shook his head in horror as the swimmers were beset by ravening crocodiles, heedless of the oncoming ships in their eagerness to take such helpless prey, but Scaurus pointed down at the oncoming fleet with an urgent shout.

'No, they're not! *That's* why they're making this attack!' On the decks of the ships not yet affected by the bombardment from the fortress's defences, men were pulling canvas covers away from machinery that had been concealed beneath their drab colours to blend with the vessels' lines, crews hurrying to man and bring them to bear on their intended target. 'It's not an assault, they have a different intention!'

Marcus stared out over the parapet at the advancing fleet, watching as the enemy bolt-thrower crews aimed their weapons up at the fortress towering over them.

'But what can they hope—'

At the roared command of whoever was commanding the fleet, the Kushites launched their first shots, aiming not for the defenders atop the walls, but at a point slightly below them. Each missile trailed a line of smoke, the Kushites having clearly decided to use the same tactics that were being exercised against them. Marcus leaned over the wall's edge to look at the bolts' point of impact, and, as the missiles impacted on the stone around the water hoist in short-lived puffs of flame, the realisation of what the Kushites' plan was came to him.

'They're trying to set a fire and burn out the hoist!'

Throwing himself at the nearest set of stone steps down into the street below, he sprinted for the entrance to the chamber in which the hoist mechanism was mounted, with Abasi and Cotta at his heels.

'You men!' A work party of a dozen legionaries, sweating profusely as they carried jars of grain from the nearest store to one of the bakeries that had been set up around the fortress, goggled at the sight of their senior centurion sprinting towards them. 'Put those jars down and follow me!'

Bursting through the door into the airy, open-fronted chamber, the centurions saw the direct evidence of what it was that the Kushite naval attack was intended to achieve. Two bolts from the first salvo had found their mark, and burning oil had sprayed across the wooden frame of the winch gear. Stepping cautiously forward while Abasi and Cotta lunged for the jars of water fortuitously positioned to provide refreshment for the hoist crew, Marcus risked a glance over its edge to confirm what he expected would be the case. More of the warships were coming into bolt range, labouring up the river with their oarsmen working as hard as they could, and on the decks he could see jars of oil alongside the bolt throwers. He pointed to the bucket, perched neatly at the platform's edge, shouting a warning to Abasi.

'If they burn the winch out we'll lose the bucket into the river!'

Abasi flicked a glance at the massive bronze bucket.

'And it's too heavy to move! You' – he pointed at the closest of the legionaries – 'go and tell Centurion Petosorapis to bring his century here, now, and to bring all the water jars they can find! The rest of you, get ready to beat out the flames if they score any more hits!'

The soldiers did as they were bidden, advancing into the chamber cautiously just as the second salvo of bolts started snapping off the stonework around the hoist room's open side, the first to sail cleanly through the wooden frame hammering into the cable drum and spraying it with flecks of burning oil, the second hitting the man who had reached up to suffocate the smouldering spots on the tightly coiled rope. Already dying, he shrieked inhumanly with the last breath in his body as the greasy tunic he was wearing ignited with a crackle, staggering away from the hoist as his body became a short-lived human torch, then fell to the stone floor and writhed with the agony of his seared skin, the chamber filling with the stink of his burnt hair. Cotta drew his sword and stepped forward, looking down at the dying man for a moment to pick the right spot to strike before stepping in and expertly delivering the mercy stroke.

Marcus looked down again, grimacing as a bolt arched down from the walls and, by some fluke of air and wind, flew cleanly into the pot of oil on the deck of a ship in the middle of the formation, igniting its contents even as it flung them across the rowing benches behind the bow-mounted bolt thrower. The ship was ablaze in an instant, burning men leaping over its sides in all directions as it veered off course and sailed into its neighbour with the last of its momentum, setting light to its timbers in turn. Both vessels, blazing furiously and without any means of propulsion, drifted slowly back down the river and into the heart of the enemy formation, herding the ships following them to left and right to avoid their deadly embrace. Presented with such inviting targets, ships packed so tightly on either side of the burning wrecks that it was almost impossible for their shots to miss, the crews on the wall above whooped at the destruction they were wreaking on the Kushite fleet. Their bolts slammed down into the enemy fleet's packed mass, raining unforgiving fire into the chaos of the disordered ships beneath them.

Peto arrived at a dead run, leading dozens of his men into the stone chamber, pairs of men carrying heavy jars of water between them, and Cotta strolled to join Marcus with a look of grim satisfaction, flicking the dead legionary's blood from his sword and sheathing the blade.

'Looks like we've weathered this one, doesn't it? Might be best not to stare out at them like a pair of fools though. It's not the bolt with my name on it that worries me, it's the one marked "to whom it might concern", right?'

Marcus smiled at the old joke, nodding his agreement as he turned and walked away from the chamber's open end with his friend and mentor a step behind him. And in the days that followed, as he replayed the scene a thousand times in his mind's eye, each time questioning what he could have done differently to prevent what happened next, he never once managed to see a way in which the terrible fluke could have been avoided. Hearing a sonorous clang, followed instantly by a loud grunt, he was in the act of turning to look back at Cotta when the veteran fell heavily against him, almost bearing him to the ground. Barely managing to hold the other man's weight up, he twisted and looked down to his friend's eyes to find them tight with pain and confusion.

'What . . .'

Putting an arm around the veteran's waist, something hard poked into his skin, and he turned the older man over onto his side as he lowered his body to the floor. The tail of a bolt was protruding from his scale armour, barely six inches of its length visible, with the remainder buried in his friend's body.

'What . . . is it?'

The lie came shockingly easily, an instinctive untruth to protect his oldest friend from the dreadful reality of what it was that had just happened to him.

'Nothing too bad. You just need to rest for a moment.'

Cotta looked up at him, snapping back into lucidity, the realisation that he was dying in his eyes. Struggling for breath, he shook his head in disbelief at the suddenness with which he had been felled.

'Bullshit . . . I always knew . . . you'd end up . . . being the death . . . of me.' He smiled into Marcus's consternation, his face deathly pale, his eyes starting to lose their momentary focus. 'And I never . . . regretted my choice . . . to follow you.'

Abasi loomed over the two men with Peto at his shoulder, shaking his head in dismay at the veteran's wound.

'You go to meet your gods, Centurion, and your ancestors.

Greet them with pride, for you have fought well. No man could ever say you wanted for courage, could they, Centurion Cotta of the Third Legion Gallica?'

Cotta grimaced up at him as a wave of pain shook his body.

'*You . . . knew?*'

The Aegyptian nodded, his gaze hardening.

'Of course I knew. Did you think that just because we stopped sending men after you in Rome we gave up all interest in you? Your association with this man' – he gestured to Marcus – 'has long been known to the men who have dragged this legion back from the brink of disaster and ridicule that it sank to after you killed our emperor. And you confirmed our knowledge with your careless use of words that my centurion here recognised as having been used by our emperor's murderer, even a decade later. Not to mention a narrowing of the eyes whenever my men mention your old legion in their marching songs.'

'*And . . . yet . . .*'

'I didn't call you out? Or have you knifed in the back? This is the best legion in the army, *Cotta*, faithful to the emperor unto death, and we had a task to perform. Had you lived to see it completed, then you and I would have had a day of reckoning, I expect.'

Cotta wheezed breathlessly, and after a moment Marcus realised that he was laughing.

'*I've . . . cheated . . . you . . . of . . . your . . .*' he coughed explosively, blood spattering the stone floor in front of him, '*. . . revenge.*'

'Perhaps.' The big man nodded dourly. 'Or perhaps I have simply lost a man with whom I might yet have declared friendship. Go well into the underworld, Cotta, and hold your head up when your ancestors look you in the face.'

He touched Marcus on the shoulder fleetingly and then turned away. Cotta coughed again, more convulsively, then stiffened in agony at the pain. He fought to raise his body to stare out of the chamber's open end.

'*Dying . . .*'

Marcus lifted his friend to let him see over the platform's edge, and Peto knelt on one knee beside him, his right hand moving from forehead to chest, then touched his left and right shoulders in turn.

'Go to God, friend, and tell of the good you did in this life. May you be admitted to heaven, to live among the righteous, where you belong.

'Fat . . . fucking . . . chance . . .' The dying centurion coughed again, spattering his armoured chest with blood. *'Should . . . have . . . realised . . . you . . . were . . . one . . . of . . . them . . .'* He convulsed, a rivulet of blood running down his chin. *'The . . . Greek's . . . new . . . boots . . .'*

Turning his head, he looked at Marcus with unfocused eyes that were almost empty of any sign of life, his last words little more than a hiss of dying breath.

'Wasn't . . . just . . . Flamma . . . loved . . . you . . . like . . . a . . .'

The last word was little more than a wheezed exhalation of his final, blood-scented breath.

'Son.'

'How did he die, Valerius Aquila?'

The scribe waited expectantly, the tip of his stylus poised over the pristine layer of the smooth, soft wax of a fresh tablet. Marcus shook his head tiredly, staring out over the rampart at the remnants of the Kushite fleet straggling away downriver towards their moorings.

'Pointlessly.'

Ptolemy frowned, the writing instrument unmoving.

'Surely you must realise that I cannot write that word in an official record of this campaign, Centurion. You are as aware as I am that the Roman public will expect such a loss to be . . .'

His momentary pause to select the right adjective was all the time a grim-faced Dubnus needed to pounce.

'Heroic? No, a noble sacrifice, is that better? Why don't you write that our friend's death was a fine example of the Roman fighting man at his best, uncaring of the risks when the empire's pride is at stake.'

'That's inspired, Centurion, exactly . . .'

The Aegyptian's praise dried up as he looked up from the tablet's wax and realised that the Briton's stare was unmistakably hostile.

'Our friend died defending a meaningless pile of stone that we will abandon to the enemy the moment it has served its purpose.' Marcus shook his head in renewed dismay. 'He was killed by the grossest of flukes, and when the battle was already won, by a bolt that struck the bronze water bucket and was directed into his back, where it penetrated his armour and lodged in his liver. My oldest surviving friend died for no purpose, and without ever seeing the means of his death.'

Ptolemy tipped his head to one side in thought, the birdlike pose that under other circumstances would have been the usual source of amusement to the friends.

'I see. Valiant to the last, he was felled by a last despairing shot from the enemy fleet that most cruelly rebounded from a metal bucket and dealt him a mortal wound. Expiring, his last words were . . .?'

Marcus looked up at him, dead-eyed.

'Write that he was proud to die for the empire. And then get out of my sight until my urge to put you over the wall for the crocodiles to feast on has abated.'

Recognising the barely restrained anger in his friend's clenched fists and slitted eyes, Dubnus took the protesting scribe by the arm with a grip that made the Aegyptian wince and forcibly led him away, explaining the facts of Marcus's relationship with his dead friend in a hissed whisper.

'The two of you were very close?' The Roman turned to find Demetrius behind him. 'I have no desire to be put over the wall and will happily withdraw if the subject is too painful.'

'I can speak of it. Indeed I have learned that discussing those we have lost helps to manage the pain of their loss. That, and other less conventional remedies.' He turned away from the view, turning his back on the straggling Kushite ships drifting back downriver. 'I met Cotta when I was only a boy. He had performed bodyguarding services for my family, and my father tasked him and a champion gladiator to teach me the skills of the arena and the legion. The gladiator gave me his guile and trickery, taught me to fight with two swords and coached my natural speed by investing it with the memory of a hundred thousand repetitions.'

He fell silent, and after a moment the Christian prompted him with a gentle question.

'And our friend Cotta?'

'Cotta . . . Cotta gave me something else. Where the gladiator was encouraging, he was challenging. When I needed to have the grim facts of life pointed out to me, he was the one to do so, like any good centurion would. They were playing roles, of course, I see that now, but at the time I hated him with a disgust as strong as any recruit for his first centurion. But he saved my life.'

Demetrius stayed silent, allowing the younger man to continue in his own time.

'When my family was murdered by the emperor's thugs, my father had the foresight to send me away to Britannia, temporarily out of their reach. But that respite would have been of no consequence had he not sent me to a friend, a senior officer in the province's army. And even that would have been of little avail if I had not got lucky on the road and met a man just like Cotta, who took me to an auxiliary cohort on the northern frontier and found me a place as a centurion.'

'You entered the empire's service as an officer?' Demetrius pursed his lips in something between surprise and disbelief. 'That must have been . . . challenging?'

'Every bit as challenging as you can imagine. But I survived it, with the help of my friend over there . . .' He nodded at Dubnus, who was, from the look of his stance, looming over the Aegyptian in a manner best described as overtly intimidatory, busy explaining the facts of military life and death to a dumbstruck Ptolemy. 'And all those years of Cotta's conditioning to help me. I was a soldier before I ever joined the First Tungrian Cohort, I just didn't know it.'

The Christian nodded his understanding.

'There is something more, I suspect?' Marcus looked at him questioningly. 'He was your last link with your previous life. The last man to have shared the time before your family's murder.'

'He was.'

Marcus fell silent again, and after a moment Demetrius sighed.

'This will not comfort you now, Centurion, but I would have you know it, and believe it, for the peace it will bring you. Your friend, if he was a good man, will have ascended to heaven to join Our Lord Jesus and his father, the almighty God of all that ever was and all that ever will be.' He raised a hand to forestall any response. 'I say this not as any sort of effort to take advantage of your grief to attempt a conversion to my religion. That will come in its own time, when the inevitable truth of my beliefs become your truth. I simply offer you that unchallengeable fact to give you whatever comfort you might take from it.'

The Roman shook his head with a slow, sad smile.

'I hope you're right, although I sincerely doubt it. But if you are, it is to be hoped that your god has a sense of humour. That, and a tolerance for bad language.'

II

'It seems that the Kushite general actually meant what he said.'

Demetrius was standing alongside Marcus, who had the second watch of the night, both men staring out over the dark expanse of the eastern plain. In the ten days that had followed since the abortive attempt to deny the defenders the use of their water hoist, no further effort had been expended on capturing the fortress. An uneasy truce of sorts had settled over the two armies, one camped like a powerful but frustrated beast, while the other sat inside impregnable walls and husbanded its slowly shrinking supplies.

'That they'll look to starve us out?' The Roman's tone reflected his uncertainty that such a plan would be the Kushite's primary course of action. 'Possibly. Although I can't shake off the feeling that there's more to him, more to that army as a whole, than just taking the most pragmatic approach.'

The Greek nodded his agreement.

'Indeed. After all, what king wants to sit idle for months, starving his enemy into submission, when some bright boy might come up with a clever way to achieve the same result without all the waiting around? Kingdoms, it seems to me, are like beautiful wives. You do well not to leave them unattended for months at a time.' He grinned at Marcus in the light of the torches that were illuminating the wall's broad fighting platform. 'No king wants to leave his kingdom unguarded for as long as this siege will take, when there are plenty of other threats to his rule, any of which might boil over like an unwatched pot if ignored for long enough.'

The Roman shook his head in mock admonishment.

'You're very free with your metaphors tonight, Christian. Is that what passes for wisdom in your church, that a woman needs to be shepherded to keep her safe from being led astray?'

Demetrius opened his hands as if to protest, but was interrupted by a breathless interjection from behind the two men.

'Centurion, there's something happening down on the river!' Marcus turned away from the view across the silent plain to find a soldier standing rigidly to attention. 'Centurion Dubnus sent me to get you!'

He followed the man down the steps and into the fortress streets below, passing the empty temple which was now a legion century's billet like most other buildings in Premnis, mounting the steps on the other side to find Dubnus leaning out over the parapet with his head cocked to one side.

'I'm not entirely sure that wall was built with your sort of weight in mind?'

'*Quiet!*' The big man ignored his friend's jibe, resuming his position and listening intently to the dark river below. 'There's *something* down there. You . . .' He waved a hand at the waiting soldier. 'Your fidgeting is putting me off, now fuck off and get Abasi!'

Marcus leaned out over the wall and listened for a long moment in total silence.

'I can't—'

Something moved on the water below them, the river's black ribbon nothing more than a complete absence of light, the sound somehow at odds with the natural susurration of wind and water.

'There!' Dubnus nudged him with an elbow. 'Did you hear *that*?'

'Yes.' The Roman stepped back, thinking fast. 'There's something down there, all right. Perhaps a small boat with muffled oars. But what can they hope to achieve when there's two hundred feet of almost sheer cliff to climb and a legion waiting for them at the top?'

Abasi appeared at his side, as immaculately turned out as ever, and not for the first time Marcus found himself wondering if the man slept in his uniform and equipment.

'This man said you wanted me. What is it, Centurions?'

'Movement on the river, First Spear. Probably a small boat, possibly a covert approach of some kind. Although to what end isn't clear.'

'Or it could just be a crocodile.'

'That too is possible.'

'But we'd be fools to ignore it, whatever it is, wouldn't we?'

Marcus nodded.

'I believe we would.'

'So, what do you propose we do? Dropping torches would work well enough to illuminate the ground on the other side of the fortress, but all we can achieve on this side is to extinguish the torch before it has the chance to show us anything, either from the drop itself or when it falls into the river.'

'A pair of men can ride down to the riverside, if we use the water bucket.'

The big Aegyptian stared at him for a moment.

'You propose to have yourself lowered down, to the river, in a bucket made from the melted-down statue of the river goddess? Do you have some sort of urge to defy the gods as many times as it takes to get yourself killed?'

Marcus met his eye and held the gaze, shaking his head slowly.

'You're accusing me of having a death wish, First Spear. Whereas the truth is that I am concerned with little more than performing my role to the best of my abilities. Whether or not that results in my death is of supreme disinterest to me. *Sir.*'

Abasi pursed his lips, clearly fighting to prevent himself from laughing.

'It's an unusual situation, for a man who has spent all his life using the title "sir" as a form of admonishment, to find himself having the same trick pulled on him, and, to make it worse, by a man who is in many ways his superior in life.' He took a step closer, standing so close to the Roman that Marcus could smell the onion on his breath. 'And in the relative privacy of here and now, with only your friends to bear witness to such a remarkable act, I can overlook it. Even be amused by it. But I assume that you do not plan to repeat insolence of such a breathtaking nature in front of the more impressionable of our colleagues?'

Marcus nodded.

'Your assumption is a safe one to make, First Spear. And forgive me, my urge to fight had the better of me.'

The Aegyptian nodded, patting his shoulder.

'A good thing, in a soldier, but officers need to understand that their role is to command, to direct, and only in the last moments to draw their sword and seek the enemy's blood. So let us pick a suitable soldier and—'

'With respect, First Spear?'

Abasi raised an eyebrow at the prospect of a further difference of opinion.

'If it *is* with respect, Centurion, you may speak.'

'I agree with all you say.' Dubnus stifled a laugh, still staring out over the river's black expanse. 'Even if, as my comrade is attempting to communicate, I have been guilty of throwing myself into the enemy on more than one occasion. But my point is a different one, if I might make it?'

'Go on. Make it quick.'

'We need the very best soldier available to do the thing I propose. The best swordsman, the best intelligence. Whatever it is the enemy are doing down there may be a matter of subtlety, and not easily discerned. And if our soldier's presence is detected, then whoever he is will need to be gifted with his weapons to survive. And with respect, First Spear, I believe I match both criteria more closely than any other man under your command. And so I submit myself for the task, knowing that I am our best chance of its success.'

The Aegyptian shook his head in disgust.

'Very clever, Centurion. Abandoning emotion and substituting logic was always likely to succeed. As it has. Very well, if you're set on this, we should get it underway before I change your mind for you.'

Demetrius took a step forward, coming to a slightly incongruous attention.

'And, with equal respect, First Spear . . .?'

'What do you want, Christian?'

Demetrius bowed.

'I cannot salute you, as I am no longer a centurion. But had you seen me when I *was* a centurion, you would have seen a kindred spirit, of sorts. But where you are as straight as a fifty-mile road, I was more . . . complex. And not, you can be assured, a good man. Which is why I seek every opportunity to restore my sense of self-worth when it presents itself.'

'And you want to go with him? What use would an old man like you be?'

The Greek grinned.

'More use than you might imagine, First Spear. I was death incarnate, when I wore the crest. I killed without hesitation, without remorse, and with consummate skill. My last act in uniform was to kill six men, and in the time you might take to properly discipline a slovenly soldier. And trust me, I still have all that deadliness bottled up inside me, ready for the day that I need it.'

'Which ignores the fact we already have a man to ride the bucket down to the river, however foolhardy that might seem.'

'One man, First Spear, is no men, if that one man can be approached from two directions. My brother-in-arms here will need a man to stand back to back with him, if he is to return from this task he has chosen to undertake.'

Abasi looked at the two men with the expression of a man discovering himself to be the victim of a confidence trick.

'Did you two discuss this before my arrival?'

'No, First Spear.' Demetrius shook his head in denial. 'Centurion Corvus had no expectation of my urge to accompany him down to the river. And neither did I, until a moment ago. But you know that what I am saying is logical. I am nobody, just a religious oddity, and I am volunteering to sell my life dearly if it will enable the Centurion to escape with his own, should circumstances turn against us down there. And I do not believe that it is my turn to die. Not yet, and not here.'

'You're ready?'

Abasi looked dubiously across four feet of empty air at the two men, grimacing at the way the massive bronze bucket was rocking slowly from side to side from their exertions in climbing into it.

'We're ready, First Spear. And I for one am happy simply to have got into this container without falling to my death. Nothing can match that for terror, not even if the entire Kushite army is waiting for us at the bottom!'

Marcus grinned at his comrade's dour tone, looking around to meet his eye and seeing the same light of determination that had animated the Christian in the moments before their attack on the riverbank scouts. Pressed back to back into the water bucket's close confines, the two men had already undergone the precarious process of inching out across a stout plank secured to the platform by heavy iron bolts and climbing into its smooth-sided confinement while poised over a two-hundred-foot drop. Marcus's heart had pounded as he had grasped the smooth metal rim with all his strength and clambered over it into the relative safety of its interior, knowing that the gently sloping rock face below would tear a falling man to shreds before dumping him into the crocodile-infested river, at best more dead than alive. Abasi shrugged, uninterested in the Greek's humour, holding up the signal cord that would play out between his fingers and be their only means of communicating with the winch house other than, in extremis, shouting at the top of their voices.

'Very well. Hoist crew, lower away.'

With the ratchet mechanism disengaged the bucket started to fall, its descent only controlled by the strength of the dozen soldiers allowing the winch capstan to turn at no more than a slow walking pace. The softly illuminated winch house seemed to climb away from the two men, as the hoist lowered them smoothly through the first dozen feet before the bucket contacted the wooden channel that had been fitted to the rock face, to allow it to progress smoothly down to the water. As the bucket's base touched the wood, a soft scraping noise that Marcus had little doubt would be audible from the river began, an unmistakable signal to anyone below that the bucket was being lowered.

'They'll know we're coming.'

Demetrius turned and spoke into his ear to be heard over the continuous scraping of metal on wood.

'So much the better. Anyone who would seek to disrupt my mission to bring the good news to these benighted barbarians needs to learn that I am ready to meet their challenge with sword and flame.'

As they continued to descend, the riverbank began to resolve itself into a faintly visible silhouette against the stars, and Marcus stiffened as he caught sight of a familiar outline.

'Look! Is that a ship?'

Demetrius craned his neck to look in the direction that Marcus was staring in.

'Hard to say. Let's stop the bucket and take a proper look?'

Marcus tugged on the signal cord, and after a moment's delay the descent abruptly halted. In the sudden silence the river's gentle sounds of lapping water were all that could be heard, and after a moment Marcus shook his head in frustration.

'I can't hear anything, and I can no longer see what I thought I had seen.'

'Nor can I.' Demetrius blew out a long breath. 'Let us proceed, but more slowly.'

The Roman tugged three times, the signal to recommence

lowering but at one third of the speed, which in turn lowered the volume of the bucket's friction against its wooden channel somewhat, but still left the two men effectively deaf. As they descended towards the river, Marcus stared intently at the spot where he thought he had discerned the shape of a boat against the river's dark surface.

'There!'

Unmistakably triangular in shape, defined against the backdrop of stars, the mainsail of a river boat was moving slowly downriver.

'It might just be a trader, looking to pass the fortress in the safety of the darkness.'

The Roman conceded the possibility with a terse grunt.

'Or it might be a Kushite naval vessel.'

Marcus looked down, realising that the narrow path along the riverbank, and the hole that had been dug to allow the bucket to drop cleanly into the water, were coming up below them.

'We need to stop!'

Tugging the cord again, the two men scrutinised the barely visible ground a dozen feet below them, neither man finding anything to give any cause for concern. Marcus shook his head in bafflement.

'Nothing, and nobody to be seen. Perhaps this is all just a little paranoid, after all.'

Demetrius shrugged.

'Your instinct was that there was something to investigate, and I say we go with your instinct. Let us continue to the ground and see what there is to be seen.'

Signalling for a very slow rate of descent with another three tugs of the cord, and a further single pull as the bucket's base touched the water, the two men used the steps built into the bucket's interior wall to propel themselves over the rim and onto solid ground. Marcus let go of the cord and left it dangling inside the bucket, examining the ground around him in the starlight for any sign of interference.

'There are bootprints!'

He skirted the bucket's bulk to join Demetrius, dropping to one knee to explore the ground the Greek was indicating with his fingertips.

'These marks are wet. Whoever made them has been in the river. Either that or . . .'

Demetrius reached out a hand to stroke the ground at their feet.

'Or working with mud!' He pulled at whatever it was that he had found, unearthing a length of rope the thickness of his wrist that had been hidden from view under a thick coating of river mud. 'I see their plan!' He pulled at the rope, dragging more of it from the closely packed mud that had been used to conceal it. 'They have laid a noose around the bucket hole, and do you see this . . . ?' He raised a knot that had been allowed to fall into the water. 'It is a slipknot. They planned to allow the bucket into the water and then to drag this trap tight, closing the noose around the hoisting rope above the bucket. And this rope is strong enough, with a big enough team of beasts, to pull the winding gear out of the hoist room!'

Marcus set down his sword and drew the dagger from his belt.

'In which case . . .'

He cut through the rope with a few swift sawing strokes of the short blade, tossing the severed noose into the river to remove the threat.

'And now let us return to the fortress and inform—'

With a sudden patter of feet on the path's hard-packed earth, there were soldiers approaching them on both sides, sprinting down the bank towards the two men, their previous stealth completely abandoned. Marcus sheathed the dagger and took up his sword, Demetrius shouting a command that made him lunge for the dangling cord.

'Send the bucket back! I will hold them off!'

The Roman tugged frantically at the cord half a dozen times and then stepped back as the bucket ascended swiftly into the darkness, setting himself to face the oncoming enemy infiltrators even as he drew breath to roar a warning up at the men above.

'They were trying to capture the bucket with a rope noose! Check the ground around the hole before you—'

A spear-armed man leapt at him out of the darkness, a barely discernible shadow whose black skin was matched by the colour of his tunic, and Marcus met him face to face, turning his spear's point aside with the spatha's long blade and then gutting him with the gladius. He threw the dying man into the water with a splash that he knew would excite the attentions of the crocodiles that routinely basked on the far bank, setting himself to deal with the attackers who would inevitably follow. Demetrius added his voice to the warning, his parade-ground roar rising over the unintelligible shouts and imprecations of the men driving their assailants forward.

'They made a noose for the bucket! Don't lower it again until you know th—'

A wave of men overwhelmed the Greek, pushing him face down into the mud even as he put his sword through his first attacker's throat, leaving Marcus alone against attackers approaching him from both sides, men hurdling the bucket hole to close inexorably on the spot where he waited, his bloodied swords raised in warning. An attacker came at him from the left, staggering away with a yelp of pain as the Roman punished his advance with a swift thrust of his gladius into his thigh, but the opening was all the time that the men on his other side needed to strike. Something hit his helmeted head hard enough to make his ears ring, and as he turned, inexorably slowly, it seemed, he was punched to the ground by a powerful blow and then smothered by bodies as both of his swords were stripped from hands numbed by the blow. In the indistinct light a silhouette loomed over him, a fist raised, and when the blow fell he saw no more.

'Wake up, Roman!'

Marcus barely registered the sting of the slaps that were being administered to his inner thighs, although a part of him knew that the pain being inflicted on him was being reduced by his weak grip on consciousness rather than any restraint on the part of whoever was striking him. His recollection of the period since he had been felled by the Kushite soldiers was tenuous at best, flashes of memory in which he had been carried onto a boat and dropped on its wooden deck with a sword at his throat, then slung over the back of a horse, powerless to move such had been the completeness of his incapacitation. An intense point of discomfort replaced the ache from the blows, the prick of an iron blade's point against the root of his phallus.

'You are awake, now get to your feet or I will use this knife to carve off your manhood and feed it to my hunting dogs!'

Forcing his eyes open, Marcus found himself face to face with a black-skinned man whose shaved head was covered by a gleaming gold helmet, his face vaguely familiar, and it took a moment's mental effort for him to realise that it was Tantamani, the Kushite general who had approached Premnis's walls after the abortive assault on the fortress. His face was contorted in disgust at some odour the Roman could not smell as he stepped back, gesturing insistently with the dagger's blade. Getting to his feet from the canvas floor of a tent, its interior barely visible in the scant light that was penetrating its thick walls, Marcus looked around him to find soldiers posted on all four sides, their ceremonial swords drawn and gleaming palely in the half-light. Standing, the soldier sheathed his dagger and barked an order over his shoulder. A pair of what appeared to be slaves, as much from their fearful demeanour as the speed with which they obeyed his command, came forward with a pail of water and a towel of sorts, and their master pointed at them.

'You have soiled yourself. Use the water to clean yourself, then wash your tunic.'

He watched impassively as the Roman did as he was bidden, waiting until Marcus had donned the damp tunic before speaking again.

'You are a prisoner of the kingdom of Meroë. You were taken on the battlefield by our men, caught in the act of an attempt to prevent us from denying the fortress of Premnis access to the river's water. An attempt that failed. Your fortress is without water now and will soon fall.'

He fell silent and stared intently at Marcus, waiting to see how the Roman would react, but Marcus simply shook his head in response, his voice still weak from the effects of the blow that had stunned him.

'I don't think so. The last time I saw that bucket it was vanishing up into the darkness. And there's no way they'll have let it back down without checking for your clever little traps first.'

The soldier stared at him impassively.

'I see that you are not to be deceived. But that might end up being your final downfall.' The Kushite shook his head dismissively. 'After all, if I cannot fool you into telling me what I need to know, I might as well have your throat cut, here and now.'

Marcus stared back at him, refusing to be the first man to break eye contact.

'You will do whatever you feel is necessary, I would imagine, given your position.'

'I will. As a general of Meroë and the master of my ruler's army. It was I who masterminded the strategy that took your port of Berenike, and I will deal with this small inconvenience in whatever way produces the fastest results.'

The Roman shrugged.

'If you are the master of strategy for this army, then it was also you who allowed us to take Premnis, deceiving you into marching north while we slid past you to the south, up the bank of the river Nilus. And as for *strategy*, I don't believe there was much tactical genius needed to take the port, was there? One five-hundred-man cohort was all you faced, a force so small as to represent nothing more than a minor obstacle to your advance, a reflection of Rome's expectation of peace with an old ally. As generals go, you're hardly in the same league as Alexander, are you?'

The Kushite's eyes narrowed at the insult.

'And you are hardly in any position . . .' He paused, and then smiled wryly. 'Ah. Yes, I see your game. You seek to provoke me into killing you, here and now, because you fear torture.'

Marcus shook his head gingerly.

'No. You mistake disinterest for bravado. Kill me now, kill me later, spare my life . . . it matters little enough.'

'You would have me take you for a fatalist?'

'I would have you recognise me for what I am. A man whose life has been dulled by the loss of one he loved above all others, and whose interests in that life have been blunted accordingly. Kill me now and send me to join her. I will not complain.'

The dark-skinned officer nodded thoughtfully.

'Truly, a fatalist. Perhaps I will have more luck with your comrade, before you are both submitted to imperial justice for your crimes against Meroë.'

The Roman laughed tiredly.

'I wish you the very best of luck with that one. If you think I'm a fatalist, wait until you see how he responds to the choice of betraying his comrades or being executed.'

After a long period of sitting on the uneven floor, prodded back into an upright position every time he tried to lie down by one or other of the spearmen surrounding him, what little light that was managing to enter the tent through its walls and the slightly open door flap dimmed to almost nothing, and was replaced by the meagre illumination of a small lamp, carefully placed well out of the prisoner's reach. Eventually, as Marcus was nodding with his body's need for restorative sleep to repair the harm done to him during his capture, the flap was opened and Demetrius thrust through it to fall on his knees. Tantamani followed him through, pushing the Christian into the circle of guards. His face was bruised, evidence of the violence with which he had been overwhelmed the previous night, but other than the marks of that initial beating, he bore no other signs of having been brutalised.

'You have told the truth in at least one matter, Roman. This man is possessed of a death wish no less strong than your own. Indeed he seems to embrace the idea of what he calls *martyrdom*.'

Demetrius rolled over onto his back with a groan.

'An uneducated barbarian like yourself would not, of course, know the meaning of the word.' He ignored the Kushite's scowl, continuing in the same hectoring tone. 'The word martyr, oh most esteemed enemy, in my language, Greek – which is of course the language of civilisation – means *witness*.'

Tantamani shrugged, turning away to examine the tent's interior with ostentatious care.

'If you seek to infuriate me, you will have to try harder than that. After all, it is not I that has allowed himself to become a captive, forced to wash himself in front of unfriendly eyes.'

The Greek laughed, unable or perhaps unwilling to control his amusement at their captor's verbal tactics.

'You think this is demeaning? You clearly wouldn't last an hour in a legion century! From the moment you join as a soldier, to the day that you manage to climb far enough up that slippery pole to get a crest and a tent to yourself, you wash your arse in front of your mates. And even if they've sworn to fight to the death alongside you, they'll still take great joy in pointing out every tiny thing about you that will make the rest of them laugh – and so you do the same to them, of course. You lot watching me wash the dried piss off my skin was about as troubling as you offering to give me a good tickle.' He shook his head in affected amusement. 'So, to return to the subject we're discussing, to be a martyr is to bear witness to the one true God, and in the act of giving one's life for him, and suffering the tribulations of that death for him, to shout belief in him to the world!'

The Kushite general raised a pitying eyebrow, shaking his head in a way clearly intended to express sympathy.

'Which would be noble, were your beliefs rooted in fact. But the fact is that there is more than one god. A whole pantheon of gods, and this we know to be true from the teaching that echoes down the centuries from the days when Kush ruled as far north as the great sea and into the lands that border it. My god, Amun, has ruled supreme over the other deities since before the earliest days of Kush, as Lord of the Thrones of the Two Lands, and it is he who oversees the crowning of our kings at Jebel Barkal, the holy mountain, where they are also laid to rest at the end of their lives, to be watched over by Amun in the next life.'

'A false god, who—'

Tantamani overrode Demetrius with contemptuous ease, his booming voice filling the tent with his power.

'The cult of my master Amun is the power that enables our kings to rule! We priests appoint them, we counsel them, we tell them when the time is right for war, or for peace! We manage their estates and foundries, we teach the arts, writing, mathematics, architecture and astronomy, sciences to rival any knowledge known to Rome!' His tone softened to that of a teacher, saddened by his pupil's lack of understanding. 'And yet, follower of your vaunted Christos, we tolerate and even encourage the worship of many other gods. Under Amun, creator of all that is and will ever be, are Geb, the god of the earth, and Nut, the goddess of the skies; Isis, goddess of motherhood; Osiris, god of the kings; Seth, the god of devastation; and Ma'at, the goddess of order and righteousness. It is Ma'at's laws that govern them all, for she is the goddess of truth, and from her we have learned our binding rules of law, morality, order and justice. Which is more than can be said for your empire, if the stories we hear from men who have travelled to the city of Alexandria are to be trusted. And at least we do not worship dead men, unlike your insistence that your emperors ascend to godhead when they die. It might amuse you to know that the head of a statue of your so-called god Augustus is buried under the temple steps in our city of Meroë, so that every man who attends to worship walks upon him. A god, indeed . . .'

The Greek smiled knowingly at him, and in the moment before he spoke, Marcus knew that the next words out of his mouth would condemn them both to death without any hope of mercy.

'Very clever. And yet, for all your pride, you are not the only people who can use a statue for their own purposes. I have watched the graven image of one of your false goddesses be broken down to provide the metal with which our water bucket was forged. And I rejoiced, priest, as I saw that graven image reduced to molten metal, rejoiced at the destruction of something so unholy!'

Tantamani's eyes narrowed in disbelief.

'You lie! No man could be so foolish as to so despoil the statue of a goddess!'

He turned to address Marcus with a look of barely controlled fury.

'Is this true, Roman? And if so, what was your part in it?'

'It is true. And while I had no direct part in it, neither did I try to prevent it. I am a follower of Mithras, not the Christian god, so I neither delighted in the act nor considered it a crime, but simply an act of necessity.'

'*Necessity?*' The Kushite was incandescent in his anger, spittle flying as he put a finger in Demetrius's face. 'You found it necessary to destroy one of the most sacred objects in the kingdom? I will have you flayed for that, your guts dropped out for you to contemplate in the brief moment before you are pulled in two by horses and your separate parts strewn across the desert for the vultures! From this moment you are a dead man waiting in terror for his own demise! I will see you executed, both of you!'

He turned to the door.

'I will leave you now and give you the time to reflect on the means by which you will die, alone and unlamented. I promise that you will die screaming for mercy, and calling out the name of the goddess you have insulted in a plea for forgiveness!' He stopped at the tent's flap. 'You wish to die, to be a witness to your god's power? Your request will be granted more fully than you could ever have hoped! I say that when you die, as punishment for your usurpation of our fortress of Premnis, it will be as a witness to his impotence, not any illusory glory that you might ascribe to him. Think on that. And prepare yourselves!'

'There's still no sign of the enemy making any use of our comrades?'

'No, Tribune.'

Scaurus reached out and put a hand on Dubnus's shoulder, the Briton nodding his thanks for the gesture of consolation. He had been standing on the wall since dawn, not even taking his eyes from the enemy camp to accept the food and water brought to him by Qadir, ignoring the burning heat of midday to keep his gaze fixed on the place where he knew his friend must be, close to the cluster of tents that had to be the Kushite king's headquarters. With the sun sinking towards the horizon, his attention was undiminished, his stare as intent as it had been half a day before.

'Well, that's something, at least. If their king had intended using them to encourage us to surrender, or just to exercise his frustration at not having succeeded in his plot to remove our ability to take water from the river, I expect he would have done so by now. And doubtless he would have done so at a point just outside ballista range.'

A pair of bolt throwers had been manned on either side of the watching centurion, their crews waiting under canvas awnings for the call to perform a task that would combine the granting of mercy with the deaths of respected men.

'You think they'll attempt to use Marcus and the Christian as hostages?'

Scaurus shook his head.

'To what end? They must know there's no way that we'll be convinced to surrender a position this strong for the sake of two men. Especially given that one of them is a religious oddity whose motives in having accompanied us here are somewhat questionable. If I were the man commanding that army, to be brutally honest with you, I wouldn't have the first idea of what to do with them.' He glanced at the Briton, whose face was set in grim lines. 'Once they've finished trying to get information from them, that is.'

Dubnus grimaced.

'And we both know that Marcus will never talk. While the Greek is more likely to be goading them, in hope of getting himself killed in some inventive way that'll get his name into the records.'

'Indeed.'

Both men looked out over the wall for a moment before the Briton spoke again.

'They're going to kill them both, aren't they?'

Scaurus sighed.

'In all probability, yes, I expect that is what will result. They're not like us, you see? We have centuries of culture behind us, philosophy that informs our morality, and standards of behaviour that apply across the civilised world. But barbarians like these? They can only be put in the same category as all the other peoples that ring the empire, forever hating us for our wealth and success, and treating each and every prisoner as an opportunity to express that frustration in the basest of ways. By all means hope for your friend's release, Centurion, but harden your heart in readiness for his death. Because to be frank with you, that is my expectation.'

'Awake, barbarians!'

Marcus sat up, bleary-eyed, starting as the point of a spear pricked the skin of his neck. He stared up at Tantamani's looming figure as the general tossed a pair of clean tunics on the canvas floor in front of the two prisoners.

'If I wasn't awake before, you can be sure that I am now. Has the time for our execution arrived? Surely a swift and clean death would be the better option for a civilised people such as you claim to be, but if you're handing out fresh garments, I can only imagine that there's an executioner waiting somewhere nearby.'

The Kushite shook his head.

'No, Roman. Once again your prejudices have the better of whatever reason you might once have possessed.'

'Perhaps it's been beaten out of me.'

Tantamani laughed.

'I like you, for the fact that you retain a sense of humour even under such trying circumstances. And no, even though I take your comrade's act of sacrilege as needing to be expunged with his own blood, the time for death is not yet upon you. I have been commanded to bring you before the ruler of Meroë, who wishes to lay eyes on men so ungodly in the hope of learning more about your people, and I am in all things the servant of the throne. So put on your clean clothing and ready yourself to meet with the most important person in both our worlds. But heed my warning, both of you . . .'

He slid a long blade from his belt, raising it for them both to see clearly in the tent's dimly lit interior.

'You will show the appropriate respect, no matter what occurs. You will keep your eyes on the floor at all times. You may not look upon the regal presence, and you may not speak, either. And be in no doubt . . .' he stepped forward, putting the knife within a foot of Marcus's face, the shuffling of booted feet telling the Roman that his escorts were ready to strike with their spears at any sign of resistance, 'I will carve Amun's name on the man who dares to cross me in this! Now wash yourselves, and dress, and do it quickly! It does not suit the ruler of all Meroë to be kept waiting!'

Washed and clad in the clean tunics, which to Marcus smelt faintly of incense, they were shepherded through the camp under the watching eyes of the soldiers that they passed, some hostile, some merely curious, Tantamani explaining their different reactions as he walked close behind them with a hand on the hilt of his sword.

'To some of these men you are little more than an oddity, paler of skin than anyone most of them have ever seen. To others you represent the death or maiming of their comrades. Were I to turn you loose among them, that would be your execution right there. Would that suit you, follower of the Christos, or did you have something more memorable in mind than being torn to ribbons by a pack of baying infantrymen?'

Demetrius wisely chose not to respond, and after another hundred paces, following a weaving path clearly intended to disorient them, the two men were admitted to a magnificent tent whose wooden floor was perfectly flat, the large open space brightly lit by dozens of lamps, and whose canvas was masked with fine materials. At one end of the tent was a dais with a golden throne placed upon it, a semi-circle of statues gathered behind it. The same scent of incense hung in the air, and, noticing Marcus inhaling the air deeply, Tantamani nodded his recognition of the Roman's reaction to the heady perfume.

'You are in the presence of Amun and all his family. The incense burns here all day, to honour and thank him for holding his protective arms over the kingdom. Now, stand here, look at the floor and do not speak, under any circumstances, without my permission. You have been warned. Now cast your eyes to the floor in readiness for the presence of the Kandake!'

Marcus frowned in surprise at the title.

'Kandake?'

His only answer was a fierce whisper, delivered so close to his ear that he felt the Kushite general's hot breath on his neck.

'*Silence!*'

Absolute quiet fell, filled a moment later by the measured footfalls of someone approaching the two men across the tent's wooden floor, the click of metal-capped heels on wood growing louder until, even with his eyes averted, Marcus saw a pair of polished boots come into view. The feet they contained were evidently small, their leatherwork intricately chased and decorated with gold inlays, while a pair of equally ornate scabbards hung beside their wearer's richly woven leggings.

'*These* are the men who were captured by the river during your latest abortive attempt to cut off their water supply, Tantamani? Dangerous barbarians who can only be presented for inspection with sharp iron at their necks?'

The voice was hard enough to belong to a king, a ruler whose word was respected as that of the gods themselves, but its tone was lighter than a man's, with a hint of amusement in its tone.

'They are, my Kandake!'

'They don't look like warriors. One of them is old enough to be my father, the other somewhat lacking in any sign of any danger.'

'True, my Kandake, and yet between them they killed three of our men before we overcame them, and another will never wield a sword for you again.'

'Did they now? Then there must be a good deal more to them than meets the eye.'

The booted feet advanced towards them, and Marcus felt the point of a knife against his throat.

'Be very still, Roman.'

The knife's point pressed upwards to dimple the skin under his jaw as the boots' wearer appraised the captives. A faint smell of perfume reached his nostrils, underlaid by the smell of horse sweat and leather.

'I can discern nothing while they stare at the floor like slaves in the market. Raise your eyes, Romans, and let me see the men you really are. And take your knives from their throats, Tantamani, they hardly pose any threat to me with their bare hands while there are thirty swords within a dozen paces.'

The man behind Marcus tensed, the movement almost imperceptible and yet unmistakable in the tent's charged atmosphere, then stepped back a half-pace.

'You may look upon the Kandake, barbarians. Do so with respect, and remain silent, or I *will* cut your throats!'

He looked up to find the Kushite ruler barely outside of arm's length, her gaze fixed directly on him. Standing behind her and on both sides were close to a dozen bodyguards, all women, hard eyes sweeping the men facing them for any sign of a threat. Armed with long spears, their armour and weapons were, like their queen's, black with silver ornamentation; each of them was equipped with swords and knives, with a small, round shield designed specifically for spear-fighting held in each woman's left hand.

'Yes, it is a shock, is it not?' The woman's expression was amused, her eyes brilliant emerald fire in an ebony face. 'You were expecting a king, regal and powerful, the man who has ripped a piece from your empire and taken it for his own. And now here I am, only a woman. You may speak, unless the shock of my sex has stunned you into silence?'

She stared at him with a raised eyebrow, clearly awaiting a response.

'I am bedazzled by your presence, Kandake, but not so much so that I am unable to reply. And yes, with all due respect to your regal achievements, I was expecting a king.'

'And?'

'And I bow my head with respect for your royal presence, Queen . . .'

Tantamani spoke from behind him.

'Amanirenas. On ascending to the throne the Kandake was advised by the gods, speaking through her priests, to take the name of her illustrious predecessor, the ruler who forced Rome to come to the negotiating table and left with the spoils of her victory undiminished.'

Marcus nodded his understanding.

'A queen who chose to become an ally of Rome, and whose successors sent horsemen and archers to the empire's aid in time of need.'

The queen stared back at him levelly.

'I have considered your empire over the years of my rule, in the ten years since my older brother died and left this burden to me. Rome is sadly diminished, it seems to me, weakened by the plague that swept the world and took my brother's life along with millions more. Your grip on your lands has been weakened, both by that blight and by your fool of an emperor, a man who fritters away the fruits of your dominion on entertainments and whores. Rome was once strong, an irresistible force with whom Kush made common cause as a mark of respect, and from necessity, but now your empire is no longer fit to enjoy the benefits of lands that were ours long before your emperor Augustus triumphed over the men of Aegyptus.'

Marcus returned her cool stare in silence, unsure as to an appropriate response, but Demetrius spoke out into the quiet despite the threat of the knives at his back.

'The blessings of the Lord Almighty be upon you, glorious Kandake! I bear the good news of his kingdom in heaven, bought for all peoples who believe at the cost of his only son's sacrifice on the cross.'

The queen raised an eyebrow.

'You are one of this cult of the Nazarene . . . what are they called now? Ah yes, I have it, you are a follower of the Christos?'

'Yes, Kandake, and—'

Amanirenas raised her hand with a flat palm towards him.

'Be silent, Christian, lest my guards mistake your prattling for an attempt to convert me to your beliefs, and murder you to prevent such disrespect. I may not keep lions to execute my prisoners, unlike my namesake, but my amazons are every bit as dangerous as the fiercest beast the first Amanirenas kept for the purpose. I call them my lionesses, and they are sworn to serve me unto death. Your death, if need be.' The Greek fell silent, exchanging glances with Marcus as the queen clicked her fingers in summons. 'Bring forth my holy man! Let us see what he makes of these barbarians.'

The tent's occupants waited in silence as a small, stooped man was escorted into its airy space by a pair of soldiers who, each holding one of his arms at the elbow, supported his progress towards the queen with gentle solicitousness, never seeking to hurry him as he paced slowly to his mistress's side. The queen went down on one knee to look up into her priest's face, speaking in their own language rather than Greek. He bowed as deeply as his bent frame allowed and shuffled closer to Demetrius, who met his questioning gaze with a direct stare and his customary smile.

After a moment's consideration of the Christian, the priest shook his head brusquely and barked a comment at Tantamani, his voice suddenly stronger than before, his tone one of warning. The queen laughed softly, shaking her head in amusement.

'Anlamani tells me that he discerns nothing of any god in you, Christian, but rather the ruthless spirit of a warrior. You are, it seems, a killer of men. He has warned my guards to be additionally vigilant in your case. And he reminds me of the fact that your faith shows no tolerance for any worship other than of your own god, and that if you had your way, our temple to Amun would be emptied of his presence, and wholly devoted to your empty promises. I believe that silence might be your wisest course from here.'

Turning away from the Greek, the priest momentarily locked stares with Marcus, his eyes widening involuntarily. Stepping closer, he reached out a hand and placed it on the Roman's face, whispering words under his breath. Nodding slowly, he lowered the hand and straightened painfully to look into the younger man's eyes for a long moment, his clear, hard gaze belying his stooped, painful frame. When he spoke, it was in slow but perfect Greek, his tone that of a genuinely surprised man.

'The mark of the goddess Nephthys is upon you, Roman, for those with the eyes to see. How is this?'

'You should answer his question.' Amanirenas smiled, evidently amused at the turn of events. 'Who knows, it might keep you alive a little longer?'

Marcus shrugged.

'I met a holy woman in Germania, a country far from here. She rescued me from the despair that ruled me after my woman died, and returned me to life by means of a herb potion that made me dream.'

The priest shook his head.

'This priestess you speak of was only a vessel for the goddess. She is the sister of Isis, goddess of birth, and sister-wife to Seth, the master of war. It is she who cares for the spirits of the dead, and for those who mourn.' He reached out to touch the Roman's face again. 'With so many tears waiting to be shed, and your woman dwelling under her wings in the afterlife . . . how could she not be drawn to you?' He raised the hand higher, touching it to Marcus's forehead, his eyes widening with shocked realisation at whatever it was that he sensed through the contact. 'You are truly gods-touched, Roman! You have been healed! It was Nephthys who bade you to live anew. I see it in you, you have been blessed by her power.'

He turned away and spoke to the queen with an animation that was at odds with his frailty. Amanirenas bowed to him and gestured to the tent's door, watching in silence until he had left the tent.

'My priest tells me that you are a man of honesty, as transparent to him as the air itself. He says that there is a purity of purpose in you, and that you are more dangerous than your companion . . . and yet more trustworthy. He believes that the goddess would never have touched a man who was not pure of heart, and he believes that your word is to be accepted as the truth. He tells me that you will not break a promise once it has been given. Whereas your fellow prisoner, he tells me, is a fanatic, a man whose mind is closed to any path but the one he has chosen, and he is marked for death.' She turned to Tantamani. 'Remove the Christian from my presence. I will speak with this man and see what light he can shed on our foes in the fortress.' Dismissing him with a wave of her hand, a gesture which seemed to elicit a momentary and swiftly concealed irritation in the general, she turned back to Marcus. 'Walk with me, Roman.'

Her bodyguard fell in around her, their entire attention focused on the Roman's every move.

'I would apologise for my lionesses' somewhat daunting behaviour, but we both know that the men who rule your empire in place of the man who should be doing the job would not hesitate for a moment to order a centurion just like you to kill me. Would he?'

Marcus smiled wryly, keeping his hands by his sides with deliberate care.

'I have read the same books as you, Queen, where an officer of my seniority is often chosen as the ideal assassin. And no, Kandake, if it would end this war in Rome's favour, then my tribune would not hesitate for an instant to issue such an order.'

'And there was something hidden behind that answer, was there not?' She stopped walking and looked him up and down. '*Are* those your orders? To allow yourself to be captured in the hope of getting close to the enemy ruler?'

'No, Kandake.' He shook his head, unable to prevent himself from smiling. 'It wasn't your veiled accusation that made me smile – but the words "a centurion like you" are grimly amusing to a man in my circumstances.'

The queen raised an eyebrow.

'Intriguing. You can explain that to me once I have shown you what it is that you face.' She led him up the slope, stopping at the ridge's crest as the sweep of her army's encampment came into view. 'All you have faced this far is a part of my strength, now you may despair at the might of my clenched fist.'

The party topped the rise, and Marcus stared out over the wide plain that stretched away from Premnis. The fortress was well over a mile distant, a squat ochre rectangle on the skyline, and, in the space between their vantage point and the maximum extent of the bolt throwers' ability to project their deadly missiles, the Kushite army was encamped. The ground beneath the cliff was black with soldiery and their equipment, a sea of tents that seemed to extend almost to the horizon. The queen's herald raised a shining horn and blew a single, piercing note that seemed to galvanise the men below them. As one man they stopped whatever they were doing and turned to face the cliff, soldiers streaming from their tents and raising their arms in salute to their queen. The horn sounded again and the army replied with a roared salute to their ruler which was repeated twice more before the men below them went back to whatever they had been doing before the horn's summons.

'Impressive, isn't it?' The queen extended an arm to gesture out over the sprawling encampment. 'Tens of thousands of men stand before you, much of my fighting strength. I left enough soldiery to ensure that my new port of Berenike could not be retaken, if this were some sort of ruse to tempt me away from my conquest and allow some other part of your army to strike without warning.'

She turned to Marcus with an appraising gaze.

'Although I do not believe that to be the case. I think that the men hiding behind those walls of mine are all of Rome's strength in Aegyptus, or all that can be spared at least, and all gambled in one roll of the dice.'

Marcus remained silent, carefully composing his face so as to give the queen no clue as to the accuracy of her surmise. After a moment she smiled, as if his very silence had given her the information she sought.

'Not that I left you very much alternative but to play this most desperate of gambits, given your lack of choices, but I expected to receive some warning of any move south. Instead of which, the men who were set to watch that route were found dead. Was this your doing, chosen one of Nephthys?'

Marcus nodded.

'I had some part in it.'

She stared at him coolly.

'My soldiers disinterred their comrades who had been sent to watch the river from the graves that had been dug for their long sleep. An act for which I am grateful. Some enemies . . . even some allies . . . might have left them for the carrion birds, rather than grant them that dignity. And in doing so, they discovered the bizarre fact that one of my officers, a servant of the temple, and well respected among the men who command my army, had had the skin of his face removed from his head. Presumably, my officers believe, to allow it to be used in some form of deception. They have sworn to have the most extravagant revenge on the man who did this, if they ever have the power to do so. It was not you, I presume?'

The Roman shook his head.

'It was not.'

He waited for the question that seemed inevitable, but the queen turned away and looked out over her host in silence.

'You know more of this than you say. But no matter. If I have your word that it was not you, then that is enough for me. For now, at least. So . . .' She raised her hand again. 'Consider this part of my army. Twenty thousand men-at-arms, all protected by the stoutest felt and linen armour, all equipped with strong, iron helmets, all armed with spears whose blades are made with the finest metal from across the eastern sea, and carrying shields faced with ebony from the south of my kingdom. In open battle, they alone would grind your legion, or whatever ragtag force it is that has chosen to squat uninvited in my fortress, into the dust of this land, and do so without any need of assistance from any other part of my army.'

Marcus nodded agreement.

'And were our men on open ground, you might be right, Kandake, although they are as disciplined and ready for war as any I have seen. You might be surprised at the damage they could wreak on such lightly equipped troops.'

Amanirenas shrugged.

'We could debate such a match, but it would be academic, for my army is more than just spearmen. There are my archers, still as famed with their weapons as in the days when my forebears sent them to assist your empire.'

'Although, Kandake, they have been unable to make much of

an impression on the fortress's defenders, who have instead used them for target practice.'

The queen shrugged.

'Your engines of death will run out of missiles to throw at us, eventually.'

'But not anytime soon, Your Majesty. We took the precaution of confiscating several boatloads of wood before your arrival, and even now the legion's craftsmen will be hard at work making new shafts for bolts, which will be tipped with the same high-quality iron used by your own smiths, intended for traders in the north but instead turned to Rome's purpose.'

Amanirenas shook her head with a broad smile.

'All of which mean nothing. I have thousands of cavalry, hundreds of my elite temple guards, each the match of five of your legionaries in any fight, and dozens of war elephants from the south lands, big, evil-minded monsters with iron-tipped tusks that would run amok through your ranks . . . but none of them will ever be needed, will they?'

Marcus remained silent, simply bowing his head respectfully to avoid any accusation of disrespect.

'I see you discern the truth in my words. I allowed Tantamani to mount an attack on the fortress, when we arrived to find my property in the hands of Rome, but it was my expectation that he would not prevail against such a strong defence. The officer who was given responsibility for making the fortress indefensible would have been banished to the distant south for the rest of his life, fortunate not to have been executed, but he begged for the chance to lead the attack from the front, knowing that he would be among the first to die. And when it became obvious that that first attack would fail completely, I commanded Tantamani to pull my army back, and spare them the lash of your defences.'

She turned to Marcus with a knowing smile.

'I will simply starve your legion out of my fortress, Roman. Two months . . . three . . . six, even. I have the luxury of all the time I need, and more, because, as we both know, there is no more strength in Aegyptus to threaten me. Your commander is a bold man, and knows his history well enough, but he will soon realise that all he has managed to do is to thrust his head into a noose of his own making. I can send half my army south, and halve the supply requirement to keep the remainder in the field, and still have enough strength to beat your legion to its knees when he eventually has to choose between battle and surrender – which means I simply have to wait for hunger to do the job of opening those gates for me.'

The queen nodded at Marcus's silent, level gaze.

'I see the confirmation of that truth in your eyes. This is all the strength Rome has to spare, and your empire will be hard pushed even to replace this legion and keep control of the grain supply on which you are so dependent, much less come south with enough men to retake a port that you can live without. Even as we stand here, I have already won this contest; indeed it was already mine before I ever made the choice to follow the urging of my priests, and restore Meroë's dignity by taking back the port. And who knows . . .'

She smiled beatifically, extending a hand to gesture at the host packed into the plain below them.

'I may yet choose to advance further north. After all, the land to the south of Koptos is of little use to Rome, and serves only to buffer our two kingdoms, which means that who controls it is of little enough real importance. Koptos will serve as a frontier city equally as well as Souan. As, for that matter, might your city of Antinoopolis, in the fullness of time. Would Rome bestir itself to recapture the city that your emperor Hadrian built in memory of his boy lover? Perhaps we will discover the truth of that, you and I, myself as the victorious liberator of lands long subjugated to Rome that once belonged to Kush, you as my captive.'

She raised a hand and stroked his cheek with a tenderness that was at odds with her martial statement of unavoidable defeat.

'Although a place for you at my side might be found, as you are so beloved of the goddess. Only good would come of having a man like you at my side, your very presence a thing of wonder. Swear allegiance to me, Roman, and renounce all fealty to your corrupt and dissolute emperor, and who knows how high you might rise in my service?' She smiled, her stare locked on Marcus's face. 'And indeed my affections.'

12

'Your time for the martyrdom you profess to desire is at hand, Christian. Do you wish to repent your faith?'

Demetrius swayed on his feet, gazing unsteadily at the temple guard with a split-lipped smile.

'You already know the answer to that question, Tantamani. I can no more repent my burning allegiance to the one God than you could renounce your worship of the multitude of false idols that soothe the meaningless agony of your existence.'

The Kushite stepped forward and sank a fist into his gut, doubling the Greek over with a grunt of pain. He had been comprehensively beaten in the hours since the general had discovered the source of the bronze used in casting the water bucket, violence made worse by his unswerving assertions that the statue had been a blasphemous false idol. The general had been abusing his prisoner for long enough that the Greek was struggling to stay upright. Tantamani had circled him with a hard face and clenched fists, striking vicious blows from every direction that had dropped the Christian to his knees several times, his footing less steady with every slow recovery from the pain being inflicted on him. The queen was watching in silence from her throne as her chief priest and military leader set out to humiliate his prisoner in front of the audience of religious statuary arrayed behind her, the gods' eyes staring impassively down at the spectacle.

'You might yet reduce the agony of your death, Christian! Will you acknowledge the existence of Amun, his wife Nut and his children whose pantheon inspires and guides our lives?'

The Christian struggled upright, shaking his head in denial.

'I cannot.'

'Or will not. The end result will be just the same. I will ask you one last time, will—'

'No!' The Greek rallied his strength, his eyes blazing with the strength of his conviction. 'I will not! Get thee behind me, you serpent of—'

Tantamani struck him again, pivoting to deliver a blow to the side of the captive's head that felled him, leaving his victim insensible on the tent's blood-spattered wooden floor, and Marcus heaved a quiet sigh of relief at the temporary halt to his friend's brutalisation.

'And you?'

His gaze snapped up from contemplation of the Christian's sprawled body to find the enemy general in his face, his blood clearly well and truly up.

'Will I acknowledge your gods?' The Roman shrugged. 'Of course. I have no problem with any other man's worship.'

Tantamani shook his head, unsatisfied with the answer and eager for a reason to visit the same treatment upon the Roman.

'And will you renounce your own?'

'Enough!' Both men turned to face Amanirenas, who had risen from the throne from which she had witnessed the protracted beating to which Tantamani had subjected the Christian. 'I have allowed you to make an example of the religious pervert, and that will be an end to it. The gods of Kush have never sought the extermination of other beliefs, not if their adherents do not seek the extermination of our own. And at no time has this captive been anything other than respectful to our kingdom. So satisfy yourself with the one man and leave the other to me. I have plans for him, whether he appreciates them or not.'

The general bowed low, shooting Marcus a glance which promised that he did not consider the matter closed. He gestured to the palace guards who had been holding Demetrius up since his eventual collapse under the sustained violence.

'Bring him. The fate I plan for him requires him to be prepared to meet his god.'

Once the unconscious victim had been dragged from the tent, the queen walked over to Marcus with a pair of her female body-guards in close attendance, their spears held ready to use as their queen circled the Roman before speaking again.

'He will die, and badly. You realise that?'

'That has already become apparent to me, Your Highness.'

She stopped in front of him, her eyes locked on his.

'Ah, that understated Roman humour that your ruling class seem to specialise in. And so tersely worded that you might even pass for a Spartan. Do they teach you that in school?'

'It is the product of years of training. When I was younger I had a habit of expressing my feelings to anyone who would listen, but I learned to control that urge at the hands of two men, one a former soldier, one a champion gladiator.'

'They taught you well. They live still, to take pride in their creation?'

'The gladiator died last year, Your Highness. The soldier re-enlisted to join me when I returned to Rome, and died in the attack from the river, with an artillery bolt in his back, a rebound from the water bucket that we forged with metal from the statue of Nut.'

'Ah. I see the hand of the god Seth, master of war, in this apparent chance death. He seeks to remind Nephthys that she may favour you, but must remain constant in her allegiance with the people of Kush, who are her devotees. Although in taking your friend in such a way, he has sent her the strongest possible message; he did not seek to chastise her as he might have done by guiding the machine-arrow to you, rather than your comrade. It seems that you truly are gods-favoured.' The queen stepped forward and took his hand, her bodyguards fidgeting at the unexpected closeness to an enemy. 'And that would explain the sorrow that my priest detected. I am sorry for your loss, even if you brought it on yourself by invading my land, and desecrating our gods – even if you did so without malice, but simply to survive.'

Knowing better than to argue, Marcus simply bowed his head in recognition of the point and held his silence. After a moment's thought, she turned to her amazons and made a dismissive gesture, issuing a spoken command whose meaning was clear enough from their unhappy reactions, then repeating the command in a tone that, even though the word was unfamiliar, clearly brooked no disobedience. Leaving only the leader of her bodyguard behind – the female warrior's eyes fixed on Marcus in a way that promised an immediate and lethal response to any attempt on her queen's life – the remainder of them left the tent. Amanirenas stayed where she was, close enough to the Roman to reach out and touch.

'You realise that I see much in you that I find . . . attractive?'

The Roman bowed slightly.

'I have come to realise that this is the case, Your Highness. And I do not believe that it is a secret to those around you either.'

The queen laughed tersely.

'Their views are of as little interest to me on this as on any other matter. I am a queen. And queens rule, Roman, regardless of the opinions of their subjects. It is some small reward for the loss of any privacy in my daily life, and for the dedication of every waking moment to my people's well-being. And when I see something I want . . .'

'You are used to taking it?'

'Indeed. Although you are not an object to be possessed, are you? You, Roman, are a man, proud, strong-willed and capable. And so I do not seek to possess you, but rather to make you my companion. You will accompany me, and provide me with the opinions of a man with a new perspective on this life, and perhaps a little of the favour in which the goddess Nephthys holds you will rub off on me, when I take you to my bed.'

Astonished, Marcus was unable to speak for a moment, and when he recovered his composure he found the woman staring at him with an unabashed hunger that was at once a source of both arousal and disconcertion.

'Madam . . .'

'I know.' She stepped closer, her breath warm on his cheek. 'The word "unexpected" doesn't even begin to describe this, does it? When I was told that you had been captured, my first instinct was that you and the Christian would make a suitable sacrifice to atone for the loss of so many of my men to your arrow throwers. And yet the moment I saw you, I knew that I would be unable to order *your* death.'

'I am . . .'

Her gaze was unwavering.

'Gratified? Flattered? After all, I am hardly unattractive beneath the trappings of war.'

Regaining some of his mental equilibrium, Marcus rallied.

'No, madam, it's fair to say that this is something of an unexpected compliment. And that which I can see of you is, I am bound to admit, of no small attraction.'

'But nevertheless I suspect that you would prefer matters if you were granted some time to consider your response? Being asked to consort yourself with a Kushite woman of any rank would be novel, but when you consider the restrictions in your freedom that would result from joining with me, the question takes on a whole new meaning, does it not? And that's before you consider what would become of you were I to tire of your company, or, worse still, die before you.'

She leaned forward, putting her lips to his in a momentary kiss and reaching out a hand to touch him, a perfume of incense and sweat making his nostrils flare involuntarily as his body responded to the unexpected provocation. Stepping back with a look of amusement, the queen smiled knowingly.

'But this is not an entirely unwelcome suggestion, I see. And I knew from the moment I saw you that we would be good together, you and I. But you may take your time. After all, you have plenty of it. My bodyguards will look after you from now on, in case some spirit of jealousy should infect my servants and inspire them to an unwise act. Think on my offer, Roman, and the multitude of benefits that would undoubtedly be yours were you to abandon your service to your tottering empire and join yourself with me.'

Led away to another tent, rather than the one in which he and Demetrius had been held captive, Marcus found himself under the unsmiling gazes and unwavering spears of two of the queen's amazons and, knowing that he was unlikely to be able to engage with them, laid down and allowed his exhausted body to surrender to the sleep it craved. Wakened after what seemed like only a short time, he was led back into the royal tent, shepherded at spear point by another pair of the queen's bodyguards whose intent, hawk-like attention was that of women who both disapproved of their mistress's choice but were at the same time committed to discharging their duty. Half expecting Amanirenas to be waiting for him, he was instead escorted through the tent's opulent surroundings and out into the harsh sunlight, on the same path along which she had led him to view her army at their first meeting.

Waiting at the ridge's edge were the queen herself, in a circle of her lionesses, and Tantamani, who was, the Roman noted, accompanied by an equal number of his own men. Uneasy glances were being exchanged between the two groups, in between whom a figure dressed in a white robe was waiting. As he drew closer, Marcus realised with a sinking feeling that it was Demetrius, his head shaved; what had at first glance looked like hair was in fact a tightly woven crown of thorns that had been forced down onto the newly bared flesh until blood had flowed down his face and neck to stain the otherwise pristine garment. Seeing Marcus's approach, the general stared with unbridled hostility as the Roman's guards guided him to a spot behind the queen's protectors, then shrugged and turned to approach the ridge's edge. What appeared to be the entire Kushite army was mustered in ordered ranks before the natural podium, a mass of armed and armoured men standing impassively under the unblinking desert sun with their attention fixed on the queen's slight figure. Nodding to Marcus with an unreadable expression, she too turned to face the host, raising her voice to be heard across the plain. Speaking in Greek, she paused after each sentence to allow her words to be repeated in her own language.

'Men of my army! You have already won a great victory for the city of Meroë! We have taken back Berenike from the people who stole it from us centuries ago! You have made the people of Kush proud again!'

She paused, and in the ranks before her, officers turned to face their men, raising their spears to orchestrate the expected roar of acclamation.

'Now the Romans have shown their deceitful nature! They have invaded land that was ceded to us a hundred years ago! They have squatted in our fortress of Premnis, uninvited! And they have destroyed a holy statue of the goddess Nut in their defiance of all that we are!'

Another pause, and the army roared its approval again, spear points and sword blades reflecting the bright sunlight as they waved in the air.

'Now we must send them a message! We must show them what will happen to them all, if they do not agree to leave!'

The queen nodded to Tantamani, and the general waved to a group of horsemen waiting at the army's edge. Raising their banners in salute, they turned towards the fortress and walked their horses forward, lowering the flags in a ceremonial display of temporary truce.

'My message to the Romans is this: surrender, or every one of you will receive the same treatment as this man!' Amanirenas gestured to Demetrius, who stared resolutely forward, ignoring the roar as her army, anticipating entertainment, shouted their approval anew. 'Bring out the means of this man's punishment and death!'

Marcus and Demetrius's eyes met, and the Greek smiled lop-sidedly in recognition of the irony that was apparently to be visited upon him. Seeing the silent exchange, Amanirenas turned to face Marcus and beckoned him to her side, her amazons parting to allow his approach but retaining their hard-eyed vigilance.

'You and this follower of the Christos are truly friends, or simply comrades?'

The Roman nodded.

'We have become brothers-in-arms.'

'Then as a mark of my favour, would-be bed partner, I will allow you to speak with him for a short time. Perhaps you can offer him some comfort before my priests enact this ceremony on which they are so set.' She looked to the leader of her lion-esses. 'Accompany him. Ensure the temple guards do him no harm.'

Scaurus watched the riders walking their mounts across the open space in front of the fortress, his face set in an expression of composure that the men around him knew he was far from feeling.

'Messengers. I will go down and meet them, since they come alone and under an offer of truce. Would you care to accompany me, First Spear?'

Abasi nodded.

'I am curious to hear what threats they might have to offer, now that they have failed to dislodge us by both land and water.'

The additional bolt throwers that had been posted to the north-western corner of the fortress had been left in place, in case the Kushites attempted any repeat of their attack, although the whole-sale destruction of their vessels had, it seemed – coupled with the gruesome manner in which the river's crocodiles had feasted on the crews who had chosen to leap from their burning craft into the water – clearly been enough to dissuade the enemy from any such thought. Tribune and First Spear made their way down from the wall, Abasi gathering half a dozen of the century guarding the portal before leading them out onto the flat, stony ground.

'Form a semi-circle around the tribune and keep your eyes open for treachery! I don't trust these devious bastards any more than I'd cuddle up to a viper!'

Approaching the waiting horseman at the head of the small party, he raised a hand to stop his men when they had advanced close enough to the riders for a spoken exchange.

'Well now, what can I do for you gentlemen?' Scaurus kept his tone light, watching as the man who was evidently the Kushite emissary climbed down from his horse. 'I have to warn you that we don't have enough space for you all, if you've come to discuss surrender terms!'

The messenger put his hands on his hips and adopted a wide-legged stance, looking up at the fortress walls before replying.

'I come from Her Majesty Amanirenas, queen and Kandake of the Kushite empire, ruler of the mighty city of Meroë and all its conquered lands, and I have a message for the officer in command of this illegal occupation of our fortress of Premnis.'

The Roman nodded, absorbing the news that he faced not a king but a queen with straight-faced equanimity.

'And I am Gaius Rutilius Scaurus, tribune of Rome and the officer commanding the emperor's Second Legion, named Trajan's Valiant Legion for its exploits in battle. And while I refute your claim to be the owner of this temporarily vacated fastness, now legally and permanently reclaimed in the name of its rightful owner, I am willing to listen to your queen's salutation.'

The messenger continued without any recognition of the challenge to his authority.

'Her Majesty's instructions are these: remove your presence from my fortress without delay and march north to leave our lands, swearing never to return, and she will overlook this transgression and the unfortunate loss of life suffered by her army in attempts to enforce her right to occupy this place. Further, she will also forgive the blasphemous destruction of a statue to the goddess Nut which, she is informed, has been melted down in order to make a water bucket – but only if your withdrawal is both prompt and permanent. If you choose to reject this generosity, however, you will receive a robust and humiliating punishment which will now be demonstrated to you by its being visited on one of the prisoners taken by the river two nights ago. Observe this man's suffering, and you will see how the kingdom of Meroë takes Amun's vengeance on those who perform sacrilege against his rule, and the sanctity of his temple's pantheon.'

Scaurus shook his head grimly.

'I cannot accept these terms. But I will offer my own. If the Kandake orders a withdrawal from Rome's port of Berenike now, and swears that neither she nor her descendants will ever again set foot on Roman soil, we can end this war, which is not of Rome's choosing, amicably. Premnis will again belong to Meroë, and the empire of Kush can once again enjoy the fruits of alliance with the world-spanning empire of Rome. Decline to do so, and Rome will summon its strength from the surrounding provinces and come to war in force. Meroë will be crushed under its boot, and the empire of Kush's long rule will be at an end. I trust we understand each other?'

The messenger stared hard at him for a moment, then replied in a tone that signalled the end of the discussion.

'I understand only that there is nothing more to be said. Actions will now speak for Meroë, and the piteous cries of your comrade as he dies will inform you as to our deep anger with the insult of your boots on our land.' He remounted, turning his horse away with a final comment called back over his shoulder. 'Send an emissary if you wish to speak again, for my queen will make no further attempt to make peace when faced with such intransigence!'

The Romans watched him ride away, the horsemen around him keeping their lances lowered in what the Romans presumed was a signal of their ultimatum's rejection. Scaurus shaded his eyes against the sun's glare, trying to discern what was happening on the ridge a mile distant.

'Surely not?' He pointed, his face creased in a frown of disbelief. 'Is that . . . a cross?'

Passing through the cordon of guards with a pair of amazons on either side, Marcus got to within arm's length of his friend before the men guarding him raised their spears to prevent any contact between the two. Close up, the Greek's face was covered in bruises, and his body trembled with the after-effects of the violence done to him, but his eyes were still as hard and bright as before the beating, and when he spoke it was apparent that his spirit was undaunted.

'So, Centurion, now we see the fate that the Lord has spared me for all these years. I am to provide an example to these heathens, and to our own men, and to inspire conversion from your collective idolatrous ways to the one true faith.'

Marcus looked around at the upright and cross-beam of a cross lying on the ground a few paces away where the men who had carried it to the spot had dropped their burden, a heavy hammer and long nails waiting beside them.

'They will make you carry that down to the place of your execution, and then they will nail you to it, just outside the reach of our artillery but close enough that your screams will be heard by the men on the walls. And you of all people must know that you will die in the slowest and most agonising manner possible. Surely you can spare yourself that indignity?'

The Greek smiled sadly at him.

'Surely, I *could*. But, equally surely, I *cannot*. Would you forego such a death, if you knew that by dying in that way you would be reunited with your loved ones, in heaven?'

'No. In truth it would be a small price to pay.'

'And there, my friend, you have it. I am to die, slowly, painfully, but gloriously. I will join the ranks of martyrs, and when my turn at the gate to heaven comes, I will walk through with my head high, redeemed of all my sins in the service of the Lord. This is what will be.' He smiled again. 'And as for you, Marcus Valerius

Aquila, go with the blessings of the Lord upon you, whether you desire them or not. I foresee great things for you.'

Marcus nodded, straightening and raising his hand in salute.

'Go well, Demetrius. I will report your sacrifice to your brothers in Alexandria, if I ever see the city's walls again.'

After a moment to organise themselves into a guard around the Christian, the temple guards ordered him to pick up the heavy wooden cross-beam. Two men helped him to seat it over his right shoulder, eliciting a grimace of pain as the wood's rough edge dug into his flesh through the flimsy tunic to draw more blood.

'Pull all the faces you like, Roman!' Tantamani strode out before the small party, raising his voice to make the most of the moment of humiliation. 'You will provide entertainment for the army of Kush in your dying, and curse your master the Christos as you follow in his footsteps!'

Demetrius smiled at him through the pain, grunting a breathless snarl of defiance.

'Harder men than you have tried to break me, heathen! Bring me your pain, and watch me revel in my martyrdom!'

A whip snaked out from the men waiting behind him, its tip carving a bloody furrow in his thigh and making him start, but, baring his teeth with the effort, he retained his grip on the cross and started walking in the direction that the men before him directed with their sword blades, a path descending to the plain below. Putting a foot on a pebble, he staggered and went down on one knee, the whip cracking again to spur him back onto his feet with a visibly straining effort that left him panting from the effort. The whip struck a third time, expertly wielded, ripping through the tunic's flimsy fabric and drawing fresh blood from his back, and with a muffled groan of pain the Greek staggered forward again, the dust at his feet spotted with red where his fresh wounds were bleeding. The soldiers standing on either side of his path through their ranks to the intended place of his execution watched in silence as the bloodied Christian made his tortuously slow progress across the plain. A dozen war elephants towered over them in a naked display of force, the stink of their faeces noisome in the sun's burning heat. Demetrius emitted what Marcus momentarily thought was a whimper of pain, and then realised was laughter – wheezing, strained, but undeniably amusement. He drew a breath and called out to Marcus, the gleeful note in his voice at odds with his dire circumstances.

'When you see Dubnus again, tell him that elephant shit stinks!'

The whip cracked again, but if Demetrius felt the pain then he showed no sign of it, seemingly focused on putting one step in front of another, as he staggered along the path between the two ranks of soldiers. After another fifty yards he slumped down again, unable to go on such was his exhaustion, and Marcus turned to the queen in silent question. Amanirenas nodded, gesturing to the helpless Greek.

'You may help your friend.'

She called to her guards, and the amazons cleared a path through the temple guards gathered around the fallen Greek to allow the Roman to get to his friend. Demetrius shook his head on seeing his friend's approach, attempting to wave him away with an exhausted, feeble gesture.

'What do you think you're doing? This cross is mine to carry.'

'I am helping a friend with his last burden.' Marcus turned to the closest of the guards. 'Carry him to wherever it is that you intend to kill him. I will carry his cross.'

The Kushites looked to Tantamani, who shrugged and gestured to the fallen Greek.

'You have saved me the trouble of ordering you to do so. Take up your comrade's burden, but do not expect to be spared the lashes that were intended for him.'

The queen's stare at her general was one of near-hatred, but Marcus shrugged and walked over to the fallen cross-beam, raising it to balance on end and then allowing it to rest on his shoulder. An experimental flex of his knees let him take the measure of its dead weight, then an upward lunge with all the strength of his thighs enabled him to lift the heavy load and stand. With a crack, the whip struck, a white-hot flare of pain on the back of his neck making him stagger before he regained control of the beam's ungainly weight, and started trudging forward behind the men who were dragging Demetrius's semi-conscious body.

'You are not built for such a task, are you, Roman? Or even accustomed to carrying such weight.' Looking sideways he saw that the general had come to walk beside him, grinning at his prisoner's discomfiture. 'It will do the Kandake good to see you struggle in this way. Perhaps it will even cure her of the infatuation that she seems to have for you.' He laughed at the Roman's attempt to present a blank expression. 'You thought I didn't know? I know everything that happens in her life, trust me on that. And can you imagine me allowing any sort of liaison between the two of you? When all this is done, and your friend there has been left for the crows to pick clean, I will have you killed, quickly, silently and without any trace of violence. All that poor little Amanirenas will know is that the white-skinned enemy she found so alluring is dead, with no known cause. She will suspect me, of course, but there will never be any proof. Kush will be protected from such juvenile stupidity in one who ought to know better, and Rome's defeat here will be final, with no risk of your influence softening her heart. Make the most of the few hours that you have left.'

Marcus laughed, ignoring the pain in his back and shoulder.

'You haven't actually seen a crucifixion then?'

Tantamani shrugged.

'No. But I look forward to seeing this blasphemer pay the price for his destruction of a sacred idol. Why do you ask?'

Marcus grimaced at the cross-beam's weight, forcing himself to keep putting one foot in front of another despite his crushing burden.

'Because it takes more than a few hours for the victim to die. It can be a matter of days, on occasion.'

'In which case I suppose you had better pray to whatever god it is that you believe in that he takes as long as possible. Because when he leaves this life, you will be following him, and not very far behind. I will tell him to tarry a while and wait for you. Who knows, perhaps the ferryman will take you both for the price of one!'

'It's a cross, all right, I can see some poor bastard carrying the cross-beam and a team of men behind him with the upright. Although I reckon they're going to nail up the man in front of him in the white robe.'

Shading his eyes against the glare, Dubnus was staring intently at the procession through the enemy army, desperate for any sign of his friend.

'What makes you say that?'

The Briton stared for a moment longer before answering Qadir's question.

'He's being carried by a man on each side, by the look of it, which means they've already beaten the shit out of him.'

The Hamian watched the distant scene for a moment, as eager to make some sense of it as his comrade.

'You're right; one man carrying the cross, another to be placed upon it. I doubt that this can be anyone other than our brother Marcus and the Christian. Is it wrong of me to hope that it is Demetrius who is to receive the martyrdom we both know he craves?'

Dubnus shook his head.

'No. As long as our boy lives another day, that's all I care about. Although how he's going to survive being imprisoned by those barbarians is a mystery to me.'

They watched as the white-robed figure was lowered to the floor, and the man they presumed to be Marcus allowed his burden to fall onto the ground beside him.

'That's where they're going to do it then.'

'Indeed.' Qadir measured the distance with a practised eye. 'Too distant for there to be any hope of an accurate shot to put him out of his misery, I'd say.' He turned to the ballista captain standing stolidly beside them. 'Any chance you could hit them from here?'

The legionary shook his head with pursed lips.

'Not even a remote chance, Centurion. I couldn't get a shot within fifty paces of him.'

'In which case, it seems, someone is going to have a long day of it.'

'Here! In full view of the fortress, but outside the reach of their arrow throwers. And do you see, Greek, I have a whipping post ready for you! Strip and bind him!'

The temple guards tore away the bloodied white robe at their master's order, pulling Demetrius's unresisting body onto the stout post, binding his hands around it to prevent him pulling away. Amanirenas watched from inside the circle of her body-guards, sphinx-like in her serene detachment from the events playing out.

'Now whip him, fifty lashes as fast and hard as possible! Let him know the anger of Amun!'

A pair of temple guards took up positions on either side of the post, shaking out their whips and judging by eye the optimum distance to stand from him, then signalled their readiness.

'Begin!'

Taking turns to strike, the two men swung their goads with all the strength in their bodies, sweat flying from their exertions. The whip blows cut thick weals into the Greek's back, and his body jerked spasmodically with every cracking impact. After twenty of so strokes he slumped against the post, pushing out his feet to remain upright, riding the incessant onslaught's waves of pain as the horrific punishment continued.

'You might just kill him, of course. That would be a shame, when he so wants to be nailed to the cross.'

Tantamani shot a sideways glance at Marcus, attempting to discern any hint of defiance to punish, but found only a stolid stare fixed on the suffering Greek.

'You are right, even if your concern is one of weakness and pity.' The general shouted a command to his men. 'Enough! He is ready! Untie him and bring forward the cross!'

Upright and cross-beam had been fixed together with nails to form a T-shape, and as Demetrius was freed from the whipping post, the instrument of his execution was placed on the ground beside him. Tantamani pointed to the newly-constructed torture frame with a gloating expression.

'Now see, Roman, how the men of Kush are every bit as learned as your own scholars! I have read Josephus, and his account of the executions outside Jerusalem in the far north was particularly instructive! I know how these things are done! Place him on the cross!'

The almost insensible Greek was laid on the wooden structure with his arms outstretched, and the Kushite walked forward to take up the hammer and nails.

'I will do this myself! Let no man say that Tantamani, warrior-priest of the temple of Amun, was not the first and foremost in punishing a man who so deeply offended our gods!'

Squatting, he directed a guard to hold the Christian's hand flat against the wooden surface before placing the point of a nail against his wrist.

'Placed just here, the nail will not pierce the veins beneath the surface. And see, I have this . . .' He showed Marcus a disc of wood through which the nail had been pushed. 'This will prevent him from simply pulling his arm free.'

Raising the hammer, he drove the nail down through flesh and wood, eliciting a groan of pain from Demetrius, the Greek's legs tensing uncontrollably against the pain as he cried out in Latin.

'Lord, forgive my sins against so many of your children! Accept my sacrifice and wash me free of my sin!'

Amanirenas looked at Marcus in bafflement.

'What is he saying?'

'He was once a persecutor of his own kind, before he converted to follow the Christos. And he is no stranger to this means of execution. He calls upon his god to forgive him for the men he did the same to, with his suffering here as a form of recompense.'

'He accepts this punishment?'

The Roman shook his head.

'No, Your Highness. He craves it.'

Tantamani drove in the second nail, securing the Greek's other wrist, stepping back to admire his handiwork as Demetrius panted with the waves of pain gripping his arms.

'Such a tidy job I have done for you, blasphemer! There will be no release from loss of blood for you!' He gestured to the guards. 'Hold his feet for me, as I showed you!' Placing their prisoner's feet on either side of the wooden upright, the temple guards watched in horrified fascination as their master placed another nail's head against the Greek's heel. 'Take a tight grip, for when I drive this nail through his heel bone, the pain will make him struggle all the more.'

He swung the hammer, forcing the iron point through the bone beneath the heel's skin, and Demetrius howled with the brutal intrusion. But as the hammer pushed the nail through his flesh and bone and into the wood, his scream of agony became a howled entreaty to the sky above.

'See my suffering, Lord! Accept my entreaty for your forgiveness!'

Marcus translated for the queen without being bidden.

'He is asking for forgiveness, Your Highness.'

Amanirenas nodded, her face a study in perplexity.

'He is being punished for his blasphemy, but calls to be forgiven for murders he committed years ago?'

'He sees himself as what the Greeks call a martyr.'

'I have read this word. He accepts suffering and death in the name of his god.'

'Yes.' Marcus winced as the last nail was driven into Demetrius's other heel, dragging another ragged scream from his bloodied lips. 'He knows the torture that now awaits – hours and days of hovering on the brink of death – and yet this is everything he has desired ever since the day he was converted to this belief in one god above all others.'

'It is indeed a strong faith.' The queen stared in disbelief as the temple guards raised the cross and manoeuvred its base into a hole dug for the purpose of allowing it to stand upright, the Greek grunting with the pain as it dropped into the improvised socket. 'He is . . . *smiling*? How can he be happy when his body is being destroyed in this way?'

'Why not ask him, Your Highness?'

The queen nodded and strode forward, her amazons accompanying her to clear the temple guards from her path. She stood at the base of the cross looking up at the Greek, who returned her gaze through eyes slitted with pain and yet was still smiling.

'Why do you smile, Christian? Surely you must know that you will rot on this cross long after your death, forgotten and abandoned?'

Grunting with the effort of flexing his arms and pushing up against the nails through his heels to prevent his body slumping, and subjecting him to the agony of asphyxiation, Demetrius shook his head.

'No man is ever alone when he has embraced the glory of the Lord our God, Queen!'

Tantamani stepped forward with a sneer.

'Ignore him, Kandake, he is a babbling fool! Where is your god now, blasphemer? How has he allowed this to be done to you if he is so omnipotent?'

The Greek smiled again.

'He is *everywhere*, idolater! Even now he is in the temples of your gods, making a mockery of your beliefs with his all-knowing, all-seeing, all-ruling power.' He coughed, hoisting his body on the nails' pivots to breathe. 'And he will bring your kingdom of lies to an end when the time is right!'

The general snatched a spear and made to thrust it into the Christian's body, then smiled slowly and stepped back, lowering the unblooded blade.

'No, that would be too easy a way out for you. And perhaps what you sought to provoke me to, I suspect. You can take your time dying, and if in the meantime you wish to entertain yourself with stories for children, be my guest!'

'That was Demetrius, no doubt about it.'

Scaurus didn't acknowledge Dubnus's statement, his attention fixed on the army paraded before Premnis's walls.

'What is your view of our tactical position, First Spear? Could we attack now, while they are distracted, and hope to win?'

Abasi stepped forward and stared over the parapet in bleak assessment of their position.

'Our strength inside these walls is also our weakness, Tribune. If I had the legion deployed and ready to fight, on level ground like that beneath us, I might just have an advantage over men fascinated with the death of a tortured captive, despite their overwhelming numbers, but by the time we could get our men out of the fortress and into line of battle, they would be over their surprise and ready to greet us. And beside that . . .' he scanned the enemy ranks again before continuing, 'I do not see their cavalry. I suspect that they would allow us to get halfway through any deployment and then sweep in from both flanks. No – speaking tactically, there is no advantage to be had here.'

'As I thought.' The Roman shook his head. 'All we can do is hope that the Christian's god chooses to be merciful to him. Although when I consider the stories he has told us as to his role in suppressing the very religion he has come to embrace, it's hard to imagine why such a vengeful deity wouldn't allow him a sizeable dose of the same agony he visited on so many others, before deciding whether to call him to his side. In either case, I suspect that he is in for a long and trying day.'

With the heat of the day fading towards the dusk, Amanirenas called for refreshments to be brought to the execution site, and commanded that her army be dismissed to their camp to eat, with men left to mount a watch on the fortress. Pinned under the relentless sun throughout the afternoon, his pale flesh rapidly turning red as it was burned by exposure to the scorching sunlight, Demetrius had struggled against his own body weight with increasing desperation. Alternately sagging from the nails through his wrists to relieve the strain on his arms, but at the cost of panting desperately for breath, he had been forced to constantly hoist himself up to breathe more freely, ever more exhaustedly. But with the onset of night he was evidently spent, slumping more than rising up, his breathing noticeably more laborious than an hour before, his legs smeared with excrement from an uncontrollable bowel movement brought on by such physical punishment.

'Perhaps your friend's time is short after all, eh, Roman? Perhaps the heat of the desert has sapped his ability to resist. I believe that he will be dead before the dawn.'

Tantamani smiled at Marcus, the murderous intent in his eyes obvious to the younger man.

'Perhaps so.' Amanirenas spoke from behind them, a cup of wine undrunk in her hand as she looked up at the Greek's weakening struggle for life. 'But I must admit that I find his example an enlightening one.'

The general turned to regard his queen with something bordering on hostile disbelief, in the moment before he managed to smooth his features into a mask of apparent indifference.

'But surely you glory in the punishment of the man who happily admitted that he took a hammer to the statue of Nut, my Queen?'

Amanirenas looked up at the Greek for a moment, taking a sip from her goblet of wine.

'I am pleased by the punishment of that crime against our gods, Tantamani. And yet I find the bravery with which the criminal has accepted his punishment a fascinating example of dedication to a cause.'

'I cannot share that admiration, Your Majesty. And neither, I expect, does your priest? Shall we ask him?'

The queen nodded her acceptance of her general's point, and

the elderly shaman Anlamani was led forward from the shaded chair in which he had dozed for most of the afternoon. Helped to stand before the cross, he looked up at Demetrius with an expression of distaste, drawing himself up to speak to the dying man.

'See, Christian, the depths of agony to which your belief has brought you? Will you not renounce your misguided beliefs, and earn a swift and merciful death?'

The Greek looked down at him, smiling through the pain as he lifted himself to breathe deeply enough to make some reply. When he spoke, his voice was hoarse from the screaming that had strained his vocal cords beyond their limit, but the strength in his words was enough to widen the old man's eyes.

'Do you see it, *idolater*? Do you comprehend the true strength of the followers of Christ? I can no more renounce my faith in the one true God than you can stop clinging to the superstition that sustains you, no matter how flimsy!'

'Blasphemer!' The priest pointed a finger at the helpless Greek, while behind him Tantamani grinned broadly, seeing the encounter play out exactly as he had hoped, as the aged cleric raised a hand in the warding gesture. 'May you die in agony! May you find yourself adrift in an ocean of darkness as your punishment in the afterlife! Amun and his war master Seth will seek you out, and flay the skin from your bones a thousand times for such an insult!'

The Christian coughed painfully, slumping down for a moment before raising himself up to spit a vehement response with the last of his strength. Straining against the nails pinning his flesh to the cross, his words were hoarse and snatched, his chest heaving as he fought for the air with which to defy the men below him.

'God will have his vengeance on you . . . for this indignity! On you and all your . . . so-called gods! This triumph . . . will be ashes in your mouth . . . when he rides to victory over . . . *your empty graven images!*'

'Kill him!' The priest turned to Amanirenas, spit flying with the vehemence of his fury. 'Do not allow him to spew his poison any longer!'

'No!' All eyes turned to the queen, who had paced forward to intervene. 'There will be no premature end to this man's life!'

Both priests turned to her aghast, the elder raising a hand in denial of her authority.

'You must not contradict us in this matter, Kandake! You do not have the—'

'I am your queen! I have supreme authority over you and every other man in this land and you will *obey* me!'

Standing behind the amazons, Marcus realised that they were ready to fight, their spears no longer held in the vertical rest position but with the blades angled towards the men facing them. Tantamani's eyes narrowed, and he looked to one side at his guards, perhaps taking the measure of their readiness to stand beside him, but before anyone could react to the swiftly changing circumstances, an urgent hail shattered the moment's deadly spell.

'My Kandake!' A dismounted cavalryman hurried into the execution circle, limping rather than striding, dried blood caking the skin of his right calf from a deep cut above his knee. 'My Kandake, Meroë is invaded!'

'*What?*'

Tantamani swivelled to face the newcomer, putting out a hand to steady him as the ashen-faced soldier stumbled, but Marcus noted that Amanirenas did not move any closer to his temple guards, instead making a surreptitious hand signal to her body-guard to close up around her.

'Invasion, my Lord! The city of Napata is afire and the temple of Amun on Jebel Barkal is sacked!'

'Who has done this? Surely Rome has no way to—'

'No, my Lord General, it was the Blemmyes! They came out of the western desert without warning, thousands strong! We are betrayed, and they have carried away the golden statues of Amun and Nut from the holiest of our temples!'

The priests stared at him, aghast, but in the moment of silence the first voice heard came from above them. Revelling in the turn of events, Demetrius grated out a hoarse laugh.

'The Lord my God has avenged me! Your boasts have proven as empty as the altars of your so-called temple!' He looked up at the darkening sky. 'Take my spirit, Lord, I am ready to join you!'

Tantamani snatched a spear from the closest guard and spun, ready to strike up at the jubilant Christian.

'*No!*'

He froze at the tone of the queen's voice, looking at her in disbelief with the spear raised, the blade less than a hand's length from the Christian's chest.

'This is *my* authority! *I* am head priest of Meroë, guardian of the temple and protector of the people, and *I* say this man *dies*!'

Amanirenas made a flicking gesture with her right hand, the index finger pointed at her general, and with the speed and purpose of long practice, the amazons standing to either side of her lunged forward and struck. One blade went high, spearing through her general's chest to pierce both lungs in swift succession, the other darting in low twice to tear through the skin of his thighs and open the arteries beneath their skin. Stepping back to set their bloodied blades in defence of the queen, they were joined by the remainder of her bodyguard in a line of sharp iron facing off against the astonished temple guards.

'*But . . .*' Tantamani staggered forward a pace, blood pouring down his legs and spluttering from his lips. '*I am your priest . . .*'

The queen stared at him with hatred in her eyes, her true feelings revealed in regal fury.

'You were both priest and general! And with that power, you forced a war upon me that Meroë neither needed nor wanted! A war whose only true aim was to make *you* stronger, strong enough to rule! Oh yes, I heard the mutterings, a man better than a woman, the glory of Kush to be restored. And so I readied myself for your treachery and waited!'

'*You are . . . undone . . . idolater!*'

Amanirenas looked up at the panting Christian, putting a finger to her lips.

'Save your strength, man of God. I will have you down from your place of torture soon enough.'

'Kandake! You cannot—'

She rounded on the elderly priest with renewed fury, pointing at the stricken general who had sunk to his knees and was staring down at the puddle of blood in which he was kneeling with horror.

'You have led me to this point of disaster just as much as that fool! And you would have connived with him to put a priest on the throne! You may live, but you will take no further part in my rule!'

She raised a hand to command the stunned temple guards, every ounce of her regal authority in the gesture and words.

'Honourable guards of the temple, you have been misled by your priests! They sought to remove your rightful queen, and place themselves on the throne in perpetuity! And in their desire for power they have left our homeland vulnerable, with the result we now see! Now you have a choice: side with the priests or obey your queen when I order you to kneel and disarm yourselves! Choose now!'

The lionesses opened their ranks without any command, giving themselves room in which to fight, and Marcus was unsurprised to see those guardsmen facing them look at each other in consternation for a moment, before first one man and then his comrades knelt and unbuckled their sword belts. Nodding grimly to her bodyguards to collect their weapons, she pointed up at the helpless Demetrius.

'Now right the wrong that you have done! Get this man down from this barbaric instrument of torture, and be careful to do him no further harm unless you wish to take his place! There is much that I wish to discuss with him, once his wounds have been tended and he has had the chance to recuperate. And now you, Roman, can accompany me to the walls of my fortress for a brief negotiation with the man whose idea it was to use its capture as a means of getting my attention. I believe that this new situation requires something of a restatement in the relationship between your people and mine!'

'There's a party approaching, First Spear!'

Staring out into the gloom in the direction that the legionary was indicating, it took the officers a moment to resolve the advancing figures from their almost dark background. Abasi was the first to react.

'Torches! Get them lit up! Bolt throwers, ready to shoot!'

They watched as the soldiers guarding the gate lit brands and hurled them out onto the stony ground while the artillery pieces to either side were cranked to their maximum depression, pointing out into the darkness beyond their semi-circle of soft, red light.

'That's close enough!' Scaurus command was pre-emptory as he stared out into the dusk murk at the unidentified enemy. 'If you come any nearer than the torches, then the only way I'll be able to make you go away will be with boiling animal fat, and I promise you that you wouldn't enjoy the experience!'

'That won't be necessary, Tribune!'

'Marcus!' Dubnus started forward, disbelieving as his friend stepped into the light of the burning brands. 'It's him!'

The young centurion waved wearily, gesturing for someone behind him to come forward, and a black, armoured figure walked forward into the torchlight.

'Allow me to introduce the Kandake Amanirenas, queen of Meroë and protector of the empire of Kush!'

He fell silent for a moment, allowing time for the man on the wall above him to absorb what it was that he had just said.

'All this was because some woman decided to have herself a war?'

Abasi raised an eyebrow at Dubnus.

'You didn't have a mother?'

'Yes, but she wouldn't—'

'She might have, if she'd been born a queen.'

'As it happens . . .' The Briton shook his head and shut his mouth, catching a hard stare from Scaurus. 'It would take too long.'

'Exactly.' The tribune turned to Ptolemy. 'You didn't know that the ruler of Meroë is a woman?'

'Indeed not, Tribune.' The scribe returned his gaze with a hint of irritation. 'The royal family of Meroë does not see fit to inform the imperial secretariat of its changes of ruler, and so it is only when the news reaches Alexandria by more conventional means, which can take months, that we discover such matters.'

'I see.' The Roman leaned over the wall to look at Marcus as closely as possible at fifty paces distance. 'You look well enough, Centurion! So tell me, what is it that I can do for the Kandake that she comes to my walls unannounced?'

The response was prompt, obviously rehearsed.

'The Kandake requests that you enter into face-to-face negotiations with her immediately, as she has a pressing matter to deal with to the south of here!' He gestured to the shadowy figures standing behind him. 'Her lionesses are jealous in guarding her, so I would suggest that you leave any weapons with your own guards?'

Abasi's voice was at best sceptical in tone.

'You want me to send my commander out onto a darkened landscape with who knows what hidden out of view?'

The woman standing next to Marcus stepped forward into full view, her armour reflecting the fire's light in gleaming red and orange.

'I am Amanirenas, daughter and only surviving child of Shabaka, king of Meroë, and I am the rightful ruler of Kush, an empire that already existed a thousand years before Rome's founders lived in a hut on a hill above a marsh! My predecessors conquered not just this land, but all of Aegyptus as well, and were known as the Black Pharaohs! We have seen off every major power that has ever chosen to confront us in battle! Saites, Assyrians,

Persians, Ptolemies and yes, Romans too, and while we have never bent the knee to any rival, neither have we ever been accused of falsehood! So hear this, Roman, and then decide whether you wish for peace or war. If you come to talk with me, here and now, I will offer my own life as surety. Aim your arrow machines at me, and if I do you any harm, then that harsh-voiced officer beside you can have me killed with a single word!' Her voice hardened commandingly. 'Shall we talk?'

Scaurus nodded decisively.

'The queen has a point. Indeed I doubt that I would have come anywhere close to these walls, were I in her position.' He unbuckled his belt and handed it to Abasi. 'Here, take my sword and dagger, and have the bolt throwers ready to shoot if needed. Will you come with me, Dubnus? You can stand behind me at a suitable distance with that axe of yours and wonder what it would be like to fight a spear-armed woman.'

'I hardly need to wonder, as I spar with Ptolemy every day' – he continued, ignoring the scribe's incensed protests – 'but I will be happy to come with you, Tribune. And you lot . . .' he paused for a moment to ensure that he had the attention of the ballista crews to either side, 'if I do get speared by some mad woman, just you make sure she pays the right price, eh?'

Walking out across the open ground before the walls that had been the only barrier between his command and certain destruction, and with only a fifty-pace circle of illuminated ground, beyond which was a darkness so complete that the entire Kushite army could have been within bow shot and been invisible, Scaurus held his silence until he had reached the spot where Marcus and his companion awaited him.

'Your bodyguard does a poor job of looking unthreatening, Legatus.'

The Roman looked back to see Dubnus leaning on his axe a dozen paces behind him, the very picture of a man attempting to look as if violence was the last thing on his mind.

'By rights he is the man you should be talking to. He's the son of a king in his own country, whereas I am merely a minor nobleman by your frame of reference.'

'And yet you do command here, and, whatever status you might or might not enjoy in your own country, here you are, it seems, the victor. Tell me, how did you persuade the Blemmyes to turn on us?'

Scaurus smiled slowly.

'You are nobody's fool, Your Highness. How did you guess?'

'It wasn't hard to make the link between your extravagantly suicidal occupation of this fortress to hold my attention and this unexpected strike from the desert, by men we believed to be our allies. What did you promise them, gold?'

'Yes, but not Rome's. I simply had an officer of mine point out to them that if I succeeded in occupying Premnis, then it would act as a magnet for you and your army. And that a fleet attacker, accustomed to moving swiftly and quietly in the desert wastes, might find the back door to your kingdom unguarded. It has long been considered a strategic weakness of your kingdom that your most holy site, and former imperial capital, is so far north, and open to attack from either side of the Nilus.'

Amanirenas nodded slowly.

'An astute plan. Although were I assessing its likely success, I could not give more than one chance in two of it succeeding. And yet here you are, with your head in the noose, waiting for the uncertainty of alliance with a desert tribe of notorious fickleness to free you. Do you consider yourself to be lucky, Tribune of Rome?'

'We make our own luck in this life, Kandake. So tell me, what terms would you like me to consider?'

The queen stared at the walls of her fortress for a moment, then spoke again in a tone that told the Romans she knew that she was beaten.

'I will remove my army from the port of Berenike and take my full strength south to deal with these treacherous allies in the manner they deserve. And in return for my surrendering my prize, you will vacate this fortress and march north to Souan. And we will both swear, face to face and on paper in the way that I know you Romans believe to be sacrosanct, never to repeat either incursion. Souan will be the meeting point for Rome and Kush, where trade will be carried out, and Rome's interests as far south as that city will be guaranteed for as long as Rome is able to muster the strength to hold Souan itself.'

Scaurus nodded agreement.

'A treaty will be required. Fortunately I have an imperial secretary in my party who will draw such a document up immediately. You will proclaim this as a victory, I presume?'

'Of course. As will Rome, I presume?'

'Undoubtedly. Kings . . . and indeed queens . . . and empires, all need such good news to keep their people believing in the justness of their rule, do they not?' Amanirenas nodded her approval. 'There is one other small matter to resolve. The Christian man who was captured on the riverbank along with my centurion here . . .'

'Will live. I have had him taken down from the cross that my treacherous general Tantamani had nailed him to. He may not walk as easily as he did before, but I will have him carried until such time as he can stand again, if he chooses to stay with me.'

'To what purpose would you seek to detain him?'

The queen smiled.

'Detain? I will not hold him against his will, but nevertheless I expect that he will come with me to Napata, and then onto Meroë itself, and gladly. I would learn more of this one god which inspires such loyalty that a man would willingly allow himself to be nailed to a cross, to undergo such an excruciating death while still calling out to his god, even in the most extreme pain. Any army of men so motivated would be a powerful force. There is a power rising to Meroë's south, the kingdom of Aksum, and unlike Tantamani and my priests, I have long believed it to be the real threat to my kingdom.'

Scaurus nodded slowly.

'If the Christian wishes to accompany you, I will happily release him from his service to Rome. But surely your people will regard him as alien, and shun his beliefs?'

'We shall see. Who knows, perhaps they will be as intrigued as I am with his devotion to just one master.' Amanirenas turned her cool gaze on Marcus. 'And you too may accompany me, beloved of the gods, if it is in your thoughts to be my companion? I think you would find the experience . . . enlightening.'

Marcus bowed.

'Without doubt, Kandake and Queen. You would be the most magnificent companion a man could desire, and yet I am firstly a servant of Rome.'

'And there is a matter yet unfinished for you in Rome, if my priest read you correctly?'

'There is. A matter of taking revenge for one I loved who was mistreated by men of power. I cannot relinquish my hopes to one day see those men face to face with their destinies.'

'As you desire, so shall it be. Take this with you, and when your task of revenge is complete, it will vouchsafe you safe passage to Meroë, should you seek refuge from pursuit.' She pulled a thick gold bracelet from her wrist, tracing the letters embossed into the soft metal. 'It bears my name and will be recognised by any royal official as having belonged to the queen. I will issue an edict that a white man bearing it is to be escorted to my side without delay. You will always be welcome in my kingdom, and in my bedchamber, beloved of the gods.' The queen turned to Scaurus. 'Have this treaty we have negotiated sent to me as soon as it is written, perhaps in the hands of your centurion here. He can bid your Christian farewell, and perhaps have one last look at the woman over whom he has chosen revenge.'

The queen stalked away at the heart of her amazons, and the Romans watched her until the darkness swallowed up her party.

'You had the chance of bedding a queen, and you turned it down to go back to Rome where one of the two men you want to kill continually plots your death, while the other lives behind an iron ring of praetorians.' Dubnus shook his head in disgust. 'If I ever needed proof that you've taken leave of your senses . . .'

Ignoring him, Marcus looked at Scaurus with new respect.

'You gambled a legion on Fabius Turbo's ability to get the desert-raiders to turn on their allies? That's pushing the odds, even for us.'

'I know.' The older man nodded wearily. 'And yet it was the only way I could see to undo the grip in which the Kandake would inevitably put us, when she discovered our occupation of this place.'

'So what now? What is your plan, once the queen has taken her army south to re-establish her kingdom's borders?'

'That's easy enough. We can return to Alexandria by river, leave the auxiliaries to garrison Souan and Koptos, and make our way back to Rome. Doubtless Cleander will be delighted to have his port on Mare Rubrum back in Roman hands, and to renew the flow of the river of gold that flows into his capacious purse. I think that some time in the capital is long overdue before we consider what we might do next, and who knows, you might just find some way to engineer some degree of recompense for the wrong that has been done to you.' He smiled sadly at Marcus. 'After all, you are beloved of the gods, are you not? And everyone knows that the gods' ability to tolerate an injustice is not infinite.'

Historical Note – the Kingdom of Kush

A quite startling amount of research was required for the author to be able to put together a story set in the Roman province of Aegyptus. I have over the last ten years become accustomed to not needing to work all that hard on my knowledge of the late second century. That was not quite so true this time, however! In the course of the year it took to write the book, it was necessary to read quite deeply into areas of ancient history, which variously encompassed the province itself, which was quite different to the imperial norm; the great world city of Alexandria; Christianity in the empire; the pyramids; the Red Sea ports and their trade with what we now call India; and, most interestingly (to the author, at least), the little-known kingdom of Kush. Any of these subjects make for interesting reading, and I'll recommend some books at the bottom of this note, but it is Kush that I've decided to talk about here.

Historians have belatedly realised that Kush was a major regional power in the ancient world. One of the longest lived civilisations anywhere, it was highly developed in terms of civil administration, religion and culture, long before Rome existed, and predates even the Greek Archaic period. Its major religious monuments dwarfed Greek achievements such as the Parthenon and Acropolis, and at its peak, when its kings ruled Egypt as the 25th Dynasty, their kingdom stretched as far north as Jerusalem and Tyre. Indeed, Kush helped to shape Egypt in much the same way that Egypt influenced Kush. Standing toe to toe with neighbouring powers, Kush managed to maintain its territorial integrity for a good deal longer than the Western Roman civilisation lasted, and left a heritage that is gradually entering mainstream historical awareness.

Kush – or Meroë, as it was known by the late second century after the death of Christ – was a power on the edge of decline by the time of this story, but was also a kingdom with a proud history, and indeed a much longer existence than that of its main competitor at that time. Whereas Rome had, according to legend, been founded in the first half of the previous millennium, some 940 years before, Kush had already existed for over two and a half thousand years in four quite distinct guises.

As the kingdom of Kerma, Kush found its first expression as a unified culture, of sorts, with the earliest urban settlement patterns in Africa to the south of Egypt, as long ago as the Egyptian Early Dynastic Period from around 3000 BCE, when Kush and Egypt began their long, intertwined relationship. By 1700 BCE, the city of Kerma was home to 10,000 people, with major buildings, palaces, granaries and storehouses, and miles of canals, all protected by a defensive wall system, and its people were already prolific traders over long distances. After a period of domination by Egypt in Lower (northern) Nubia the power of the pharaohs waned, and Kerma went on the offensive, but this only served to harden Egypt's resolve, and the kingdom was invaded and conquered, its king displayed hanging from the mast of the pharaoh's flagship as he sailed back to the north. Becoming increasingly Egyptianised over hundreds of years, inevitable in a lengthy occupation, the people of Kush nevertheless retained enough independence to re-establish their own kingdom when the Egyptian New Kingdom collapsed in 1075 BCE. And it was from this point that Kush began its rise to greatness.

By 750 BCE, a Kushite king by the name of Kashta had invaded Upper (southern) Egypt and captured Thebes, and his successor Piye went on to finish the job and capture the entire length of the Nile Valley. The so-called 'Black Pharaohs' ruled both Egypt and Kush as the 25th Dynasty, seeing themselves as maintaining the classic Egyptian culture and religion in the pharaonic trad- ition. With a wider influence than just the area of their new domain, they took tribute from Levantine trading states and competed militarily with the Assyrian Empire, but their evident territorial and political ambitions were to lead to disaster. In 671 BCE the Assyrians, having been bested in battle more than once against the Kushite king Taharqa, broke a thirty-year losing streak against the now ageing ruler, invaded Egypt and sacked his northern capital, Memphis. His successor's brief recapture of the kingdom's northern territory was in vain, and the Assyrians advanced to capture Thebes in the south, and may even have penetrated as far south as the holy city of Napata. It is in this period that the centre of gravity of Kushite authority began to centre more on Meroë, to the south, and Kushite culture began to become more African in nature.

The Assyrians were succeeded by the Persians, ruled by Cyrus the Great, but his successors were unsuccessful in their efforts to take Kush, overcome, it seems, by the triple scourge of the huge distances involved, the desert's inhospitable nature and the Kushite army's ability to resist. As was often the way in such a stalemate, Kush and Persia exchanged gifts and made peace, with Persian silver being found in elite Kushite burials and 'Aethiopians' serving in Xerxes' invasion of Greece in 480 BCE. Kush, meanwhile, continued to exist despite external pressures, combining Egyptian tradition with their own culture, religion, writing, architecture, aesthetics, trading methods and military organisation, and by 330 BCE had consolidated its grip on southern Egypt as far north as Aswan. It was at some point in this period that the seat of govern- ance formally moved south from Napata to the less vulnerable Meroë, where it was to remain until the kingdom's fall.

Initially ejected from southern Egypt by the resurgent Ptolemaic Egypt, ruled by the descendants of Ptolemy, the king who had arisen from the Macedonian leadership with the death of Alexander the Great (who had conquered Egypt and founded Alexandria), relations between the two great states normalised into cooperation, with joint hunting expeditions in search of war elephants on the steppe to the south of Meroë, and Kush became somewhat Hellenised in the process, just as did Egypt to an even greater degree. But, by 200 BCE, the Ptolemaic kingdom had declined so far that Rome, seeing an opportunity, stepped in to prop up the failing state and secure the valuable grain supply. It was an inevitability that, in the fullness of time, the first emperor, Augustus, would declare its annexation as his own province, to be governed by his chosen representative in order to safeguard this critical role as Rome's breadbasket. In the process of securing the province, Rome re-established control of the long disputed area of southern Egypt, land which had been Kush's for a century, with the unwelcome effect for Kush of depriving its southern neighbour of lucrative tax income, and setting the scene for the war to come.

As evidenced by the *Res Gestae Divi Augusti* (the Deeds of the Divine Augustus), the emperor's funerary inscription which detailed his illustrious achievements, a war duly took place, with Rome deeming itself victorious over enemies in both Ethiopia and Arabia – although the reality was a little more nuanced than the simple statement that 'very large forces of the enemy of both races were cut to pieces in battle and many towns were captured'. In his book *Geography*, the contemporary scholar Strabo recorded the events of the Kushite-Roman war, which in simple terms were these: the Kushite king Teriteqas invaded Upper Egypt in 27 BCE, taking border towns and pulling down statues of Augustus wherever they were to be found, a grave insult and clear signal of intent. Rome counter-attacked with, it seems, only ten thousand men to face thirty thousand Kushites, but these were battle-hardened legionaries fresh from the civil war that had put Augustus on the throne; their equipment and tactics were probably also superior to those of their enemies, in addition to their high level of motivation and experience. They sacked Napata, the Kushite holy city, and both the king and his son Prince Akinidad were killed at some point in the campaign. His wife, the Queen Amanirenas, took up the fight with vigour, pursuing the withdrawing Romans back to Premnis, a fortified hill-top city which has (just) barely survived the flooding brought about by the Aswan dam. A stalemate resulted from the Roman use of massed legion artillery to cancel out the Kushite numerical advantage on the empty ground before the fortress, and Augustus's general Petronius, probably acting on orders from above, sent a diplomatic party from Kush north under escort to meet with the emperor on the island Samos. The resulting peace terms seem to have been highly generous to Kush, perhaps understandably so given Augustus's need to end the war and avoid being forced to fight on too many fronts. Rome and Kush chose to co-exist, and even became military allies to some degree, and the presence of a trade-hungry neighbour seems to have invigorated Kush for some time. Intriguingly, however, while most of the statues of the emperor which had been taken were returned, at least one was not, its head (now in the British Museum) being buried under the steps of a temple in Meroë in perpetual insult and defiance, to be discovered almost two thousand years later.

Meroë was still close to the peak of its magnificence at this time, the city's crops irrigated by the Nile and bordered by forests, a classical city whose broad thoroughfares were lined with statues, but the seeds of its downfall had already been planted. The death-blow came not from the north, the traditional source of competition, but from the south. Around 330 CE, Kush's southern neighbour, the kingdom of Axum, invaded and sacked Meroë, a blow that would leave it deserted within twenty years, but even before this (and probably at the root of the weakness that allowed such an invasion), Kush had been approaching the end of its sustainability. Its forests denuded by the amount of wood needed to create charcoal and fuel the iron industry, its fields overgrazed and over cropped, the city had already been at significant risk of collapse. Intriguingly, it was during this period of decline that the religion which the kingdom had shared with Egypt began to face competition from the upstart faith that was sweeping the ancient world around the Mediterranean, Christianity. Whether this was a factor in the fall of Kush is impossible to say, although the collective opinion is that Kush's successor, Axum, became Christianised from the fourth century onwards, and such religious disruption might have been a factor in Kush's slide into disaster.

After centuries of scholarly neglect, and indeed some racism in the historical writing of previous centuries – such as statements that the amazing pyramids of Napata and Meroë (sadly despoiled, in some cases with explosives, by Europeans in search of burial treasure in the late nineteenth century) must have been built by 'whiter' North Africans – the kingdom of Kush is emerging into general consciousness of the ancient world. I can thoroughly commend those interested to read into the depth of knowledge available with regard to this vibrant regional empire. A unique polity that underwent several phases of existence, variously conquered and conqueror, with distinct religion, culture and trade, well known to and respected by its neighbours, it is very much worth knowing more about.

Recommended reading on the subject has to include the following amazing web page (and yes, I realise that this is a hostage to fortune given it might not exist in years to come) – *https:// wildfiregames.com/forum/index.php?/topic/21602-the-kingdom-of- kush-a-proper-introduction-illustrated/* – if you can be bothered to type all that in, I promise you that the page, for as long as it exists, is a visual and historical treat. Its author, Malcolm Quartey, has done a truly magnificent job of providing not only wargamers but also the rest of us with the most magnificent – and stupen- dously compendious – account of Kush's history, complete with illustrations. Just read it, you'll thank me! And if you're looking for a book on the subject, try *The Kingdom of Kush: Handbook of the Napatan-Meroitic Civilization*, by László Török.

If you'd like to know more about Christianity in the Roman world, then I can recommend *The Christians as the Romans Saw Them* by Robert Louis Wilken, and *The Darkening Age – The*

Christian Destruction of the Classical World by Catherine Nixey is quite an eye-opener on the subject of the way that the new religion literally changed the world.

And if you're curious about Roman Egypt I'd point you to *The Oxford Handbook of Roman Egypt,* edited by Christina Riggs, while *Soldier and Society in Roman Egypt* by Richard Alston digs deeply into how the Roman army was a fundamental part of the province's governance.

The Roman Army in AD 182

By the late second century, the point at which the *Empire* series begins, the Imperial Roman Army had long since evolved into a stable organisation with a stable *modus operandi*. Thirty or so legions (there's still some debate about the Ninth Legion's fate), each with an official strength of 5,500 legionaries, formed the army's 165,000-man heavy infantry backbone, while 360 or so auxiliary cohorts (each of them the rough equivalent of a 600-man infantry battalion) provided another 217,000 soldiers for the empire's defence.

Positioned mainly in the empire's border provinces, these forces performed two main tasks. Whilst ostensibly providing a strong means of defence against external attack, their role was just as much about maintaining Roman rule in the most challenging of the empire's subject territories. It was no coincidence that the troublesome provinces of Britannia and Dacia were deemed to require 60 and 44 auxiliary cohorts respectively, almost a quarter of the total available. It should be noted, however, that whilst their overall strategic task was the same, the terms under which the two halves of the army served were quite different.

The legions, the primary Roman military unit for conducting warfare at the operational or theatre level, had been in existence since early in the republic, hundreds of years before. They were composed mainly of close-order heavy infantry, well-drilled and highly motivated, recruited on a professional basis and, critically to an understanding of their place in Roman society, manned by soldiers who were Roman citizens. The jobless poor were thus provided with a route to a valuable trade, since service with the legions was as much about construction – fortresses, roads and even major defensive works such as Hadrian's Wall – as destruction. Vitally for the maintenance of the empire's borders, this attractiveness of service made a large standing field army a possibility, and allowed for both the control and defence of the conquered territories.

By this point in Britannia's history three legions were positioned to control the restive peoples both beyond and behind the province's borders. These were the 2nd, based in South Wales, the 20th, watching North Wales, and the 6th, positioned to the east of the Pennine range and ready to respond to any trouble on the northern frontier. Each of these legions was commanded by a legatus, an experienced man of senatorial rank deemed worthy of the responsibility and appointed by the emperor. The command structure beneath the legatus was a delicate balance, combining the requirement for training and advancing Rome's young aristocrats for their future roles with the necessity for the legion to be led into battle by experienced and hardened officers.

Directly beneath the legatus were a half-dozen or so military tribunes, one of them a young man of the senatorial class called the broad stripe tribune after the broad senatorial stripe on his tunic. This relatively inexperienced man – it would have been his first official position – acted as the legion's second-in-command, despite being a relatively tender age when compared with the men around him. The remainder of the military tribunes were narrow stripes, men of the equestrian class who usually already had some command experience under their belts from leading an auxiliary cohort. Intriguingly, since the more experienced narrow-stripe tribunes effectively reported to the broad stripe, such a reversal of the usual military conventions around fitness for command must have made for some interesting man-management situations. The legion's third in command was the camp prefect, an older and more experienced soldier, usually a former centurion deemed worthy of one last role in the legion's service before retirement, usually for one year. He would by necessity have been a steady hand, operating as the voice of experience in advising the legion's senior officers as to the realities of warfare and the management of the legion's soldiers.

Reporting into this command structure were ten cohorts of soldiers, each one composed of a number of eighty-man centuries. Each century was a collection of ten tent parties – eight men who literally shared a tent when out in the field. Nine of the cohorts had six centuries, and an establishment strength of 480 men, whilst the prestigious first cohort, commanded by the legion's senior centurion, was composed of five double-strength centuries and therefore fielded 800 soldiers when fully manned. This organisation provided the legion with its cutting edge: 5,000 or so well-trained heavy infantrymen operating in regiment and company-sized units, and led by battle-hardened officers, the legion's centurions, men whose position was usually achieved by dint of their demonstrated leadership skills.

The rank of centurion was pretty much the peak of achievement for an ambitious soldier, commanding an eighty-man century and paid ten times as much as the men each officer commanded. Whilst the majority of centurions were promoted from the ranks, some were appointed from above as a result of patronage, or as a result of having completed their service in the Praetorian Guard, which had a shorter period of service than the legions. That these externally imposed centurions would have undergone their very own 'sink or swim' moment in dealing with their new colleagues is an unavoidable conclusion, for the role was one that by necessity led from the front, and as a result suffered disproportionate casualties. This makes it highly likely that any such appointee felt unlikely to make the grade in action would have received very short shrift from his brother officers.

A small but necessarily effective team reported to the centurion. The optio, literally 'best' or chosen man, was his second-in-command, and stood behind the century in action with a long brass-knobbed stick, literally pushing the soldiers into the fight should the need arise. This seems to have been a remarkably efficient way of managing a large body of men, given the centurion's place alongside rather than behind his soldiers, and the optio would have been a cool head, paid twice the usual soldier's wage and a candidate for promotion to centurion if he performed well. The century's third-in-command was the tesserarius or watch officer, ostensibly charged with ensuring that sentries were posted and that everyone know the watch word for the day, but also likely to have been responsible for the profusion of tasks such as checking the soldiers' weapons and equipment, ensuring the maintenance of discipline and so on, that have occupied the lives of junior non-commissioned officers throughout history in delivering a combat-effective unit to their officer. The last member of the centurion's team was the century's signifer, the standard bearer, who both provided a rallying point for the soldiers and helped the centurion by transmitting marching orders to them through movements of his standard. Interestingly, he also functioned as the century's banker, dealing with the soldiers' financial affairs. While a soldier caught in the horror of battle might have thought twice about defending his unit's standard, he might well also have felt a stronger attachment to the man who managed his money for him!

At the shop-floor level were the eight soldiers of the tent party who shared a leather tent and messed together, their tent and cooking gear carried on a mule when the legion was on the march. Each tent party would inevitably have established its own pecking order based upon the time-honoured factors of strength, aggression, intelligence – and the rough humour required to survive in such a harsh world. The men that came to dominate their tent parties would have been the century's unofficial backbone, candidates for promotion to watch officer. They would also have been vital to their tent mates' cohesion under battlefield conditions, when the relatively thin leadership team could not always exert sufficient presence to inspire the individual soldier to stand and fight amid the horrific chaos of combat.

The other element of the legion was a small 120-man detachment of cavalry, used for scouting and the carrying of messages between units. The regular army depended on auxiliary cavalry wings, drawn from those parts of the empire where horsemanship was a way of life, for their mounted combat arm. Which leads us to consider the other side of the army's two-tier system.

The auxiliary cohorts, unlike the legions alongside which they fought, were not Roman citizens, although the completion of a twenty-five-year term of service did grant both the soldier and his children citizenship. The original auxiliary cohorts had often served in their homelands, as a means of controlling the threat of large numbers of freshly conquered barbarian warriors, but this changed after the events of the first century AD. The Batavian revolt in particular – when the 5,000-strong Batavian cohorts rebelled and destroyed two Roman legions after suffering intolerable provocation during a recruiting campaign gone wrong – was the spur for the Flavian policy for these cohorts to be posted away from their home provinces. The last thing any Roman general wanted was to find his legions facing an army equipped and trained to fight in the same way. This is why the reader will find the auxiliary cohorts described in the *Empire* series, true to the historical record, representing a variety of other parts of the empire, including Tungria, which is now part of modern-day Belgium.

Auxiliary infantry was equipped and organised in so close a manner to the legions that the casual observer would have been hard put to spot the differences. Often their armour would be mail, rather than plate, sometimes weapons would have minor differences, but in most respects an auxiliary cohort would be the same proposition to an enemy as a legion cohort. Indeed there are hints from history that the auxiliaries may have presented a greater challenge on the battlefield. At the battle of Mons Graupius in Scotland, Tacitus records that four cohorts of Batavians and two of Tungrians were sent in ahead of the legions and managed to defeat the enemy without requiring any significant assistance. Auxiliary cohorts were also often used on the flanks of the battle line, where reliable and well drilled troops are essential to handle attempts to outflank the army. And while the legions contained soldiers who were as much tradesmen as fighting men, the auxiliary cohorts were primarily focused on their fighting skills. By the end of the second century there were significantly more auxiliary troops serving the empire than were available from the legions, and it is clear that Hadrian's Wall would have been invalid as a concept without the mass of infantry and mixed infantry/cavalry cohorts that were stationed along its length.

As for horsemen, the importance of the empire's 75,000 or so auxiliary cavalrymen, capable of much faster deployment and manoeuvre than the infantry, and essential for successful scouting, fast communications and the denial of reconnaissance information to the enemy, cannot be overstated. Rome simply did not produce anything like the strength in mounted troops needed to avoid being at a serious disadvantage against those nations which by their nature were cavalry-rich. As a result, as each such nation was conquered their mounted forces were swiftly incorporated into the army until, by the early first century BC, the decision was made to disband what native Roman cavalry as there was altogether, in favour of the auxiliary cavalry wings.

Named for their usual place on the battlefield, on the flanks or 'wings' of the line of battle, the cavalry cohorts were commanded by men of the equestrian class with prior experience as legion military tribunes, and were organised around the basic 32-man turma, or squadron. Each squadron was commanded by a decurion, a position analogous with that of the infantry centurion. This officer was assisted by a pair of junior officers: the duplicarius or double-pay, equivalent to the role of optio, and the sesquipilarius or pay-and-a-half, equal in stature to the infantry watch officer. As befitted the cavalry's more important military role, each of these ranks was paid about 40 per cent more than the infantry equivalent.

Taken together, the legions and their auxiliary support presented a standing army of over 400,000 men by the time of the events described in the *Empire* series. Whilst this was sufficient to both hold down and defend the empire's 6.5 million square kilometres for a long period of history, the strains of defending a 5,000-kilometre-long frontier, beset on all sides by hostile tribes, were also beginning to manifest themselves. The prompt move to raise three new legions undertaken by the new emperor Septimius Severus in AD 197, in readiness for over a decade spent shoring up the empire's crumbling borders, provides clear evidence that there were never enough legions and cohorts for such a monumental task. This is the backdrop for the *Empire* series, which will run from AD 192 well into the early third century, following both the empire's and Marcus Valerius Aquila's travails throughout this fascinatingly brutal period of history.

THE CHAIN OF COMMAND
LEGION

LEGATUS — LEGION CAVALRY (120 HORSEMEN)

BROAD STRIPE TRIBUNE

5 'MILITARY' NARROW STRIPE TRIBUNES

CAMP PREFECT

SENIOR CENTURION

10 COHORTS
(ONE OF 5 CENTURIES OF 160 MEN EACH)
(NINE OF 6 CENTURIES OF 80 MEN EACH)

CENTURION

CHOSEN MAN

WATCH OFFICER   STANDARD BEARER

10 TENT PARTIES OF
8 MEN APIECE

The Chain of Command
AUXILIARY
INFANTRY COHORT

LEGATUS

PREFECT

(OR A TRIBUNE FOR A LARGER COHORT SUCH AS
THE FIRST TUNGRIAN)

SENIOR CENTURION

6-10 CENTURIES

CENTURION

CHOSEN MAN

WATCH OFFICER   STANDARD BEARER

10 TENT PARTIES OF
8 MEN APIECE